HALTING STATE

'*This isn't a game*, Jack. You don't want to find him! You want the police to dealwith it. Don't worry about evidence, there are two security cams in every room and hallway.'

You feel embarrassed: she's absolutely right. You're also feeling a little shaky. You don't know quite how you expected Wu Chen to react, but trying to stab you and making a run for it – if he'd had a real sharpie instead of a penknife, or if he'd missed the keyboard, which you're going to have to replace, dammit – it's outside the playbook and there's no GM to appeal to. 'Crap,' you mumble.

'You can say that again.' Elaine pauses. For a moment you made naked eye contact with her, unscreened by enhanced reality: it's acutely embarrassing, the kind of out-of-context behaviour that business etiquette is intended to avoid. She looks shaken, too, but she's keeping a good lid on it. 'Come on, let's get you patched up,' she says, taking a step backwards, and breaking whatever information transfer it was that was going on between you via some kind of sub-verbal mammalian protocol layer.

Then she takes you by the undamaged hand and leads you back into the real world.

BY CHARLES STROSS

Singularity Sky

Iron Sunrise

Accelerando

Glasshouse

The Atrocity Archives

The Jennifer Morgue

Halting State

Saturn's Children

HALTING STATE

CHARLES STROSS

orbit

www.orbitbooks.net

ORBIT

First published in the United States in 2007 by Ace, an imprint of
The Berkley Publishing Group, Penguin Group (USA) Inc.
First published in Great Britain in 2008 by Orbit
This paperback edition published in 2008 by Orbit
Reprinted 2008 (twice), 2009

A CIP catalogue record for this book is available from the British Library.

ISBN 978-1-84149-665-8

Typeset in Garamond by M Rules
Printed and bound in Great Britain by CPI Mackays, Chatham, ME5 8TD

Papers used by Orbit are natural, renewable and recyclable
products sourced from well-managed forests and certified
in accordance with the rules of the Forest Stewardship Council.

 Mixed Sources
Product group from well-managed
forests and other controlled sources
www.fsc.org Cert no. SGS-COC-004081
© 1996 Forest Stewardship Council
FSC

Orbit
An imprint of
Little, Brown Book Group
100 Victoria Embankment
London EC4Y 0DY

An Hachette UK Company
www.hachette.co.uk

www.orbitbooks.net

In Memory of Datacash Ltd.
and all who sailed her, 1997-2000.

ACKNOWLEDGMENTS

Books do not get written in majestic isolation, and this one is no exception. Certainly it wouldn't exist in its current form without valuable feedback from a host of readers. I'd particularly like to single out for thanks Vernor Vinge, Hugh Hancock, Greg Costikyan, Ron Avitzur, Eric Raymond, Tony Quirke, Robert Sneddon, Paul Friday, Dave Bush, Alexander Chane Austin, Larry Colen, Harry Payne, Trey Palmer, Dave Clements, Andrew Veitch, Hannu Rajaniemi, Soon Lee, and Jarrod Russell. I'd also like to thank my other test readers, too numerous to name today. Finally, thanks to the publishing folks without whom the book wouldn't have been written: my agent, Caitlin Blasdell, my editor at Ace, Ginjer Buchanan, and my copyeditors, Bob and Sara Schwager.

PROLOGUE:
WE KNOW WHERE YOU LIVE,
WE KNOW WHERE YOUR DOG
GOES TO SCHOOL

Mail-Allegedly-From: recruitment@DO_NOT_REPLY.round-peg-round-hole.com
Subject: Attn Nigel – job offer
Auto-Summary: A job offer, vaguely menacing.
Spam-Weighting: 70% probable, but worth a look.

Hello. We're Round Peg/Round Hole Recruitment. We want to offer you a job on behalf of one of our clients.

You didn't send us a résumé? Of course you didn't – that's our job! We know all about you, Nigel. You are an underpaid 29-year-old Maths and CS graduate from Edinburgh University. You've been employed by SprocketSource for one year and four months, and you're three months overdue for a pay review. Your programming skills in Zone/Python 3000 and your expertise in distributed combat systems have generated an impressively high domain-specific reputation on WorldDEV Forums and HackSlashBurn, but does your line manager care? No. Bill does not care. He does not adequately appreciate you. And there's a reason for this.

Here at Round Peg/Round Hole, we don't just passively trawl a boring old database full of CVs for matches against our client's boilerplate job descriptions. We install a Google box on their corporate network, build a Google Directed Semantic Map™ of their internal dialogue, then use our revolutionary new JobInformant™ distributed-agent technology to search the web for potential conscripts. And when we've found them we work out how to motivate them. Like this:

You've been wondering why your boss isn't paying attention to you, and you've probably noticed your colleague, Sonia Grissom, putting in unusually long hours recently. She's being a little bit distant towards you, too. And there's a hiring freeze.

What you don't know – because you don't have access to our JobInformant™ distributed-agent technology – is that your lying shit of a boss is sleeping with his junior combat programmer, and he's looking for an excuse to fire you and promote her into your shoes. Sonia is a workplace player, and you are not. You have no employment tenure because you have been in the job for less than two years, and nobody hires grunts who get themselves remaindered. You'll be industry road-kill.

You might as well face it: you have no future with your current employer.

But there is an alternative.

You, my friend, are the exact person our client, a prestigious international gaming consultancy, has been looking for. (And if you're not, we'll pay you €2000 to spend a day with us helping us understand where our data analysis went wrong.)

Your obsession with reward feedback loop modulation and fractional reserve magic banking – which Bill does not understand – is music to our client's ears. The rest of your skill portfolio is attractive, too. Our JobInformant™ SatisFactor™

package predicts a 72% probability that you will synergize effectively with their coevolutionary operations group, rising to 89% if you are allowed to indulge your preference for working from home and using an avatar for customer-facing situations. That's cool with them, and on that basis they have authorized us to offer you a 25% pay rise, and a generous stock-option package. Not to mention the opportunity to stick it to Bill so hard he'll be picking pieces out of his back teeth for years to come.

To claim your new job, or book your €2000 one-day head-hunting research consultancy, reply to this email . . .

SUE: GRAND THEFT AUTOMATIC

It's a grade four, dammit. Maybe it should have been a three, but the dispatcher bumped it way down the greasy pole because it was phoned in as a one and the MOP who'd reported the offence had sounded either demented, or on drugs, or something – but definitely not one hundred per cent in touch with reality. So they'd dropped it from a three ('officers will be on scene of crime as soon as possible') to a four ('someone will drop by to take a statement within four hours if we've got nothing better to do'), with a cryptic annotation ('MOP raving about Orcs and dragons. Off his meds? But MOP 2 agreed. Both off their meds?').

But then some bright spark in the control room looked at the SOC location in CopSpace and twigged that they'd been phoning from a former nuclear bunker in Corstorphine that was flagged as a Place of Interest by someone or other in national security.

Which jangled Inspector McGregor's bell and completely ruined your slow Thursday afternoon.

You're four hours into your shift, decompressing from two weeks of working nights supervising clean-up after drunken fights on Lothian Road and domestics in Craiglockhart.

Daylight work on the other side of the capital city comes as a big relief, bringing with it business of a different, and mostly less violent, sort. This morning you dealt with: two shoplifting call-outs, getting your team to chase up a bunch of littering offences, a couple of community liaison visits, and you're due down the station in two hours to record your testimony for the plead-by-email hearing on a serial B&E case you've been working on. You're also baby-sitting Bob – probationary constable Robert Lockhart – who is ever so slightly fresh out of police college and about as probationary as a very probationary thing indeed. So it's not like you're not busy or anything, but at least it's low-stress stuff for the most part.

When Mac IMs you, you've just spent half an hour catching up on your paperwork in the Starbucks on Corstorphine High Street, with the aid of a tall latte and a furtive ring Danish. Mary's been nagging you about your heart ever since that stupid DNA check you both took last year ('*so the wee wun kens his maws ur both gawn tae be aboot fer a whiule*'), and the way she goes on, you'd think refined sugar was laced with prussic acid. But you can't afford to be twitchy from low blood sugar if you get a call, and besides, the bloody things taste so much better when they're not allowed. So you're stuffing your cheeks like a demented hamster and scribbling in the air with the tip of a sticky finger when a window pops open in front of the espresso machine.

SUE. MAC HERE.

He's using an evidence-logged CopSpace channel, which means it's business. *Blow me,* you think, as you save the incident form you're halfway through filling in and swap windows.

SUE HERE. GO AHEAD.

With a sinking feeling, you look at your half-finished latte, then glance sideways at Bob. Bob raises an eyebrow at you.

GOT A 4 4U. SMELLS FUNNY. CHECK SOONEST.

You swallow convulsively and take a swig of too-hot coffee, burning the roof of your mouth. It stings like crazy, and you just know the skin's going to be peeling by evening when you rub it with your tongue.

MAIL ME THE TROUBLE TICKET.

There's a musical ding from over by the doorway, and a mail icon appears on your desktop.

ON DUTY, you send, giving the latte a final wistful look. 'Bob? We've got a call.'

'Eh, boss . . . ?' Bob lifts his cup and hides whatever he's been working on – probably Solitaire.

'Bring it along, it's nae the blues.'

You file the email as you leave the coffee shop. Bob trails after you. The destination shows up, as a twirling diamond just visible over the buildings on the far side of the road as you get in the car.

It's a short drive from Corstorphine to the incident site, but it's up the steep slope of Drum Brae, hemmed in by shoebox houses at the bottom of the hill and the whirring prayer wheels of the wind farm at the top. By the time you're heading downhill again, you're worrying that the map is confused: 'Turn right in one hundred metres' it tells you, but all you can see is an urban biodiversity coppice. 'What's the scene?' asks Bob.

'I dinna ken. The skipper says it's a weird one.' You feel a flash of irritation – but your shift is a car short today, which makes it a stupid time for a prank – and right then you spot an open driveway leading into the trees, and your specs are flashing green. 'Eh, look at that lot, will you?'

There are a bunch of cars parked at the end of the drive, and as the Forestry Commission doesn't hand out Bentleys and Maseratis, it's a fair bet that you're in the right place. But the building they're parked outside of is a raw contrast to the posh wheels: it's more like a 1950s public toilet than a corporate office, just four concrete walls propping up a flat slab of characterless roof that seems to scream *Asbestos!* with all the force its wheezing, mesothelioma-ridden lungs can muster. *Maybe it's some kind of up-market cottaging club for the tech start-up crowd?* You shake your head and climb out of the car, tapping your ear-piece to tell your phone to listen up: 'Arriving on SOC, time-stamp now. Start evidence log.' It's logging anyway – everything you see on duty goes into the black box – but the voice marker is searchable. It saves the event from getting lost in your lifelog. Bob trails along like an eager puppy. Eight weeks out of police college, so help you. *At least he's house-broken.*

The door to the premises is a retrofitted slab of glossy green plastic that slides open automatically as you approach, revealing a reception room that's very far from being a public toilet. *So much for the cottage scene.* The lighting is tasteful, the bleached pine impeccably renewable, and the vacant reception desk supports a screen the size of Texas that's showing a dizzying motion-picture tour of an online game space, overlaid by the words HAYEK ASSOCIATES PLC. It stands sentry before a raw, steel-fronted lift door with a fingerprint reader. *Naturally.* But at least now you know this isnae going to turn into another bleeding community relations call. You've had more than a bellyful of them, what with being one of the few overtly heterosexually challenged sergeants in C Division.

'Anyone here?' you call, bouncing on your heels with impatience.

The lift door whispers open and a Member of Public rushes

out, gushing at you and wringing his hands: 'It's terrible, officers! What took you so long? It's all a terrible mess!'

'Slow down.' You point your specs at him in full-capture mode. Your specs log: one Member of Public, Male, Caucasian, 185 high, 80 heavy, short hair, expensive-looking suit and open-collared shirt, agitated but sober. He's in that hard-to-guess age range between twenty-five and forty-five, used to being in control, but right now you're the nearest authority figure and he's reverting to the hapless dependency of a ten-year-old. (Either that, or he's afraid you're gonnae arrest him for emoting in public without a dramatic license.) He's clearly not used to dealing with the police, which gives you something to play on. 'May I see your ID card, sir?'

'My card? It's, uh, downstairs in my office, uh, I guess I can show you . . . ' His hands flutter aimlessly in search of a missing keyboard. 'I'm Wayne, by the way, Wayne Richardson, Marketing Director.' Wayne Richardson, Marketing Director, is clearly unused to not being in control of situations. His expression's priceless, like you've pointed out his fly's undone and his cock ring is showing. 'Ever-everybody's in the board-room; we've been waiting for you. I can, uh, take you there, Constable . . . ?'

You give him a not terribly warm smile. 'Sergeant Smith, Meadowplace Road Station. This is Constable Lockhart.' Richardson has the decency to look embarrassed. 'Someone here reported a theft, but I'm a bit unclear as to what was stolen.' You blink up the trouble ticket again: yes, this guy was one of the two names the dispatcher logged. *Something about a safety deposit box. Boxes.* 'Who noticed the item was missing? Was it yourself?'

'Uh, no, it was the entire security trading team!' He looks at you with wide-open eyes, as if he thinks you're about to call him a liar or something. 'It was on all the screens, they couldn't miss it – there must have been thousands of witnesses all over the shard!' He waves in the general direction of the lift. 'There's a crisis meeting in the boardroom right now. We captured the intrusion on-screen so you can see for yourself.'

They watched it happen on video instead of trying to intervene? You shake your head. Some people will do *anything* to avoid a liability lawsuit, as if the thief tripping on a rug and sticking their heid in the microwave is more of a problem than being burgled. Or maybe the dispatcher was right? *Off their meds an' off their heids.* 'Show me the boardroom.' You nod at Bob, who does a slow scan of the lobby before trailing after you.

Richardson walks over to the lift, and you note there's a thumbprint scanner in the call button. Whoever stole the whatever, there'll be a logfile somewhere with their thumbprints on file. (Which from your point of view is good because it makes detection and wrap-up a whole lot easier. The warm glow of a case clean-up beckons.) As the doors open, you ask, 'What exactly happened? From the beginning, please. In your own time.'

'I'd just come out of the post-IPO debrief meeting with Marcus and Barry, they're our CEO and CTO. We were in a three-way conference call with our VC's investment liaison team and our counsel down south when Linda called me out – she's in derivatives and border controls – because there was something flaky going down in one of the realms we manage for Kensu International. It's in the prestige-level central bank for Avalon Four. There was a guild of Orcs – in a no-PvP area – and a goddamn dragon, and they cleaned out the bank. So we figured we'd call you.'

The lift stops, and you stare at Wayne Richardson, Marketing Director, in mild disbelief. The jargon can wait for later,

that's what your interview log is for: but one name in particular rings a bell because Mary says Davey's been pestering her
for an account. 'Avalon Four? Isnae that a *game?*'

He swallows and nods. 'It's our main cash cow.' The doors
slide open on an underground corridor. The roof is ribbed with
huge concrete beams painted in thick splashes of institutional
cream, and it's startlingly cold. There are bleached-pine doors
on either side, a cable duct winding overhead, and posters on
the walls that say LOOSE LIPS SINK SHIPS. For a moment you
wonder if you've blundered into some kind of live-action role-
playing thing, a cold-war re-enactment maybe but just then
your phone chimes at you that it's gone offline.

'Uh, Sarge?' asks Bob.

'I know,' you mutter. You must be too far underground, or
they're not carrying public bandwidth, or something. You
force yourself to take it easy. 'The signal in here's poor: I'll
probably end up having to use a pen,' you warn Richardson,
pulling out your official evidence phone. 'So I may havtae
back up or slow down a wee bit. Begin statement. On scene' –
you rattle off the reference in the corner of your eye – 'attending to Wayne Richardson, Marketing Director.'

He leads you down the passage towards an open doorway
through which you can hear raised voices, people with posh
accents interrupting each other animatedly. The doorway is
flanked by two potted rubber plants, slightly wilted despite
the daylight spots focussed on them. 'Ahem.' You clear your
throat, and the conversation in the boardroom dribbles into
incontinent silence as you stick your head round the door.
Behind you, Bob's got both his handcams out as well as his
head cam, and he's sweeping the room like a cross between the
Lone Gunman and a star-crazed paparazzo: it's policing, but
not as your daddy knew it. You're going to have to have a word

with the lad afterwards, remind him he's a cop, not a cine-matographer.

There's a fancy table in the middle of the room, made of a transparent plastic that refracts the light passing through it into a myriad of clashing rainbows, and there's a lot of light — it may be a cave down here, but these yins have LED daylight spots the way papes have candles. The chairs around the table are equally fancy: they look like they belong in a squadron of fighter jets, except ejector seats don't usually come with cas-tors and a gas strut suspension. Shame about the way their occupants are letting them down, though. There are six of them. Two slimy wee maggots in ten-thousand-euro suits are clogging up the end of the table wi' their status-symbol tablets: they're the ones that were yammering at each other until they saw you. No ties; maybe it's a dress code thing. There's a lass in a suit, too, but she's too young to be a decision maker. *Secretarial/Admin,* you guess. And then there's the other guys who are, frankly, geeks. It's not like they've got blinking red navigation lights on their heids, but two of 'em are wear-ing sandals and the other's enough to make you wish your Little Database of Charges had a section on Fashion Crimes: the stripes on his shirt are interfering with your specs, and the evidence cam is picking up a nasty moiré effect. 'Ahem,' you repeat, as a holding action, then stare at Wayne Richardson, Marketing Director. Let *him* sort this out.

'Oh, excuse me.' Richardson takes his cue. 'This is, uh, Sergeant Smith and Constable Lockhart. The sergeant's here to take a statement.'

'That's enough,' you cut in. 'If you can introduce everyone? Then ye'd better show me what happened.'

'Uh, sure.' Richardson points at the suits with the slits for their owners' dorsal fins first: 'Marcus Hackman, CEO.'

Hackman gives Richardson the hairy eyeball, like he's sizing him for a concrete overcoat, but only for a second. Then he turns the charm on you with a nod and a great white smile that reveals about two hundred thousand dollars' worth of American dental prostheses that he probably wears because it's the only way to stop the bairns from screaming and running away before he can eat them. *Clearly* by calling the Polis, Wayne has pissed in Hackman's pint, but he's too much of a professional to let your arrival perturb him. 'We're grateful that you could come, but really it's not necessary—'

'And Barry Michaels, our Chief Technology Officer.' Michaels is plump and rumpled in an old-Fettes-schoolboy-Boris-Johnson sort of way, with a port nose and a boyish cowlick of black hair: you peg immediately that he's probably as bent as a three-bob note, but unlike Hackman, he's not some kind of toxic-waste-eating Martian invader from the planet Wall Street. He nods nervously, looking like he's eaten something disagreeable. 'This is Beccy Webster, our Market Stabilization Executive.' The twentysomething hen's a high-flyer, then? 'Mike Russell, Sam Couper, and Darren Evans' — the latter is the one with the anti-webcam shirt — 'are our senior quants.'

'Excuse me?' You raise an eyebrow.

'Sorry. They're our economics wizards, they do the market programming around here that's the bread and butter of our business. It's just what they're called.'

You take a deep breath. 'Right. I understand Mr. Richardson phoned in a report of a theft from your company. He tells me that you got it on video, and it's something to do with a game. What exactly was stolen?' You take a wild guess: 'Was it the source code, or something?'

'Oh dear.' Michaels emotes like a sweaty-handed old theatre

queen. 'Anything but!' He sits up in his ejector seat – you're certain, now, that you've seen one just like it in the air museum at East Fortune – and takes a deep breath. 'Did you tell her it was the source code, Wayne?'

'No, I—'

'What *did* you tell the police?' Michaels demands. He sounds very upset about something. *Okay, pencil him in as number two on your list of folks who don't like airing their smalls in public.* (And remember for later: *There's no smoke without a source of combustion . . .*)

'Nothing, I just called them because we've been robbed!'

This is getting out of hand. 'What was stolen?' you ask, pitching your voice a bit louder.

'Everything in the central bank!' It's Webster. *At last,* you think, *someone who gives simple answers to simple questions.*

'Central bank where, on the high street?' You can't be sure while you're offline, but you don't think there are any banks at this end of Drum Brae—

'Show her the video,' Hackman says wearily. 'It's the only way to explain.'

You're looking out across a verdant green rainforest canopy that sprawls across the foothills of a mountain range so tall that the peaks are a vulpine blue haze in the distance, biting at the smaller of the three moons that chase each other across the sky. A waterfall half a kilometre high shimmers and thunders over the edge of a cliff like molten green glass, shattering into rainbow-clouded fragments as it nears the lake beneath. Brilliantly plumed birds soar and swoop across the treetops, occasionally diving towards the waters of the river that flows from the lake. The effect is more than real: it's as supernaturally vivid as an exotic holiday ad, banishing the rainy

Edinburgh afternoon outside to the level of a dreicht grey parody of reality.

You're about to ask what you're meant to be seeing here – a bank robbery in a package holiday ad? – when the camera on the rainforest pans back and up, and you realize you're not on Earth anymore.

There's an island in the sky, a plug of rock set adrift from its mooring in the sea of reality, like a painting by Roger Dean come to life. Beneath it, ghostly violet and green lights flicker, buoying it up on a wave of magic. The camera rises like a helicopter and pans across the island. Although there are trees atop it, it's mostly given over to buildings – constructions with uneven stone walls and steeply pitched roofs, some turreted and a few supported by classical colonnades. The ground rises near the heart of the flying island, peaking at a low hill that is surmounted by the battlements and towers of a gigantic castle. The battlements flash and glitter in the sunlight, as if they're made of a glassy substance: rainbows shimmer in their recesses.

'This is the Island of Valiant Dreams. It hovers above the Lake of the Lost, in the foothills of the Nether Mountains in Avalon Four. The Island is home to the city called Roche's Retreat, and it's supported by ancient magicks. Among other things, it is home to the central bank of Avalon Four, which we manage under contract.'

Aye, reet, you tell yourself, as the viewpoint rotates and zooms in on the island, diving towards the cobbled streets and crowded alleys that thread the city. There are a myriad of folk here, not all of them human. You weave past the heads of giants and around the sides of a palanquin borne on the back of a domesticated dinosaur led by lizard-faced men, loop around a timber-framed shop that leans alarmingly out across the road, leap a foot-bridge across a canal, then slow as you enter a huge stone-flagged city square, and dive through the doorway of a temple of Mammon that puts Parliament to shame. *So this is what the wee one thinks he's getting for his birthday?* It's all very picturesque, but the column of exotic dancers high-kicking their way between two temples tells you that Davey'd better have another think coming.

'This is the central bank. Our task is to keep speculation down, and effectively to drain quest items and magic artefacts from the realm to prevent inflation. One way we do this is by offering safe deposit services to players: Avalon Four runs a non-persistent ownership mode so you can lose stuff if you're killed on a quest and respawn, and the encumbrance rules are tight.'

It's not much like your local branch of the Clydesdale. Demons and magicians and monsters, oh my! – a bizarre menagerie of unreal, superreal entities stand in small groups across the huge marble floor, bickering and haggling. Here and there, a flash of light and a puff of smoke erupt as one of the staff invokes an imp or servitor to take this or that item to the safe deposit vaults, or to check an adventurer's possessions out of their custody and return it to their owner.

'The time is just past ten fifteen . . .'

Your viewpoint jerks, then slews round to face the entrance to the bank. The doors are three times as high as a tall man, carved from giant ebony beams clasped in a frame of some silvery metal: the hinges they turn on are as thick as a body-builder's arms. But they're not silvery now – they're glowing dull red, then a bright, rosy pulse of heat lights them up from the outside, and the doors begin to collapse inwards on a wave of choking black smoke.

In through the smoke marches a formation of monstrous

soldiers. They're larger than life and twice as gnarly, prognathous green-skinned jaws featuring tusks capped in gold. Their uniform is a mixture of brown leather and chain-mail, and their helmet spikes bear the impaled heads of their trophies, nodding above the points of their pikes. *Just like Craigmillar at chucking out time on a Saturday night,* you figure, *only not as ugly.*

There are many of them, for the column is at least ten rows deep: and something vast and red and reptilian looms behind them, ancient and malign.

Then the picture freezes.

'You are looking at an Orcish war band. There are at least forty of them, and they're a very long way from home. The thing behind them is a dragon. They seem to have brought him along for fire support. Which is impossible, but so is what happens next.'

The picture unfreezes.

The Orcish warriors spread out and adopt a spearheaded formation. Their leader barks a sharp command, and the pikes are lowered to face the denizens of the bank, who are turning to watch with gathering astonishment and anger. Here and there the bright glamour of incantations shows a spell-caster winding up to put the intruders in their place. And then –

A wave of darkness descends across the room, and the occupants freeze in their tracks.

'This is when *something* – we're not sure what – nerfed our admins back to level zero and cast a Time Stop on everyone in the room. That's a distressingly high-powered spell, and it normally affects just one target at a time.'

Flashes and flickers of light fitfully stab into the darkness. The Orcs are dispersing, fanning out with the speedy assurance of stage-hands moving the furniture and props while the stage

lights are dimmed. They move between flicker and fulmina-
tion, snatching up leather sacks and ornately decorated chests,
seizing swords and swapping their cheap leather armour for
glittering plate. Over the space of a minute they denude the
floor of the bank, snatching up the treasures that are inexplicably popping into view from the ethereal vaults.

Finally, their leader barks another command. The Orcs
converge on his banner, his helmet nodding high beneath its
column of five skulls – and they form up neatly into columns
again, and march out through the mangled wreckage of the
doors. As the last one leaves the threshold, the darkness
disperses like mist on a summer morning. A couple of the
braver warriors give shouts of rage and chase after their
stolen property – but the dragon is waiting, and the smell of
napalm is just the same in Avalon Four as on any other silver
screen.

'We've been robbed,' says Richardson. 'Got the picture
yet?'

It's time to rub your eyes and start asking hard questions. *So
someone found a bug in your game, and you called the Polis?* Looks
like a good place to start. While these tits are wasting your
time, ordinary folk are being burgled.

'You said the Orcs were a long way from home. How do
you know that?'

Sam Couper – the middle geek – sniggers. 'Traceroute is
my bitch.' He shuts up immediately when he sees Hackman
sizing him for a side order with fries.

'My colleague is trying to explain' – Beccy Webster's subtlety of emphasis is truly politician grade; she probably mimes
to Wendy Alexander videos before breakfast every morning –
'that they were controlled by a bunch of gold farmers in a

sweatshop in Bangladesh. But we lost them when they ran over the border into **NIGHTWATCH**.'

'We could have nailed them if that ass-hat Nigel would show his sorry ass in the office once in a while.' Russell is clearly pissed about the missing Nigel, but you can follow that up later.

'**NIGHTWATCH** is another game?' You're in danger of getting a cramp in your raised eyebrow.

Webster nods, sparing a warning glance for the three stooges. 'Yes, it's operated by Electronic Arts. They in-source quant services behind their own iron curtain, so we don't have admin privileges when we go there.'

She pauses, mercifully, and you think of your upcoming evidence session and fail to suppress a groan. 'So why did you call *us?*' you ask. 'It seems to me this is all internal to your games, aye? And you're supposed to be the folks who *stop* players from, from' – you shrug, searching for words – 'arsing about with virtual reality. Right?' Wasting Polis time is an offence, but somehow you don't think the skipper would thank you for charging this shower. *More trouble than it's worth.*

'You listen to me.' When Hackman speaks, you listen: he's got the same sense of menacing single-mindedness as a Great White homing in on a surfboard. 'The exploit isn't as simple as robbing a virtual bank of virtual objects. The way Avalon Four is architected means that someone had to leak them a private cryptographic token before they could change the ownership attributes of all those objects.' He clears his throat. '*You* shouldn't have been called.' He spares a paint-blistering glare for Richardson: 'This is a job for SOCA, not the local police . . . But seeing as you're here, you might as well note that not only has an offence been committed subject to Section three of the CMA, as amended post independence in 2014' – *shite, he's got you* – 'but we just completed our flotation on AIM three weeks ago last Monday, and our share price this morning was up nearly twenty-seven per cent on the post-IPO peak. If we don't find the bastards who did this, our shares are going to tank, which will rip the shit out of the secondary offering we were planning to make in six months. The timing's too cute: this isn't just a hacking incident, it's insider trading. Someone's trying to depress our share price for their own financial gain.'

'What's the current damage?' asks Richardson, unable to control his stock-option twitch.

'Down two point four, word doesn't seem to have leaked yet.' Michaels sounds like he's reading an obituary notice. 'But when it goes, if we lose, say, thirty per cent – that's twenty-six million euros.'

Hackman unleashes his fish-killer grin again: 'Thirty per cent? We'll be lucky to get away with ninety.' He glances at you, and you see that the smile doesn't reach his eyes. 'Now, would you like to borrow a telephone? So you can, I don't know, maybe call in the real detectives?'

You don't want to let the gobshite see he's rattled you, but €*26 million* puts a whole different complexion on things: normally robbery doesn't score too high on the KPI matrix, but something on this scale has the potential to go Political. So you stare him down while you put on your best Morningside cut-glass court-appearance accent. 'I *am* a detective sergeant, Mr. Hackman. And I'm afraid that due to current force-manning constraints, we can't just drop everything and start an immediate large-scale investigation. I have to file an incident report with my inspector, and he has to take it to the chief constable; then it's *his* decision whether or not to call in

SOCA.' (The Scottish Organised Crime Agency, who will slot the job into their priority tree somewhere between chasing international plutonium smugglers and rescuing kittens from window ledges.) You smile, oh-so-friendly, and let him see *your* teeth. 'So I'm going to start by interviewing everyone in this room separately, then I'll prepare my report, and as soon as it's ready, I'll send it up the line.' (Right after you finish with your plead-by-email recording.)

'Now. Who's first?'

ELAINE: Stitch-up

En garde!

You are standing in the nave of a seventeenth-century church, its intricately carved stone surfaces dimly illuminated by candles. Your right foot is forward, knee slightly bent, and you can feel the gentle curve of the worn flagstone beneath the toes of the hand-stitched leather slipper you're wearing. Your right arm is raised, and your hand extended as if you are point-ing a gun diagonally across your chest, muzzle wavering towards the roof of the west wing. With your left hand, you support your right, just as if you're holding a heavy pistol. Heavy pistol about sums it up – the long sword may be made of steel and over a metre long, but it weighs no more than a Colt Python, and it's balanced so that it feels like an extension of your fingertips.

You are facing a man who is about to try to kill you. He's wearing a black Kevlar-reinforced motorcycle jacket with lead weights Velcro'd to it, plus jeans, DMs, and a protective helmet with a cluster of camera lenses studding its blank-faced shell. Like you, he's holding a long sword of fifteenth-century design, its steel cross-guards shielding his hands, which are, in turn, raised, like a baseball striker poised ready for the ball. But you don't see the biker jacket or DMs because, like your opponent, you're also wearing a full facial shield with head-up display, and it's editing him into a full suit of Milanese plate, the Renaissance equivalent of a main battle tank.

'Let's try that again,' you offer, tensing.

'Sure.' He rocks slightly on the balls of his feet, and for an instant you have the surreal sense that he's not holding a sword at all – it's a cricket bat, and he's got it the wrong way up.

'Your mother wears army boots!'

You're not sure that's the right thing to say to a late fifteenth-century main battle tank, but he takes it in the spirit you intended – and more importantly, he spots you changing guard, lowering the point of your sword. And he goes for you immediately, nothing subtle about it, just a diagonal swing, pivoting forward so he can slice a steak off you.

Of course, this is just what you expected when you twisted your wrist. You dip your point and grab your blade with your left hand, blocking him with a *clang*. He tries to grab your blade with his left hand, but you keep turning, raising the point – you're using your sword like a short stabbing spear now – and hook the tip into his armpit like a one-and-a-half-kilo can-opener while hooking his knee with your left foot.

Unlike a modern main battle talk, the old-fashioned version can fall on its arse.

'Ouch! Dammit. Point to you, my lady.'

'That's your brachial artery right there,' you comment, taking a deep breath as you watch the bright gouts of virtual blood draining from him.

You take a step back, and your enemy does likewise as soon as he's picked himself up. Both of you let your blades droop. 'How did you know about the army boots?' he asks.

Whoops. 'Lucky guess?'

'Oh. I thought maybe you knew her.' There's disappointment

in his voice, but the sealed helm opposite doesn't give anything away.

'No, sorry.' Your heart's still pounding from the stress of the moment – thirty seconds of combat feels like thirty minutes in the gym or three hours slaving over a hot spreadsheet – but a certain guilty curiosity takes over. 'Was she a Goth or a hippy?'

'Neither: she was in the army.' His foot comes forward, and his sword comes up and twitches oddly, and before you can shift feet, it thumps you on the shoulder hard enough to let you know you've been disarmed – literally, if there was a cutting edge on these things. 'Ahem, I mean, she was *into* the army. New Model Army, dog-on-a-string crusties from Bradford.'

'I know who they are,' you snap, taking two steps back and raising one hand to rub your collar-bone, which is not as well padded as it ought to be and consequently smarts like crazy. 'And in a minute I want you to show me what you just did there.' *No camisole tops at work for a few days,* you remind yourself, which is kind of annoying because you can live without the extra ironing and the knowledge that Mike landed one on you. (You overheard him telling a newbie 'She's got reflexes like a greased whippet on crystal meth' the other week, and you were walking on air for days. It's true, but Mike's got extra reach and upper-body muscle, and all you have to do is let yourself get distracted, and he'll teach you just what that mediaeval MBT can do.) 'But first, let someone else use the floor.'

You retire to the pews at the left of the aisle, sheathing your sword and stripping your headgear as Eric and Matthew take your place, joking about something obscure and work-related. You drop out of haptic space and without your eyewear continually repainting him in armour, Mike reverts to his workaday appearance, a biker with a borg head transplant. Then he strips off the battered Nokia GameCrown to reveal a sweaty brown ponytail and midthirties face, and shakes his head, presumably at seeing you as yourself for the first time in an hour, rather than a femme fatale with farthingales and a falchion. (And that's not so flattering, is it? Because you may not be overweight, but let's face it, dear, people mistake you for a librarian. And while you work with books, you're not exactly involved in publishing.) 'I was wondering if I could have a word of your advice, Elaine,' he says as he slouches onto the unforgiving bench seat.

'What, a technical issue?' You raise a damp eyebrow. Mike's been doing this stuff years longer than you have, since before AR and OLARP games began to show, practically since back in the Stone Age when you either did dress-up re-enactment or actual martial arts (and never the twain shall meet); and aside from your oiled-canine reflexes, he's basically just plain better than you'll ever be. 'I suppose . . .'

'It's not about that,' he says, sounding uncertain. The penny drops, just as he goes on to say: 'It's about the car insurance.'

You get this from time to time, although there are blessings to be counted: it's not like you're a lawyer or a doctor or something. 'I don't work that end of the business,' you remind him.

'Yeah, I know that. But you know Sally was in a shunt on the M25 last week?' (Sally is Mike's wife: a bottle-blonde middle-management type who tolerates his night out with the lads once a week with an air of mild, weary contempt. You suppose they must see something in each other, but . . .) 'We got this bill for the recovery truck and repairs, then the other driver's claiming private medical expenses, and the thing is, she swears there was another car involved, that didn't stop.'

You've got a sinking feeling that you know what's coming, but you can't just leave Mike dangling so you restrict yourself to a non-committal 'Hmm?'

Eric and Matthew are poised on the floor in front of you, almost motionless, knees and elbows occasionally flexing slightly. None of the chatter you and Mike go in for. A couple of the others are working out, warming up in the vestry, and you can hear Jo's boom box thudding out an obscure Belgian industrial stream as they grunt and groan about another day at the office. 'She was driving along in the slow lane near junction nineteen, heading towards Heathrow, behind the guy she tail-ended. Doing about ninety, there weren't any trucks about, but traffic was heavy. Anyway, she says a white Optare van overtook them both, pulled in front of the Beemer, and braked, and by the time she was on the hard shoulder there was no sign of it.'

'Hmm.' You carefully put your sword down, then nudge it under the bench where nobody will trip over it. 'You haven't said "swoop and squat" yet, but that's what you're thinking, isn't it?'

'Yes.'

'What's the damage?'

'Well, Sally's carrying six points on her license and she had that car-park smash last year. She'll lose her no-claims discount, which'll cost us about eight hundred extra when we renew the insurance.'

'Ouch.' Your bruised clavicle throbs in sympathy. Driving's an expensive pastime even before you factor in diesel at €5 a litre, speed cameras every quarter of a kilometre on all the A-roads, and insurance companies trying to rape the motorists to recoup their losses on the flood-plain property slump. 'Who are you with?'

'Nationwide.'

Well, that's a relief – an old-fashioned mutual society, instead of a pay-by-credit-card web server owned by Nocturnal Aviation Associates Dot Com (motto: 'We fly by night') out of the back of a cybercafé in Lagos. 'That's good news. What's the Beemer trying to dun you for?'

'Sixteen thousand in repairs – listen, it's not a current model, Sally said she thought it was about ten years old – two thousand for roadside recovery, and, you're going to love this, nine thousand in fees for orthopaedic treatment. They're claiming whiplash injury.'

'I see. Nearly thirty grand?' You shake your head. Mike's right, that's nearly an order of magnitude over the odds for a simple tail-end shunt on a motorway at rush hour. Even at ninety kilometres per hour. And whiplash – 'Listen, all BMWs have been fitted with head restraints since forever, and they've had side-impact and frontal air bags for at least two decades. That kind of claim means they're talking surgery, which means time off work, so they're gearing up to hit you with a loss-of-earnings. I expect they'll try to drop another thirty grand on the bill in a month or two.'

Mike's face was sweaty to begin with: now it's turning the colour of the votive candles they'd be burning if this was still a functioning church. 'But we've got a ten per cent excess . . .'

'Right. So you've got to make sure the other guy doesn't get his hands on it, don't you? You're right about it sounding like a swoop and squat, and that medical claim is a classic. Medical confidentiality is a great blind for snipers, but we can poke a hole in it if there's a fraud investigation in train. Now, Nationwide still have some human folks on the web in the Customer Retention and Abuse groups, and what you need to do is to get this escalated off the call-centre ladder until a human being sees it, then you need to hammer away.'

'But how do I . . . ?'

You start checking off points on your fingertips. 'You start by getting Sally to offer them her car's black-box log. Once you know exactly *where* she was when the incident happened – the black-box GPS will tell you that – you tell them to serve a FOIA disclosure notice on the Highways Agency for their nearby camera footage – if they won't listen at first, I'll talk you through doing that yourself. That will tell you whether the Optare was involved, in which case you can kick Abuse into opening a fraudulent claim file on the other driver. Then you can go after the medical side. If the other driver has a doctor's note, pull their BMA records and see if they're legit – I'll bet you a bottle of Chardonnay there's a reprimand on file because doctors who're willing to diagnose fictional ailments for cash rarely stop at one. Once you've got that, you can go after the vehicle with a statutory vehicle history disclosure notice – that's what the police use on you if they think you're driving a chop job – and then you can query the vehicle's book value. At which point, if you're right and it's a swoop and squat, NU will hit up their insurer for the full value of the claim and blacklist them, while indemnifying you. Your insurer should do all of this automatically if you get their Abuse team's attention, but you don't have to wait – the forms are all online, you can do it from your phone, and once you've got the ball rolling, your insurer will pick it up.'

Mike goes glassy-eyed halfway through your explanation, but that's okay: he's nodding like a parcel-shelf ornament, which means he's got the essential message that he's anything but helpless. Civilians confronted by an alien bureaucracy always feel helpless at first, but once they realize there's a way to get what they want, they usually recover. 'I think I got some of that—'

'I'll email you tomorrow.' From the office, in your copious free time, you'll off-handedly throw him a FAQ: Nailing Petty Insurance Fraud 101. Mike asking you to help with Sally's fraudulent car claim is a bit like calling in an air strike to deal with a primary-school bully; but he's your friend, and besides, if anyone in the office notices and makes a fuss, you can point out that it's good public relations.

'Thanks, ever so.' With classic English understatement, he looks more grateful than he sounds.

While you were talking, Eric and Matthew have somehow gone from twitching slightly to Matthew lying on his back with the tip of Eric's sword touching his stomach. As you watch, Eric brings up his point in salute and backs out of the duelling space. You stand up, feeling an itchy urge to claw your way back out of your work headspace, and turn to Mike: 'Best of three rounds?'

JACK: Steaming

Debug mode:

You are sitting, half-asleep, in an armchair. Your eyes are closed, and you feel very unsteady. Your head's full of a post-viral haze, the cotton-wool of slowed reflexes and dulled awareness. In stark contrast to the normal state of affairs, you can hear yourself think – there's just one little voice wobbling incessantly about from side to side of your cranial prison, which is no surprise after the amount of skunk you just smoked. In the distance, the chiming clangour of tram-bells sets a glorious harmony reverberating in icy splendour across the rooftops. And you are asking yourself, like the witchy-weird voice in a video of an old Laurie Anderson performance:

'What am I doing here?'

Restart:

There's a ringing in your ears. *Oops, must have drifted off.* That's the trouble with smoking shit to help yourselves forget –

Yourselves? Well yeah, there's you, and there's Mitch, and there's Budgie. Tom couldn't come because he was busy being newly married and responsible, but between you and Mitch and Budgie, you're three of the four corners of the former Social Networking Architecture Team, and you've flown out here on a budget shuttle from Turnhouse to get falling-down legless and scientifically test all that research into whether cannabis destroys short-term memory, because god help you, it's better than remembering how badly you've been shafted.

Which is how come you're sitting in a half-collapsed armchair, stoned out of your box, on the narrow strip of flagstoned pavement alongside the Prinsengracht canal, listening to alarm bells –

And contemplating the wreckage of your career, after four years in the elite Dirty Tricks wing of LupuSoft, working on special projects for nobbling your corporate master's rivals, then a transfer to the relatively clean game-play side of **STEAMING**. Four years of top-secret death marches and psychotic deadline chases in beige-walled cubicle hell (when you'd rather have been sailing the wine-dark seas); frenzied developer boot camps held in sinister wire-fenced floodlit compounds in the Grampians; weekends spent following the team at home and away events with a laser range-finder and a dynamics package (and wasn't it fun trying to avoid that big ned from Portobello who'd got it into his head that you're some kind of headhunter from down south who's gonnae gut his side, and kept trying to get his posse to stomp your head in?). And all the while you're living off peanut-butter sandwiches and stale sushi take-aways while your waistline expands and your visual range contracts as you stare at a screen the size of a secondary-school whiteboard all day long and half of the night.

Then there were the dying weekends, weekends stolen from the company management by sheer bloody-minded smackdowns with HR so you could go back to Rochdale to spend some time with your ma, who was in a bad way from the lung cancer, or visit Sophie and Bill and the nieces. Until one day Ma wasn't there anymore, and the rest of it, and that's *you* in that corner there, you with your sixty-thousand-euro salary and your legacy that went partway to a poky wee place in the Colonies and a mortgage you won't pay off before you retire, and no fucking life whatsoever. (Well, there's your knitting habit and your criminal record: but that's just fodder for your OCD.) This is your life, it's been your life since you clawed your way from CS graduate to start-up seven years ago, and your so-called life is such a bijou bourgeois piece of shit that there's no room for anything but work in it, so you've been keeping yourself too busy to care until –

Last week they cancelled **STEAMING** and told you to clear your desk at half an hour's notice. *Here's your next month's pay in lieu, now get the hell out of here, you freak!* And you suddenly realise that you haven't got a life. Even though they made you learn more about Scottish Premier League fitba than the captain of the national squad, the bastards.

'Excuse me. You cannot be sleeping here—'

Restart:

The worst thing about it all is that you *hate* football.

Of course, to have admitted that you hated football while you were working on **STEAMING** would have been a bit like one of the US president's staffers confessing to thinking religion was overrated, abstinence didn't work, and what the country really needed was a short sharp dose of communism with a side order of Islamic extremism to go. It's one of those things that you just couldn't talk about at LupuSoft, not while they had the exclusive rights to both the Hibs' *and* Rangers' fan club franchises and were trying to milk the surplus income out of all the assorted bampots, neds, and ne'er-do-wells who figured that a LARP where you get to play at football hooligans among consenting adults was better than the other kind of live-action role-playing. (In which you played at football hooligans with *non*-consenting adults, while the combined manpower of Lothian's finest and the Rock Steady Crew played collar-the-radge back atcha with CS gas and tasers.) On the other hand, you were able to suppress or sublimate your hatred without too much difficulty. You're a bourgeois liberal geek who thinks 'team player' is a term of abuse, but you believe in society, you believe in checks and balances, you believe in getting your own back on the thick-headed sports jocks who made life excitingly unpleasant for you in school . . . and as it happens, while you were working on **STEAMING** you could convince yourself that you were *doing your bit*, because any job that gets the brangling thugs playing a game on their mobies instead of lobbing tinnies and chibbing innocent bystanders up the high street has got to be a good thing. Network-mediated LARPs have been the gaming story of the decade, ever since **SPOOKS** came along and gave actuaries a chance to live a secret agent life on the side; **STEAMING** was set to ring the cash register again and take the nutters off the street. And it paid the mortgage, besides.

At least, that's how it had been before the Bologna cup final disaster, and the double whammy of the social psych study in *The Lancet* the very next week that stuck the proverbial sharpie in and twisted, hard. Questions were asked in the lumpy-looking construction site down Holyrood Road, and the ministers did wax worthy and serious and proceeded to apply the tawse of uptight self-righteousness to the rump of the dead equine of games industry self-regulation with gusto and vigour. At which point LupuSoft management revisited the risk-value trade-off inherent in defending their investment in a second-division virtual-world football-hooliganism game against a class-action lawsuit, and decided the professional thing to do was to downsize your team's sorry ass.

Maybe it could have gone the other way in the boardroom if the Polis hadn't uncovered a network of Little League serial killer wannabes who were using **STEAMING** to rehearse next Saturday's riot over on Easter Road: but *that* was the final nail in the coffin. All the suit-wearing world loves a geeky scapegoat, and you boys were going down in flames. So there was only one thing to do: fly out to Amsterdam and get absolutely steaming drunk for the weekend, not to mention so stoned you're having auditory hallucinations to the sound of the tram bells.

'Excuse me, sir, but you cannot sleep here.'

You open your eyes. The auditory hallucination is peering at you through her surveillance goggles as if she's never seen a stoned tourist before. She's been so polite that for a moment you feel a flash of perverse gratitude until the weed clears enough for you to realize that she is a member of the Politie and quite capable of summoning a vanful of black-clad accomplices who will vanish you into some concrete custody cell faster than you can snap your fingers if she chooses officially to notice that you are not terribly conscious.

You try to say, 'Please don't arrest me, I'm just a sleepy tourist, I won't be any trouble,' but it all runs together at the back of your tongue and comes out as something like 'nnnghk.' You tense your arms and prepare to lift yourself out of the armchair – standing up would seem like the right thing to do at that point – but that's when you realize the armchair is situated adjacent to a street sign on a pole, to which your friends have kindly handcuffed your left wrist. And that goddamn ringing noise won't stop – it's not in your ears at all, is it?

'Um?' you say, dully staring past the cop in the direction of the antique shop on the other side of the pavement. There's something odd about the window, the pattern the lights make as they reflect off it – or don't, as the case may be. *Broken,* you tell yourself sagely. Someone has broken the antique shop window and dragged this annoyingly *gezellig* armchair out onto the pavement for you to sit in. Talk about game scenarios gone wrong: it's like something you might end up dumped into in **STAG NIGHT: THE PURSUIT** if you started griefing the bridesmaids.

'Does this chair belong to you, sir?'

Sometimes when you laugh you come out with a burbling, hiccuping sound, like a hyena that's choking to death on its food. You can hear it right now, welling up out of your shirt pocket, tinny and repetitive. It's the ultimate custom ring-tone, as annoying as a very annoying thing indeed, except this particular piece of intellectual property isn't owned by a bunch of gouging cunts.

"Scushe me, tha's my phone . . . ' Your right hand is free, so you try and insert your fingers in your shirt pocket and play chase the mobie. Somehow in the past hour your hand has grown cold and numb, and your digits feel like frankfurters as the handset slips past them, giggling maniacally.

'Pay attention, sir. Did you take that chair from the shop? Who handcuffed you to the NO PARKING sign? I think you'd better blow into this meter, sir.'

She's a sight easier to understand than the local Edinburgh Polis, which is no bad thing because the voice at the end of the line is anything but. 'Jack? Hi, it's Sophie! Are you alright? Are you busy right now?'

'No, not now—'

'Oh that's a shame, I'm really sorry, but can you do me a favour? It's Elsie's birthday the Tuesday after next, and I was wondering—'

You breathe on the end of the cop's torch as she holds it

under your mouth, then swallow. Your sister is tweeting on the end of the line, oblivious, and you really need to get her off the phone fast. You force unwilling lips to frame words in an alien language: 'Email me. Later . . . '

'But it's important!' Sophie insists. 'Are you alright Jack? Jack?' The plangent chords of her West Midlands accent form brassy patterns of light on the end of the torch, where an LED is glowing red, like the call disconnect button on your phone.

'I think you'd better come with me, sir.' She has a key to the handcuffs, for which you are duly grateful, but she wants you to put your phone away, and that's surprisingly difficult, because Sophie keeps going on about something to do with your oldest niece's birthday and Confirmation – hubby Bill wants Elsie and Mary to have a traditional upbringing – and you keep agreeing with her because *will you please put the phone down, a Dutch cop is trying to arrest me* isn't a standard way to break off this kind of scenario. (If only families came with safewords, like any other kind of augmented-reality game.) Things are stuck at this point for a tense few seconds as you mug furiously at the officer, until she raises one index finger, then unlocks the handcuff from around the pole, twists your arm around the small of your back, wheechs the mobie out of your grasp, and has your wrists pinioned before you can say 'hasta la vista.'

It's shaping up to be a *great* weekend, make no mistake. And there's always Monday to look forward to!

INTERLUDE
CIA WORLD FACTBOOK, 2017

SCOTLAND

Location: 54 38 N, 1 46 W – Western Europe, occupying the
northern two-fifths of the island of Great Britain.

FLAG

Description: Sky-blue background with a white Cross of St.
Andrew (diagonal) superimposed. As a member state of the
EU, the EU flag may also be flown.

. . .

NAME OF COUNTRY

Conventional long form: Republic of Scotland

Conventional short form: Scotland

Data code: SCO

Type of government: republic, EU core member state

Capital: Edinburgh

Independence: 1 January 2012

Constitution: 13 March 2011; adopted 1 January 2012 at
formal independence

Legal system: based on Roman law and traditional Scottish law,
substantially modified by indigenous concepts; compliant
with EU *corpus juris*; compliant with EU

. . .

ECONOMY

Economic overview: The economy is small and trade dependent. Offshore oil and gas, once the most important sector, is now dwarfed by industry, which accounts for 32% of GDP and 46% of export and employs 25% of the labor force. The financial sector is still large, and accounts for 24% of GDP and 40% of exports; Scotland is home to a disproportionate percentage of the former United Kingdom's banks and insurance companies. Since independence and EU membership, the country has benefited from substantial EU assistance in developing its poorest regions. Inflation is low and there is a regular annual trade surplus. Unemployment remains a serious problem in regions formerly dominated by smokestack industry, and is a major focus of government policy.

Politics: Scotland is noted for its ingrained left-wing political bias and rejection of the liberal economic and conservative social policies encouraged south of the border – this tendency contributed to the breakup of the former United Kingdom. The ruling Scottish National Party is nevertheless providing aggressive assistance to inward-investing companies and has established an industrial development office to encourage small indigenous firms. The model pursued has been described as 'following Ireland and Norway,' and Scotland is widely viewed as being one of the 'Atlantic Tiger' group of small but healthy economies on the western rim of the EU . . .

SUE: EARNING OVERTIME

You've been on scene for an hour already, your stress levels are rising, and it's taken you this long to figure out just one thing: you're going to be late for your evidence 'cast thanks to Wayne Richardson, Marketing Director and Prize Twat, who sits wittering and wringing his hands on the other side of his desk while you try to figure out how to investigate a crime that was committed by a radge bunch o' faeries in a place that doesn't exist. Your smartphone's nagging you about hitting your transferrable overtime limit, and you've already blown your quota for time off in lieu this month; if this goes on you're gonnae have to put it on unpaid hours and file for a time credit from Human Resources. It's even threatening to snitch to the Occupational Health Department that your Work/Life Balance is out of kilter: if this goes on, it'll be off to the compulsory Yoga and Aromatherapy classes with Stress Management for you. Inspector Mac will gently chide you in that calm and measured tone of voice that's fifty times worse than being screamed at by a tanked-up ned: politely enquiring why you didn't talk the idiot into going straight to SOCA instead of dropping his pants on your desk (and Mac's by proxy). And speaking of neds, that's exactly what there's going to be one more of back on the streets if the sheriff fails to see your testimony in their browser when they come to that case.

Congratulations. You've got the investigation from hell to add to your desk load: one that's probably going to run and run for weeks and months, suck in scarce resources from all over, and likely as not will never deliver a clean-up because the festering cunts who go in for high-order stock scams and use botnets in Pakistan can also afford silver-tongued barristers. So your clean-up metric is about to take a nose-dive in the shitter, and all because Wayne Richardson, Marketing Director, panicked and phoned 211 instead of listening to his boss and emailing his company lawyers.

Things are just about coming together in an investigatory sort of way. You've borrowed the MD's office, and they've hooked you up with access outwith the corporate DMZ so you can talk to the station again. Along with the formal caution, you tipped them the nod that they'll get their shinies back after the ICE take a gander at them, which may take some time, so they should kick back and relax. With any luck, that should stop them from getting all upset while the Information Crime Executive play with their toys. (You wouldn't bother except they're Victims, and Victims of Class at that, and the Victim's Charter Ombudsman can have your guts for downpipes if you piss them off: so don't do that, alright?) You've called the said scene-of-crime boys and told them to get their arses down here, and you've uploaded that first barking boardroom scene up to the station server, and you've tasked Bob with getting statements, fingerprints, and DNA swabs from the other witnesses.

You're getting ready to take a deposition from Wayne Richardson, Prize Twat, and you're beginning to feel like it's all under control, when your phone rings. It's on voice-only and with a sinking feeling you see it's the skipper. 'I ken I'm late, sir, but there's nothing to be done about it, this one's doing my head in. If you've been following it . . . ?'

'Aye well, I have that, Sue.' Mac sounds unnaturally phlegmatic about the whole business. 'It's not your fault you're running late. How many statements have you got lined up?'

You take a deep breath. 'There's eight o' them in the shop, and another who works from home. They're trying to call him in but he isna answering his phone or IM. There was no signal down here 'til I got them to give me a line, so I went manual at first. I've sent you the boardroom shoot, that's our formal complaint. I was about to have a talk with Mr. Richardson from Marketing, to get the statements going. The alleged crime . . . I've just uploaded a copy o' their video grab; I figure it speaks for itself. I've called ICE in, but they're swearing blind about how the crime happened on a bunch of mobile phones all over the planet, so I figure we're just going to have to hope there's some evidence for them to find when they lift their laptops. Just getting a straight story about what it is these folks do for a living is giving me a migraine. Anyway, even with Bob helping, interviewing this shower is going to take me a couple of days, and I'm not afrit to say, I'm in over my head, sir.'

Which is the honest truth. Collaring neds for breaking and entering is one thing, managing the gay community outreach program and training constables is another, but international cybercrime in a nuclear bunker under Drum Brae is *right* off the map. It's not something they teach you how to tackle in the coursework for the sergeant's exam. You don't mean it to come out sounding like a whining plea for help, but it does: 'What do you want me to do next?'

Inspector McGregor, bless him, isn't old-school and doesn't believe in hanging his officers out to dry. 'Ach, well, you've made a good start simply by hanging in there and taking names.' He pauses for a moment, then his voice deepens slightly, his tone confiding. 'I just got word from Division that they've had a notification of serious financial crime served by a bunch of solicitors working for a shower called Tiger Investments in London. Meanwhile, a different firm working for Hayek Associates PLC – who would be your mob, I'm thinking – are yammering on the phone about hacking and insider trading, so it looks like the shite's already hit the fan, and everyone's lawyering up for a pie fight. Consider yourself lucky the *Scotsman* hasn't already sent a news crew. Anyhoo, Liz Kavanaugh and her firm are on their way over as soon as they can extricate themselves from a meeting, so look busy and secure the area. All you need to do is stop anyone leaving, log any traffic, start the interviews, and hold the fort until she takes over, and you're out of there with full marks. Are you okay with that?'

You breathe a sigh of relief. Detective Inspector Kavanaugh is a high-flyer who's got her teeth well into the local heavies; let her break her skull on this one. 'Aye, that's doable, sir. But, about the Hastie case—'

'That's your wee ned, is he not?'

You feel a stab of gratitude that he picked up on it: 'The very same, sir.'

'I'll get on to the Sheriff's court and try to buy us a week. If they're not having it, and you're still tied up I'll send someone round to record you on-site, but I'm not taking you off the SOC until X Division have got their feet on the ground. Is that alright by you?'

'Aye. Sir.' You breathe another sigh of relief. You'll probably be late coming off shift, and you're going to spend a good part of Friday hanging around here – you know *all* about those X Division high-flyers and their meetings – but that's the least of your worries right now, and what with the paperwork this is going to generate, you'll make it up in desk time over the next week. 'I'll get right to it.'

'Bye.' He ends the call, and you open the door. The pacing stops suddenly: Wayne nearly jumps out of his expensively manicured skin as he notices you.

'Mr. Richardson? If I can have a few minutes of your time?' You smile politely, not showing him your teeth.

'Um, I was about to call our US office, fill them in on the picture—'

It's two hours to shift end and it's Mary's night off, which means she'll be annoyed if you're not home in time to keep Davey under control when the wee pest gets home from school. *If? When.* You can just see this one running and running, so you drop the velvet glove treatment for a moment: 'This is police business, Mr. Richardson. I want to take a formal statement from you *right now.* Your colleagues can wait.'

'Uh . . .' He's doing the fluttering thing again. 'Alright.' He shuffles towards the office as if he thinks you're going to arrest him. Which isn't actually on the agenda yet, but . . .

You point him at the visitor's chair. 'Look. Sit there. Yes, like that.' You put your phone on the desk and aim it at him. 'This is a phone, okay, I know it looks clunky an' old-fashioned, that's because it's shielded, ye ken? I want you to look at this camera. Alright, what's going to happen is this. First, I'm going to officially caution you. This is routine, and it doesn't mean I'm going to charge you with anything, but a crime has been committed here, and you're on the scene, so it's routine to caution everyone. Then I'm going to formally ID you, and we'll have a little chat, which will be logged under rules of evidence. At the end of this session, I'll email ye the raw file. About three days later you'll get a transcript in the email. What you do is you sign it in ink and bring it to the station within seven days, with your ID card, where we take a saliva sample, register it, and it goes into the file as evidence. That's so it can be brought up in court.'

He frowns, looking worried.

'What?'

'What if, uh, what if the transcript's wrong? Or something?'

You can't help yourself: you snort. 'The transcribers can be pish, sometimes, I'll give ye that, it's what you get when you farm out half the office jobs to Lagos and the other half to a buggy AI, but you're allowed to correct it before you sign it. It's *your* statement to *us*, ye ken. Just don't spread it around.'

(You don't feel the need to remind him that failure to sign and return the affidavit within 7 (seven) working days is a summary offence under the Criminal Justice Reform (Scotland) Act (2012), failure to present a valid biometric ID card is a more serious offence under the Identity Cards Act (2006), and fiddling with the statement may be an offence under the Criminal Law (Consolidation) (Scotland) Act (1995). Because, well, as a law-abiding citizen it's his job to know these things, and you've a not-quite-teenage son to be riding herd on besides.)

'Okay, I guess.' His shoulders droop. 'Where do we begin?'

'Well. Now we're on the record' – you pause to tell the button on the phone to save a time-stamp – 'in your own words, would you mind explaining to me exactly what is it that your company does and what went wrong today?'

ELAINE: Death or Coffee

It's a Friday morning in a North London suburb, and you haven't won the lottery yet, and nobody's drafted you for the King's Musketeers, so it's off to work you go. (Actually, you don't buy lottery tickets in the first place. You ran the figures back when you were seventeen and, wishful thinking or no, you're not *that* stupid. But that's not the point, is it?) It's a Friday morning, you're on the job, and Chris left an email on your mobile about a 10 a.m. crisis meeting. *Crisis, what crisis?* There was none on the horizon when you left work yesterday evening. Hopefully it's just HMRC querying the executive bizjet account consolidation file again.

You check out your shoulder in the bathroom mirror. That's quite some bruise Mike landed on you at the club. The pint and a half of Budvar in the Frog and Tourettes afterwards let you sleep without noticing it, but it's stiffening up now, and you're going to have to work that shoulder carefully for the next few days. So it's the black blouse and the grey suit today. Which will need washing by the end of the week because the Tube seats are filthy these days. TfL can't afford to clean them because they're in crunch mode, buying their way out of their Infraco PPPs to avoid bankruptcy. The mess defederalization has left the country in has really come home to roost this decade: what the cooked books give, the cooked books taketh away. Isn't that the way the world works?

Breakfast is a hastily munched Kellogg's bar washed down with a glass of organic apple juice. You grab the latest copy of *Accounting, Auditing and Accountability* and stuff it in your briefcase, along with the usual: pen, iPod, your father's antique pocket calculator, and a dog-eared copy of Tobler's manual of sword-fighting that you borrowed from Matthew. You visit the bathroom briefly for a smear of lipstick and eyeliner, then you're out the door.

Early May used to be the chilly tail-end of spring, according to Mum. And it certainly used to be cooler. Now the savage summer kicks in weeks earlier, and everyone who can afford it is fitting air-conditioning. (Which in turn is doing no good for the country's ECB stability pact compliance – *no, cut that out! They're not paying you to daydream fiscal policy risk analyses on the commute time, are they?*)

Harrow is its usual sweaty, smelly self, cramped and cluttered with cars that seem to get bigger every year, in a weird race with the price of petrol: look who can afford to fill the bigger Chelsea tractor. It's already five to eight, and the Tube's in full-on rush hour mode. You manage to elbow your way into a carriage at West Harrow and, miracle of miracles, there's a seat edge to perch on all the way to Baker Street (by which time the temperature has got to be pushing thirty degrees and there's a solid wall of bodies between you and the door – good thing you're not claustrophobic). Then it's another half hour on the Hammersmith and City line, rattling and breathlessly hot all the way across London to Whitechapel, and finally fifteen minutes strap-hanging on the DLR south towards Wapping, through the weirdly cyberpunk landscape of geodesic glass dildo-shaped skyscrapers alternating with decaying left-over Olympic infrastructure and cookie-cutter housing developments. You've got it timed down to the nearest minute, and it still takes you ninety, minimum, to do the door-to-door. Count the working days lost – you spend fifteen hours a week commuting, seven hundred and fifty hours a year draining down the sump hole of the capital's crap transport infrastructure. If you could afford to move east you would, but the bits you can afford are all doomed: you've seen the flood maps for the Thames Gateway suburbs and know which insurance firms are whistling past the graveyard . . .

Because you're dead good at your job. Now if only you had a life, too, eh?

The office opens its doors and swallows you off the street. Once upon a time it started life as an unassuming Georgian town house; but today, the garden is overgrown with Foster Associates geodesics, the roof is covered in solar tiles, and the door scanned your RFIDs and worked out who you were while you were still halfway up the street. The HQ of Dietrich-Brunner Associates is probably worth more than some Third World countries. You hole up in the ladies' for a minute to freshen up, then it's up the lift to the third floor, where the junior associates swelter under the low eaves.

After you drop your briefcase you head straight for the coffee station. It's turning half nine, and there's a queue of thirsty associates, ordered by pecking order, waiting for Jessica or Esmé or whoever it is from Admin to quit fiddling with the cartridge and get out the way. A bunch of the associates are glassed-up and fiddling with spreadsheets or in ludic colloquia, but you didn't think to strap your office to your face before you headed for your fix, which leaves you open to the kind of petty irritation that comes with being forced to stand and queue with no distractions. Your spirits droop: then they droop further when you notice Adam Elliot (or he notices you). He's the wrong kind of distraction. But something tells you that a couple of the other associates are logging everything. Certainly Margaret Harrison, up front in the queue, has her associate partner specs on but isn't doing the in-meeting hand-dance. So maybe he'll keep his needling to himself for once.

'Hi, Xena!' he chirps, 'Killed any commuters today?' You try to ignore him: being rude wouldn't be constructive, and *constructive* counts for a lot around here. Adam fancies himself as a big swinging dick in risk analytics: leave out the 'big' and 'swinging' and he's right. But he won't let go. 'How did your quest turn out?'

You know there's no advantage to be gained by murdering idiots – it doesn't teach the idiot anything and it might give onlookers the idea that you take them seriously – but you haven't had your double ristretto yet, so you muster up the coldest stare you can find and say as steadily as you can: 'My private life is none of your business, Adam.' A minor imp of the perverse prompts you to add, 'If you keep passing unwelcome comments, I'm going to have to consider logging these incidents for future action.'

'Hey, that's not nice! I'm only kidding.' He turns passive-aggressive puppy-dog eyes on you. 'You know it's just fun, don't you?'

'Why should she know that?' Margaret interrupts sharply. That gets his attention: she's fortyish, formidable, and probably due to make full partner any month now. She sounds annoyed. 'Go pick on someone your own size, Mr. Elliot. Or at least someone with a compatible sense of humour.'

'But I was just—'

'Making an idiot of yourself in front of the peanut gallery.

Do yourself a favour? Find yourself something constructive to do with your time.' You cross your arms, and Adam slinks away empty-handed. If you ever decide to go postal in the workplace, you'll be sure to start by showing him your first-class letter-opener: in the meantime, though, Margaret deserves some thanks. 'What was that about?' she asks you.

You feel your cheeks heating. 'Adam's got some ideas about me, and he likes to needle.'

'Really?' She raises an eyebrow. 'I'd never have guessed. What about, exactly? I may be able to help.'

Oh bugger. This is exactly what you didn't want to happen, but there's no polite way to put her off. 'In my *copious free time*' – you make sure the ironic emphasis is obvious: if there's one thing that shows disloyalty to the partnership, it's spending your energy outside of work on something that *isn't constructive* – 'I have a hobby. I used to be into gaming, but I drifted sideways into historic re-enactment.'

'Gaming?' She raises an eyebrow. 'Historic re-enactment?'

'Live-action real-time role-playing. Then sideways into mediaeval German sword-fighting,' you clarify. This is the point at which most people's eyes glaze over, which is the reaction you're hoping for. But Margaret doesn't take the offered bait.

'Gaming? That's interesting. Would you have played' – she pauses to twitch at a user interface that's invisible to you – 'Dungeons and Dragons at some point?'

Whoops. 'Not really. I was heavily involved in **SPOOKS** at one time, but . . . ' The woman from Admin finishes fiddling, there's a clunk and clatter from the machine, and the queue moves forward. Margaret seems to have sacrificed her place at the head just so she can interrogate you. 'It tried to eat my life, so I cut right back.'

'That's useful to know.'

'It's old news!' The queue moves forward in lock-step again as Eddie from Phone Support gets into place with a cup holder for the black gang downstairs.

'I'm sorry, I didn't mean to sound patronizing, I really meant it may be useful – are you on the facial Chris called?'

You nod.

'Good, I thought so. Look, all I know is that it has something to do with the Tiger Investments account. Chris said to be on the lookout for gamers because we'll need them, God only knows why. Come to think of it, maybe that's why your name came up.'

'Looking for gamers?' *For the Tiger Investments account?* Even through the haze of embarrassment – that bastard Adam *has* been talking behind the bike shed – it sounds bizarre. 'That's what the crisis group call is about?'

The queue ratchets forward again, bringing her to the front. She smiles patronizingly. 'Look, terribly sorry, must fly. See you in half an hour?'

You force a brittle smile in return. You've got a feeling you're going to need that caffeine.

JACK: REVENGE OF THE MUMMY LOBE

You have been in police cells precisely twice in your life — there was that total disaster when you were fifteen, then going back even earlier there was that time when you were a wee thing and Gav and Nick got you to moon the Lord Mayor when he was up for opening the new drop-in centre. Gav and Nick could run faster than you, which is why — you now realize, with perfect twenty/twenty hindsight — they suckered you in. Both times you were too young to really figure out how bad the situation was. It's somewhat less obvious to you how you ended up being booked into an Amsterdam cop shop at zero dark o'clock last night, largely because you were too addled on skunk and strong Continental beer to know which way was up — but by morning you have made up your mind that despite their laid-back reputation, Dutch police cells are no more fun than English ones. Especially with a hang-over.

If you hadn't been arrested, you'd have ended up spending Friday and Saturday nights in a cramped room at the Bulldog — a hosteller's inn notorious for its remarkably low prices and dubious furnishings. Instead, you spend the night in a cell with a foam mattress, a light bulb, and a stainless steel sink-and-toilet combination by way of furniture. It's actually bigger than the room at the Bulldog, and the stains on the mattress are probably not much worse, but there's no soap, no Internet, and no munchies to distract you from obsessively worrying about your miserable fate. Because, you know, you're doomed. This is the second time you've been arrested in your entire life, and your stress levels are so high that were a bunch of black-robed inquisitors to file chanting into your cell and lead you down a stony tunnel lined with manacled skeletons to a cavern furnished with an electric chair, it would come as a relief. You don't have a clue what to expect, so when the door rattles and opens, you nearly jump out of your skin.

'Mr. Reed. Please come with me.' It's a different cop, built like a rugby jock, and looking extremely bored.

'Um, where?'

You must look confused, because he speaks very slowly and loudly, as if to a half-witted foreigner: 'Step out of the cell and proceed to the end of the corridor, until I tell you to stop.'

'But my—' You glance down at your feet, then shrug. They took your shoes, your belt, your jacket, and your mobie, then made you sign a form: and now some rules-obsessed part of your hindbrain is yammering up a fuss about going out without your shoes on. It's probably the same lobe of your brain that makes sure your fly's zipped up and your nose wiped – the mummy lobe. 'Okay.' You force yourself to take a slippery sock-footed step forward, then another. Your head throbs in time to your heartbeat, and your mouth tastes of dead rodents. Now you notice it, the mummy lobe is nattering at you about brushing your teeth . . .

There's an office room with a desk in it, and a Politie sergeant, and a bunch of indiscreet cameras in luminous yellow enclosures labelled EVIDENCE in English and Dutch. (They must get a lot of tourists here.)

Not to mention a shoe-box containing your mobile, your jacket, your belt, and your shoes. 'Mr. Reed. Please sit down.'

You sit.

'Did you, on the evening of the twentieth, throw any items at the window of the antique shop at 308 Prinsengracht?'

You frown, trying to remember. The mummy lobe is about to say 'I don't think so, but I might be wrong' but you catch it in time, and what comes out is a strangled 'No!'

The cop nods to himself and makes a note on his tablet. 'Did you take the armchair that the owners of 306 Prinsengracht had placed by the side of the road for a municipal waste pick-up and move it so that it was outside the antique shop at 308 Prinsengracht?'

That's an easier one. You don't remember anything about the armchair before you woke up in it. 'No.'

Another squiggle on the tablet. The cop frowns. 'Do you remember anything about last night? Anything at all?'

At this point the mummy lobe makes a bid for freedom and control over your larynx, and instead of saying 'Where's my lawyer?' you hear yourself saying, 'No, not until I woke up in that chair. I was in the Arendsnest earlier in the evening and we had a bit to drink, then we moved on, and things got vague. Then I woke up chained to the street sign.'

'When you say "we", who were you drinking with?'

'I was with Mitch and Budgie. Tom couldn't make it, he was on paternity leave—'

'Alright.' The cop makes another mark on his tablet, then pushes it aside and gives you a Look. You quail: your balls try to climb into your throat. 'Mr. Reed. You appear to have been the victim of a prank that got out of hand. Your DNA was not found on the stone that broke the shop window, or on the window itself, and camera footage shows three other persons carrying you and the chair before handcuffing you to the street furniture. So you are not suspected of vandalism or theft. However, let me be clear with you: that level of drunkenness is a public order offence, and I believe we have sufficient evidence to obtain a conviction. Because it's a minor charge and you are a non-resident EU citizen, if you agree to plead guilty to *"Dronken orde/veiligheid verstoren op openbare weg,"* a drunk and disorderly public order offence on the public highway, for which there is a fine of two hundred and fifty euros, I can release you immediately. If you choose to deny the offence you have the right to a trial before the sub-district court.' He leans back and crosses his arms.

That's pretty harsh for the Amsterdam Politie, but you'd heard they were having a crack-down: just your bad luck to be caught in it. 'What are the consequences if I plead guilty?' you ask.

'As this is an administrative offence, there will be no subsequent proceedings or criminal record if you agree to the fine.' He looks bored. 'It's your decision.'

The offer, it's a no-brainer. Pay €250 and that's the end of it – it's not as if they're going to put you on a sex offender's register or send you to prison or something. The alternative is to face the uncharted waters of finding a lawyer and going to court, where they'll probably find you guilty as charged and send the black-robed chanting inquisitors to lead you down a stony tunnel lined with manacled skeletons to a cavern furnished with an electric chair, just for wasting their time. 'And face it,' the mummy lobe reminds you, 'you *were* drunk, weren't you?'

You nod, then wince as your forehead reminds you about the hang-over. 'Do you take PayPal?'

'Of course.' The cop gestures at the box on the table. 'You will receive an email with instructions for pleading guilty.' He pauses. 'You should remember that failing to plead by email and not attending a court session are much more serious offences than public drunkenness, and the Scottish police will prosecute you on our behalf.'

That you don't need. 'Okay. I'll pay the fine,' you say hastily.

'That concludes this interview. You may leave when you are ready,' says the cop – and he stands and walks out the door, leaving you staring after him with one shoe in your hand and the other on your left foot.

'Don't forget to tie your shoelaces,' chides the mummy lobe. 'Remember, it's a serious offence!'

You emerge from the Politie station blinking robotically, like an animatronic ground-hog with a short circuit. The hangover has intensified so much that you're trying not to move your head in case it falls off. Waves of pain throb in stereo from either temple, and your skin feels two degrees too hot and two sizes too small. It's a bright Saturday morning, and the light isn't making your eyes hurt so much as giving them the *chien andalou* treatment, slashing razor blades of pain through the puffy red-rimmed windows of your soul. It cools down a little once you get your glasses on and the overlays up, but all of this is as nothing compared to the *my-fly's-undone* sensation you get when you carefully look over your shoulder at the front of the station. It is to angst as déjà vu is to memory. If you'd only not let Mitch and Budgie—

Do what?

You shake your head and whimper quietly, then cast around for a tram stop. A plan is hatching. You're going to sneak into your room, sink a couple of ibuprofen and a can of Red Bull as you throw your shit in your bag, then you're going to tiptoe out and hot-foot it all the way to Schiphol and throw yourself aboard the first flight home. Damn the expense. Your phone's already trawling the travel sites for bargains: once home, you will break into your neighbours' house while they're at work, find their cat, and somehow persuade the beast to bury your head in its litter tray. *That* should cure the hang-over, or at least put it in perspective: and then—

The fragile porcelain of your newly cast plan shatters into a myriad of pieces as you remember the phone conversation with Sophie. Something about a party for Elsie? You're supposed to send her a birthday pressie? Forget about sticking your head in the litter tray, it wouldn't do to go birthday-shopping for your eleven-year-old niece while smelling of ammonia. Dammit, home you will go, and knowing your luck, you'll have a job in a bank lined up by next week, fixing broken spreadsheets while wearing a suit with one of those strangulation devices, what do they call them . . . ?

Clean up first. Okay? At least it went a hell of a lot better than the *last* time, when you and Amanda Parker got yourselves into trouble at school.

Amsterdam doesn't do mornings, especially at weekends. You pull your glasses on, tell your phone to show you the road to perdition, and stumble dizzily past shuttered boutiques and sleeping cheese shops, across cobbled streets empty of traffic, towards a tram stop, where you wait for ten minutes until a rattletrap streetcar squeals to a halt beside you. A quick web search shows you that one of the bargain-basement budget airlines has seats home for just €200, one way, plus carbon duty and airport tax. The sea-cat ferry from Rotterdam to Edinburgh is a whole lot cheaper, but you have a sudden queasy vision: *This is your stomach, and this is your stomach on the ocean wave.*

The Bulldog is open, so you sneak up the claustrophobically tight staircase to the floor with your room. You've only brought an overnight bag, and you barely bothered unpacking. Minutes later you're out of the backpacker zone and onto the street, heading for the Centraal Station and a fast train to the airport.

Amsterdam may not do mornings, but the Centraal Station never sleeps. You find yourself standing in the plaza in front of the station with your eyeballs burning from the reflected sunlight jangling off the canal. Motor-scooters and kamikaze cyclists keep trying to kill you, and the place is full of menacing junkies and beggars trying to bum a note off the tourists. The square smells of stale beer and dog turds and hot metal overlaid by the fart-laden exhaust fumes of bike engines. The tram bells in the background set off a cacophonic echo in your head, and birds flock overhead, hunting for victims to dive-bomb. You're still busy trying to buy your flight home, and your glasses can't keep up with the flashy graphical interface the airline uses: cookies keep timing out and your session resets itself. The bandwidth is crap here, and the whole scene has turned out to be one gigantic bummer. You want home, and you're dying for that train back to Schiphol: you'd hoped to get away from the whole **STEAMING** mess once and for all, but the dying snake of a crashed and burned game plan has trapped you in its coils, and it feels like it's choking the life out of you. You really need to go home and get a job interview nailed down.

You wonder who your next corporate master is going to be.

SUE: WAYNE'S WORLD

**STATEMENT BY MR. W. RICHARDSON, MARCH 20, 2018
(RAW TRANSCRIPT):**

'We're Hayek Associates. We were founded three . . . no, four years ago. Just over four years ago. We're a diversified economics consultancy and market-maker. We run virtual central banks for ORGs [massively multiplayer online role-playing games]. We stabilize the economies of seventeen imaginary realms with a combined VM2 – that's, uh, a measure of the total virtual money supply – about the same size as Japan's. We're primary contractors for a tier-one game, **VIRTUOUS GOLD**, that has almost 12 million players, paying €120 a year for access and averaging another €260 on extras. We're primary contractors for three tier-two games in the one-to-five-million-player range, including Avalon Four: also for four tier-three games, a bunch of small fry, and a couple of big development projects I can't talk about right now without violating commercial confidentiality. What it boils down to is, we're responsible for ensuring that 20 million players who spend roughly €6 billion a year to participate in our clients' games don't see their virtual stakeholdings vanish into mid-air.

'I joined Hayek about eighteen months ago when Barry and Bo Pierson – Bo founded the company, he sold his shares to Marcus last year for a couple of million just before I arrived – figured they needed someone to re-engineer their in-game vision. In my last job I was senior market intelligence officer for Kensu International's Scottish distributor. I used to work for Disney Corporation's intelligence unit before that. Marketing and intelligence analysis are closely related anyway, and Hayek needed both. Marcus was on the phone a lot because he was just setting up our working arrangements with Kensu, and we got talking and I did some freelance campaign development work for him, and one thing led to another. Working in this industry is a bit like *Desperate Housewives*, all looking for the right start-up who's going to marry you and make you a millionaire . . . that's the IPO, I guess. Or am I thinking of the unapproved options scheme? No, the IPO is like pregnancy, the options are the . . . hell, it's Barry's metaphor, he can explain it to you.

'You asked about the business? We manage economies in order to maximize player draw – to make it a compelling experience that sucks players in. Imaginary worlds with millions of players don't obey quite the same economic rules as the real world – or I guess they obey them differently, because rather than running on money, games run on fun. I mean, if the players aren't having fun, they'll leave, and then what'll we eat? We plug into Maslow's hierarchy of needs at a different level from a traditional economic system, but a lot of the principles are the same. Money and treasure is always flowing into the game space because you need to reward the users for playing – complete a quest, pick up the treasure. Do you play any games . . . ? No? Just CopSpace? That's not a game, that's a metaverse like Real World or Second Life . . . Sorry, I'll get to the point, I'm just trying to explain what we do, like you asked. Modern games are infinitely scalable in size and number of players. When a customer clicks through the license conditions to play the game, they're agreeing to add their phone as a node in a distributed server. More players equal more servers – not for themselves, I might add, we *never* run a server node for any given game on the same host as a client for that game, that would be asking for trouble – but at the back end, we're in the processor arbitrage market. The game programmers' biggest problems are maintaining causality and object coherency while minimizing network latency – sorry, I'm just telling you what our clients obsess over. Necessary background, okay?

'Anyway. One problem with using users' machines as distributed-processing nodes is that they always try to hack the service. No need to be shocked, it's just a fact of life. They're always trying to get into someone else's gaming pants, and not even running the distributed-processing nodes in a separate VM will stop them. So, to prevent fraud, every item in a distributed game space has to be digitally signed and every significant event in the local game is voted on by at least three peers, and we rely heavily on the phone's trusted processing infrastructure. Incidentally, this means we're into the same authorization and authentication business as your credit card company. Because if somebody finds a way to change stuff without our authorization, they can create value from nothing, then sell the results on IGE or eBay. Which is ultimately deflationary, not to mention being a howling whirlwind of No Fun At All for everybody who's trying to play the game by the rules.

'That's one way of looking at the picture. Not only is there this whole raft of mind-numbing automated administrative stuff that goes on every time you add a player – which is what the game developers worry about – there's *inflation*. Inflation happens when money and loot flow into the game. But to keep the customers happy you have to keep rewarding them. Playing the game is inflationary because they keep burgling the tombs of dead gods, breaking into the governor of Jamaica's dungeon vaults, colonizing the Andromeda galaxy, and so on. And you know, you can't tax them or make the money decay, because that would be No Fun, and if the game stops being Fun, why play? That's the difference between in-game economics and the National Bank – the bank doesn't have to worry about whether we're enjoying ourselves. So we have to control this tendency towards galloping stagflation, and we typically do this by offering short deposit accounts for starship captains, controlling the after-market in magic wands, providing mortgages for prestige-rank necromancers wanting to build their own crypts, and all that sort of thing.

'Then there's immigration and border controls. Most modern multiplayer games run on a couple of distributed-processing platforms – Zone runs on Symbian/GDF and Microsoft Arena runs on .NETSpace – and they've standardized on a common client engine so they can focus on developing new content. Competition is fierce. They've all got scrapers and immigration incentives to persuade customers to migrate from one game to another, taking their characters and loot with them. It's against the terms of service, but no game vendor is willing to cut their own throat by enforcing it – that'd piss off the customers. So, you've got out-of-band merchant sites like IGE and eBay's Gameboard, and a whole bunch of coyotes who make their living by providing tools to migrate avatars from one environment to another, using the exit game assets as arbitrage against a position in the entry game. Which in turn means there are exchange rates between games – and not just game-to-game, I'm talking game-to-euro rates, game-to-yuan, game-to-rupee. All the strong currencies, you name it, even US dollars. So there's currency speculation and an external market in gaming currency hedge funds, not to mention the Magic bugs who believe in keeping their loot in the most powerful magic items they can buy, like the guys who keep their savings account in a roll of gold coins under the bed. There's dirty stuff, too, dirty tricks some of the game companies play on each other, hostile speculation and attempts to dislodge or recruit each other's customer bases, but we don't do any of that stuff at Hayek Associates. We play strictly by the rules.

'One way we take currency out of circulation is to sell imaginary real estate. Another is to provide safety deposit services so that players can stash their gold or loot with us for a fee – this works in game spaces with encumbrance rules. If we spot a deflationary sump, we have to create liquidity until we can plug the gap – this is something a real bank can't do – so we can start offering interest on deposits, handing out free resurrections, that kind of thing. And while all this is going on, we have to keep an eye on how the customers are enjoying their market experience. If people start grumbling, we've got a problem.

'My job – well. I commission in-game campaigns to track customer satisfaction, establish hedonic goal posts, and set targets so our programmers and quants know which way to drive things to maximize fiscal stability. It's like being chancellor of the exchequer, except you can substitute "fun" for "profits" – up to a point, until interdomain currency conversion and hedge funds come into the picture. In monkeyspace – sorry, I mean, outside the games – I'm also in charge of marketing and sales liaison with our corporate clients. We each wear three different hats here at Hayek Associates. Making a single sale, even to a tier-three game, is potentially a multi-million euro contract for us, so a lot of work goes into it . . .

What? Yes, I work with Marcus on closing new accounts. Yes, he's senior to me . . . I suppose you could say that [he's in charge]. No, I'm the Marketing Director. I'm only worth .5 per cent of the company's market cap. I'm insignificant, obviously beneath your notice . . .

'Okay, yes, I understand that. Sorry. No more sarcasm.

'Let me see . . . at about a quarter past ten this morning, I was in a meeting with Marcus and . . . why the hell am I repeating this? You've seen the stream. I've seen the stream . . . No, I can't swear that it really happened because it's something I saw on a screen. What I *thought* I was seeing was a bunch, thirty, maybe forty, Orcs – they're a character race in Avalon Four – march into the central bank. It's in a magic castle carved out of a diamond the size of a hill, in a city floating on a mauve cloud near the Spinward Mountains, and the bank vaults are – look, they're not a real physical vault, it's just a database table that stores a bunch of cryptographic hashes on objects that are registered as being lodged in the bank, okay? The objects are stored in a holographic database on the players' smartphones and the game engine keeps track of them for us. No, I can't tell you whose phone stores a given item. They move around a lot, and there are usually copies on three or more phones at the same time. The bank is a different matter, the root authentication keys are locked down and stored in a trusted database on a server . . . yes, where else would you put a bank? *That's* why we're based in a nuclear bunker. It's good public relations. Yes, the root keys are signed by the Bank of Scotland in monkeyspace. The real security is all in the firewalls, and the data integrity schemas. Nobody ever imagined a band of Orcs would steal a database table . . . '

END RAW TRANSCRIPT

ELAINE: A CATASTROPHIC
LOSS OF GOODWILL

You enjoy facials about as much as you enjoy visits to the dentist. One of these years, when you're *really* rich, you plan to set aside a week and turn yourself over to a dental surgeon who will put you under general anaesthetic, yank out all your pearlies, and install ceramic-and-titanium memory-metal implants socketed into your jawbones. Once you get over the hang-over you'll be able to say good-bye to fillings, secure in the knowledge that you're going to go to your coffin wearing an enigmatic diamond smile. And won't *that* fuck with the archaeologists' heads?

Unfortunately, there's no such easy cure for facials, but you've acquired various coping strategies over the past four years in DBA: a ristretto and a trip to the bathroom first, so you're awake and comfortable; a copy of the agenda and a full battery charge on your old-fashioned folio, so you can scribble notes on it and do what-if modelling on the fly; and a chunk of time allocated ahead of schedule so you know what the hell you're meant to be talking about.

But sometimes they call the meeting at short notice, and there's no agenda on the server, and your folio's fuel tank is half-empty. So then you have to tough it out, like having a cavity drilled out without local anaesthetic. It's all part of *being constructive*.

The sudden-death summons to an agenda-less face-to-face meeting about the Tiger Investments account does, it must be admitted, suggest something interesting is afoot. Chris handles their business, and while you haven't had anything to do with it before, you sort of knew what it was about. TI is an angel specializing in high-tech start-ups, your typical Web 3.1415 outfits, and TI contracted DBA – in the person of Chris Morgan, full partner (and Director of Risk Management) – to produce full pre-IPO investment reports on their clients. Now one of them appears to have gone spectacularly pear-shaped.

'I got a call from TI yesterday evening,' Chris explains. He's got that post-augmented crash look, as if he's been burning bandwidth all night. He's in his midfifties, with heavy black eyebrows and a perpetual worried expression behind his thick-rimmed glasses, as if he's certain he's forgotten something important. 'Their latest clients have had a catastrophic intrusion. More to the point, their lead programmer is missing, and they're screaming about an inside job. I don't have the full picture yet, but it appears someone called in the police, and I understand the local force are escalating it to SOCA. TI have mostly cashed out, and obviously they'll be under suspicion of ramping. Our direct liability is capped at five million, but the implication that we missed something is clearly there.' He pushes his specs up his nose. (He may be one of the last generation who grew up with PCs with glass tubes, but he's kept abreast of the times: those high-resolution Armani displays conceal lasik-enhanced eyeballs.)

Brendan clears his throat. 'What's the plan?' he asks mildly.

'You're the plan: all of you.' He grins quickly. You glance around the table, seeing surprised faces: Faye, Mohammed, Fred, Brendan. The only person who's nodding is Margaret, an indicator that speaks volumes. 'We're going up there tonight on the sleeper train. Jessica's booking rooms and a secure conference suite for us in the West End Malmaison. I expect we'll be there for about a week, so pack your bags accordingly. I've taken the liberty of clearing your schedules as this is now our number one priority.' He looks directly at you, and you raise an eyebrow. 'Yes, Elaine, you're off the Croatia job. Any questions?'

Mohammed, diffidently: 'It's Friday . . . '

'I know.' Chris looks as if he's bitten a lemon. 'But the police are already in attendance. We can't barge in and expect anyone to give us the time of day right now. Monday is another matter, so we're going up there tonight. You've got Saturday to decompress, and Sunday we'll hold a planning session so that when we go in mob-handed on Monday morning, we've got some idea what we're doing.' He pauses. 'By the way, you're all free to go home after this meeting. You'll be needing time to make appropriate arrangements.'

'What *are* we going up there for?' you ask. 'I mean, what can't we do from down here?'

'She's right,' Mohammed agrees. He glances at you nervously.

'I don't see why you need *me*,' Brendan adds waspishly. 'Scotland's got a different legal system. I'm not qualified to practice up there.'

'Hayek Associates are incorporated in London, under English law,' says Faye. 'Isn't that right?' She looks unnaturally pleased with herself.

'That's right,' says Chris. To Mohammed, with a shy grin: 'There's no escape!'

You can't help yourself: 'But I still don't see why we need to be there in person.'

Chris screws up his face and opens his mouth, but Margaret gets there first. 'If I may?' she asks.

Chris nods.

'This doesn't happen very often.' Margaret's lips are as thin as a black line on a balance sheet. 'I know what you're thinking, Elaine. Usually we don't need direct access. The trouble is, usually we're looking for inconsistencies in the audit trail.' She glances at Chris to back her up. He nods thoughtfully. 'Normally we have a good idea whether the data we're being supplied with is sane: we're looking for someone siphoning assets out through the backdoor, but we're pretty sure the building exists in the first place.'

Chris nods again. 'But I'm told this breach took place in, in a *game*.' He glances at Margaret. 'I'm still trying to work out the implications,' he admits. You shiver, as it becomes apparent: Chris and Margaret don't have a clue what they're doing! They're trying to work it out from first principles. Which means this really *is* something unusual. 'We don't know whether there even *is* an audit trail. Or what an imaginary bank robbery in a virtual space means to our client. That's what we're going up there to establish.'

'So why are you dragging Faye and Brendan along?' you ask.

Margaret snorts. 'To figure out whether we were sold a bill of goods by Hayek's board. Chris doesn't want to lose the TI account. Or Lloyds,' she adds pointedly.

Oh. 'You think they're going to be unfriendly?'

'I'm certain of it,' Chris says gloomily. 'If this goes wrong, we could be looking at a catastrophic loss of goodwill, not to mention the Avixa account.' Avixa is a really big contract that's too damn similar to TI for comfort. 'So the plan is, we turn up unannounced on Monday.' He nods at Brendan. 'Gene is drawing up an application for an Anton Piller order' – he still uses the old term for a court search order – 'and a freezing injunction behind it, which we'll be serving on our arrival, I hope. Mohammed, you're familiar with HA's business structure and accounting procedures; we're going to go over them with a nit comb. Margaret, Fred, and Faye will tackle business work flow, managerial competence, and anything else that springs to mind. Brendan, you're there to serve the orders and liaise with our Scottish counsel if necessary. Keep our toe in the door. Elaine, Margaret tells me you've got some background in gaming. The asset loss took place inside a game supervised by Hayek Associates. I want you to go in and audit the bank inside the game. Can you do that?'

Your mind goes blank. It's like one of those horrible nightmares, turning up late at school to sit an exam in a subject you haven't been studying for and finding you're the only person wearing clothes because everyone else is naked – 'You want me to *what*?'

'Bank robbery inside an online game. Banks have accounts. Robberies leave a forensic trail. Yes?'

You blink stupidly for a few seconds. 'Yes, I . . . see. I think.' He glances away, obviously ready to proceed to the next item on his agenda, so you raise an uncertain hand. 'I think you got the wrong end of the stick,' you say hesitantly. 'This is an online game, right?'

It's Chris's turn to blink. Did he think you were some kind of game wiz? 'Well, yes. Why?'

'I'll need an interpreter,' you explain. 'I don't know as much about this stuff as I'm going to need to know' – no point saying you know *nothing at all*, that wouldn't be *constructive*, and it's being constructive under pressure that gets you promoted to partner, although seeing what that Stepford-esque process does to people over the past couple of years has taken the sheen off it — 'and you said their head programmer has gone missing. Is he a suspect?'

'I wouldn't want to prejudice your investigation,' Margaret says with a funny little smile. 'Draw your own conclusions.'

'Well then.' You smile right back at her. *Bingo. They think the programmer did it.* Which means it's probably an inside job, a crime inside a game. *Whoopee.* 'Well, let's pull this missing guy's CV and hire someone *just like him* so I've got a native guide. A gamekeeper to find the poacher. Right?'

'Right.' Chris nods, slowly. Then he makes a note on his pad. 'I'll tell Jessica to get onto CapG right away about matching a body to that skill set. I'm sure there was something about him in the pre-IPO filing. CapG should have — or be able to find — somebody on contract if we light a fire under them. Happy?'

You nod. 'Yes.' If you're getting a gamekeeper to guide you through the undergrowth, you're not being set up to take the fall. Which is good to know because you were getting anxious there for a minute.

'That's settled, then.' Chris momentarily forgets to look worried. 'Any other questions?'

JACK: MOUTH→INSERT(FOOT);

By daybreak on Monday morning you are no longer in Amsterdam or hung-over, but you are still unemployed. It's already light when you stumble downstairs, scrubbing at your face with the shaver (hard enough to raise welts – it needs a recharge), to spoon half-stale coffee into the filter cone. It's the Big Day today, but your sole interview-worthy suit is three years out of fashion, none of your shirts are ironed (or made of fabric with no-wrinkle, for that matter), and your one-and-only tie has somehow acquired a big brown beer-stain while lurking at the back of the sock drawer. *Sod it.* You ask yourself: *Am I that desperate yet?* Well yes, maybe you will be: but this is only day one of your unemployed life, business is booming, the recruiters know you're a techie, and if the interviews go badly, you can hit up your credit card for a new outfit afterwards. So you pull a not-too-stinky black tee out of the washer/dryer, round up yesterday's jeans, and slop UHT and sugar into the chipped Microsoft Office mug on the kitchen work-top as you try to wake up. Then, just as you're thinking about hitting the job boards, the phone rings.

'Hello? Is that Jack Reed? This is Mandy from AlfaGuru. You posted that you were available on Thursday? We've had a job opening come up, and I wonder if you'd like to interview for it—'

Thirty minutes later you've done a quick change into your interview suit and you're walking along parking-choked Glenogle Road, heading towards the bus stops and picturesque boutiques on Queensferry Road. You've dumped all your usual game-space overlays except for Google Local and Microsoft RouteMaster, and the sky is stark and clear above you; the ghost world is almost empty but for the crawling trail of an airliner outbound towards North America, and a twirling red tag tracking your bus across the city towards you.

Replaying the call from Mandy at AlfaGuru is almost enough to get you into a work-a-day frame of mind again. Mandy says the assignment's to do with some kind of insurance-agency work and lists a skill set that matches yours. This comes as a big surprise. Since when do the finance industries code their payroll runs in Python 3000 and execute them on a Zone VM? She wants you to drop in on an office in Charlotte Square for an interview with the primary contractors, CapG Financial Services Consulting. If you get the job, AlfaGuru pockets 15 per cent from the customer for resourcing you. The more you think about it, the more likely it seems that Mandy has made a mistake. ('Games developer, accountant, what's the difference?') Unfortunately, she didn't actually say who the ultimate client was, so you can't Google them to be sure. Chalk it up to practice for the real job interviews you'll be doing in a week or two. Why not play along? The worst they can do is tell you your suit sucks, and you knew that already.

Meanwhile, in other local footnote news (digested from the dailies by your agents, after they prioritize the important stuff about industry mergers, devkit point releases, and new game announcements): the ongoing squabble between Holyrood and Westminster over who pays for counter-terrorism operations is threatening to turn nasty (because nobody north of the border *really* believes that Scotland is some kind of terrorism magnet, whatever the bampots in London think). The first minister is making some kind of high-profile announcement about re-introducing free schooling to encourage the birth rate. And a Russian illegal immigrant has been necklaced down in Pilton, the victim of a suspected blacknet gangland slaying. It's your usual Embra Monday morning rubbish, aside from the Brookmyre special.

The bus snakes up the road in due course, flanks rippling with Hollywood explosions advertising Vin Diesel's latest attempt to revive his ancient and cobwebby career. You climb in and grab the overhead rail, another anonymous traveller among the late flexitime commuters, the young ned females with baby buggies and streaked ponytails, and the buttoned-up Romanian grannies with shapeless wheelie-bags. At least there's nobody on the bus with an ASBO warning flag twirling above their head.

Charlotte Square marks the West End of the New Town (so-called because it was new when it was built in the 1760s: Edinburgh has history the way cats have bad breath). One side of it is linked to Princes Street and George Street by the short umbilical of South Charlotte Street. The central grassy square and man-on-a-pillar memorial is surrounded on all sides by looming grey town houses infused with the solidity of the Scottish Enlightenment and the gravitas of their seven-digit price-tags and Adam fireplaces. Nobody actually *lives* in these houses; they've long since been turned into very expensive offices, roosts for firms of solicitors and professional bodies and head-hunters: like CapG Consulting, to whose hallowed meeting facilitation centre you have been summoned.

'Good morning, Mr. Reed!' chirps Fiona-on-the-front-desk, discreetly arphing your details from your ID card. 'Are we here for our interview?' She addresses you with the chirpy condescension of a dentist's receptionist talking to a sullen three-year-old.

You briefly weigh the pleasure of making her cry against the potential damage to your credit rating and bite your tongue. 'I guess I am.'

'Let me just see where you need to go . . . ' She has a traditional terminal on her desk, and makes a big show of tippy-tapping the keys and clicking the mouse. 'Ooh, that's interesting. The client is Dietrich-Brunner Associates, and according to AlfaGuru you're an *exact* match for the skill set they're looking for! Isn't that exciting?'

'Um,' you say, hoping to buy time. You can already feel an imaginary tie – you're not wearing your beer-enhanced relic – squeezing your carotid artery shut. CapG is one of the really big outsourcing/rightsizing/bullshitting groups. They don't employ game developers, they employ Excel macro monkeys and very expensive systems-management consultants. And whoever these Dietrich-Brunner people are, they don't ring any bells from the gaming end of the industry. They sound more like a firm of up-market cat burglars, or maybe venture capitalists. 'What exactly are they asking for?'

There's obviously been some kind of mistake. Maybe Fiona-on-the-front-desk is looking at someone else's records.

'Let's see.' She squints at the screen and traces one finger down it, moving her lips. 'CS degree, upper second honours or better. Lots of Python 3000 and also Zone administration on Symbian/GDF or .NET-Space. In your personal interests you're down as a keen gamer – is that right?'

You stare at her, open-mouthed, while she stares back at you as if she's wondering if you need a nappy change.

'That's me,' you admit. 'Are you sure you got the company right? They don't sound like a gaming development house to me.'

More clickey. 'No, there's no mistake, Mr. Reed. They're insurance fraud investigators. I've got a couple of senior placement executives who're dying to talk to you about the client's requirements.' She puts her professional smile back in place: 'According to your NI records, you're resting between contracts right now. Would you like me to put your interview down against your Jobseeker's Activity for this week?'

You boggle for a moment. *CapG are plugged into the social security database?* The Jobseeker's Activity requirement – the number of interviews you do per week – is one of the mandatory hurdles they put in your way before coughing up unemployment benefit. 'I, uh, suppose so. So, there's an interview?'

'Yes, they'll be with you in a few minutes if you just take a seat in interview room five?' She clearly can't wait to get you out of her nice clean reception area. She's probably afraid a real customer will walk through the door any moment now and mistake you for someone who actually *works* here.

Room 101 is on the first floor, opposite the lavvy. You trudge up the stairs with a sinking feeling. It's about the size of a toilet cubicle and there's a smell of leaky drains to underscore the resemblance. Inside, you find the usual: multifunction printer, thin terminal, speaker-phone, and a desk they probably stole from an old primary school while it was being demolished. The only windows are the ones on the antiquated screen. All in all, it's a typical agency teleconferencing suite. You settle down in the chair and wait for your call, wishing the cheap bastards could stretch to a coffee robot.

You'd do some digging for background on Dietrich-Brunner, but there's an unaccountable lack of signal in this room: you're completely offline. *Nice.* You're remembering why you don't like temp work. CapG's paranoia about – horrors! – their contractors actually *talking to their clients* without them being able to eavesdrop ('heaven knows what'll happen, maybe the client will *offer them a job* without giving us our cut?') turns these interviews into a bad time-travel trip: you've heard that this is what it used to be like for *everybody* back in the twentieth century, tied down by fixed land-lines and corporate firewalls.

The screen rings, saving you from your Dilbert re-enactment experience. 'Yes?' you ask, sitting up and centring your head in the mirror window.

'Jack Reed?'

The caller window expands to show you a much larger room and a couple of Suits. They're sitting side by side behind a polished conference-table: call them Mr. Grey and Mr. Pin-Stripe for now, using the cut of their cloth as a reference point.

'Yeah, that's me.' You force yourself to smile. There's a bit of echo in the pipe, so clearly CapG are trying to anonymize the routing. Either that, or they're trying to convince you they're a bunch of spooks trying to look like a body shop. *Willy-warmers.* 'You're looking for someone to do a number on a client called, um, Dietrich-Brunner Associates?'

'Yes.' Mr. Pin-Stripe looks down his nose at you. 'We understand you've worked on short-term trouble-shooting contracts before?' He's about forty, immaculately turned out, greying at the temples, and to say he sounds dubious is an understatement.

'Yeah. Before LupuSoft I did some temping.' Which is a

polite euphemism for university vacation work and desperation stuff between real jobs, but with any luck they won't ask for the gory details. 'Fessing up to three months on a front-line tech support desk might not be too convincing. 'I prefer longer-term commitments.' Which is true enough, and it implies loyalty, you hope.

Mr. Grey is about ten years younger, has blond fly-away hair, and is just as frozen-faced as Mr. Pin-Stripe. He cuts in rapidly.

'It says on your CV that you've got a high reputation score on WorldDEV, is that right? And you spent the past nine months engineering an agile swarming combat model for a commercial product – **STEAMING**, is that the name? Is that right? At LupuSoft?' His voice is almost supine with a boredom completely at odds with his words: they're obviously using an emo-filter on the voice stream. 'I used to play **PREM-IERSHITS**. They make really good games.'

You nod, wearily. Echoes of your Sunday hangover chase the cob-webs and tumbleweed around your Monday morning head. 'I was team leader on the extreme conflict group. We were implementing a swarm-based algorithm for resolving combat between ad hoc groups with positional input from their real-world locations—' You weeble on for a minute or so, playing buzzword bingo. Mr. Grey nods like a parcel-shelf novelty, hanging on your every word. The poor bastard looks like he still harbours secret romantic ideas about the gaming biz. Trapped in an outsourcing consultancy, writing requirements documents for a living, he imagines that if things were just *slightly* different, he could be cutting loose and hanging tough in some laid-back-but-dynamic programming nirvana. Little does he suspect . . .

Eventually, Mr. Pin-Stripe takes over. (He's been listening, his face completely expressionless all the while.) 'I'm sure you've memorized all the Java APIs,' he says, unintentionally dating himself in the process. 'But we've already made enquiries with LupuSoft, about the projects you worked on.' *Oh shit. Does that include the special stuff we don't talk about?* you wonder. But he moves swiftly on. 'What do you know about Avalon Four?'

You rack your brains for a moment before you remember. 'That's a distributed realm running on Zone. Made by, um, Kensu? Out of Shanghai? It's basically a fairly faithful implementation of Dungeons and Dragons, fourth edition D20 rules. Just like the old Bioware series, except it's a Zone-based Massive.' Mr. Pin-Stripe's face is still a rigid mask. You begin to wonder just how much image-processing horsepower is going on behind the screen – *his* voice is slightly fuzzed, too. Maybe they think you've got a speech-stress analyzer concealed in your belly-button? 'With modern rules updates, of course. They had to ditch a lot of the Cthulhu stuff after Chaosium was acquired by Microsoft, but the world doesn't really need another squid-shagger MORG . . . there's money in AD&D, it's a reliable cash cow, and that's what Avalon Four is supposed to be.'

'Have you ever played Avalon Four?' asks Mr. Pin-Stripe, his face still unreadable. You stare at the screen. There's no sign of a pupillary reflex – in fact, his eyes are slightly fuzzy, at below-par resolution. *Yup*, what you see is definitely not what you get. For all you can tell, on the other side of that fat rendering pipeline Mr. Grey and Mr. Pin-Stripe could be naked, middle-aged, Korean housewives.

'Sure.' You shrug. 'I OD'd on D20s back in my teens, to tell the truth. It's something to go back to for old times' sake, but I don't usually play more than the first level of a new game, just to cop a feel and eyeball the candy. Um, to see how they've implemented it. Zone's full of MORGs, and it's my job to add to them, not get lost playing them.'

You are getting a queasy feeling about this set-up: some-thing's not right. CapG's client – *damn them for shielding this room so you can't Google on Dietrich-Brunner* – need a game engin-eer. They know jack shit about game development, so they hit up their usual outsourcing agency, which turns out to be CapG. Who, *what a surprise*, also know jack shit about game development, so they go to AlfaGuru and Monster and all the other bottom-feeding body shops with some CV they got off the net, and you just happen to be the first person they found who matches the search criteria. Trouble is, it sounds like a complete clusterfuck waiting to happen. Neither the client nor the resourcing agency knows what the hell he's doing. You'll probably get there and find out they really want an airline pilot or a performing seal or something. And wouldn't that be bloody typical?

While you are having second thoughts, Mr. Pin-Stripe seems to come to some sort of decision. And he opens his mouth:

'As you have no doubt already realized, this is an unusual contract for us. One of our clients, Dietrich-Brunner Associates, are in some distress. They are a specialist reinsur-ance risk analysis house; they negotiated the guarantees for a venture capital corporation that backed a very promising game industry company that went public a few weeks ago. It now appears that a complex crime has been committed inside Avalon Four, and to cut a long story short, certain parties are liable for an enormous amount of money if the details come out.' He pauses. 'Have you signed our non-disclosure agree-ment yet?'

'You want an NDA?' You shrug: 'Sure.' Everybody demands NDAs. Probably Fiona-on-the-front-desk was supposed to nail you for one on your way in the door. That's okay, you can sort it out later.

'Good.' Mr. Pin-Stripe nods, jerkily, at which point the brilliantly photorealistic anonymizing pipeline stumbles for the first time, and his avatar falls all the way down the wrong side of uncanny valley – his neck crumples inwards disturbingly before popping back into shape. (You can fool all of the pixels some of the time, or some of the pixels all of the time, but you can't fool all of the pixels all of the time.) 'Dietrich-Brunner Associates have assembled a tiger team of auditors who are about to move in on the target corporation. Their goal is to prove criminal culpability on the part of Hayek Associates' board, which has implications for the size of their liability – they also want to give the police any necessary assistance in bringing the criminals to justice. However, DBA are not a games company. They lack specialist expertise, and one of their analysts has asked for someone with a skill set almost identical to yours.' You sit up straight. *He can't be thinking about* that, *can he . . . ?* It's not something you list on your CV, other than in the vaguest terms – some of the projects they had you working on back before you shifted sideways into **STEAMING** are dual-use, quite close to violating the law on hacking tools.

'If you accept this contract – which will be a strictly shortterm one, billable hourly – you will be assigned to their team as a domain-specific expert to help them understand what happened. You will be working under condition of strictest secrecy, before and after the job. You started when you walked in the door of this office. Is that acceptable?'

You take a deep breath. The moment crystallizes around

you – the grubby paint, the underlying sickly-sweet smell of blocked drains, the two false faces on the desktop before you – and your headache and sense of world-weary fatigue returns. The mummy lobe reminds you that you've got six weeks' salary in your bank account: you don't have a car or a girl-friend, your only real outgoing expenses are the house and the residual payments on the mortgage from Mum's chemo, and you've been working so many eighty-hour weeks that you haven't had time to spend your 60K-plus-bonuses package on anything else. You don't *need* the kind of political turdball that you can see rolling down the gutter towards you on the leading wave of a flash-flood. You especially don't *need* a couple of smug suits leaning on you to take it on the cheap because you've been unemployed for all of forty-eight hours in the middle of the biggest industry bubble since AJAX and Web 2.0. The mummy lobe is telling you to say *no*.

So you open your mouth and listen to yourself say, 'I want eight thousand a day. Plus expenses.'

This is the polite, industry-standard way of saying 'piss off, I'm not interested.' You did the math over your morning coffee: you want to earn 100K a year, what with those bonuses you've been pulling on top of your salary. (Besides, a euro doesn't buy what it used to.) There are 250 working days in a year, and a contractor works for roughly 40 per cent of the time, so you need to charge yourself out at 2.5 times your pay-roll rate, or €1000 a day in order to meet your target. Not interested in the job? Pitch unrealistically high. You never know . . .

'Done,' says Mr. Pin-Stripe, staring at you expressionlessly. And it is at that point that you realize you are well and truly fucked.

SUE: GAINING ACCESS

It's Monday morning, and you are semi-officially PO'd.

Thursday was bad enough – you didn't wrap up until Liz Kavanaugh and her firm were well installed, grilling the MOPs one-on-one. Before you clocked off, Liz took you aside for a little off-line time. 'Sergeant Smith? Mind if I call you Sue?'

You nodded cautiously, because you always found it hard to tell where Inspector Kavanaugh was coming from. (She looks like she's heading for politician-land, with her law degree and tailored suits, but what she wants along the way – who knows? She's still a bloody sharp cop.) Whatever, pissing her off was a very low priority on your check-list, and if she wanted to be friendly, that was fine.

'Nice to know.' She smiled briefly, more of a twitch than anything else. 'I'm short-handed, and you were first on scene, so you're already up to speed. I've got a feeling that there's a lot more to this than meets the eye because I'm getting a ton of static already. Holyrood is really rattled, and a whole bunch of interested parties are about to descend on this mob. And I'm going to lose Sergeant Hay and DC Parker to the Pilton murder enquiry tomorrow. So if you've got nothing more urgent to do' – which translates from inspector-speak into *this is your number one priority as of now, sunshine* – 'I'm going to ask you to stick around for the time being.'

To which all you could do was shrug and say, 'Could you clear it through Mac first, Inspector? He's my skipper, an' I wouldn't want him to think I was deserting the ship.'

Kavanaugh nodded briskly and book-marked your request, and that was your Friday case-load blown out the water, not to mention your monthly clean-up rate: Jimmy Hastie would just have to wait until someone else could collar the little gobshite for something. But at least you wouldn't have to tell the skipper yourself.

Friday was worse than you expected. You turned up at nine o'clock sharp, frazzled from a breakfast argument with Mary over who was going to fetch Davey after school – with the wee scally himself making a bid for beer money by offering to take himself down to Water World if only you'd give him the read-ies – only to find that Mac might have detached you, but he was hanging on to Bob. So you headed over to the bunkerful of crazies on your lonesome, only to find a very inspectorly Liz Kavanaugh briefing a reporter from the *Herald* outside the bunker doors, and a couple of suits from X Division skulking around out back for a quick fag. They were very old boy's club, and you barely got the time of day from them: *arseholes*. So you went inside and buckled down to interviewing the help, except you couldn't get a handle on whatever it was they were speaking: it *sounded* like English – they were all southern transplants – but the words didn't make any sense. After the third shot at getting Sam Couper to explain how he knew the Orcs were Pakistani Orcs (and not, say, Japanese Orcs, or your more reliably radge subspecies from Dalhousie), and getting a different reply each time – culminating in your having to ask him how to spell 'multiswarmcast minimum-latency rout-ing' – you excused yourself and went to find the inspector.

'I don't understand these folks' tongue, Liz. They're space

aliens from the planet IT industry. Maybe someone from ICE can talk techie to them? It's like the joke about the post-modernist gangster who makes you an offer ye canna understand. More to the point, I don't know what I'm supposed to be looking for, an' that's a wee bit of a handicap. I mean, with your average wee ned, it's pretty clear what's gan on, what mischief they're up to, but this shower don't tick like that. Can you not give me some guidance?'

Kavanaugh fixed you with a baby-blue gaze so pointed you could have booked her for carrying a sharpie: 'You're recording everything, aren't you? I know you're not a specialist. *They* know that, too. Just do the interviews, and someone who knows what to look for will go over them later. We'll get a full gesture and voice stress breakdown, not just what they're mouthing off, and if we're lucky, someone will get over-confident and forget they're not just talking to you. Understand? Once we know who's not telling us everything, we can roll it up from there.'

You nodded. Not that understanding made it fun, but at least you weren't wasting your time. 'Okay, I got that. You figure it's an inside job, and maybe we can flush our bird by playing dumb.'

'You mean, *if* it's an inside job.' The inspector's façade cracked for a moment: she looked tired. 'Of course, it might not be. In which case we're in a deep pile of dogshit, and it's going to take SOCA to dig us out of it. Have you got everyone pencilled in on your list yet?'

You zoomed a GANT chart you'd been working on and zapped it in front of her: 'I've not met this Nigel MacDonald yet. He wasn't in yesterday, and he isn't here today. Works from home, according to Richardson. Some kind of programmer. I phoned his number, but he isn't answering.'

'Well. If I were you, I'd go round and bang on his door.' She grinned. 'Rattle some cages. Within reason,' she added hastily.

Within reason.

Which was the rub: way back when you were doing a social psych module for your degree in police studies, you went through a period when you used to try and nail every damn category of offender to one of the steps of Maslow's pyramid of needs. Take your common-or-garden ned (or chav, if they're from south of the border): you know what motivates them. It's basic stuff, a couple of steps up the hierarchy – beer and sex, mostly, and maybe the need to have a bigger boom box in their tinny wee shitebox of a jacked-up hatchback. Fitba's a bit too intellectual for that bunch, except for the tribal element. And neds are the bread and butter of community policing: domestics and public order offences and drugs plus the odd bit of petty theft. Pencil that in as physiological/safety stuff, with a dusting of sex on top. So you got a certain kind of crime that fit their needs, and a certain type of motivation, and figuring out how to join up the dots was mostly quite straightforward.

Whereas . . .

Where the hell did stock options fit in hierarchy theory? Or designing a better fire elemental? It was all right off the map, tap-dancing on the self-actualization pinnacle of the hierarchy. Your neds wanted to eat, get drunk, or fuck, and the bad things they could do were quite predictable – but the double-domes in the bunker were all at the top of the food-chain already – they either didn't need or didn't want that stuff. Forget boom boxes for the motor, half the staff drove Mercs or Maseratis, and the other half didn't drive at all, probably thought it was a Crime against Gaia. What recondite shit could they get up to in pursuit of self-actualization? Especially in a business that made money, near as you can tell, by refereeing a game?

It's enough to make an honest cop's head hurt.

Being politely thick at the gearheads was getting to you, so after lunch you got in the car and trundled over to Mr. MacDonald's house, which turned out to be a top-floor flat in Bruntsfield, just off the Links. Which would have made for a nice side trip, but by the time you'd found somewhere to park and then climbed four flights of stone steps – like most of Edinburgh, the tenement he'd chosen to live in predated the invention of the steam engine, never mind lifts – you were deeply unamused to find yourself facing a locked oak door with a discreetly reinforced frame and an unanswered doorbell.

Standing on the wicker door-mat, you speculated for a few moments: *maybe the sly bugger's legged it to Dubai to spend his ill-gotten gains?* (Assuming for a moment that the ill-gotten gains existed – you weren't too clear on that.) You glanced up. There was the usual sky-light over the stairwell, but you were buggered if you were about to go shinnying up on the roof, twenty metres up, just to try and sneak a peek through the shutters. *If Liz wants me to break my neck, she can write me a memo.* Instead, you put in a request for a UAV overflight and some pix: lowest priority so it wouldn't come off your budget, just something to add to the task list of the next one of the force's spy planes to overfly the neighbourhood. You tagged the flat as not responsive to officer in CopSpace, time-stamped it, scribbled out a paper police access form, and jammed it through the letter-box, then headed back to the bunker, so you could spend the rest of your afternoon being talked down to by nerds.

At least you got Saturday and Sunday off for your sins.

Which brings you around to the here and now of Monday morning, and the team meeting Liz has called while you're sipping your latte in Starbucks (as usual). Mac released you to her almost by return of IM, so now you're stuck working with the old-school suits from X Division, not to mention a new boss who's too smart by half. *Wonderful* . . .

'I think we've got preliminary coverage of all the parties on the scene of crime. Not that it makes much sense to talk about the scene as such, but Grant tells me the imaging is complete, so we've got an evidence sandbox with a complete snapshot of Hayek Associates' IT set-up as of Thursday evening, with traffic inputs since then.' The inspector shrugs elegantly. You're not sure whose office she's sitting in with her cam, but it's plusher than yours. 'Now for the follow-up.' She pauses and looks straight at the phonecam, for all the world as if she's reading from a teleprompter. 'Mark, if I read my tea leaves correctly, we're going to get a shitload of interested parties descending on the scene today, from insurers and underwriters on down. I want a complete visitor log and report on what they want with the target. Maybe we'll get something back from shit-storm analysis this time.' Mark – Sergeant Burroughs – grunts something semi-audible.

'Yes, I want a full background on everyone.' Kavanaugh raises her coffee mug (genuine ceramic, none of your recyclable cardboard nonsense). 'You and Grant can go camp out in the bomb shelter this morning. I'll be along later. Sergeant Smith.' (You stiffen unconsciously.) 'It's been forty-eight hours. Have we heard from your missing party?'

'No mam.' It's out of your mouth before you realize it. 'I emailed, phoned, IM'd, left a paper note, and banged on his door, if that's what you're asking. And I started the clock.'

'Well then.' She smiles. 'He works from home, we have reason to believe he's got material evidence relating to an ongoing investigation in his possession, and he isn't answering the door after forty-eight hours. Meet me at the Meadowplace station in half an hour. It's time to call in the ram team.'

Warrender Park Terrace. To your left, the Links, grassy meadow with cycle paths and ancient trees spreading their boughs over the parked cars. To your right, your typical Edinburgh tenement block; roughly carved stone blocks, rickety doors on the common stairwell shared by a dozen flats, and no sign of what's going on behind those politely drawn slatted blinds and net curtains. It could conceal genteel working-class pensioner poverty, or a space-age bachelor pad. A loudly arguing family of five or a solitary bloater rotting in an armchair in front of a dusty TV.

CopSpace sheds some light on matters, of course. Blink and it descends in its full glory. Here's the spiralling red diamond of a couple of ASBO cases on the footpath (orange jackets, blue probation service tags saying they're collecting litter). There's the green tree of signs sprouting over the doorway of number thirty-nine, each tag naming the legal tenants of a different flat. Get your dispatcher to drop you a ticket, and the signs open up to give you their full police and social services case files, where applicable. There's a snowy blizzard of number plates sliding up and down Bruntsfield Place behind you, and the odd flashing green alert tag in the side roads. This is the twenty-first century, and all the terabytes of CopSpace have exploded out of the dusty manila files and into the real world, sprayed across it in a Technicolor mass of officious labelling and crime notices. If labelling the iniquities of the real world for all to see was enough to put an end to them, you could open CopSpace up as a public overlay and crime would vanish like a hang-over. (If only half the tags weren't out-of-date, and the other half was free of errors . . .)

You park up behind the Tranny just as Kavanaugh and Sergeant Gavaghan are stretching their legs and the ram team are getting their kit-bags out. She nods at you, and Gavaghan makes eye contact. He's okay, you've worked with him before. 'Where is it?' asks the skipper.

'Up here.' You point. A couple of uniforms you don't know start hauling their bags towards the steps. 'Whoa, it's the top-floor flat. Let me show you.' One of them mutters something under his breath. You pretend not to notice.

It's a warm day, and the smell of cut grass and pollen from the horse chestnuts on the Links tickles your nose. By the time you reach the top of the stairs, you're breathing a bit faster than you should be. You bend down and examine the letter-box. Your access form is still in place. More to the point, the *Evening Post* is jammed halfway through. The freesheet comes out on Thursdays, clinging grimly to its declining circulation. The inspector's right behind you. You point at the letter box and she nods. 'Not a good sign. Very well. Sergeant Gavaghan, would you like to inspect the premises before we go in?'

Gavaghan glances over his shoulder. 'Jimmy, you got the X-ray specs?'

'Yes, sir.' Jim leans against the wall directly under the sky-light and rummages around in his kit-bag. 'X-ray specs coming right up.'

They're not spectacles and they don't run on X-rays, but the tera-hertz radar box can see through walls well enough to fit the bill. Bob switches it on, pointing it at the stone floor, and opens up a new layer in CopSpace. The skipper finger-types a label: MACDONALD RESIDENCE. 'Let's see what's in there.'

Jim points his box at the door and fiddles with it. Then he starts swearing. 'I'm not getting a signal, mam. Nothing at all.'

Kavanaugh raises an eyebrow. 'Is it working? Give me a quick peek sideways.'

'Just a sec . . . ' He takes the box off-line from CopSpace, then swings it round for a moment, to point at the neighbour's door. 'Yes, it's working okay.' He points it back at the absent programmer's front door. 'If I didn't know better, I'd figure there was shielding in there.'

Kavanaugh raises her eyebrow higher. You make eye contact. She's smiling, but there's no humour in it. 'He's sharp,' she remarks to nobody in particular. 'That's a distinct possibility. Put your box to sleep. We're going to have to do this the old-fashioned way.'

Jim looks up at the ductwork where the electricity and gas pipes enter the flat. 'Shite,' he says succinctly.

'Constable Rogers,' Gavaghan mutters, 'the rams, please. Overalls, everyone.' He turns away and starts talking to dispatch, asking them to find out who owns the utility feeds and get them shut off.

Rogers – and Jim – hand you a disposable overall, then get the door jacks and battering ram assembled. The latter is about a metre and a half long, and has a transparent face shield and sixteen evidence cameras hanging off it. While they're doing that, Gavaghan drafts you to help with the duct tape and nylon sheeting, improvising a loose tent to cover the front door and keep particulates from escaping.

'Everyone record full lifelog, please,' says Kavanaugh, standing at the back of the cocoonlike white tunnel. Even wearing a blue polythene bag, she manages to look coolly managerial.

Jim glances at you as Rogers makes busy with the horizontal ram, jacking the uprights of the door-frame apart to help pop the lock's tongue out of its groove. 'You got your Girl

Guides' badge in battering rams?' he asks. *Are you going to get in the way?*

'Nah.' You shrug. 'What you want me to do?'

'Get back and stand oot the way. We'll take two practice swings first. Don't get too close, I wouldna want to put you in hospital.'

'Okay.' You line up behind his back, looking at the door over his shoulder, through the thick Lexan shield.

'One – two – three!' The impact is jarring, but the door takes it. 'Jesus,' Rogers mutters disgustedly. 'Again! One – two—'

The door topples inwards with a loud crash. It's one of those flats that has a windowless room for a hall, everything else opening off doorways to either side. This being the top floor, it has a skylight, and what light there is comes streaming through the open Varilux window and the door to the living room, which is ajar. The floor's bare, and the walls are an odd golden colour, papered with a curious design.

For a moment you fixate on the step-ladder and the rope dangling through the skylight and think, *Oh shit, he's hanged hissell.* Then you blink it into perspective as you follow the ram crew onto the top of the fallen door, and you realize there's no body, and the rope is a bundle of cables that reach the floor, then trail into the living room. It's a suicide scene without a suicide. *Aw fuck, I should'ha gone up the roof after all,* you think. You sniff suspiciously. The air smells musty, and there's an unpleasantly familiar undernote to it.

'Samples!' calls Constable Rogers, and there's a clicking noise up and down the ram as its forensic air samplers snap closed on a million microscopic dust particles floating in the air. Some of them are hooked up to the sniffer on his belt, and if anyone's been smoking the whacky baccy, you'll hear about it in a minute: others go to the real-time LCN profiler and its online link to the national DNA database. 'Down ram!'

You step around the guys as they lower the heavy ram. Ahead of you, Gavaghan and his crew are opening doors and glancing inside. The inspector's busy with a tripod and some kind of laser surveying tool. You put your best foot forward and shove the living-room door open, camera first.

It's your typical tenement living room. Three-metre-high ceiling, fireplace, and a huge bay window with wooden shutters, from back when daylight was cheap and electric lights were unheard of. Some of these buildings are older than Texas. There's a cheap sofa with too many cushions, and a big recliner, but that's where the normality ends. Because what kind of weirdo fills their living room with office equipment, then trashes the place?

'Sue.' You nearly jump out of your skin at the inspector's tone of voice: 'If you don't mind?'

'Sorry, I was just capturing the scene . . . '

She slides past you, shaking her head. 'Spare me.' Then she gets an eyeball of the big office desk lying on its side and the PC with its guts spilled across the floor. 'Log this to evidence, *don't* touch anything—'

'Skipper?' It's Gavaghan, calling through the hall, his voice hollow. 'You'll want to see this.'

'What. Now?' She's out of the living room like a cat after a moth, and you trail along in her wake, cams still chowing down on every stray photon around you.

'Kitchen,' he calls. Flags are going up everywhere, ghostly signs tagged to doorways like BATHROOM and BEDROOM 2, and Liz dives towards KITCHEN. 'Hold it!' There's something in his voice that brings the inspector up sharply.

'How bad is it?'

'Need SOCO to tell us, skipper. It's not like there's a body or anything—'

'Then why are you—'

'We're too late: it's already been sanitized.'

ELAINE: BEING
CONSTRUCTIVE

Saturday morning finds you rolling out of a sleeper train berth bright and early, in Edinburgh. Capital of the People's Republic of Scotland, jewel of the north, biggest tourist trap in Europe, and a whole bunch of other things. The first not-so-subtle hint you're not in England is the row of flags flying over the railway station concourse – pale blue background, white diagonal cross. They're feeling their new EU-regional *cojones*, the Scots. It's a puzzler, but at least they're not insisting you clear customs and immigration: thank Brussels for something.

The taxi ride to your hotel rubs in the fact that you've come to another country. It's the old-fashioned kind of black cab, with a real human being behind the wheel instead of a webcam and a drone jockey in a call centre. Your driver manages to detour past a weird building, all non-Euclidean swoops and curves (he proudly declares it to be a parliament, even though it looks like it just arrived from Mars, then confides that it cost a science-fictional amount, confirming the Martian origins of its budget oversight process). Then he takes a hyperspace detour round the back of a bunch of office blocks and into a rural wilderness, around the grassy flank of an extinct volcano so pristine that you half expect to see a pitched battle in progress between ghostly armies in kilts. Finally, you pop back out into a stonily pompous Victorian satellite town centre: except that back home, buildings don't usually have battlements with cannons carved into them.

Okay, so maybe they're feeling their *cojones* because they've invented hyperspace travel. You ease your death grip on the black cab's grab rail and twitch your map overlay into life. 'Malmaison,' says the driver.

'Uh . . .' You blink. The hotel does indeed appear to have gun turrets. And gargoyles. Then your tourist map twitches and rearranges itself in front of your eyes as the overloaded Galileo service catches up with you. 'This is the, uh, Niddrie Malmaison. I wanted the West End one?'

'Oh, *reet*. Ahcannaebemissingthe—' You blink at the subsequent stream of consonants interspersed with vowels that sound subtly wrong. Maybe you'd have been better off waiting for a call-centre-controlled limo. But evidently no reply is expected: the driver hits the pause button on his meter and engages the mysterious fifth wheel that allows taxis everywhere to turn on the spot. And you're off again, into a bizarre grey maze of steep streets and steeper buildings, with or without battlements. Eventually you find yourself in front of what your map overlay insists is the right hotel, and you can relax and bill it to the company account. The frightening numbers suddenly feel a lot less threatening when you remember you're being billed in euros, not pounds.

This hotel also has crenulations, towers, and flagpoles, but they seem to have missed out on the more alarming architectural excursions and the lobby has a reassuringly familiar interior, furnished in international hotel-chain glass and chrome.

Negotiating the front desk isn't hard, and once you've installed the contents of your suit carrier in the bijou closet and parked your laptop on the beautifully arranged desk, you suddenly realize that it is barely nine o'clock in the morning: you're in a foreign capital city, you don't actually have to check your work email until tomorrow, and once you've showered the sleeper-induced kinks out of your neck and shoulders, you've got an entire day in which to do touristy things. The prospect is inexplicably frightening and alluring. So, of course, you do it.

On Sunday you deal with a mild hang-over, a business-planning facial in the conference suite that staggers on for six and a half hours, and the inexplicable realization that the previous day you purchased a five-foot-long claymore from a dodgy pawnshop on North Bridge, and you have *no idea* how to get the thing home through the metal detectors at Euston without being arrested for carrying an offensive weapon, viz., a two-handed sword.

It must be something in the water.

On Monday morning you awake with the dawn, a mild sense of dread gnawing at your stomach. It's performance anxiety, the kind you get when you're about to be plunged into an unpredictable situation. So you dress, grab a light breakfast in the hotel restaurant, then collect your briefcase and go down to the lobby to meet up with Chris and Brendan and the others at nine thirty sharp.

"Lo, 'Laine,' says Mohammed, grinning behind his glasses: he's got them dialled all the way to opaque, and with his dark suit, he looks more like a historic mob hit-man than an accountant. 'Are we ready to rock?'

'Speak for yourself,' snorts Maggie, making him jump. 'Elaine, have you heard from—'

You spot the unopened email, hovering in your peripheral vision like a discreet butler. 'Not before breakfast,' you say. Flicking a finger, you open it. It's from CapG, and they've found a native guide for you. 'Yes, thanks.' You skim the message. 'That looks okay,' you concede.

'He'll be over here after lunchtime,' Maggie adds, proving she's more networked than you are. 'If I were you, I'd take him off-site for orientation before you move in.'

'Well, yes.' Does she think you were born yesterday? *Or, your sneaky bone prods you, is she trying to keep you out of the loop for some reason?*

'Mohammed, you and I are going to have a little chat with Mr. Michaels and Mr. Hackman.'

'Have you brought your garlic and holy water?' asks Chris, kibitzing from the side-line.

'Ha-ha, very droll.' Maggie gives him a long stare.

'I'm not kidding. If you haven't met Hackman . . . he's like Lamb, John Lamb. From HSBC.'

Maggie shudders. 'Really.' *The Silence of the Lambs* is a company in-joke around the coffee station.

'Yes.' Chris claps her on the shoulder, lightly. 'If that's our first taxi . . .'

A couple of minutes later you find yourself knee to knee with Faye and Brendan in a driverless black cab, hurtling around cobble-stoned mews like a one-half-scale model of Knightsbridge. It's raining, and condensation from your breath coats the taxi window beside your head. Faye is busy with a spreadsheet, you see from her glasses and the keyboard laser-projected across the conference folder on her lap. 'Have you ever been in on a search order before?' asks Brendan.

You shake your head. 'Not much to it,' he says cheerily. Tapping the side of his glasses: 'We serve the court order on the defendant and go in. The law's near enough the same, it dates to the eighties and nineties, back before the locals got uppity. If they try to stop us, we find the nearest police officer and point out that they're disobeying a court order to prevent the destruction of evidence. A little bird tells me the cops are already camping out on the doorstep, so we won't have far to go. Meanwhile, I've got a second order ready to go in on their telco – Fred's handling it – to cut off all their communications if they don't play ball.'

You shake your head. 'They're a net company. That'll leave them dead in the water.'

'Oh yes.' He nods cheerfully: 'Take them down for two working days, and they'll probably go out of business. They're on the sharp end of quality of service guarantees with teeth. It's our nuclear option.' From the way he's stroking his brief-case you have an uncomfortable feeling that he hopes he's going to get to push the button.

'Brendan—' Faye warns, fingers tap-tapping at her lap.

'Sorry.' He doesn't sound it. You smear the condensation with your sleeve and look out at the traffic. Four euros a litre for diesel up here, and the road's still jammed.

An uncomfortable minute of stop-go traffic later, the taxi takes an abrupt left, then left again, and grinds to a halt. All you can see out of the window is a muddy car-park surrounded by dripping trees, but when you call up your overlay, you see that this is it: unless the address is wrong, you're in the right place. Brendan waves his company card at the scanner, the doors spring open, and you immediately put both your feet in an ankle-deep icy puddle. 'Shit.' You bite back on your anger as you hop forwards, hoping your shoes aren't ruined.

Louder swearing from the other side of the taxi tells you that the whole car-park is a mud-bath. You reach dry land and see a building ahead, two police cars drawn up in front of it – *that's the offices of Hayek Associates?* It looks more like a brightly coloured garden shed. Raised voices: 'I'm sorry, sir, but you can't come in unless the inspector says—'

There's a thicket of twirling tags above the entrance: Chris, Maggie, Mohammed, and a blue diamond marker blinking blues and twos. Your heart sinks as you hurry towards the shed, hoping to get out of the rain. Inside the entrance you find a strange little scene. The shed is tricked out like the lobby of a corporate office, but there's no office building attached, just a bank of lifts. Which are being guarded by a very bored-looking policeman, who is giving Chris and Mo the I'm-sorry-sir-you'll-have-to-come-back-another-day story while scanning your face with his evidence-locked life recorder's camera.

'We've got a court order,' says Chris. 'Mr. Kadir, if you'd care to show the gentleman . . . ' He's using the stilted, formal language smart people use when talking to police with evidence cams.

'Sure.' Mohammed opens his conference folder and pulls out a document. 'This is a compulsory search order, served by—'

'I'm sure it is, sir, but you'll have to stop right there.' The cop looks flustered. 'This is a criminal investigation. I'll call the inspector immediately, and she'll sort you out as soon as—' He stops, then fidgets with his earpiece. 'Oh.' He nods to himself. 'Uh, Sarge? If I can . . . ? I've got a group of visitors here with a solicitor and a compulsory search order demanding immediate access. What should I . . . okay, I see, right, I'll do that . . . It's what? Aw, no! Right, right. I'll do that, sir.' Behind the CopSpace glasses and the flickering pixelated reflections off his eyelids, his face tells its own story. *Grim news.* He shakes his head and takes the court order from Mohammed. 'I'm sorry to break it to you gentlefolk, but I'm going to have to take your identity cards. Then you can go in an' do what you must, but before you leave the site, I must take DNA samples and verify your identity.'

'DNA *what?*' Maggie squawks indignantly, and you are inclined to agree: being photographed and fingerprinted for the ID card is all very well, but this isn't normal.

The cop sighs. 'Orders,' he says. 'So we can exclude you from our enquiries.'

'But it's a fraud case. What use is DNA evidence?'

'Not *those* enquiries.' He furrows his brows at Harrison. 'The missing person investigation.'

JACK: IN HELL

The Martians from CapG are not wholly inhumane: the clock starts ticking when the one o'clock gun sounds from the castle battlements. You take yourself off to the designer shops on George Street to do something about your wardrobe – for eight thousand a day it'd be stupid not to – and by the time you hear the distant thud, you've acquired a new suit, some lunch, and a precarious determination to bluff your way through to the bitter end. You've even bought a tie, soup stains optional.

When Mr. Pin-Stripe texts you, you're dodging through the lunchtime crowds on your way towards the West End: **GO TO [LOCATOR: SEE ATTACHMENT]. ELAINE BARNABY WILL MEET YOU IN THE LOBBY**.

Oh great, you think: *Who the hell is she?* Then you glance at the locator. Some hotel or other. *Wonderful.* You're still shaking your head as you hail a taxi – *CapG are paying,* you remind yourself – and tell the driver where to go.

The hotel is a modern conversion. Edinburgh's planning laws are strictly dedicated to keeping the capital looking like a time warp from the eighteenth century, so the developers bought an old stone warehouse and gutted it, erecting a glassy cube of modernity inside the hollow shell. You wander into the lobby and glance around. *Who am I looking for?* vies with

What am I doing here? There are skinny people with very expensive glasses and/or very thin laptops sitting on non-Euclidean sofas under tastefully arranged halogen spotlights, but no way of knowing which one of them is your contact. Which is annoying. So you stand around aimlessly for a minute, then put your brain into gear and walk over to the reception desk. 'Hi. Is there an, um, Elaine Barnaby staying here?'

The receptionist fakes a smile. 'I'm sorry, but we don't disclose guests' names—'

'Could be,' a woman's voice says from behind your shoulder. You begin to turn. 'Did CapG services send you?'

'Uh, yeah,' you say, finishing the turn –

'Oh I'm sorry,' apologizes the receptionist –

'Well, you're late.' She looks like a librarian. Mousy hair, black plastic spectacle frames, and a sternly disapproving expression. 'Like the rest of this circus,' she adds, taking some of the sting out of the words. 'Come on.' She turns and stalks towards the lobby staircase, not bothering to wait for you.

Ah, fuck it. She can bitch all she wants for a thousand an hour. *A thousand an hour! Jesus, they're paying me a* thousand *an* hour *for this?* You follow her in a hurry.

She pauses at the top of the stairs, on the mezzanine that looks out across the city towards the international conference centre from behind the cunningly designed false frontage. 'By the way, what's your name?'

'Jack. Jack Reed. And you are Elaine Barnaby? From, uh, Dietrich-Brunner Associates?' *Who are you and what do you do?*

'Two out of two.' Her smile is less insincere than the receptionist's, but you can tell it's concealing the core message: *Who is this slob, and is there some kind of mistake?* 'You're not like the normal run of consultants CapG send us.'

You shrug. 'That's because I'm not one of their normal consultants.' She starts moving again, up the staircase towards the first floor like she's got chromed pistons inside those trousers instead of legs. She probably cycles everywhere. You manage to keep up, but you're breathing heavily by the time she barges through the fire doors and into a corridor on the second floor. 'Much farther?'

'Just in here.' She waves you towards an office door, which unlocks with a *clunk* as she approaches. 'Sit down. I want to get some things straight.'

Ah, right. This is where your thousand-euros-an-hour mirage evaporates on contact with the white heat of reality. *Well, it was nice while it lasted.* 'Yeah, well, this job smelled funny from the first. I mean, CapG isn't a game-development consultancy, so I was wondering why they were looking for someone with my skills. So I guess the disconnect was with the requirements you sent out?'

Barnaby shakes her head, then pushes a stray lock back behind her ear. You notice that she's got very fine, fly-away hair. 'One moment.' She flexes her hands, airboarding – there are subdermal chips in each of her finger joints, she can probably type two hundred words per minute without RSI. It's an office world input method, not a gamer interface, but . . . 'Let's see. You're a senior developer, formerly employed by LupuSoft, working on games that run on ZonePhones. Right?'

Ding! You nod, still having trouble believing in it.

'Cool!' she says, a big fat grin spreading across her face like sunrise in the arctic spring. It's a happy smile, too wide for that narrow face, and it makes her look unexpectedly attractive. 'I wasn't sure they'd find one in time.'

'But—'

'I need a Zone programmer,' she explains, 'because I've got to audit a bank that's located inside Avalon Four.'

'Audit a *bank*?' You know that's got to be what Mr. Pin-Stripe was talking about, but it didn't quite register at the time. '*Inside* a game?'

'Yes.' She picks up a leather conference folio that was sitting on the table and opens it. 'It's been robbed.'

'The bank. Robbed . . . ?' All of a sudden the solid ground under your mental feet has turned into a solipsistic ice-sheet. 'Hang on, that's impossible. I think.'

'Right.' She nods, vigorously. 'That's what everyone I spoke to at Hayek Associates said. But they would say that, wouldn't they?'

'Let me get this straight. Hayek Associates are a stabilization house, aren't they? And they've been stabilizing Avalon Four—'

'A stabilization house would be a company that manages the in-game economy, wouldn't it?' She's making odd gestures with her hands, and for a moment they distract you because it looks like knitting, only nobody would use a two-hundred-millimetre needle.

'I think we're using divergent terminology, but yes. I say "second-tier industry subcontractor", you say "bank". But the thing is, if it's properly designed, robbing the bank should be impossible.'

'Why? It's a database server, isn't it? Someone grabbed a bunch of entries from a table and deleted—'

'Not exactly.' This is giving you a headache. 'Zone games don't run on a central server, they run on distributed-processing nodes using a shared network file system. To stop people meddling with the contents, everything is locked using a cryptographic authorization system. If you "own" an item in the game, what it really means is that nobody else can update its location or ownership attributes without you using your digital signature to approve the transaction – and a co-signature signed by a cluster of servers all spying on each other to make sure they haven't been suborned.'

'So it's not physically on a server?' You can see her trying to keep up. 'Could someone forge the signatures?'

'Not really.' You're racking your brains now, because the authentication architecture of Zone isn't something you've really studied, but a couple of old university courses are raising dusty echoes in the back of your head. 'It's based on the old DigiCash protocol, invented by a cryptographer called David Chaum, back in the eighties and early nineties. He figured it could replace credit cards on the Internet – it was designed to allow anonymous transactions but prevent fraud, and cryptographers had been whacking on it with clubs for twenty years before the Zone consortium picked it. The signature mechanism is very secure – you'd need to suborn the root keyservers for the entire Zone game space . . .'

You trail off into silence. *Whoops,* you think, and kick yourself. Suddenly a grand an hour doesn't seem like very much money at all. Ms. Barnaby is looking at you with an expression you last saw in primary third, when Mrs. Ranelagh didn't deign to notice your wee waving hand in time to give you a toilet ticket.

'*Yes?*' she asks, compressing so much data into the twenty-four-bit monosyllable that if you could patent the algorithm, you'd be set for life.

'Well, uh, I . . . wow,' you manage. 'Why did you want *me?*'

She unwinds by a fraction of a degree. 'You've got the same background and experience as the programmer who's missing from Hayek Associates.' *Programmer who's – shaddup, Jack.*

'Everyone else is focussing on HA's business-level organization, they dumped the gaming stuff on me, and I'm not really an expert.' She gives a little self-deprecating laugh that raises the temperature back above zero. 'So I asked for a native guide.'

Ah. That explains it. Well, no it doesn't, you realize, but it goes at least a third of the way towards it. 'What do you do?' you ask her.

'I'm a forensic accountant.' She pulls that prim, mousy, librarian face again as she taps a bunch of papers in her folio into line.

'Oh. Well, ever done any gaming?' There's always a chance. Some of the deadliest GMs you ever ran into back in your table-top days were accountancy clerks by day.

'Not *that* kind. Why, do you think . . . ?'

You glance at the blank white walls of the conference room. *Perfect.* 'Now's your chance. Do you have a line of expenses?'

'What are you suggesting?'

It's still only a vague thought, but . . . 'We could go have a sniff round Hayek Associates, but we'll only get the cold shoulder, and, besides, they'll be logging everything you do. I think we ought to go have a word with this programmer of theirs when he goes into work—'

'Can't do that, he's *missing*.'

'You mean he's vanished?'

'The police say he disappeared, probably over the weekend.' She makes it sound like he pulled a sickie. You shudder. There's a lot of money in a hack on Zone's DigiCash layer, but enough for that? 'We can't get access to HA's offices until the police finish whatever it is they're doing, so we're stuck sitting on our thumbs for today, anyway.'

'Oh. Well then.'

'Well?' She looks at you expectantly, and you realize she

can't be all that much older than you. The librarian act is elaborate camouflage. Behind it, who is she really?

'Well, if that's the case, can your expense budget run to a taxi out to PC WORLD and a pair of high-end gaming boxes?'

'Yes, I think it would,' she says slowly. 'What have you got in mind?'

'A guided tour of Avalon Four, from the inside, so you know what you're getting yourself into. Are you game for it?'

Limbo. In mythology, it used to be where the dead babies were stacked like cord-wood, awaiting a bureaucratic salvation. Limbo: the dusty front porch of hell. In Zone terminology, Limbo is the hat-check desk.

You've configured yourselves for spatial proximity, so you step into reality next to the unformed noob. The noob's not got as far as adopting any specific species or gender, so they're present as a humanoid blob of mist floating above the marble floor of the temple. 'Can you hear me?'

'Yes. You mean through my headset?'

'That's right.' You take a look around while she's fiddling with her senses. The temple is vaguely classical, Doric columns and marble floors around a raised central area with your traditional altar, columns of flickering light rising from it towards the airy dome of the ceiling. There's a ghostly choir improvising atmospherically in the background. 'Found the controller yet?'

'I think so—' The noob jolts violently, then sprints across the floor, slamming face-first into a pillar. 'Ouch! What just happened?'

'I think you set your acceleration too high.'

An hour later she's still fiddling with her hair, and you're wondering if maybe you would have done better to give her an off-the-shelf identity: answering occasional questions and helping the noob work out who she wants to be is intermittently amusing, but it's not exactly getting the job done. On the other hand, you've got to admit that those asp-headed dreadlocks are very cool indeed, and more to the point, she's not going to be able to do her job if she doesn't at least have some idea of why people invest so much time and effort in their characters. 'I think we should get moving,' you suggest.

'You think?' The noob turns to look at you and, to your surprise, raises an eyebrow: obviously she's been exploring the somatics while your mind was wandering. 'How does this look?'

'It looks fine.' *For a first attempt.* The tools for creating a character in Zonespace are a lot finer and more subtle than those offered by the older MMOs, but by the same token, they're harder to use well: some people make a tidy real-world living just by fine-tuning other players' avatars. What Elaine has come up with is a passable attempt at an anime medusa, with brightly textured skin like vinyl, big brilliant eyes, and colourful clothing. 'Okay, to start with, you'll need this.' You hand her a short-sword that she's skilled up for. 'And this.' A chain-mail vest, slightly rusty. 'You wear them like *so*.' The noob nods. 'And now you either need to learn how to navigate – there's a tutorial garden outside the door over there – or I can teach you.'

'Which do you recommend?'

She's either being very patient or she's actually enjoying the novelty of it all. 'I'd do both. Stick with me for now, then go online yourself tonight and mess around with the tutorial.'

'Okay.' She sounds sceptical. You glance sidelong out of game space and see her as she is, focussed completely on the game box's dual screens, her glasses shutting out anything that isn't part of the reality in front of her. *Totally* intent, finger-joints twitching oddly as she turns the L-shaped controller around in her hands. 'How long does this usually take?'

'What? Oh, the tutorial garden outside that door over there is designed to give you the basics of how to control your body in about half an hour to an hour. Then if you pick one of the shards, there are a bunch of solo quests you can run that will train you up until you can play competitively in about a week, um, twenty to thirty hours of on-line time. But if all you want to do is tag along with me, then just get through the tutorial in the garden.'

'You've got a whole load of kit.'

'Yeah. I'm Theodore G. Bear. The G. stands for Grizzly, and I'm an *ursus*.' You rear up and look down your nose at her from your full three metres, then pull out the huge, brass-barreled blunderbuss you carry in your pack and sling it around your neck where she can see it: 'I believe in the right to keep and arm bears.' It's about the size of a five-pounder carronade off of one of Captain Kidd's frigates, and it's been personally blessed by the Spirit of the Age, which gives it a serious edge against superstitionists and darklings. You wait for the groan, then add, 'The best way to do this is if I carry you, so I'm going to sit down now, and then I want you to try the mount command.'

'You've got to be kidding.'

'Nope.'

She fiddles around for a minute, then suddenly she's sitting on your pack, which has sprouted stirrups and a natty little leather saddle. 'Hey! I can ride?'

'It's a standard skill for epic characters. Don't try it on anyone you aren't campaigning with, they might get pissed off. Okay, time to wander.' You stand up and head for the big double doors at the front of the temple, keeping it slow. 'This is the Temple of Newborn Souls on the Island of Is, which sits in the Nether Sea just off the coast of the main continent, which is called . . . Hell.'

Hell lies outside the universe, and is thus largely exempt from the laws of physics. Its geometry is a Dantesque parody, for while the Nether Sea is flat, the entirety of the continent lies below sea-level, a vast trumpet bell some thousands of leagues wide stretched out across the knife-sharp line where the sea meets the swirling vacuity that forever hides this realm from Heaven.

How do you describe a continent of pain that has been hollowed out into a frozen whirlpool, forever held below the cliffs of roaring, glass-green waves that somehow flail at the abyss, without ever curling over and toppling over to inundate the red-glowing wilderness?

How do you describe the turbulent flocks of the venal, swirling like starlings in the autumn air above the muddy fields of the Somme? How to picture the power-pylon ranks of impaled, damned souls marching in synchrony across the deserts of the fourth circle? The searing black-iron skyscrapers of Dis, windows glowing with diabolical light?

It's like something out of Hieronymus Bosch, of course. Bosch, as pastiched by a million expert systems executing code that procedurally clones and extrapolates a work of art across a cosmic canvas. Procedural Bosch, painting madly and at infinite speed to fill in the gaps in a virtual world, guarded by the titanic archangels of Alonzo Church and Alan Turing, spinning the endless tape . . .

It's funny how it takes game space to bring out the poet in you. And it's even funnier how you're embarrassed about letting it show.

'That's Hell. Don't worry about it, it's just a little joke that got out of hand.'

'You're shitting me.'

'Not at all!' You lumber forward onto the stony path that meanders around the temple, heading downhill towards the beach front. 'What happened was, the original set-up is where you go to acquire a body; hence, Limbo. Then a couple of the procedural content guys got bored and decided to have fun with the back-drop. This was all pre-alpha, back in the pioneering days, but they'd seen the movie' – and bloody awful you thought it was, too: an aging Patrick Stewart as Satan, hamming it up for the jeezmoid market – 'and somehow managed to grab a chunk of scenery rights by a back-door licensing deal. So we're in Limbo, on the hill overlooking a sinkhole estate. And we're about to teleport ourselves down to Earth, just as soon as I find the, ah—'

You find the right sacred grove, and flop down on the holy mosaic, which lights up in response: *Standard Lambent Radiosity Tint #2*, if you're an accurate judge of such things.

'But why is it still here?'

'It's somewhere we can banish persistent griefers.' The damned souls in this particular hell are there for violations of game law – ranging from beating up noobs and stealing to more recondite offences against virtual reality. All they can do is lie, broken and impaled upon their wheels, screaming abuse at the robot devils until their sentence is done, and they can go back to the game. 'Okay, hold on. We're going down to Vhrana.'

The sky turns deep blue, the world freezes, and a progress bar marches slowly across it from horizon to horizon. Ethereal runes written in aurorae six hundred kilometres high scrawl across the heavens, updating reality, and for a moment your skin crawls with superstitious dread. *Someday we're all going to get brain implants and experience this directly. Someday everyone is going to live their lives out in places like this, vacant bodies tended by machines of loving grace while their minds go on before us into strange spaces where the meat cannot follow.* You can see it coming, slamming towards you out of the future, like the empty white static that is all anyone has ever heard from beyond the stars: a Final Solution to the human condition, an answer to the Fermi paradox, lights on at home and all the windows tightly shuttered. Because it's a thing of beauty, the ability to spin the cloth of reality, and you're a sucker for it: isn't story-telling what being human is all *about*?

And then your claws click down on cobble-stones and the horizon implodes into the uneven Tudor timber-framed frontages of the high street in Vhrana.

Vhrana is the capital city of Cordua, in northern Breasil on the continent of Mu. It's about two kilometres in diameter, built atop a mushroom-shaped dome of limestone that has come adrift from its foundations and floats about a kilometre up above the rain-forest-covered flanks of Mount Panesh. Enterprising adventurers have quarried out vast cellars beneath their picturesque guild-houses, and for a pittance you can descend through the endless passages until you come to a wicker platform overlooking the jungle. Then you can rent a bamboo-and-silk hang-glider and descend to the surface or, if you are Adept, levitate by the power of will alone.

Vhrana is a mess of clashing architectural styles, but the Duke has imposed a certain uniformity over it all by restricting the supply of certain building materials – not unlike Edinburgh, come to think of it. Thus, the timber-framed Tudor look hunches cheek by jowl with lighter wood-and-wicker buildings, some of them thatched, and the odd

eruption of elvish structures – tediously similar to late-medi-
aeval Japan, in your opinion, but at least it doesn't clash too
violently. There aren't many people out on the streets yet, for
it's still morning in most of North America, but as you make
your way towards the northern market hall, you pass a number
of hawkers selling their stuff.

'What are you looking for?'

'Voodoo board. I'm pretty sure it's near the north end of
this market. We're in a no-PvP zone, by the way, you can hop
down and explore if you want: nobody's going to jump you.'

'Oh. Okay, then.' She manages to dismount without impal-
ing herself on a street sign while you sniff around among the
market stalls – a lot of their keepers are in zombie mode,
crying out their sales spiel in a loop – and look for the board.
Eventually you find it, tucked away between the Golden Lotus
Peace and Justice Co-operative (actually the local chapter of
the Assassins Guild) and the Temple of Ru'aark. You scroll
through flashing names and blinking icons, looking for –

'The missing guy. What's his name?'

'Nigel MacDonald, aka Nigel Reliable. Not.'

'I meant, his Zone name. Names. Any inkling?'

'What, you mean what his character was called?'

'No, his *true* name. The one that's attached to any character
he's playing, so his friends can find him. Like, I'm currently
being Theodore G. Bear, but my Zone handle is JackReed.
You're currently being Anonymous Coward – sorry, that's a
generic, you haven't named your noob – but when we logged
you in we created an account with the Zone handle
ElaineBarnaby. Yes?'

'Oh, right. Wouldn't he just be NigelMacDonald?'

'Nope. For one thing, that's a common name. I only got
JackReed because I've been playing since the early days, and

I pulled a few strings; name squatting is a national sport hereabouts. And for another, I'm thinking if we want to trace Mr. Reliable, we need to know what his handle was.' You think for a moment. 'What his handles were . . .'

She's sharp. 'Plural?'

'You got it.' You stare at her noob. There's a faint *ding* as a name finally appears over her asp-haired head: Stheno. *Good, she's cluing up.* 'Listen, it's a quarter to five, and if we don't get hold of his handle real soon now, we're not going to be able to get any further today. Assuming he was hiding something, we need to know who we're looking for. So. Got any bright ideas?'

'Yes. Let's run through that tutorial you told me about. We'll worry about finding MacDonald's name tomorrow; first I figure I need to know what I'm doing. Or did you have other plans for the evening?'

SUE: VICTIM LIAISON

Being first on scene has its little perks, and one of them is that under the Victims of Crime (Restitution) Act (2010) – a hangover from before the independence vote went through – if an offence has been committed against a designated Victim of Crime with a pecuniary value of blah or a custodial sentence of wibble, the designated VOC must be assigned a Victim Liaison Officer, to do the touchy-feely hand-wringing shit and dial the Samaritans for them. You were the first responder to Hayek Associates, you're not part of Liz's trained and certified gang of murder puppies, and the pecuniary value is clearly well outside the two-thousand-euro threshold, so she patted you on the head and told you to run along and be a good little VLO for Hayek Associates.

But how the fuck do you counsel a corporation that's been mugged?

'Hello, I'm your Victim Liaison Officer. I understand you're a bit upset about it – share price down in the dumps, third quarter figures looking a bit dodgy, that kind of thing – would you like to talk to someone sympathetic? A cup of tea, perhaps?'

So you go back on site, nip down the fire stairs and through the blast doors round the back, and bang on the Great White Chief's door.

'Who is it?'

You open the door. 'Sorry to disturb you, Mr. Hackman, but I was wondering if you'd have the time for a wee chat.' You smile, making friendly.

Marcus Hackman's office is all done up in chrome and black like an eighties bachelor pad. Mary has a thing for design magazines, and you recognize the Eames chair and lounger, and you'll swear you've seen that desk somewhere famous. One wall is cluttered with photographs and certificates and the sort of shit the terminally insecure use to reassure themselves that they really matter; or maybe it's what aggressive office sociopaths use to browbeat the terminally insecure into thinking that *they* really matter. The shark bares his teeth at you in a not-too-cannibalistic manner. 'I can spare you five minutes.'

'Thank you, sir.' You smile right back at him. 'First things first, are you aware of your rights under the Victims of Crime Act?' You blink the relevant paragraphs up in front of your right eye, just in case: 'As a Victim of Crime, you have the right to a Victim Liaison Officer, and I thought you'd be pleased to know that I'm here to help everybody deal with any unpleasant consequences emerging from the incident.'

His cheek twitches. 'You mean, to spy on us,' he accuses.

'I wouldna put it like that, sir. Victims of Crime can be quite upset by the process. They need support, they need regular updates on the progress of investigations, and it helps just a little bit to make sure that they don't get the feeling they've been dumped. We wouldn't want anyone to get any ideas about taking the law into their own hands, either—'

He raises a hand. 'Please. Let's be honest and *open* here.' He smiles with exaggerated bonhomie at the brim of your hat, mugging for the camera. 'A financial institution managed by my *company* has been robbed, and a member of my management team fucked up by inviting you in rather than going through the correct channels. Quite obviously, your boss thinks it's an inside job, so she's sent you to snoop around and see if the insider freaks and makes a run for it.' (He puts his hand down on the pile of papers cluttering up his desktop: you try to eyeball them discreetly, zooming for an image capture, but his hand's in the way.) 'That's fine and dandy. You just don't need to play the happy clappy let's-all-hold-hands script at *me*. I've got more important things to worry about.'

'Like what?'

He looks at you briefly, then makes a flicking motion with his fingertips.

'You want to say something off the record?' you ask.

He nods. *Interesting.*

You shrug. 'This is *most* irregular,' you tell him as you pull out your phone and hit the big red button labelled OFF. He doesn't need to know that it's not your only camera.

Hackman leans forward, across his desk. 'You know we've been served with two search-and-seizure orders in the past day? One's from a specialist risk-consultancy agency. The other's from our insurance underwriters. They're going to be coming through here in hobnailed boots over the next couple of days, and believe me, you haven't seen victims until you've seen what those thugs are going to leave behind. They mean to prove negligence on our part: there's a lot of money at stake. If you're poncing around in the background, trying to get my people to open up and go all weepy on your shoulder, then potentially you are going to do me a lot more harm than the initial incident.' His shoulders are quivering with something very like anger but so tightly controlled that all that comes across is a sense of desperate urgency. 'There are going to be people running around these offices, people I can't legally keep out, bottom-feeding scum who are *not friendly*. Like you, they're investigators. Unlike you, they're not investigating the crime in order to find the perpetrator; they're looking for an excuse for a deep-pocket lawsuit. They want to take everything I've built here and steal it, and if they can find a legal pretext to do so, they will stop at nothing. They're trash and I wouldn't cross the road to piss on them if they were on fire – but I can't *legally* stop them, even though I'd like to break their arms and legs and, and—'

Hackman pauses for breath, pauses to collect himself: he's red in the face and breathing deeply. You force yourself not to recoil. You're used to MOPs venting at you, but what's freakily weird about this time is that as far as Hackman is concerned, you're just a bystander, a convenient audience for his theatre of hate. For a moment you wonder if he's having a heart attack, or maybe an orgasm, but then he pulls together another of his slick smiles and aims it at you, and it's Game On again, with the charm ray turned all the way up to eleven. 'Obviously, I'd be overjoyed if you could find the weakest link here and nail their hide to the front door. If nothing else, it would get me off the hook with the bottom feeders. But I do not want you snooping around in a manner that . . . *encourages* them. They're hostiles, and they don't know anything that can contribute to your investigation; all they can do is smear shit on the walls and steal the carpet. *Am I clear?*'

You stare at Hackman, taken aback by his ferocity. He's still doing that shaky-trembly thing again; but it's not anger that you can see in him now, it's pure and simple hatred. The big man's got his radge on, hasn't he? Fascinating! Not to mention scary enough you'd be calling for backup if he was in the high street wearing a hoodie. Here in the executive office suite, and him wearing a suit, it's only a bit less scary: but you know how to deal with this kind of customer, and anyhow, he's not going to get violent at *you*, is he? Unlike 90 percent of the scum you get to deal with on the street, physical violence is the last thing you're likely to encounter from Hackman. (Which only makes him all the more dangerous.) 'You've been completely clear, sir. Thank you very much. If you don't mind, I'm going to turn my mobile on again.' You reach up and hit the phone's button. *Stick* that *on the station evidence server and let Liz suck it.* You smile at him reassuringly: 'I'm here to help *you*, sir. You don't need to worry about bystanders.' Then you back out of his office, very slowly, not taking your eyes off him, not giving him an opportunity to attack.

Okay, so you're the designated Victim Liaison Officer for a corporation that's been mugged. But what do you do when the CEO's a psychopath who's out for revenge?

You hear from Liz around five o'clock, just as you're about to go off shift. 'Can you drop in the station on your way home? Verity's called a facial over the MacDonald business, and he wants your input.'

Typical, you think, but you swallow it: she's the skipper, and you've got to admit, this business is turning into a real pile of shit. With blood on the carpet and a programmer who went missing right about the time his employer reported a multi-million-euro hit, things are not looking good; the pressure is going to be telling on Liz from Verity, if not the chief. It's still just a missing person case leg-humping a white-collar fraud, but with the amount of money at stake (and the Sexy! New! Technology! angle), there's going to be Media Attention landing on your collective ass real soon now, if it hasn't already, and the chief constable takes a dim view of media whores who don't deliver. So you drive over to Meadowplace Road and mooch into the conference room with its tatty wallpaper and ancient flickering fluorescent lights, by way of the coffee machine on the second floor.

Liz is sitting at the front of the table with an expression like someone peed in her miso soup. Jimmy the X-Ray Specs and Roger the Ram are gassing about the morning's breaking and entering, while a whole bunch of heavy SOCOs are nattering over their notes and a couple more sergeants from X Division are trailing you in. One of them you recognize as one of the standoffish suits who was up at the bunker the other morning. All told you're out on a limb: you're not normally involved in this kind of incident meeting, and indeed you're one of only a couple of uniforms in the bunch. 'Alright, folks, let's get started,' Liz calls, just as the door opens and another suit walks in. 'Sir, we were just getting started. Would you like a chair, or . . . ?'

'No, you carry on,' says Chief Superintendent Verity, and you cringe slightly: he's got a voice like a rat-tail rasp, and rumour says he's not long for the shop, the lung cancer's not responding to treatment very well. For him to have dragged himself out to this session suggests that arses are being well and truly kicked all the way up to the top in officer country, if not the Justice Ministry. Trust that bastard Hackman to have friends in Holyrood.

'Alright, everyone. I assume you all know what this is about. We started off with a white-collar crime, a CMA special, last Thursday at Hayek Associates over in Granton. A whole bunch of money went missing. We got the call by mistake – one of their managers panicked and dialled 211 instead of trying to shovel things under the rug, and I think there's a story in that. But anyway, on Friday we discovered a member of staff wasn't answering the phone. As of this morning, things get slightly worse insofar as we now have a missing person on our hands, with a bunch of evidence that points to it being murder: his flat's been done over, there're signs of a struggle, and I believe Bill has got something to tell us about his movements. Take it away, Bill.'

Bill stands up, shuffling his tablet and a bunch of papers in a conference portfolio. He's one of the suits from the woodshed the other day: fortysomething, salt-and-pepper moustache, dour puss with lips like he's bitten a lime expecting nothing better. 'Aye, well. The subject, one Nigel MacDonald, has no previous. He came to our attention in the course of the on-going investigation at Hayek Associates, who employ him as a programmer.' Which is a load of bollocks, if you're to believe what Wayne and the others are pointedly *not* saying: it's like describing a brain surgeon as a first-aider. But the evidence is there in cold figures on their payroll, and the way everyone at Hayek tenses up and goes close-mouthed when you ask how they're going to fill his boots. 'Mr. MacDonald works from home an awful lot, and nobody's seen hide nor hair of him since last Wednesday. By which I mean nobody's seen email or spoken to him on the phone.'

Bill unfolds a fat swatch of paper from his portfolio. 'I ran a query through NCIS' – the National Criminal Information System, not yet disentangled from the English one, even after eight years of IT-mediated divorce proceedings – 'and then when that came back empty, I asked for a banking trace. That's empty, too. He hasna spent a cent since Wednesday except for direct debits on his bank account. So I applied to NIR for a transaction log. Mr. MacDonald hasna presented his ID card to an Authorized Agency' – one with a direct line to the National Identity Register – 'in more than three years. In fact, he hasna ever been stopped and checked. He *did* use it to open bank and credit accounts when it was issued, and he used it to apply for the mortgage on his hoose, but aside from that he's the regular Invisible Man. He doesna drive a car or own a bus pass, so there's nothing to be done aboot his movements. I havena pulled the street cameras yet, but if we have tae do it, I wouldna bet on his mug showing up.' He stepped down from the podium, an expression of disgust on his face.

'Thank you, Bill,' Liz says drily. 'Scene of Crime next. Dr. Tweed?'

The 'doctor' isn't medical; Tweed is a lab monster with a Ph.D. and a perpetual air of mild amusement. Inevitably, he wears a sports jacket in the offending fabric, complete with corduroy elbow patches. And unlike Bill, he feels no need to stand up or parade around the front of the room. 'I'm glad you called me for this one, it makes a nice change from the usual ned domestics turned messy.' He fiddles for a moment with his laptop, then you see the entire back wall of the conference room vanish into CopSpace, replaced by a walk-through ludium – the entire scene digitized and uploaded into virtual reality.

'Let's start here, in the front hall. When the ram team laid the door down, they covered the dust and print evidence from the last people to traverse the hall. When the initial survey was over, Marge and Hal from Fettes Row came in and took an impression in aerogel foam. There's lots of dust there, and a couple of partials, but the most recent footprints are useless because whoever left them was using disposable polythene overshoes with some kind of vascular lining. Just like Marge and Hal, in fact.'

You sit up and start paying real attention. You had the idea that MacDonald and his friends were a wee bit paranoid, but this is right out of order.

'It's the same throughout the flat. It's been turned over by professionals. Mr. MacDonald appears to have had a serious gadget habit, not to mention some apparatus on the roof that I'll get to shortly, and the hardware is still there. But every last piece of personal memorabilia has been removed. The place is unnaturally clean, except for the kitchen. There's no food apart from the fridge, for example. No personal items: no photographs, no paintings or posters, no books or magazines or newspapers, no toothpaste or painkillers in the bathroom cabinet, no nail clippers, no toilet paper. Someone took the time to vacuum behind the washing machine. If I didn't know better, I'd say nobody lived there at all, except for the kitchen. Basically, the crime scene has been thoroughly sanitized by somebody with more than a passing knowledge of forensics.'

You glance sideways to see how the others are taking it. Doubtless this is old news to Liz and explains her headache, but the chief is looking very down in the dumps, and no mistake. And then Dr. Tweed mouses over to the kitchen and clips through the door to the scene beyond.

'This is the kitchen. It's been sanitized, too, and I'd be very surprised if it's been used for its notional purpose in the past couple of years. Real kitchens are lovely places, they can tell us a lot. From the type of grease and particulates retained in the extractor hood over the cooker, to the foodstuffs in the refrigerator, and the contents of the bin, they can be a gold mine. A surprising number of burglars help themselves to a snack on their way through, so it always pays to check the rubbish . . . but anyway. The fridge is, um, see for yourselves.' The door on the virtual refrigerator blinks magically open to reveal a pristine interior. 'It's been cleaned out. This is how we found it. There are no contents; the brown stain on the side is a povidone iodine hospital scrub. Meanwhile, over *here* we have a patch on the work-top where you'll see there's a faint out-line – matches a microwave oven. Why the hell anyone would leave the electronics in the living room but take the microwave oven is, well, your guess is as good as mine. But that's what they did: they scrubbed the fridge out and lifted the microwave. Maybe they'd been using it for toasting RFID tags or something. But the whole thing's been thoroughly sanitized.'

'*Sanitized?*' Verity explodes. 'Are you telling us you can't get anything?'

'Yes, I am – at least, so far.' Tweed nods like a dashboard ornament. He starts counting off fingers. 'There are no human traces in the place that haven't been thoroughly cleaned or scrambled. When the LCN results came back, it was a smeared mess – we got a DNA sample alright, one from about three hundred people in parallel.'

'What else doesn't fit?' asks Liz.

Tweed shrugs. 'The bedding has been stripped down. I lifted debris samples on the mattress debris, but that's been contaminated, too.'

Verity snorted. 'How do you contaminate DNA evidence?'

'We work with really tiny samples, so you – the bad guys – just give us too much evidence. Best bet is whoever sanitized the flat spent a couple of hours on the top deck of a bus with a small vacuum cleaner. We all shed skin particles like mad wherever we go. Blast dust from a bus seat cushion all over a crime scene, and it's like smearing over a fingerprint on a glass by passing it around the entire population of a night-club – all I can lift from it is a horrible mess.'

'Bah.' Verity crosses his arms. 'What else?'

Liz raises an eyebrow. 'I'd like to give everyone a quick overview. If you don't mind, I'm going to pass the baton to Joe from ICE. Unless there's anything else that's important, Doctor?'

Tweed sighs. 'Nothing that changes the overall picture.'

'Joe?'

Joe's a weedy little pencil-necked geek, almost a self-parody act. 'Hi!' he squeaks. 'You want to know about the servers? Okay, here's the story: we've got nothing. It's a really nice pile of kit, all of it less than two years old, professional business gear rather than SOHO – but there are no manuals, removable media, or licenses, and the fixed media, hard disks and flash, have all been nuked. I mean, it's scrubbed, right down to the bare metal, using a tool that conforms to DOD 5220.22-M. That's what we use when we're decommissioning confidential but non-classified kit. Someone *really* didn't want us taking a look at their video library. Which is a bit of a head-scratcher because if we want it back, it's a fair bet that not even GCHQ will be able to help.'

'The roof-top garden,' Liz prompts.

'Oh, *that*.'

'Yes.' Liz nods to the chief's raised eyebrows – waggling like a pair of hairy caterpillars arguing over a tasty leaf – 'Here's the fun bit.'

Joe nods eager affirmation. 'This is where it gets weird. Our boy had gone up through the skylight and stuck a satellite dish on his roof. An illegal one; it turns out he didn't have a building warrant and it's over a metre in diameter. Um. Actually it's a metre and a half, on a powered azimuth mount, and it's an uplink. We don't know where it was pointed because when we gained access, it was parked in the vertical position, but it was plugged into a bunch of black boxes in the hall. I'm still not sure what half of it is, but there's also a cell antenna on the roof, and *that's* plugged into what appears to be a custom GNU radio box, and they're all switched through the server rack in the living room.'

'Explain GNU radio,' says Liz, in a tone of voice that says she's already been here, and it doesn't get any better.

'Sure. It's a soft radio. You plug a sufficiently fast digital signal processor onto the back of an analogue-to-digital converter and a wire, and simulate the radio procedurally. Run a program and it's a TV receiver, run a different program and it's a cellphone base station.'

'Isnae that illegal?' calls Bill, from the back.

'Well spotted.' Joe flashes a grin, suddenly assertive now he's on his own ground. 'Firstly, it's free – you can download it from just about anywhere – and secondly, you can run it on just about any PC with the aid of about thirty euros' worth of off-the-shelf kit. So the actual state of the law – not being a complete ass – is that *using* it is illegal under *certain circumstances*. Not having the contents of his media, I can't tell you what he was doing with it, but using the box he was running it on as an illegal satellite TV decoder would be like shaving with a katana. Twenty to one he was doing something naughty.'

'Such as?' prompted Verity. 'What sort of stuff would a man like that be doing in his spare time?'

Joe twitched. 'This isn't spare-time kit, I'm afraid. Current best price I could find on the hardware is somewhere north of twenty thousand euros. He might have been sucking down naughty satellite broadcasts and feeding them to his friends, but . . . well. He might have been snooping on phone calls for the Russian *mafiya* or running an anonymous cellular phone remixer to bypass the security services. I can't tell because whoever turned him over wiped all the media, but I can tell you what it *looks* like. Do you suppose it could be something to do with that murder in Pilton?'

'Very possibly,' says Liz. For his part, Verity looks like he's bitten into an apple and found half a worm. 'I wasn't going to put it in so many words, but the roomful of kit makes me think that we may be up against a blacknet here – possibly the same one we had all that trouble with last year.' There are groans all around the room, especially from the old-school detective suits at the back. 'What we found in the flat fits the pattern, and MacDonald's disappearance would also fit if you view it as an elimination followed by sanitary measures.'

'It does that,' Verity grates, letting the words out reluctantly, 'so we'll consider it. *Fuck*. Alright, it's showtime. Bill, get onto facilities and book an incident room. Liz, I trust ye've started a new HOLMES instance? Email everyone the URL and start getting this all into it. Pencil me in the SIO slot and keep me updated. Who's handling the Pilton murder, isn't it Fergus? Let's get this linked into that data set and see what we can fish up . . . '

You realize with a sinking feeling that everybody else around here knows what Liz and Verity are speaking about – and from the long faces it's bad, very bad indeed. But you didnae get to be a sergeant by sticking your pinkie up and saying *Please miss, what blacknet was tha'?* So you get yourself into CopSpace and go hunting it, and when you see what comes back, you just about boak.

Because if Liz is right, that poor bastard MacDonald won't be giving you a witness statement. And that's just for starters . . .

ELAINE: Stitched Up

You don't know what you were expecting from the body shop, but it certainly wasn't a rumpled-looking bear-driving gamer called Jack. (Alias Teddy or otherwise.) And while you *do* know what you were expecting from the investigation, it wasn't spending a rainy afternoon in a hotel conference room playing swords'n'sorcery games.

But at least Jack's congenial, and he seems to know how the game works, which is the main thing.

You're about halfway through the tutorial, learning how to pick locks, sneak across butterfly floors, and turn small furry critters to stone with your Mad Powerz, when your phone rings. You put the game on hold for a moment: 'Yes?'

It's Chris Morgan. 'Elaine? We're breaking for a bite to eat now, and it's a good excuse to get everybody up to date. Want to meet me in the lobby in ten minutes?'

You spare a glance for the mouse you're trying to turn into a stalactite. 'Can do.' A thought strikes you. 'Should I bring Jack?'

'Jack? The body shop guy?'

'The consultant,' you correct him.

'Hmm. Yes, bring him along. I'm not sure what he can contribute, but you never know.'

You hang up, glare at the wee sleekit, cowrin', timorous beastie, and try the gesture again. *Voilà*: instant stone-baked rodent. Well, at least *that* worked. You log out, then tap Jack on the shoulder. He jumps. 'Yes?' he asks.

'Finish whatever you're doing, we're going for dinner. On the company.'

'What – okay, yeah.' You can just about see his eyes twitching behind the opaque disks of his gaming glasses. 'Ten seconds . . . right.' He slides the glasses off. 'What should I expect?'

'We're going for dinner,' you repeat patiently. 'You know, a chance to have a meeting without starving to death.'

'Yes, but who with? You're the only person I've met so far,' he adds.

'Oh, right. I guess I should have introduced you – well, the rest of the team was in a meeting when you showed up, so it wasn't exactly practical. Now's your chance. Unless you had something else on?'

Jack looks momentarily perplexed. 'No, nothing doing,' he says ruefully. He lays his glasses down carefully on top of the gaming laptop – the screen's a shimmery blur from where you're sitting. 'I have no life.' He chuckles, trying to make a joke of the obviously defensive reaction, and you feel a stab of unworklike empathy.

'Well, let's go.' You stand up. 'I'll introduce you to everybody.'

Chris is down in the lobby with Mohammed and Brendan. They've shed their ties, which is a bad sign – either there's zero probability of any client action today, or Chris is planning on leading an overnight death march. But at least it'll be a well-fed death march, you figure, as he leads you all into the hotel bistro. The manager has already sorted out a table at the back. A minute later Margaret and Faye show up and the forced small-talk and time-filling silences stop.

'Brendan, why don't you fill us all in on the time line?' Chris suggests, once introductions are made and starters are ordered.

'Sure.' Brendan stares at his water glass dourly for a moment. (Another sign that things are going badly: Chris didn't start by ordering a couple of bottles of stockbroker's ruin. He wants everybody sober.) 'It's a mess. Here's what we know. Last Thursday someone at Hayek managed to get the police *interested*. They were supposed to be keeping a lid on it pending a proper investigation, but someone panicked, and to make matters worse, it's local plod, not SOCA or the Serious Fraud Agency. Then the police discovered that one of Hayek's people, Nigel MacDonald, is missing. The latest update – don't ask me for details, and I shall tell you no lies – is that it's a full-on missing person investigation. Seems the plod went to call on Mr. MacDonald at home and found signs of a struggle: they're treating it as a possible murder case.'

You look around the table as your soup arrives: there are long faces all round. 'That isn't very helpful,' Margaret says carefully. Damn right it isn't: having to work with the police getting underfoot is bad enough, having the police actually threatening to *do their job* . . .

'Indeed not.' Brendan sounds ghoulishly pleased with himself. 'Can I continue? It appears to be an inside job, the insider in question has vanished, the police think he may be dead, and to add to the fun, they're treating the offices as a secondary crime scene. If MacDonald *is* dead, that turns this into a murder investigation, and they pull out all the stops.' His glance takes in Jack, who is sitting next to you, shoulders slightly hunched as he chews on a crust of garlic bread. 'Obviously, they're going to consider the robbery in Avalon Four as a likely motive for the hypothetical killing, so if that happens, we won't be able to move without tripping over a dibble.'

Margaret smiles and puts her soup spoon down. 'What did you achieve today?' she asks you. And you think: *I should have seen this coming.*

'I—' You corpse for a moment. *What the* hell *are you going to say? I played games for four hours straight?* It must show on your face because Margaret's smile becomes slightly fixed as she waits. 'I, uh . . .'

'Um. May I?' asks Jack. You nod, speechless. 'We obviously couldn't get access to Hayek Associates, so we decided to use the time productively by setting up a high-performance Zone client network, then covering some essential familiarization material. We also discussed ways and means of tracking Mr. MacDonald's history in Zonespace, because – as you're no doubt aware – most inside jobs also involve an external partner who can launder the merchandise, and finding the outside connection is our best hope for discovering what actually happened inside Hayek Associates.'

He then launches into a spiel of explanatory technobabble that leaves you agog with admiration. It's not so much the ten-euro words that do it as the polished professionalism with which he slots them together. For a moment, you almost know what it must feel like to be a Thames Gateway resident talking to a flood insurance salesman. 'That's about it,' you add, shrugging, when he nods at you. 'Any questions?' You hold your breath, hoping nobody calls your bluff.

Margaret is studying Jack as if he's your pet sheep-dog and she's just caught him reciting Shakespearean sonnets. At least *you're* off the hook. 'No, no questions,' she says thoughtfully. She looks at Brendan. 'When can we get access?'

'I've asked London to try to get someone to talk to the

police.' He drives a piece of bruschetta around his plate in pursuit of a puddle of olive oil. 'Hopefully, tomorrow morning if we can just get through to this Inspector Kavanaugh's boss.'

'Right.' Chris leans back in his chair and smiles lopsidedly. 'We'll have to wait on it, then. Meanwhile, here's something for you all to bear in mind. If it turns out that Nigel MacDonald was working on his own, or with an external partner, but essentially trying to rip his employer – then we're off the hook. The HA business plan is exonerated, our remit doesn't include criminal background checks on junior employees, and we're out of here. On the other hand, if there's evidence pointing to a member of the board, we're still potentially in trouble. So we have a good idea what we're looking for, don't we?'

You nod, even though you've got a nagging feeling that this doesn't entirely add up. *Does Chris have some kind of hidden agenda here?* But then he takes a sip of water and continues.

'Whatever the cause, though, we need to know enough about what happened, and how, to ensure it doesn't bite us again. So, Elaine, finding out what *actually* happened is still your absolute priority, while the rest of us make sure it was just a rogue employee.'

Oh, *now* you get it. Chris is setting up to pull everyone else out, just as soon as he's confirmed that none of Hayek Associates' board were in on the robbery. You're going to get left with the clean-up, and doubtless he'll cut a deal to subcontract your services out to Hayek's insurers, or maybe even the local cops, for a tidy sum. *Stitch-up.* You're going to be stuck up here in Edinburgh hunting needles in virtual haystacks while Chris and Margaret go home, announce the job's all done, and move on to the next project. Lovely!

*

After the meal, there's a general drift towards the hotel bar, where Chris has announced his intention of buying a round. It's the usual team-building thing, and it's the last thing you feel like taking part in, constructive attitude or no. But Margaret corners you in the lobby, all the same. 'I hope you don't think you're being singled out for something bad,' she says, a calculating light in her eyes. 'It's not like that at all. Chris got word from above that he's wanted down south, and I agreed that we need someone with a steady hand to tidy this up, and we really need to get back to London before Avixa or GenState notice we're gone. Chris trusts you; otherwise, he wouldn't have put it in your hands.'

You manage to force yourself to smile. *Okay, so it* is *a stitch-up.* You don't score points inside DBA for being the lone gun on a trouble-shooting mission, out in the cold where nobody can see you. 'That's perfectly alright, Margaret. Chris was completely clear on what he wanted. I'll see it gets done.'

'Good. Between you and me, Chris misread this situation, and he knows it. Unless it turns out that we're all in the shit together, Chris overreacted massively. I think the stress of juggling six cat-A clients simultaneously may be getting to him.' That's enough to make you raise an eyebrow, and you file it away for future reference: normally even full partners don't handle more than two or three cat-A's at once, plus a handful of smaller jobs.

Margaret glances across the lobby. 'That native guide of yours. Doesn't look like much, but that was a very slick line of bullshit he sold us.'

'It wasn't bullshit,' you say defensively. 'He's from the games industry. He probably bought that suit this morning, but he knows his own field like the back of his hand – what did you expect?'

'Not that.' She smiles unexpectedly. 'Good luck with your insider hunt. And don't let the natives pull any wool over your eyes.' She turns and stalks off in search of other minions to intimidate, leaving you flexing your fingers and trying to decide whether you want to strangle her or go down on your knees and beg for lessons.

Right now, you don't much feel like going along with Chris and the gang and making nicey-nicey. Then you spot Jack across the lobby. He's dithering around the doorway. You move to intercept him. 'Hi.'

'Hi.' He looks uncertain. 'I was just heading off.' He looks like an overgrown kid who's been caught not doing his home-work.

For a split second you teeter on the cusp of a choice. You have two options: do you tell him 'I'll see you tomorrow,' and go back to your hotel bedroom to watch downloads and brood? Or do you take him in hand, and say, 'The evening's young, and I need to get out of here for a bit. Fancy a glass of wine?'

Mm, decisions.

'I need to get away from work for a bit. Do you know any good wine bars at this end of town?' A moment later you kick yourself: *What if he thinks it's a come-on?* But Jack is timid, and well trained or sufficiently domesticated to simply nod.

'Beats doing the ironing.' He smiles to show he's just kidding about comparing you to a pile of rumpled shirts.

'Well, cool.' He holds the door open, then heads off down the street. It's late enough that the sun's low and dazzling, forcing you to keep your eyes down rather than goggling at the insane architecture.

'Have you been to Edinburgh before?'

'No. This is my first time in Scotland.' There's a shop window full of garish tartans and a discount bookshop with a window full of those blue-on-white Scottish flags. They're big on flags here, almost as big as the Americans: something to do with their new franchise independence, probably. As long as they keep voting the British federal line in Brussels, that's all the English establishment want: but perhaps things look different from this side of the frontier. 'Where are we?'

'This is the West End of the New Town, so-called because they only built it about two hundred and fifty years ago. It's a world heritage site, hence the manky stonework that keeps falling off the buildings and crushing tourists.' He glances at you swiftly. 'Not often, you'll be pleased to know.' He's got his glasses on, and they're lit up, washing the whites of his eyes in kaleidoscope colours.

'I'm reassured. Hey, we're out of the office. This isn't billable, you don't have to keep working.'

He looks startled. 'What, my glasses? No, I was just checking the eating-out guide.'

'I thought you lived here?'

'Yeah, but . . .' You come to a corner and he pauses, waiting for the traffic lights to change. 'Wine bars aren't my usual scene.'

'Oh, it doesn't need to be a posh wine bar. Anywhere that's not the hotel bar will do right now – I just wanted to get away.'

He brightens, visibly. 'I'm better at pubs.' He pauses as the traffic stops, and the green man lights up. 'Um, you seem a little tense.'

'You could say that.' You hurry across the road and realize the house-front you're walking past is actually a branch of Boots. 'I hate that kind of scene. When they break the bad news to you while you've got your mouth full, so you can't tell them exactly what you think.'

'Hmm. It *was* a stitch-up, then? I'm not used to your kind of work, it sounded like one but I wasn't sure . . . '

'Oh, it's a stitch-up alright.' You take a deep breath. 'Nothing to be done about it, I guess. Chris and Margaret are going to take the kiddies home and leave me to sort out everything while they take the credit for it. At least, I *think* that's what's going on – assuming Chris doesn't have some kind of covert agenda—' You realize you're babbling at a near stranger and shut up. That's a bad sign. And your feet are putting you on notice that wearing five-centimetre heels on the Edinburgh streets is probably not a good idea – everywhere seems to be uphill. 'Where's this pub?'

'Not far.' He gestures at another pedestrian crossing and another damned uphill road. 'See?' And indeed you do: there's a pub nestling between a newsagent and a charity shop on the other side of the crossing.

While Jack orders stuff at the bar, you pin down a bench seat at a table in one corner of a big, lino-floored room and take a look around. There's a TV on a curious inner vestibule over the door, and lots of dark wooden panelling, but it looks less like a pub and more like a railway waiting room from a seventies historical drama. Only the huge row of whisky bottles behind the bar, and the odd, pillar-shaped dispensers suggest that someone other than British Rail does the catering here. Even the games machine is an antique, curved-glass monitor and all. The bar's almost empty, except for a couple of dour old men hunched over one end of the bar as if they're afraid of being recognized.

Jack appears, clutching two pint glasses. 'I hope this is okay,' he says, 'CAMRA rate it highly on their local wiki.'

You look around. 'It's half-empty. Isn't that usually a bad sign?'

'The evening's young.' He slides a glass towards you. 'And it's a Monday.'

'Don't remind me.' God, four more days of this before you get a chance to dash home for the weekend. You'll miss combat on Wednesday, your evening class on Thursday, and Mum phoning you on Friday to nag you about whatever comes to hand. 'Maybe tomorrow we can actually make some headway . . .'

'Yeah, well.' He takes a mouthful of beer. 'Have you thought about paying for a background search on the elusive Mr. MacDonald?'

'Office hours.' You sip your beer. It tastes light and remarkably bitter, but not in a bad way. 'Do yourself a favour, don't carry the job home with you.' You don't know why you're warning him off this way – maybe it's just because he seems a little lost among the sharks – but what the hell.

He sighs. 'You're talking to the wrong guy. I've had three years of death marches and no life. If I switched off easily, I'd have fallen by the wayside ages ago.'

'Well. Different workplaces.' You pause, wondering what you're doing sitting in a pub with a strange man you met this morning at work. 'How did you get into it?'

'Oh, the usual. I was about eight when Dad gave me an old box and tried to teach me how to program it in BASIC. He gave up trying to keep up after I discovered assembler. I went to university in Edinburgh, ended up studying CS because it was interesting, nearly failed my course because I spent too much time playing games and working with a couple of friends on an attempted start-up that didn't go anywhere, and had to get a job. Luckily, one of my other friends was already working for Nutshell Productions and got me an interview, and it went from there.'

All of which is factual but doesn't tell you anything about what makes him tick. 'And?'

'And then' – he looks lost for a few seconds, then blinks rapidly – 'my mother got lung cancer. Looked like a treatable one at first, but turned nasty – she ended up needing leading-edge immune system treatments that hadn't been approved by NICE, so I paid for them. Sophie kicked in a little as well, but she and Bill had the kids to look after. For a time it looked as if Mum was in remission, but then she caught multidrug-resistant pneumonia, and that was it.'

He shudders a little as you mentally kick yourself for being a prying bitch: it's not the explanation you were after, but it puts things in perspective. *Change the subject, dammit.* 'Writing games pays that well?'

He stares at his glass. 'It pays pretty well. I should consider myself lucky, that's what Sophie – my sister – keeps telling me. It just doesn't seem . . . ' He takes another mouthful of beer. 'Here, look. This glass. There's about half a pint in it, right? An optimist: it's half-full. The pessimist: it's half-empty. Right now, for the past year, I've been looking at a half-empty glass. Then last week my employers poured piss in it. This morning, the fairy godmother at AlfaGuru just handed me a shot of single malt. I'd like to apologize in advance if I look a bit green about the gills, it's been a hell of a roller-coaster ride.'

Shit. You choose your next words carefully: 'The glass isn't half-empty or half-full. What you're looking at is half a pint of depreciable assets sitting in a pint of capital infrastructure that can be amortized over two accounting periods.'

Jack chuckles. 'That's the finance version, is it?'

'I think so.' You pause. 'Is there an engineering one?'

'Let me see.' He stares at the glass. 'Yes! It's quite simple:

that's half a pint, all that's wrong is the glass is twice as big as it needs to be.'

'Right.' Your own glass is going down, you notice. 'The re-enactor's version: the glass should be made of pigskin and the beer's historically inauthentic.'

'The police officer's version—' There's a maniacal cackling noise from Jack's pocket. "Scuse me.' He pulls out his phone. 'Yes? Who is – hello?' *Pause.* 'Hello?' *Pause.* 'This isn't funny,' he says, in an odd tone of voice. 'Who are you? What do you want?' *Pause.* 'Hello? Hello?'

He puts the phone down carefully, as if he's afraid it'll bite him.

'What was that?' You ask.

'I don't know.' He picks up his glass and chugs half the content straight down. 'Number withheld. If it happens again, I think I need to talk to the police.'

'What?' You stare at him. 'Have you got a stalker, or something?'

'I don't know.' He looks puzzled, now. 'It was – it sounded like a school playground, you know? Kids shouting, for about five seconds. Then a voice said, "Think of her children," and hung up.' Puzzlement is turning into perplexity on his face. Whatever the caller might have thought, Jack clearly doesn't know what it's all about. And neither do you, you realize, with a hollow feeling in your guts.

'Any ex-girlfriends?' you ask, trying to keep your tone light.

'Not since Mum got sick.' He twitches and you think, *You poor bastard*: there's a nasty little story there, of that you can be sure, but now's not the time to go digging. 'Before you ask, no, I have never been married, and I don't know any raging bampots of the first water who hang around playgrounds recording . . . voices . . . ' He trails off.

'What is it?'

'Nah, can't be happening,' he mumbles to himself. 'Nobody'd be crazy enough to try to make me drop this job by threatening Elsie and Mary, would they? Sophie's daughters,' he adds after a second. 'They'd have to be nuts, wouldn't they?'

You're gripping the edge of the table *way* too tight, tense with unwelcome memories that he's just summoned like spirits from the vasty deep. 'I think you'd better report this to the police,' you hear yourself telling him, as if from the other end of a dark tunnel. 'Just in case.' And hope to hell that's all it is, a wrong number, a prank call. Because the alternative isn't something you want to think about.

JACK: DESIGNS ON YOUR DUNGEON

You don't want to stay in the pub after the poison phone call and the bitter memories it dredged up, but it's too early to go home, and you don't much want to be on your own with nothing else to think about. Besides which, while you've had a bellyful of hanging out with folks from work recently, Elaine is different. She's pretty intimidating in a work context, but right now she seems to want company. She's an odd mixture of spiky stand-off-ishness and— Well, maybe she just wants company because she's suffering from new-city syndrome, right? But you're inclined to go along with it anyway, for your own reasons.

Before you leave the pub you nervously call the Polis – but they're deeply uninterested in a terribly bureaucratic kind of way. They take a detailed statement, asking you to spell your name, the name of the pub you were in, the people you were with, your cat's name, and your mother's blood group, then they promise to email the phone company a request for their call logs: but due to some quirk of the Regulation of Investigatory Powers Act, as Amended, even though you routinely record all your calls, they can't actually use it as evidence of anything. 'I've got your complaint on the system, Mr. Reed, and if it happens again, you just text us on this number, citing this case reference . . .'

Bastards! Squeaks the mummy lobe, outraged at their unwillingness to enforce the full majesty of the law on your behalf. (After all, every time you've had a run-in with them before, they've had no trouble enforcing it against you, have they?)

After that, you move on by mutual consent to a less-fore-boding venue, a city centre pub with HAPPY HOUR signs and a jukebox and loud after-office revellers getting it on. It's not fun, exactly, but it beats the alternative. One pint is enough to calm you down again, but it also seems to be enough for Elaine, who is beginning to look twitchy. 'Look, I need to be up tomorrow without a hang-over if I'm going to do the face thing with Hayek's people. How about we call it an evening and you meet me at their offices at nine thirty sharp?' She beams you the address and you stick a push-pin in your phone's map display.

'Okay, I'll do that,' you say, stifling a groan at the idea of the up-with-the-larks timing. (It wasn't like this at LupuSoft: breakfast at noon, so to speak.) 'I'll walk you back to the hotel.' You stand up and hold the door for her, and at the hotel she makes her awkward goodbyes and strides through the door. Then the whole thing comes crashing down on your shoulders like a suit woven from slabs of slate. *Jesus fuck.* The panicky urge to phone Sophie is sudden and nearly irresistible – but then, what if you're wrong? You don't want to tear holes in the Potemkin village of her reality. So you decide to play games instead.

It's zero dark o'clock and you're coiled up on the futon in your living room like a basket case, goggles glued to your face by a mixture of sweat and determination. Your hands are twitching and spazzing from side to side, and you're muttering under your breath like an old alkie communing with his invisible pink proboscidean. At least, that's how it would look to a time-travelling intruder in your wee house who didn't know what was actually going on – the body adrift in the grip of a weird compulsion while the mind decays inside it. A time-traveller from the 1980s or later might notice the winking LED status lights on the boxes under the flat-screen telly and guess at the significance of the glasses, and from the early nineties onwards they'd stand a good chance of understanding the muse whose arms you dance in: but to a visitor of Wellsian or earlier vintage, it would be wholly incomprehensible other than as some weird display of vile degeneracy.

(You vile degenerate, you and your hundred million cyberspatial compatriots!)

Not that you're much given to probing the time-travelling condition when you can go rushing around bashing goblin brains with your clan buddies, which is what you're doing right now – a bit of mindless recreational hack'n'slash to distract yourself until you're tired enough for bed.

You're running around as Oberon, a high-level warlock of more or less human origins who you've been developing for a while, out of idle curiosity – he's well optimized for playing in a variety of fantasy zones, mostly ones that branch off the old dungeon paradigm – and you've hooked up with a trio of adventurers you just met in the guild-house to go and kick short green butt in a cave complex somewhere north of Castle Greyhawk and east of the rising sun. Alice (on morningstar and clerical anti-undead duty), Helmut (on war-axe and attitude) and Fantomas (lock-picking and garottes) are reasonably experienced players, for which you are grateful: so far the goblins have just been a minor nuisance, but you've got a feeling there's more to this cave complex than meets the ultravision-augmented eye up to now. Which is why you've got half a dozen defensive spells locked and loaded, a neon-red knife missile floating above your left shoulder, and a serious case of paranoia as you tiptoe after Fantomas towards the running water you can hear ahead.

It's a cave *complex*, of course, because you don't generally run across anything as small as a mere cavelet in Greyhawk. There will be underground rivers, vast and wide, and huge cavernous killing zones with mist-wreathed stalagmite islands and waterfalls thundering into the subterranean depths – and stepping-stones and brokeback bridges to traverse under fire from the chittering hordes. Plus at least two side-quests to fulfil if you want to acquire the plot coupon to open the door to the money shot on the third sub-basement level guarded by the Klingon security detachment – except you made that last bit up: whimsical, but that's how the automatic scenario generators work, they've got all the subtlety of a play-by-numbers adventure book or a Hollywood motion picture.

Still, you can enjoy the artwork. Someone put a lot of effort into the music score, which is variations on a vaguely classical theme with a trance background: and the stony footing actually looks as if someone who'd been down a limestone karst or two in their day designed it, bedding planes and all. It doesn't look like off-the-shelf tiles, and you're almost beginning to wonder whether someone at Wizards of the Co$t has finally cracked procedural sedimentary rock formation in Zone when you run up against Alice, who has stopped and is crouched behind a boulder.

'What is it?' you ask, using your private chat channel.

'Someone else ahead. Don't look like NPCs.' That's Fantomas talking. He's got a thick Yorkshire accent, which is pretty weird coming from a halfling swathed in black assassin's silks.

'Eyeballs, oh great mage?' That's Helmut. There's a suspicious buzz to his voice that bespeaks either a suspiciously lossy routing or a voice remixer – the latter's most likely, so you peg him as a transvestite, but that's his privilege – but the sarcasm comes through undimmed.

'Certainly. Give me one second.' You hit on a spell slot and the knife missile shimmers with a shield of invisibility, then you send it forward into the dark cavern that vaults across the underground lake on whose shore you are playing hide-and-seek.

There's a beach about fifty yards out across the expanse of black liquid, and a rickety wooden pier running out from it to a gondola-like boat that rocks slightly in an invisible breeze. You look through the missile's eyes as it closes in on the boat, then, as if by magic (as if! In a place like this!) it pierces a shield of some description, and a small horde of bad guys appear beneath you. There are at least twelve of them, lumpen green-skinned warriors in heavy iron armour, skull-helmets and horsehair fringes nodding above beetle-browed faces: and they all bear a red ideogram on their shields. But they're sure as hell not NPCs – you can hear a low-key conversation, the strange (to your Western ears) nasal-sounding intonation of mandarin speakers, and they're equipped like adventurers, and that one in the sorcerer's robe is an—

'Oh *shit*,' you manage to say, just as the enemy mage looks up expressionlessly, stabs his staff of power at your knife missile, and you lose contact. 'Hostile clan, look like dark-dwellers, at least a dozen' – and then you flip back to your local context and look around and everything's going to pieces around you. Half a dozen of the skull-helmed intruders march up out of the placid lake waters at the double, shedding their magical gills as they lower their halberds. You begin to trace a rune of protection, but you're too late: a cross-bow bolt, burning with alchemist's fire, takes you in the back, from the trio of archers who have appeared from cover in the passageway behind you.

That pisses you off, and you're a sufficiently powerful sorcerer that you don't have to take that sitting: so you turn and prepare to zap a fireball at them as your magic armour comes online.

But nothing happens. You twitch. 'Give me fire support!' yells Alice. 'Someone heal Helmut—'

You line up another fireball and let rip. *Nada. Huh?* Something's clearly wrong.

Another hostile steps out from behind the archers. This one is wearing a suit of powered battle armour and carrying a small tactical atomic grenade launcher from **SPACE MARINE**. Which is just *not possible* in Zone – it's a tech-level transgression, not to mention a red flag to the moderators – but the last thing you see of your enemies is the red-glowing ideogram floating in the depths of his helmet face-plate as he pulls the trigger.

And brings the curtain down on Oberon the Warlock as neatly as any game you've ever lost.

Fucking cheats!

The next morning you awaken in a breathless near panic, one of those *I'm-late-I'm-late-I'm-late* tension dreams you get just before the alarm tweedles. You bounce out of bed too fast, get dizzy, stagger to the shower, begin getting dressed, and realize you only bought the one dress shirt to go with the suit. So you end up being ten minutes late out the door, unshaven and wearing a grand's worth of pinstripes over a **STEAMING** tee-shirt that promises to bam yer pot, Jimmy.

You hop the bus from the high street out to Drum Brae, shifting the time with a wee dip into Ankh-Morpork. The bus trundles past ominously looming hunchbacked houses, cars replaced by noisome horse-drawn wagons, pedestrian commuters by a mixture of dwarfs, golems, werewolves, and humans from various periods of History-Land™. There are only a couple of icons spinning over players' heads, though – Discworld™ isn't too popular among the nine-till-five set. It's all a bit drearily boring, so you drop out of the overlay and into your newsfeed for the rest of the trip.

The Hayek Associates' offices – well, you'd heard about the old government nuclear command/control bunker out near Corstorphine hill, but you weren't sure you believed in it until now. The car-park is full of Porsches and Bentleys, plus a Police van: all it needs is a bathroom with a jacuzzi full of brightly coloured machine parts to make your day. You head for the entrance, where a big guy with a badly trimmed moustache and a suit that screams 'cop' in sixteen different languages steps into your path.

'Hold on, son. What are you here for?'

You swallow. 'I'm a contractor, working for Dietrich-Brunner Associates, who I'm supposed to be meeting here' – you check your glasses – 'ten minutes ago.' *Damn.*

Mr. Moustache pulls out an ancient smartphone that bristles with keyboardy goodness. 'Just a mo. Can I see your ID card?'

You resist the urge to get shirty and open your wallet. 'Yup.'

'Okay.' He checks his phone. 'In you go, Mr. Reed.'

'Thanks—' You pause, suddenly realizing something. 'Who are you?'

'The tooth fairy, son.' His cheek twitches, then he reaches into his suit pocket and produces a warrant card. 'In you go.'

'You can never be too sure,' you say, risking it, and scurry inside before the mummy lobe can scream and faint at your scandalous temerity in questioning his authority.

The bored temp on the reception desk stares at you like you're something she trod in by accident: 'You're late,' she says. 'Second level, room 110.' She points at the lift opposite, then hands you a badge. You get the message, and head straight for room six (having figured out – unlike the temp – that *of course* the lunatics at Hayek Associates number everything in binary).

Room six turns out to be a boardroom. The door's open, and as you slide through it crabwise in an unconscious attempt to render yourself invisible you find Elaine, half the gang from last night, and a bunch of strangers, some of whom have that geek vibe to them. Chris, Elaine's boss, is speaking. You sneak in and stand at the back like a naughty schoolboy while Chris rolls on in an imperious tone of voice, telling the bunch of strangers that he's got the legal equivalent of a carrier strike group zeroed in on them, and they'd better give him access all areas, or else. Which goes down about as well as you'd expect.

'What you're asking for is impossible,' snaps the leader of the enemy faction, a big silverback marketroid with all the charm of a Gitmo interrogator. 'The audit can be arranged, if you're willing to pay for it and contract with a mutually acceptable third party who will be bound by our standard NDAs, but the rest is right out. You're asking for a complete copy of our database and transaction log, plus core mission-critical systems so you can perform a hostile audit while we're trying to keep our business running in the face of an external hack attack: that's just not practical, unless you've got a few hundred petabytes of storage kicking around and a data centre to run the sand-box in.'

The vaguely rat-faced guy from last night – Brendan – raises a document wallet. '*This* says you're going to give us access. Why not just get it over with?'

'Give me that,' the silverback says contemptuously. He sniffs a couple of times as he reads it. Meanwhile, you fidget with your specs. There's a new layer on the room, and a whole bunch of documents. *It's lawsuit-space: cool!* You glance at the auths and see that you're on the Dietrich-Brunner case folder – they've listed you as staff, so you can edit their files. 'Chris, I'd appreciate a word with you and your counsel in private with me and Phil.' He glances at a cynical thirtysomething who is doodling notes with a pen on a yellow legal pad. 'Just to clear the air.'

Chris turns round. 'You heard him, everybody take ten.' He smiles, but it doesn't reach his eyes. Thinking you might as well beat the rush, you slide out the door about five seconds ahead of Elaine.

'What's going on?' you ask.

'Chris and Hackman are trying to outasshole each other.' Her lips underscore the dry disapproval of her tone. 'When they finish posturing, the lawyers will broker a deal, and the winner gets to dry-hump the loser's leg.'

You roll your eyes. It's not exactly a novelty, but . . . 'Why is it that the further up the greasy pole you look, the more childish the games get?'

She examines you with clinical interest, as if looking for signs of life on Mars. 'Let's go find the coffee station. I think they'll be at it for at least half an hour. Got to make it look hard-fought.'

As it happens, Elaine is out by less than four minutes. You're just finishing a polystyrene cup of mechaccino from the robot caffeine dispenser in the Mess Hall (that's what it still says on the door) and you've just about gotten round to thinking *why me?* for the third time this morning when Cynical Phil sticks his head round the door. 'It's safe to come back, the shooting's over,' he mutters, then withdraws in a hurry. Everyone puts their coffee down and troops obediently back to the boardroom, where the Chris-and-Hackman show has dropped the final curtain.

'You've got a week,' says Hackman. He looks like he wants to bite someone's throat out: no wonder his lawyer didn't want to hang around. 'Your tech heads can poke around as much as they need to, and Rebecca and Mike will give them what they need.' A subtle emphasis on the last word there. 'Wayne will act as gatekeeper. You want something, you ask Wayne, he's got the authority to say yes or no. Your accounts team can dupe our personnel files and accounts and look at them off-line, subject to nondisclosure arrangements. But I don't want you underfoot. Two bodies, one week, that's all you get to plant down here.'

One week? Chris smiles lopsidedly and nods at Elaine. 'That should be sufficient,' he says confidently. 'I've got every faith in you, Elaine.' And that's you, and your eight grand a day, *right there.*

Midafternoon finds you attending a business meeting in a dungeon under Vhrana, with a gorgon called Stheno and a dark elf archer called Venkmann. Venkmann is one of the house avatars, currently being driven by Mike Russell. He has black-enamelled armour, an elaborately engraved skull-faced helmet, a twenty-centimetre-long Fu Manchu moustache, and an evil laugh – and that's just the visible assets. 'Where do you want to start?' he asks.

'The Orcs.' You ground your blunderbuss on the uneven, rubble-strewn floor of the cave and lean on it. 'They were bearers, right?'

'Pretty much.' Venkmann raises one bony finger. Its tip glows green as he commences writing notes that hover in the air behind him. 'Encumbrance, one hundred and ten pounds each before they hit a movement penalty.'

'Did you go hunting their registered owners?'

'Yup.' Venkmann scrawls another check mark in mid-air. 'All forty were signed up via a botnet in Malaysia, using stolen credit cards. The cost of a tag in Avalon Four is low enough that their banks just authorized the transactions without doing a fraud check.'

The gorgon is looking a little bit lost. Periodically, she shrugs or twitches, stereotyped body language untouched by mortal puppeteer. 'Where did the card numbers come from?' she finally asks.

'Who knows?' Venkmann shrugs. 'It's petty crime at this level – fifteen euros here and there. We told the cops, who made a note of it, but—'

'No, I mean, did all the numbers come from the same source?' she asks. 'If some web storefront got themselves hacked, that might tell us something. Work it from the other end, find the hacker, find who they sold the numbers to.'

Venkmann looks perplexed. 'Is that possible?' he asks.

You shift your weight between feet and rumble bearishly. 'Of course it's possible,' you point out. 'There's a *real world* out there, Mike. Maybe we ought to ask the cops if they've covered that angle yet.'

'The cops will take the details and give you a pat on the head, then they'll ignore you,' predicts Stheno. 'It's a volume crime, they don't investigate small frauds individually, it's not cost-effective.' A small buzzing insect, no doubt attracted by the smell of blood, flies too close to her, and one of her asps snaps at it. The snake-lock misses, but the fly drops to the floor and shatters like glass. 'If you expect them to share intelligence, you're mistaken. The rule is, information flows into an investigation, never out of it. Break the rule, and you risk tipping off the target.'

Venkmann walks over to the Iron Maiden that leans up against the far wall of the dungeon. He idly spins the hand-crank that winches the lid up. 'Whatever. We got forty Orcs. They didn't act like a bunch of macro zombies. When I reran the footage, they were acting too random, too human – making mistakes and cancelling out of them, that kind of thing. They were following their leader, and when they ran, they ran back here.'

'Orcs. Treasure. How did they get into the bank?' you ask.

'Someone gave them ownership privs on the loot.' Venkmann sounds annoyed. 'The same someone who nerfed the gods, presumably.'

'Could someone have cracked Hayek Associates' root certificate from outside?' you ask. 'Or do you think it was an inside job?'

Venkmann winches the Iron Maiden's lid all the way open. What's inside lies in darkness. 'What I think is, there's a bug in Kensu's shitty Chinese code. It might be a memory leak – someone left a fence-post error in a copy-on-write primitive or something – or maybe something more exotic, but someone figured out a privilege-escalation attack that works. If you can get deity level rights, you can probably de-escalate other folks, too. The question is, who got root? And what did they do with the loot, anyway?'

You snort. 'Treasure is treasure. That's what eBay is for.' It's worth whatever someone is willing to pay for it – like bank-notes, which used to carry the words, *I promise to pay the bearer on demand the sum of ten pounds.*

'Yes, but they haven't shown up there yet. This is stolen goods, I think we might get a stop put on the auction a bit faster than usual.' He clears his throat. 'Anyway. After they got here, they, well, they made an unorthodox exit.'

He gestures at the Iron Maiden.

'You have got to be kidding,' you say. If you die in-game, your body – and what it's wearing – stays where you fell. You reincarnate in your bare scuddies and you've got to run if you want to re-equip before some scavenging farmer grabs your kit. But the Iron Maiden is tagged as a shredder – it's got the permanent death attribute, a creepy purple glow surrounding it in your admin-enhanced vision. That's pretty damned unusual in this kind of game space; it doesn't just kill you, it shreds you beyond resurrection. 'What would be the point of that?'

'Well, obviously it killed them fatally. More importantly, it surrendered ownership of their in-game assets to, to whoever was waiting here. The Fence.'

'Ah,' says Stheno, sounding as if she's just achieved enlightenment.

'So let's replay the entry log for this shard and see who came here,' you suggest, 'before the Orcs showed up with the loot.'

'Ali Baba and the Forty Thieves,' says Stheno.

'Huh?'

'Open Sesame!' she cries. And the Iron Maiden starts flashing.

'What the fuck?' says Venkmann.

'Go on, open it up,' Stheno urges.

'Not likely, it might be a trap.'

Venkmann's risk-averse attitude bugs you, so you put your mad skillz to work. Bringing up the in-game debugger in your field of view shows a whole bunch of scripting cruft attached to the torture implement. 'Hey, this thing is really over-engineered for a simple killing machine, huh?'

'What? What's—' Venkmann can see what you're seeing, and you get the feeling that back in his office Mike is twitching with something other than a caffeine jag. 'Hey, that's not right. It says it's signed by . . . ' He trails off, muttering to himself, and the Venkmann avatar lolls on its feet like a hanged puppet, only its jittery fingertips showing that it's not dead.

WHAT'S HE DOING? Stheno IMs you.

'There's about' – you run a quick compile/syntax check on the tree – 'about fifteen thousand lines of code attached to that thing, where there should only be a couple of hundred. They're digitally signed using the Hayek corporate certificate, too, which means that someone at HA put them there. Numpties.'

'You're telling me they didn't even check? Before now?' the snake-woman hisses at you.

'Yeah, looks like.'

'Jesus.' She glances at you. 'How do you know this?'

'You've got access to a built-in debugger and development suite whenever you're running in god mode' – a nasty thought strikes you – 'and there was a bunch of core database code in that thing: if someone's planted a trigger in a public table and a watcher somewhere else in Zonespace—'

There's a brilliant blue flash of light from the Iron Maiden, prompting you nearly to sprain a thumb bringing up a bunch of defensive spells you keep ready for just such occasions. 'Shit!' yells Venkmann. Darkness gathers, fulminating, in the corners of the room, a smoky penumbral effusion spilling from the crack that has opened up in reality. You power up the Shield of Steel Focus and the Dome of Defence in a hurry, watching the world around you blur into watery unfocus as figures with too many limbs step out of the corners, moving in insectile stop-go jerks.

Venkmann is frozen over the gaping maw of the Iron Maiden, held in place by some unseen force. You turn to confront the intruders and realize that Stheno is outside your zone of protection. *Shit.* This is going to be ugly. There are four of the things, like gigantic anthropomorphic toads with strangely articulated limbs and great horned heads. You crack open a vial of Neverslow and inhale the bitter fumes, then unsling your blunderbuss as the world around you seems to slow, jerking in stop-frame animation. The gun's already loaded with coarse-ground silver filings and lead shot, and when you pull, it bangs deafeningly in the confined space, blasting a cloud of smoke and sparks at the nearest of the demonic intruders, who yells raucous rage at you but doesn't even stop coming. You can see the haze of improbability spiralling around its head, the madness in its eyes – *it's a fucking slaad of some kind! What are they doing here?* – and then it raises its webbed hands in a spell-caster's gesture, and a vast bloom of emerald fire envelops you. Which is a huge relief because it tells you you're up against a bot; no human player – not even a total noob – would do something that stupid.

Two of the slaad's fellow gate-crashers run into your Dome of Defence from either side, rattling your teeth as you invert the blunderbuss and reload as fast as you can. Reflexes left over from your munchkin days take over, and you blaze away, trying meanwhile to figure out what it all means. (You were

looking for a clan of cannon fodder, not a booby-trapped artefact that triggers a teleport routine to drop a gang of pissed-off
midlevel demons on you: who put it here, and why?) 'Stheno,
you still alive?'

'Yes! What's going on?'

'They're trying to kill us, and they're a whole lot more
powerful than Orcs. Get behind me, I'll handle—'

'No you won't.' Stheno steps daintily around the Iron
Maiden – Venkmann still wired to it with blue sparks flashing
off his hair – and draws a long sword she found somewhere.
Her status icon shows that she's trying to go into some weird-
ass haptic combat mode, something only idiot LARPers use,
and you swear quietly as you dump a handful of Dust of
Dispelling down the smoking maw of your gun and raise it
again. One of the slaadi is going for her, which means –

A huge fountain of blood squirts across the room in arterial
gouts. *Shit, exit one auditor, dashed bad game-play, do you want to
reincarnate in the middle of a fight?* You shrug and drop the
hammer on the demon as it scrabbles with ichor-dripping
claws at the edge of your dome. Stupid fuckers, they've got a
magical arsenal all of their own: played straight, they could
take you down in minutes. *Magic stick go Bang* and you can see
daylight – okay, torchlight – through the beastie's rib-cage as
it takes a tumble. *Good.* You turn to the next one, only to find
that Stheno's still in the game and has got in ahead of you with
that sword. She's holding it at a weird angle and as the slaad
screams and launches itself at her, she twists it and hops sideways, as if that's going to achieve anything. The predictable
thing happens – it takes a swipe at her but misses, probably
because she's accidentally triggered her Tumble talent and
gone cartwheeling face-first into the wall.

What the hell? You're supposed to be in quick time thanks

to the dust you snorted, forcing the local Zonespace servers to crank down the time base for everyone else within the game's event horizon (meaning, this room). Maybe Stheno's LARP-addled mode can only do real-time, and the god mode Venkmann dropped on you both so casually has stopped the game engines from downgrading her movement rate. Or something like that . . . You're still turning towards the next pebble-skinned party pooper as Stheno twists sideways and jabs her frog-sticker at him, misses, and does a neat back-flip. The slaad twitches, roars, then takes a swipe at her. 'Why can't I touch the fucking thing?' she yells frustratedly.

'You're not equipped for it! And he's got too many hit points!' you yell back at her, reloading in a hurry because bad guy #4 is sneaking up behind her with malice clearly in what passes for its tiny mind. 'Clear the area! No, duck!'

She ducks, still holding on to her hilts like grim death, and you blast a cloud of buckshot across her shoulders and into frogface's maw. He sneezes, green goop flying, and begins to Incant. That's a bad sign, those things have big death-magic mojo. So far, the bot's been playing them clumsily, using a tank to run over individual infantry instead of shelling them from the next county over – but if it gets its shit together, you're going to be in a world of hurt. As if that's not enough, you hear a low-pitched warning buzz: your Shield of Steel Focus is nearing the end of its life, and any moment now you're going to be unprotected.

You begin to back towards the Iron Maiden, hoping to use it as an obstacle, when Stheno leans over the supine slaad and starts horse-whipping it with her snake-headed dreadlocks. Which, surprisingly, works – the thing must have been pretty near to dead already. There's a crackling tinkle as the grotesque frog-statue rolls over on its side, and then she vaults over it towards bad guy #4. He's still busy Incanting – these spells take time – so you follow her, pitching in with all four paws in the faint hope of breaking his concentration roll. Only, no dice. Stheno has another momentary lapse of co-ordination and goes head first into the far wall, limbs spazzing wildly. Slaad #4 emits a strange howl and points, and all hell breaks loose – in the direction of the thoroughly immobilized Venkmann.

You whack the demon alongside his head with an ursine pawful of claws. That gets his attention: he turns and clumsily gouges at you with a scaly hand, gobbling and gurgling incoherently. You whack him again while Stheno leans forward and makes stabby to no particular avail. The gobbling rises towards an angry, incoherent peak, then stops, breaking up like a bandwidth-choked voice call. Another whack, and the slaad subsides in a twitching heap, oozing corrosive juices that eat away at the tiled floor.

'It didn't work,' she says plaintively. 'I kept trying to go into haptic contact-mode, and it wouldn't work!'

'Whoa,' you wheeze. 'You mean, like, full-body input? That doesn't work in Avalon Four without a hack pack on the side.' Typical noob trick, trying to use an esoteric interface and going arse over tit, instead of simply whaling away with the plus-three Axe of Decerebration. 'Let's check on Venkmann.' You shamble over towards the Iron Maiden, kicking dismembered amphibian parts out of your way. Venkmann's still wired into the shredder, kicking and twitching, so you call up the debugger console again and drop a break point on the thing. He falls away from it, collapsing on the floor. For a moment you think he's dead, but he magics up some hit points from somewhere and is back on his feet.

'What the *fuck* was that all about?' he demands, irritably.

'When I catch the motherfucker who invented those—' He rambles on angrily for some time while you examine the code hooked into the Iron Maiden, which is still sparking and fulminating on an al fresco basis. Interestingly, it seems to have erased itself. If you hadn't had a devkit buffer open before the extradimensional mugging, you wouldn't even have noticed the missing twelve thousand lines of code. 'What happened?'

'Who's got write access to your version control system?' you ask Venkmann.

'Huh? What's that got to do with it?'

'Plenty, I think.' You stare at the Iron Maiden, then tweak a couple of resources. The cascade of sparks and the violet pulsing aura go away. 'Should be possible to look inside that without triggering the trap, now.'

Venkmann leans forward. 'Either of you got a familiar?'

'Um.' You should have thought of that: just because you disarmed the trap doesn't mean that it's safe to look. 'I'm fresh out of 'em. How about you?'

'I've got a snake,' Stheno offers uncertainly.

'Badger,' says Venkmann. He turns round and begins to incant. There's a bang and a cloud of purple smoke as a confused-looking badger appears.

'What . . . ' Stheno begins to ask.

'It's a familiar. He can see through its eyes, okay?' Venkmann continues to incant. A moment later, the badger shimmers and warps into invisibility. 'Now it's an invisible badger – the best kind of camera.' Venkmann bends down, picks something up, and leans over the Iron Maiden before releasing it.

'Well, there's a surprise!'

'What's down there?'

'It's a rabbit-hole,' he says slowly, looking around as if at a different landscape.

'Where's it go?'

'Looks like Zhongguo shard, going by the map. Which is part of Hentai Animatics' zone, and we don't have an admin contract for that. I think you've just uncovered an illegal-immigrant tunnel.'

SUE: CHOP SHOP

Hackman's weird outburst has haunted you all through the case team meeting up at the station, despite your hasty cramming on blacknets and anonymizing peer-to-peer crime networks and the people who set them up and skim off the profits; in particular his admonition not to have anything to do with the 'bottom-feeding scum'. Bottom-feeding scum are, you might say, something of a professional specialty – and not just when you're hauling bodies out of the Water of Leith; all you need is to think back to the last open evening at the wee one's school, and it's there fair and square in the playground with a squint and a buzz cut to go with the sharpie in its back pocket. It disnae matter whether they're bottom-feeding scum with a chib and a crack habit or the up-market kind who book the assassinations of their business rivals via blacknet. So, with the inspector's encouragement, you head back to Hayek Associates' bunker – where by now they're hunkering down under their concrete eaves to avoid the barrage of writs and journalists' inquiries whistling down on them from parts north, east, west, *and* south – to go Liaise with some Victims.

It's early afternoon when you park next to the muddy pothole at the edge of the car-park. First off, you check the Mess Hall to grab a coffee and see who's there. A couple of the

quants are hanging around the coffee machine: your glasses –
now configured for off-line browsing – remind you of their
names, Couper, Sam ('traceroute is my bitch') and Evans,
Darren. You walk up behind them. 'Sam, Darren,' you say,
with a smile, 'how are you doing today?'

They both nearly jump a mile: they may be thick as thieves,
but they lack the reflexes of the pathologically non-law-abid-
ing. Turning these nice middle-class nerds inside out and
shaking them until the pips squeak would be so easy it'd make
the baby Jesus cry: they're still terrified of parking tickets.
Clearly neither of these two are running an illicit blacknet.
They haven't even been exposed to the long arm of the law
often enough for it to lose its dreadful majesty. 'Fine! Fine!
What you want?' Darren asks, too eager for his own good.

'A regular coffee, hold the sugar,' you suggest, and damn if
Sam doesn't turn and make a pathetic lunge for the control
panel, so eager to oblige that if you slid an unsigned confession
under his fingers, he'd be in for the high jump tomorrow.
Aye, this one would have been blackboard monitor in junior
six, right enough. Not to mention the class swot. Which may
actually make the job at hand harder – they'll drown you in
irrelevant details if you give them the chance. 'I was wanting
to interview both of you later today, get your account of what
happened. Are you free later on?'

'Uh, yeah, just not right now.' Darren is recovering his
composure faster than Sam. 'Busy fighting fires, covering for
that asshole Nigel. He hasn't updated the group-reconciliation
files since last Wednesday, and we're going to be in the shitter
if we don't get it under control before the weekly M4 policy
session.'

'Your coffee, miss . . . ?' says Sam.

'Sergeant, actually.' You smile at him as you take the cup.

'Sergeant Smith.' That's right, grind it in, define your authority now so he bends the neck later. 'When's the policy session?'

'Uh, Wednesday, actually,' volunteers Darren, getting his act together. 'I guess I can make some time late this afternoon or maybe tomorrow morning, but right now we've got to patch Nigel's—'

The door opens, and another quant comes in, along with two suits whom your specs unhelpfully identify as VISITOR 1 and VISITOR 2. 'That's okay,' you say. 'Tomorrow will do. Ten o'clock?' He nods. 'Okay, see you then.' You nod at Sam, also, and he seems to take it as a dismissal and scuttles away with his tail between his legs. Which leaves you with an opportunity to check out the visitors before you move on. You put your smiling meet-the-people face in place and turn to face them.

'Hello,' you say. VISITOR 1 is male, late twenties, overweight, badly shaved, and that suit *really* doesn't go with the faded black tee-shirt. VISITOR 2 is female, skinny, somewhere in that vague period between late teens and midthirties, and looks like she knows far too much about spreadsheets for her own good. Black suit, very corporate, well-coordinated. Verdict: they're technical/clerical citizens. Sub-type: probably law-abiding, apart from the occasional furtive joint. 'I haven't seen you around here before. Are you from' – you nudge up the case database – 'Dietrich-Brunner Associates?'

VISITOR 1 is of a kind with Sam, but VISITOR 2 is made of sterner stuff: she sniffs and gives you an old-fashioned look. 'Could be,' she says. 'Who are you?'

You stare back at her: she's a bit mousy, but you've met her type before – usually giving you a nasty grilling on the witness stand.

'I'm Detective Sergeant Smith,' you tell her, 'working out

of Meadowplace station.' You drop the smile. 'You *are* from Dietrich-Brunner?'

VISITOR 2 continues to make with the long stare, but VISITOR 1 caves. 'Um, yeah, we are. She's the organ grinder, I'm just the performing monkey.' He mimes shaking a hat.

VISITOR 2 elbows him in the ribs, sharply. 'No, you're a dancing *bear*. Do try to get the right species!' She faces you: 'I'm sorry we seem to have gotten off on the wrong foot. I'm Elaine Barnaby, and yes, I'm from Dietrich-Brunner – I'm a forensic accountant. Jack here is a game-development consultant, and he's acting as my guide. Now, what can we do for you, Sergeant?'

'You can help yourselves to a coffee, then maybe tell me why Marcus Hackman might not want people such as yourselves, um, crawling around on his turf?'

She raises an eyebrow. 'Ah, that *is* an interesting turn of phrase. *His?*'

Good, that's got her attention. 'Depends. What are you doing here? I mean, in Hayek Associates' offices?'

'Oh, that.' She sniffs. Jack bends over the coffee machine, mumbling to himself, then starts punching buttons like it's a Game Boy. Your fingers are itching to stick their names into CopSpace and see what comes back, but that might be a wee bit too obvious if you did it right now . . . 'I'm *supposed* to be conducting a security audit on a bank in an online game. At least, that's what I thought the picture was yesterday. In practice . . . I take it you're here because Wayne or Marcus or someone reported the intrusion last week? That'll have gone on your case-load as a crime, possibly hacking, possibly theft or fraud – whatever. Well, DBA got sucked in because one of our senior partners vetted Hayek's board before their IPO the other month, and this stinks of an inside job. So Chris panicked and dragged a team of us up here to do something about it. Now there's a programmer missing and that's . . . well, it's enough to get him off the hook, so he's pissing off back to the City, but my job – and Jack's – is to confirm that it really was this Nigel MacDonald that did it, dot the i's and cross the t's. I *think* Chris may even be planning to pull strings and get NFIU to take us on as specialist subcontractors, if he can sort out the cross-border jurisdictional voodoo.'

That sets you back on your heels: the Crime and Rehabilitation Office hires civilian specialists from time to time, it's true, and the technical side of this investigation is going to the National squad as soon as anyone notices it – does that make these people bystanders or fellow cops? *Leave it to Liz to sort out the turf wars, you decide.* 'Ah, well, I cannae be telling you anything until someone tells me you're to be working on the case,' you temporize. 'But if there's anything ye've found about the situation, and especially about Nigel MacDonald, I'd love to hear it.'

'Yes, there's—' Jack begins eagerly, before Elaine gives him a look that could strip paint. There's some interesting chemistry going on there, if you're any judge of such things.

'I think what he means to say is, we'd be happy to co-operate with your investigation purely on a professional peer-to-peer basis with appropriate confidentiality safeguards in place for a pooling of information,' she picks up, facing you like she's holding a royal flush. And, indeed, she is. So you smile and take a mouthful of too-hot coffee. One point to her.

'Well, that's a start.' You pause a moment. 'You said something about knowing what you were meant to be doing yesterday. What's changed since then?'

'We're trying to track down where Tricky Dicky hid the loot,' says Jack, ignoring the warning look Elaine sends him.

'Seeing he's not here for us to ask. Hmm. Do you have him in custody yet?'

You weigh your answer carefully. 'Not yet. In fact, if you should see him, I'd appreciate it if you'd IM me. My colleagues do indeed have some questions we'd like to put to him.' *Starting with, how'd you come back from the grave? Assuming you existed in the first place?* But there's no call to go frightening the horses just yet, so you keep that thought to yourself.

'I think we can do that,' Jack says, seemingly oblivious as Elaine raises the energy level from Defrost to Nuke. 'Problem is, it could be anywhere in Zonespace, or even out of it. Avalon Four isn't the only game sharing this platform, and whatever was stolen, if they can get it out of Avalon and into somewhere else . . .' He trails off.

'What is it?' Elaine asks sharply.

'eBay.' He pulls on a pair of thick-rimmed glasses. 'Assuming this was a real bank robbery, what do you do with the goods?'

'The goods?' You look perplexed. 'Banks hold *money* . . .'

Jack shakes his head. 'This is a game, remember.' He glances at Elaine, who nods slowly. 'The bank's not somewhere that manages risk; it's somewhere that stores value. You can only carry so much crap around with you in Zonespace without becoming encumbered, which slows you up. So Hayek run the bank and sell safety deposit storage. This gives players who haven't bought themselves a castle yet a place to stash their goodies while they're running around on quests, and it also siphons money out of the game stealthily, in bank charges. Anyway, what was stolen was the contents of about three thousand safety deposit boxes. Actually, the real crime was that someone corrupted the digitally signed ownership certificates for objects in the database, turning them over to some third party: the Orcs were just warm bodies to carry the loot away. Once they had it, the ownership certificates got swapped around again via a remixer to stop Hayek or Kensu International from figuring it out – they don't routinely log all ownership changes, it'd be like running a supermarket chain's stock control system – then got the hot goods out of Avalon Four and onto another shard via the rabbit-hole.'

This sounds horribly familiar. 'You think there's a fence somewhere?'

Jack scratches the side of his nose, then takes the glasses off and polishes them on his tee-shirt. 'The whole scenario makes no sense at all *unless* there's a fence.' He examines the glasses. 'In-game auction-houses won't touch stolen goods, but if they've got a conduit set up, say in another real-world juris-diction or even in another Zone partition, they could sell the loot on eBay. The trouble is going to be getting a list of the stuff that's been stolen, then checking for all the possible auction-houses. And that's before you start to wonder if the stolen prestige items have been hacked on by someone with crafting skillz . . . '

It *is* horribly familiar: there's a wee garage down in Cramond that Mac's been trying to shut down for years – the owner's a big ned, done time in Bar-L for receiving, and the inspector swears blind he's running a chop shop – but he's never been able to pin anything on it. You've got unfond memories of spending nights and mornings keeping an eye on his back yard via spy cam, trying to spot a delivery. And on a larger scale, it's what those blacknets you were reading up on are supposed to do – antisocial networking sites. 'Where would you go to look?'

'I'd start by trying to find out what's been stolen,' says Jack. 'And then I'd write a bot, to go round all the online auctions trying to match a shopping list against what's on sale. Drill down, cross-correlate the merchants' – he's going all cross-eyed, and you're not the only one who's staring at him as if he's turned into some kind of delphic oracle – 'see if any names keep coming up.'

Barnaby snaps her fingers, a dry, popping sound. 'Time series analysis on the transaction log from the auctions,' she says, leading you to wonder whether you're surrounded by complete nutters or just very, very strange detectives.

Jack shakes his head. 'I'd better go see if Mike's got a list—'

You reach a decision. *Funny how Marcus Hackman's* bottom-feeding scum *are a lot more human than he is, isn't it?* 'No you won't. *We* will. Because if you find anything, and there are names attached, I'll be wanting a wee word with them.'

It turns out that nobody actually knows what's been stolen.

'You've got to understand, it's a distributed database,' says Couper, looking flustered – when you and Jack found him he was hunkered down in a nest of big flat screens full of tiny coloured text with a ragged left margin, and it took a tap on the shoulder before he'd look up – 'we don't track everything centrally.'

'What about the journal logs?' asks Jack. Someone behind you snaps their fingers.

'Well sure, but we're typically tracking close to a million transactions per minute. Good luck if you expect us to grep *that*.' He kicks his chair back from his workstation and turns to face you. 'You'd have to track the user handles from when they logged in—'

'Can't you put up a notice somewhere?' asks Elaine. 'Ask for information.' She pauses.

Couper doesn't give her a breathing space. 'Sure, but nobody would—'

'Tell them it's to register an insurance claim,' she interrupts, raising her voice. *Someone's been taking assertiveness classes,* you realize. 'That Hayek Associates are trying to get the items back, but will be unable to return unclaimed items.'

'But they'll claim all sorts of shit that they never had!'

'Really?' She gives Couper a withering look: 'I'd never have guessed. Poor innocent me, nobody told me that people *lie* while I was studying for my master's in forensic accountancy . . .'

'But what use is it?' Couper looks upset, more than anything: 'It doesn't make sense!'

'It's simple enough. Most people will tell the truth, especially when we tell them we just want to know their five top items, so we can verify them against our database.'

'But there isn't a database—' Couper stops dead.

Elaine nods, smiling a little smile. 'But they don't know that, do they?'

'Oh. Right, well then.' Couper shakes his head.

'I'll need admin access to the auction-houses,' Jack adds.

Couper splutters. 'You can't be serious! They're in this to make money. They could sue us into the ground if we let you mess with their stock—'

'Read-only,' Jack says firmly. 'I need to write a scraper that can trawl their database for hot property.'

'Talk to Wayne, or Beccy. I can't give you access without their say-so.' Sam crosses his arms stubbornly. 'Go on. I can't help you.'

Elaine looks at you and raises an eyebrow. 'Sounds like a plan,' you tell her. The thought of giving Wayne Richardson, Prize Twat, a bad case of indigestion holds a curious appeal for you. 'Let me handle this.'

ELAINE: GAME OF SPOOKS

It's about eight fifteen when you finally get out of Hayek Associates' offices and summon a taxi to whisk you back to your hotel room. You are, not to put it too pointedly, dog-tired. On the plus side, at least you made some progress. That cop, Sergeant Smith, looks like she's going to be a useful contact, and Jack is certainly paying his way. When you left him back at the bunker, he was elbow deep in whatever it is that programmers do, oblivious to everything else. Which is kind of annoying, because he's about the only person up here who you know who isn't a co-worker, and now you've got to face an evening in a strange city on your own, but what the hell. They call this place the Athens of the North – there's got to be something you can do by yourself on a summer night, hasn't there?

Well, no.

Back in your room, you have a quick shower, then check the eating-out guide, by which time it's past nine and you're half past hungry. You're not keen on going back to the places you went into with Jack, not on your own, and the room service menu looks okay, so you order up a big green salad in penance for yesterday's business meeting, then it's ten, and the hotel gym's closed, and *where the fuck did the day go?* It's even worse than a weekday in London – at least there you can break the commute home in a cocktail bar with some friends.

It's ten thirty and you're glumly contemplating an early night and a seven o'clock session in the gym when your phone rings. You look at the display with a sinking feeling: it's a particularly tedious LARP called **SPOOKS**, a real-time game in which you're acting your parts in a shadowy pan-European intelligence agency locked in a struggle for global hegemony with the forces of Chinese military intelligence, the Russian FSB, and, of course, the CIA.

'Yes?' You try not to snap.

'Elaine Barnaby? This is Spooks Control. Are you busy right now?'

You glance around your beautifully decorated and utterly sterile worker cell: 'Not particularly. You know I'm in Edinburgh?'

'That's why we're calling.' Your nameless Control sounds drily amused. 'On behalf of our sponsors.' The spooks at the centre of the organization in the game you play. 'Your authenticator is—' He rattles off a string of nonsense words, just to prove he's got access to your Control file.

'I'm on business . . .'

'So are we. We were hoping you could do us a small favour while you're there.'

'How small?' As usual, there's no face to go with the call, just the eye-in-a-glass-pyramid-in-Docklands logo. If this was a video call, at least you could glare at him. 'It's half past bloody ten!'

'We need a small parcel delivering.'

'A small parcel. What's wrong with FedEx?'

'Well, as you just pointed out, it's half past ten at night. The parcel's sitting downstairs in your hotel lobby. It needs delivering to—' He rattles off a set of Galileo co-ordinates. 'That's about half a kilometre away from where you're sitting.'

'Humph.' You look at the phone speculatively. 'What's it worth?'

'To you? A twenty-minute walk before bedtime. To the recipient? Priceless.' Control sounds smug. You can picture him sitting in some bedsit, working through his check-list of in-game tasks in order to convince himself he's got a life.

There's no easy way to say no without giving offence, and anyway, you were thinking about doing something before bed – 'I'll do it.'

'Thank you. I've been told to tell you, Agent Barnaby, that a hell of a lot depends on this package being in place before midnight local time.'

'Sure.' You hang up, pull your shoes and glasses on, grab your jacket, and go downstairs.

It's dark outside, and there's a single tired-looking clerk on reception. You smile at him tentatively. 'I understand you've got a parcel for me? Barnaby, room 214.'

'I think so, let me just go and see . . .' He shuffles off into the back office, then returns, holding a DHL package. 'If you'd sign here, please?'

'Sure.' You swipe your phone across his reader and thumbprint the signature. 'Thanks.'

Outside, the evening air is cool and smells faintly of the cherry blossom that's piling up in the gutters at the side of the pavement. You pull on a disposable plastic glove then pull the tab on the parcel. *This recording will self-destruct in thirty seconds.* Rumour has it that the first **SPOOKS** campaign got the beta-testers arrested and questioned for a week under the Terrorism Act before the police realized it was a game; that's why you carry a special endorsement on your ID card. The parcel turns out to contain a bland-looking matte black plastic box about the size of an old-time DVD case, and some heavy-duty outdoor bonding pads. There's also a brief, printed note on paper. 'Attach to front of building above eye level facing the street. When attached, initiate pairing with your phone to "unnamed device 1142." Passcode is 46hg52Q. Once paired, dial ##*49##*, and leave the area. When home, text Control.'

Bloody typical. You pocket the bugging device, or whatever it is, key the co-ordinates into your specs, and let the overlay guide you along the pavement towards the target building. This sort of nonsense is partly why you've been thinking of retiring from **SPOOKS**; it's almost tediously realistic. Not James Bond swigging cocktails by the pool in Grand Cayman, just 'pick up package X, transport to location Y, phone number Z.'

Location Y turns out to be an impressive crescent of Georgian stone town houses. They've got flights of steps like stone drawbridges, jutting out over a dry stone moat with windows in the basement – and steps down to them, for these are garden flats. You hunt around for a few minutes until you find the right set of steps, then approach the door. There's a row of ten buzzers next to the entrance, and right at the top of the row someone has chalked a blue rectangle with your **SPOOKS** cell warchalk sign. You take out the box and the adhesive pads, position it carefully, and jump through the digital hoops to switch the thing on. (It's probably just a ten-euro inventory tracking phone and a camera to snap the back of another player's head as they leave for work tomorrow: but what the hell.) You wait till you're halfway home before you text Gareth.

You're just keying in a brief message when your specs vibrate for attention. You glance up: the **SPOOKS** overlay is active, and it's telling you **TWO-PERSON TAG TEAM DETECTED**.

The dictates of the game require you to take it seriously, even though you're too tired for this shit, and you want to go to bed. Besides, **SPOOKS** tries to map non-player characters onto real local objects – and you can really live without two strangers trying to follow you. You speed up slightly, not glancing round – that's your glasses' job – and mumble quietly, calling up a course into the densely occupied area around the corner of Princes Street and Lothian Road. You change direction, darting into a side street, and behind you the blips on your head-up display turn to follow you.

This isn't good. 'Phone, get me a taxi,' you mutter, and break into a jog. The side street is almost deserted, cars parked on either side of its cobbled quaintness, but you can see lights and hear traffic ahead. There are footsteps behind you, and you accelerate, running –

And a taxi's headlights show up, swerving in towards the kerb in front of you. 'Where to, miss?' asks the driver, as you pull the door shut. 'Hotel—' You try to remember. 'Hotel Malmaison . . .'

Behind you, the tail team falls away in the darkness as the taxi carries you back to the illusion of security.

JACK: MEAT MACHINE

It's like that first Alcoholics Anonymous meeting: 'Hi, my name is Jack. And I have a code problem.'

You're a grown-up, these days. You don't wear a kamikaze pilot's rising sun headband and a tee-shirt that screams DEBUG THIS! and you don't spend your weekends competing in extreme programming slams at a windy campsite near Frankfurt, but it's generally difficult for you to use any machine that doesn't have at least one compiler installed: in fact, you had to stick Python on your phone before you even opened its address book because not being able to brainwash it left you feeling handicapped, like you were a passenger instead of a pilot. In another age you would have been a railway mechanic or a grease monkey crawling over the spark plugs of a DC-3. This is what you are, and the sad fact is, they can put the code monkey in a suit but they can't take the code out of the monkey.

Which is why you more or less missed out completely on a very entertaining barney between Elaine and some weedy intense-looking marketroid in casual-Friday drag and fashionable specs who seemed most upset about something. You were off in your own head, trying to figure out a strategy for reducing the Himalayan pile of junk data that your query agents are going to pull out of the Zone database, and you just wished they'd all shut up so you could go back to drawing entity-relationship diagrams on the walls in green crayon. In fact, you were so far out there that the mummy lobe forgot to threaten to set Sergeant Smith on you on account of your overdue library books. You even managed to forget about the weird phone call last night. You were, in short, coding.

'What's up with him?' you remember the cop asked Elaine.

'Not sure. If I didn't know better, I'd say he was stoned, but he keeps twitching his fingers: I think he's in keyboard withdrawal or something.'

So you surfaced for long enough to explain what you needed, and they got the marketroid to tell Sam to log you on to the code repository and give you the authentication tokens, then they found you a nice padded beige cubicle and parked you in it so you could design a tool for the job of trawling through several million transactions.

An indeterminate time later, an irritating voice inserted itself into your awareness. 'Jack. Hello? Have you got a spare minute?'

'No—' You shook yourself. 'Uh.' Your bladder was threatening to go on strike, your left calf was standing in for a pincushion at a convention of Belgian lace-makers, and your eyes ached. 'Hang on a moment.' You check-pointed the project and pulled your glasses off, then leaned back and stretched your arms over your head. 'Okay, I've got a spare minute now.'

Elaine leaned against the door-frame. She looked tired and irritable. 'It's nearly six thirty. Are you getting anywhere?'

'Give me another three hours or so, and I might be ready to switch it on. Assuming you posted the insurance ad?'

'Yes, that's been authorized.' She fidgeted with her hands, clasping one palm in the other and flexing her wrist back and forth, then the other. 'We've already got some responses. I thought you said this would be fast?'

'Give me a file of magic items and miscellaneous loot in well-formed Structured Treasure Language, and I've got a tool that can search one or more auction-houses for stuff resembling each item in it, and give you back a proximity metric and some information about the seller. I've got one auction-house plug-in nearly completed and four more to write, but they're all variations on a theme after the first one. Trouble is, your responses won't be in STL, so I'll have to run them by hand. Best thing would be if you give me five or ten sample items, and I can leave it crunching overnight on the test data. Then if it works, tomorrow I can set the rest going.'

She rolled her eyes. 'Okay.' She sounded unconvinced, and *that* got your attention; it was the sound of €1000 an hour slipping away.

'Ever written a large spreadsheet?'

'Yes.'

'And then tested it? Making sure that what comes out is what's meant to come out?'

'Yes, but—' She stopped.

'What I'm doing here is like working up a pivot join, then some complex statistical break-downs across six or seven different tables, a couple of which are in different formats. If I rush it, it'll come out wrong. Worst case, it'll come out *looking* right but full of plausible garbage.'

'If it's like writing a spreadsheet, then' – she raised an eyebrow – 'what do I need you for?'

'Because you don't have a couple of years to learn the Zone APIs and the Python 3000 language for scripting it. How long did it take you to write that spreadsheet?'

'Ah.' You could hear the *clunk* as the gears engaged between her ears. Then she smiled, reassured. (*Advanced Programming 401: managing the managers* – first of all, figure out how to tell them what you're doing *in their own language*. Writing a big spreadsheet with lots of macros was a bit Mickey Mouse, but you had to admit it wasn't too far removed from what you were doing. It was all data reduction when you got down to it.) 'Okay. I'll email you the data I've got. If you can run a test tonight . . . when will we know?'

'If it doesn't crash and burn, first thing tomorrow. At least we'll know something, even if there's nothing but smouldering wreckage – if we're lucky we'll hit pay-dirt overnight.' If it didn't work, you'd fix it, then run it tomorrow with all the insurance claims you could get.

'Good. I need to go get something to eat: I'm starving.' She paused for a couple of seconds: 'Well, see you tomorrow, then.'

You smiled. 'See you.'

A minute later you sat bolt upright in your chair and swore at yourself for missing a hidden query – but you're more at home with SQL than socialization: innuendo wasn't a language they taught in CS lab.

Ah well, you thought. You were just going to have to face up to another night with only a fish supper and your games console for company. It could have been worse: you might be unemployed as well.

When you finally stretch and kick back from the laptop keyboard, it takes you a minute or two to remember where the hell you are. There's the usual moment of disorientation, a kind of existential dizziness as you re-enter the everyday time-stream in which most people spend their lives: hours have slid by unnoticed, feeling like minutes (except for the ache in your neck and the gritty heat in your eyes). Sometimes you doubt that any time has passed: but when you look at your clock you realize it's nearly ten at night. Chucking-out time. But at least the search'n'sniff program you threw together is running. The laptop is plugged into Hayek Associates' own router – physically connected by actual *wires* – and is trawling through the distributed database, distilling tens of gigabytes per minute into useful candidates.

You switch off your glasses and blink as you stumble out of the office, noticing for the first time that you're really hungry. HA have inherited the office layout of the former government military bunker – not much point in trying to tunnel through steel-reinforced concrete walls half a metre thick – but they've replaced the old wooden doors with transparent lexan panels that darken to opacity at the touch of a fingertip, replaced ancient fluorescent strip lights with smart OLED panels that brighten in front and dim behind you. The effect is strangely claustrophobic, surrounding you with a pool of carefully sculpted daylight as you walk towards a shadowy exit.

Most of the offices you pass are empty and dark, but a faint rime of light frosts the night ahead of you as you near it. Glancing sideways, you see that the door is set to opaque; the light barely leaks out around the edges, and if the passage hadn't been dark, you'd never have noticed it. You hesitate as you reach it, on the verge of knocking out of sheer curiosity, but then you hear the ugly voices.

'—right off! We're in deep shit if this goes on. They raided the MacDonald tenement, did you know that? And those bastards from DBA are digging too deep. If they keep on going, it'll be obvious what's going on.'

'And I'm telling you that if we chill and sit still until the put options vest, they won't be able to prove anything. It's running on rails, yes? And we *haven't* done anything. So, we're being targeted. Luckily they don't know what they're looking for, and they can't prove anything. So, just – chill. Stop fretting. Lie low and wait for it to blow over.'

'What about your friends? Can they do something for us? Arrange a distraction, maybe? Muddy the water?'

'I've got them working on it already, but I can't promise anything. Leave that side of things to me. What I want to know is, can you hold up *your* end?'

Pause. 'I'll do my best. It's just, with these fucking pests sniffing around underfoot, they keep getting in my face. If we don't get them out of here soon . . .'

'Leave them to me, I said. My friends are working on getting them pulled out.'

The voices fall, and you suddenly realize you're standing here outside the door, and the mummy lobe gooses you with a red-hot trident: *Don't you know it's rude to eavesdrop?* It screeches in your ear. You wince, and tiptoe guiltily away, trying not to think too hard about what whoever they were were talking about. It wasn't entirely clear, but it sounded like they were simply talking about ways of getting Dietrich-Brunner to pull out. And if you were in their shoes, what else would you do?

Up on the surface, you let yourself out of the office, and the door swings shut behind you before you realize that you've got no way back inside. The last vestiges of daylight stain the sky a pale blue above the black silhouettes of the trees. You haven't booked a taxi, either. You trudge down Drum Brae towards the distant rumble of traffic from Queensferry Road, bringing up a bus map overlay on your glasses. You've just missed one by three minutes, and they're down to three an hour at this time of evening. *Great.* At least it's a warm night, without any real risk of a spring deluge.

When you get home, you find a letter lying on top of the

pile of spam on the floor just inside your front door. (At least, it looks like a real piece of correspondence – lately the junk mailers have been wising up, disguising advertising come-ons as tax demands and gas bills.) It's addressed to you by name and they used a real old-fashioned postage stamp. You tear it open and four glossy photographs fall out.

Heart pounding, you pick them up and hold them where you can see them properly, under the hall light. The first photograph is the entrance to Hayek Associates' offices. You flip past it to the second. This one looks like a primary-school playground. There's a cluster of wee ones playing in it, and you don't need the dotted red circle someone's helpfully Photoshopped into the image to tell you you're meant to be looking at Elsie. You feel sick, but you can't stop yourself looking at the third picture. It shows the front door of a house you know quite well, and that was your sister on the doorstep, her and Mary in her school uniform, in the early-morning light, looking very young. The picture's a little blurry, as if the photographer was trying to conceal the camera. As well they might, because as soon as you get a good look at the fourth picture, you put them all down and speed-dial the number the policeman gave you after the dodgy voice call, hyperventilating and trying not to panic.

The last photograph shows an empty butcher's slab.

SUE: Heavy Mob

You're still eating your breakfast the next morning when you get an IM from Liz: **SHIT DUE TO HIT FAN AT 0915 MEET ME AT INGLISTON**. It's so unexpected you blow orange juice bubbles through your nose, much to the wee one's amusement, then end up swearing at the pain in your sinuses. You don't have a car today, but you get your move on anyhow, and you make sure you're on the tram out to the airport in time for Liz's promised faeco-ventilatory intersection.

It's the tail-end of the morning commuter rush. Liz is stalking up and down outside the entrance to the shiny new terminal on what used to be the highland show-ground, her face pinched and tense: she's smoking a cigarette, which surprises you – you didn't think she was the type. When you approach her, she drops it, pulls a face, and grinds it into the tarmac. 'You're late.'

'I don't have a car.'

'You don't? Ah – shit.'

You blink back red overlays – the airport is a kaleidoscopic blur of too much information in CopSpace – and focus on her. She looks tired, as if she's been up since too early in the morning. 'What's going on?'

'Visitors from Europol,' she says absently, shoving her specs up her nose. 'Some kind of special operations team from

Brussels. Here, have a look.' A huge, indigestible dollop of something descends on the centre of your desktop, and you just have time to read the title of the opening page before she adds, 'Didn't mean to bite your head off. Looks like they're here.'

She turns and marches into the concourse, and you hurry to keep up, trying not to go wall-eyed as you skim the summary. Corpus juris, Europol agreements, bilateral treaty of secession arrangements for justice, law, and order – it's all bullshit. What it boils down to is –

Six men and women in dark suits and dark glasses marching towards you from the EU arrivals exit: the heavy mob converging from London and Brussels with stainless steel briefcases and secure identities. 'Inspector Kavanaugh,' says their leader, not extending a hand. 'Our cars are waiting. Who's this – ah, I see. Good morning, Sergeant Smith. You will come with us.'

A fleet of driverless BMW SUVs appear, bouncing slowly over the traffic pillows, and pull in next to you, flagrantly ignoring the red route markings and security notices. They've got diplomatic plates. Doors spring open, and you find yourself gently inserted into the empty driver's seat of the third vehicle as Liz and the leader of the hit squad slide into the back. The steering wheel twitches hesitantly, then as the doors click shut it spins hard over and the yuppiemobile accelerates fast. You try not to shudder: you hate the whole idea that some bored drone pusher in a remote driving centre has got your life – and half a dozen other lives – in his hands. At least on the motorways the cars steer themselves, that's within the capabilities of today's AI. 'Please switch off your personal electronics,' says the man in dark glasses. 'The car is shielded, but this is to go no further.' His English is as perfect and accentless as an old-time BBC presenter's.

You peel off your glasses and hit the Judas switch on your phone, then the antiquated TETRA terminal, and finally – when he clears his throat impatiently – your cameras and bio-monitors. 'Which department are you with?' asks Liz.

'Officially, you'll find the plaque on our door reads *"Organisation pour Nourrir et Consolider L'Europe."'* You're watching the Man in Black in the driver's mirror, and his cheek doesn't twitch. Behind him, in the jump-seat in the cargo area, his companion is opening up a Peli briefcase and exposing an array of hardware that you're really not supposed to fly with. 'It's our little joke – the only one. We're not the Man from UNCLE, and this isn't a game.'

Liz, and you've got to give her credit for keeping a level head, is having none of it. 'Then you'd better tell me *precisely* who you are and what the hell you think you're doing here. Because right now you are on my patch, and you are breaking the speed limit, violating at least three different firearms regulations, and if you don't pull over on my request, I'll have to add kidnapping two police officers to the charge sheet.'

You carefully move your left hand to your belt and make sure there's nothing in the way of your wee tinny of whooping gas. Because if the skipper puts it like that . . .

'You have nothing to worry about,' says the spook. 'My credentials.' He pulls out a passport with a white cover, then a fancy ID badge. Liz takes them.

'You know damn well I can't verify these while I'm off-line,' she snaps. 'The name's right, but how do you expect me to confirm you're the real thing? Tell me, *Kemal*, assuming that's your real name, where are you taking us?'

The man in the back finishes screwing the stock onto his weapon – it looks like a cross between a sawn-off shotgun and a paintball gun – and puts it down on the case.

'It relates to your current case, unfortunately. We're going to visit a warehouse in Leith,' says the head spook. 'My colleagues have already instructed your SO6 to seal off the area while we raid it. You are here to witness and act as local liaison because you are already familiar with this case. My colleagues in the next car' – he nods at the vehicle immediately behind you – 'are going to proceed to a collocation centre in the Gyle in order to shut down the main backbone between here and the south. The fourth car is going to visit the emergency control centre and serve a crisis note. Their job is to shut down all communications in the target area. Finally—'

'You're going to *what?*' Liz explodes.

'Finally, the Royal Danish Air Force have kindly consented to let us use one of their E7C aircraft, assigned to ERRF for infowar duties and counter-terrorism support. In case the target is defended.'

By this point your jaw's hanging open; you've just about forgotten the can of Mace, or your indignation about being more or less kidnapped. 'What's in the warehouse?' you ask.

Kemal – if that's his name – leans back. Now *he's* the one who looks like he's had a sleepless night. 'Your investigation into the disappearance of Mr. Nigel MacDonald, and the report of your findings in his apartment, attracted our attention. Have you identified the body in your ongoing murder investigation from the graveyard on Constitution Street yet?'

'No.' Liz looks grim. 'If you know something—'

'I am sorry I cannot identify the body for you, but I can *definitely* assure you that it does not belong to Mr. MacDonald. And your speculation about a blacknet, possibly owned by the Moscow *mafiya*, has been noted.'

'You'd better explain.'

'The equipment you discovered in Mr. MacDonald's

apartment was cloned by your ICE officers. When they logged the details of what they found on NCIS, we were alerted. We cannot tell you what the equipment was for, but two similar installations have been recovered in Prague and Warsaw in the past four months. The installation appears to be operated by a non-state actor for illegal purposes—'

'Are you talking terrorism here?' Liz interrupts.

Kemal's expression is stony. 'Life would be a lot simpler if we were dealing with a cell of simple-minded religious obsessives with a grudge against the modern world. I'm afraid it may be something much worse—'

'Because this is my city you're talking about, and I happen to have a duty to protect its inhabitants and uphold the law. *Is public safety at stake?* I need to know!'

'Not' – Kemal pauses as the car speeds up, hurtling uphill to merge with the morning traffic heading for the city by-pass – 'hmm. That question is difficult to answer. I think it's safe to say that there is no immediate threat, and there are no biological, chemical, or nuclear weapons involved; but failure to isolate the warehouse and impose a *total* communications blockade will, at the very least, allow some extremely dangerous information to escape. There is also some uncertainty as to whether the warehouse is occupied, and if so, whether the people inside it are armed. Our worst-case scenario is that we are facing a foreign Special Forces unit with emplaced defences and demolition charges – but if that's the case, we're fucked anyway.'

'Who's fucked? Us? Your department?'

'No, Inspector: the European Union.'

Either the car's air-conditioning is fierce, or your skin's crawling. 'Why are you dragging us into this, then?' you demand, your voice rising. 'We're the Polis, not Mission bloody Impossible!'

'You're already involved, and we want to keep this as quiet as possible,' Kemal explains. 'You will need these phones and glasses, please put them on immediately.'

'Why—'

'Your CopSpace has been compromised. So has your TETRA network, but at least you can dispatch backup by voice control. Please? This has already been arranged for. We need you tied into our grid before the operation commences.'

He passes you a pair of heavy, black-rimmed military spectacles and a ruggedized phone. You make eye contact with Liz, in the mirror, and she nods, minutely: you put the glasses on and boot them. There's a brief flicker as they check your irises against their preloaded biometrics, then the world outside the BMW is drenched in unfamiliar information all the way to the horizon. You glance to your left, out to the north, where a green diamond is orbiting above the Kingdom of Fife. A quick zoom shows you that it's real, a lumbering wide-body airliner in military grey, the knobbly outlines of high-bandwidth antennae studding its flanks like barnacles on a whale. Or at least, these goggles have been programmed to *think* it's real. Once you accept someone else's augmented reality, there's really no telling, is there? For all you and Liz can tell until you're plugged back into the comforting panopticon of CopSpace, this might just be some kind of elaborate live-action role-playing game.

The convoy is past the gyratory and heading towards Queensferry Road way too fast, probably racking up speeding tickets at a rate best measured in euros per second. All the traffic lights are switching to green in front of you as the steering wheel twitches from side to side: red info bubbles above anonymous grey roadside boxes inform you that they've been 0wnZ0red by the Royal Danish Air Force. You rest your hand on the wheel, and it shivers like a live animal. 'What do you expect to find?' asks Liz. 'And who is the adversary?'

'Hopefully, just a warehouse full of servers. Maybe a satellite dish or two.' Kemal is soothing. 'I'd like nothing more than for this to be a false alert. In which case, we shall make our apologies, pay our speeding fines, and be on our way without further ado.'

Liz snorts. 'That'll be the day.' She reaches for her phone: 'Now I've got to call the chief—'

'Not until we arrive. As I said, your terrestrial trunked radio network has been penetrated.'

ELAINE: ALONE IN THE DOME

Despite the late-night chase through the darkened streets of the New Town, you sleep like a log and awake refreshed and ready to face a new day. You spend a brisk half-hour in the health suite, then shower and hit the hotel restaurant for some breakfast. Chris and the others have cut and run back to the big smoke already: well, tough. You've got Jack and his magic code to give you some leads, and you've got access to Hayek's offices, which is enough to be getting on with.

You've still got the office suite that Chris paid for, so you go down there and start going through the backlog of office email and project notes that have been building up since last Friday, when reality got put on hold for the duration. By twenty past nine your mood is sinking, and you're mildly annoyed when you realize that Jack is late. So you text him, and get no reply – and no delivery notification. *Odd*.

With Jack off-line – and therefore no access to the results of his overnight trawl – you're at a loose end. So you go out into the mezzanine and attempt to convince the coffee machine to give you something drinkable, and while you're waiting for the bubbling and clanking to stop, you get an incoming call. From Jack, of course.

'Where've you been?' you demand.

'Sorry – I had to go to the police station. I got another

nastygram, this time on paper: they wanted to examine it and look for prints.'

Oops. You wince even though he can't see you. 'Oh. Where are you now?'

'Stuck in traffic, but I should be with you in about five minutes. I thought I should call ahead, though. The overnight run was mostly a success, and it found something interesting. There's a likely-looking auction going on in one of the clearing-house sites; the stuff on sale looks to be an exact match for some of the stolen magic items. What makes it interesting is the ping latency to the current owner of the items — he's in Glasgow. If we can get Hayek to twist Kensu's arm into disclosing their customer contact details, we may be able to pay them a visit.'

'Oh, that's *good* news.' You're slightly startled to discover how eager you are. 'IM me what you've got, and I'll get onto Wayne immediately. What do you suggest we do?'

'Don't know yet. See where the lead goes, I suppose . . .' Twenty minutes later you're holed up in the office with Jack on the line, a couple of half-empty coffee cups and some half-baked theories. Wayne is being a pain: his phone insists he's in a meeting and refuses to put your call through. But at least Jack's got his lead. 'The insurance claim request got fifty-one responses before I kicked back last night. I fed them in and set the spider running on the two largest auction sites that handle cross-game Zone trades. Twelve of the items turned up immediately, in a single stash that KingHorror9 is trying to shift. KingHorror9 is currently logged as active in Forgotten Futures, and a quick ping test suggests they're local — latency is under ten milliseconds. So I think if we can get their name and address, we can go collar them immediately.'

'*If* they're local,' you warn him. 'Because—'

Your phone butts in: 'Mr. Richardson is holding. Do you want to talk to him?'

'Yeah, put him through.'

'What do you want now?' he begins. 'Because I'm in a meeting—'

'We've got a lead on the stolen goods,' you tell him before he can wind up to hang up on you. 'I need to pull the registration details of a user called KingHorror9, their true name and street address and so on. If you can do that, we can go and pay them a visit right now.'

'Oh, let me just open a new stickie . . .'

Suddenly Wayne turns helpful. A minute later you're off the phone with the distinct feeling that Progress is being Made, or at least an order has gone in to the production department, who are thinking about setting a delivery date sometime next week. A minor miracle . . .

The door opens as you get to the bottom of your coffee cup. It's Jack. He's remembered to shave, but his tee-shirt is even more faded than yesterday's. 'Morning.' He plants himself in the other office chair and turns the laptop sitting on his side of the desk to face you. 'You might find this interesting.'

'Uh, what?' He's grinning.

'I logged in before I got here.' He points to a big aerial photograph of a city, something like a spy satellite image. 'While I was stuck on the bus, I wrote a plug-in to map the IP addresses of the auction site users into an overlay for Google Earth. I figured that being able to visualize where they were would be . . . well. It's not guaranteed accurate – they could be tunnelling in from elsewhere, or covering their trail in some other way – but what I found was interesting.' He flicks a couple of commands at the air, and the pointer tracks across the screen as the image zooms in until you're looking at a gleaming metal building that looks like a gigantic wood-louse. 'Glasgow SECC – the conference centre.' A bunch of green triangles appear, clustered heavily around one end of the building. 'That's where the local hot spot is. There's another stash here' – he zooms out, dizzyingly, the city dwindling to a pimple on the side of Scotland, then the entire British Isles receding towards the horizon of a curved sphere, spinning round and zooming in again somewhere near the northern end of the Bay of Bengal – 'but I figure Glasgow's easier for us to get to than Dhaka.'

'Glasgow? You sure about that?' It doesn't entirely make sense to you.

'Yeah.' He twitches over to another window. 'The hot spot of auction offers is hanging off the centre's local switch. That's where they're selling their loot. There's a lot of game activity there, looks like' – he's blinking and twitching behind his glasses – 'there's a gaming con there. It's a bank holiday on Friday, isn't it? But midweek, that doesn't make sense unless . . .'

'What's the con-convention?' you ask, trying to sound only appropriately interested. Not that you know much about such things – you've done a few re-enactment events, but hotels and hucksters and hordes of socially inept fanboys don't tempt you.

'Let's see.' He Googles for a minute. 'Oh, right – yup, it's a business convention. Sponsored by blah, foo, and Kensu International, oh what a surprise. Hmm. Today's a public day. Tickets are fifty euros.'

Your mailbox whistles for attention: a note from Wayne has just come in. 'First things first. Phone, get me Sergeant Smith.' You wait expectantly for a few seconds, but it dumps you into a voice mailbox. 'Oh. Hello, Sergeant. Elaine from

Dietrich-Brunner here – can you call me when you get this? I believe we've got a lead for you on the items that were stolen from Hayek Associates. Bye.' You disconnect, then turn back to Jack. 'Alright. You're the local – how do we get to Glasgow from here?'

Glasgow turns out to be a fifty-minute train ride away from Edinburgh. Worse, the SECC isn't next door to the station – it's a trek out of the centre, several stops away on the toytown model underground system. So after spending a futile ten minutes trying to scrape various badly designed railway company websites, Jack suggests taking the first available connection, then catching a taxi at the other end if necessary. The train turns out to be your usual tired old nag of a commuter service (the shiny new maglev doesn't open for another two years), and by the time you're halfway there – staring out of the windows at an implausibly damp landscape outside Falkirk – you're beginning to wish you'd simply flashed the company Amex and hired a helicopter.

Jack, for his part, sits head down in the seat opposite, rattling his fingertips on a virtual keyboard, so oblivious to the real world that you have to poke him on the shoulder when you want to ask what he's doing. 'Adding another plug-in for Sativa,' he says, as if that's an explanation. So you go back to skimming the dump of Hayek's monthly statements that Chris and the gang dug out of them before the incursion, looking for suggestive anomalies. Of which there are many, especially in the petty cash – what on earth is an economics consultancy buying voodoo dolls for? Or paintball guns? – but they're not the *right* kind of suggestive to ding your bell.

Eventually the train rolls through a grim landscape of warehouses and high-rise apartments, before diving into some kind of tunnel and surfacing in a huge, vaulted Victorian station. You find yourself in a strange concourse, facing a curved wall that seems to be carved out of a cliff of red sandstone; there are inward-looking windows set in it, and gargoyles about to take flight hunch their wings beneath the cast-iron buttresses that support the arching roof. For some reason there's a small gingerbread town perched on the platform, entire buildings complete with roofs and gutters untouched by rain. 'What the hell is that?' you ask in disbelief.

'Glasgow Central.' Jack positively beams. 'Let's get a taxi!'

Ten car-sickening minutes later (Glasgow seems to be built on a grid system dropped across a bunch of hills, and its roads are populated exclusively by automotive maniacs), the driverless taxi drops you in a concrete wilderness near a river. Before you, a huge glass wall fronts a fifty-year-old concrete groundscraper. Someone's unrolled a grubby cherry-coloured carpet onto the platform, and put out a notice-board. INTERACTIVE 18 flashes across it in gold letters and PUBLIC WELCOME below, in a somewhat more subdued font. There are people visible inside – greeters and business types in smart-casual drag – and booths.

You were having misgivings about this trip because it seemed to have all the ingredients of a wild goose chase except for the goose: but you're here now, and it can't be helped. You square your shoulders and follow him in. 'Two public day passes,' Jack tells the bored attendant on the desk.

'That'll be fifty euros each, or you can fill in these surveys for a free, complimentary pass,' she tells you in an accent so thick you could use it as a duvet.

You glance at the survey: it's the usual intrusive rubbish, so (with a malign sense of glee) you answer it truthfully. No, you don't buy any RPGs or subscribe to any MMOs. Yes, you're a financial services industry employee. Yes, you make buying decisions with an eye-watering bottom line. Then you change your sex, age, date of birth, and name, just to be on the safe side before you hand it in and accept your free, complimentary (thanks for the market research data) badge.

Inside the wide concourse, everything looks like, well, the kind of trade show that attracts the general public. There are booths and garish displays and sales staff looking profession-ally friendly, and there are tables with rows of gaming boxes on them. There's even a stray bookstore, selling game strategy guides printed on dead tree pulp. 'Check what it looks like in Zone,' suggests Jack, so you tweak your glasses, and suddenly it's a whole different scene.

The concourse is full of monsters and marvels. A sleeping dragon looms over a pirate hoard, scales as gaudy as a chameleon on a diffraction grating: it's the size of a young Apatosaurus, scaly bat-like wings folded back along its glit-tering flanks like a fantastic jet fighter. Beyond it, a wall opens out into the utter darkness of space, broken only by the curl-ing smoke-trail of a nebula and the encrusted flanks of a scabrous merchant spaceship trolling the final frontier for profit or pleasure. Half the sales staff have morphed into gaudy or implausible avatar costumes, from caped and opera-hatted Victorian impresarios to swashbuckling adventurers. 'How are we going to find anyone in this?' you ask helplessly, as a whole company of wolves trot past a booth where a group of sober-looking marketers are extolling the virtues of their firm's reality development engine.

'Check your email . . . '

He's right. There's a note from Wayne, giving you name, rank and serial number on the elusive KingHorror9. It's prob-ably not strictly legal – there are data protection and privacy laws to tap-dance around – but then, what KingHorror9 is doing isn't strictly legal, either. And they're here somewhere. You look around. Then it occurs to you that if there's a whole bunch of Zone servers running here, and you've got a Zone character, you might as well use it. So you tell your phone to load Avalon Four, log yourself in as Stheno, and look around again.

The dragon's still there, but the gaggle of Victorian maidens in big frocks have vanished, replaced by a huddle of warty-skinned kobolds; the walls have morphed from concrete to the texture of damp granite, and the huckster tables and booths have been replaced by broken-down wooden shacks and brightly painted gypsy carriages. The developers' booth has decayed into a mausoleum occupied by a grisly vanguard of skeletons and zombies, who hang on the every word of the livid witch-king who stands before the sacrificial altar. Somebody has spray-bombed one side of it with a big neon arrow (it really *is* glowing) and the words, AUCTION IN FOUR MINUTES. 'Ah. I get it,' you say. There's no reply. When you glance round, Jack's vanished.

JACK: THIS IS NOT A GAME

For the first time, you have a target and a true name: Mr. Wu Chen. Never mind which is the family name and which the personal, at least it's a name. And it's attached to a credit card number, although you've only got the last four digits. *Gentlemen, start your search engines.* Elaine is wandering along behind you with the slightly stunned expression of a Mormon missionary at a Pagan Federation summer camp – it obviously *looks* like a target-rich environment – but the set of co-ordinates attached to Wu Chen's badge (which, like all the attendee badges at this shindig is bugged with seven flavours of RFID – you checked your privacy at the door when you filled out that marketing questionnaire, unless you remembered to pack a tinfoil wallet) is moving slowly through the huge auditorium at the back of the building.

You lock Wu Chen into the map widget hovering over to the left, then simultaneously log all your Zone IDs on simultaneously, collapsing their various shards into a single mish-mash view. Why stick with a single reality when you can walk through a multiverse? Most people are only running avatars in one realm or another, and viewing them all simultaneously is an exercise in whimsy: here's an astronaut talking to a devil, next door to an Orc buying a book from à vampire. It's like being stuck inside a bazaar of the bizarre. A lecture or talk or some kind of interview is breaking up in the room to your right and there's a coffee stand to your left, starkly mundane between a timber-framed stately home and a parked flying saucer. Then you look closer. Someone's tagged it: AUCTION IN FOUR MINUTES. As you look, the four changes to three. The tag references a certain eBay auction . . . A quick glance at your map widget confirms that Wu Chen is in room 112, which is up an escalator on the left and down a corridor.

You take off up the hall fast, shouldering your way between a troupe of baboons and a Waffen SS officer who glares at you with ill-concealed annoyance. Mr. Wu Chen owes you some answers, and you're going to get them. But lurking behind your surface preoccupation with the Dietrich-Brunner job, there's an unpleasant realization gnawing away at your guts. Someone is sending you nastygrams – someone who seems to know you're working for Elaine and who's getting all their information about you via the net is trying to get at you via your nieces. *You* don't have kids, or a partner, or much of anything – all your friends are absent – but whoever they are, they've sunk their claws into the nearest soft spot they can find on the net. You're not by nature a violent man, indeed usually you go out of your way to avoid confrontations – but that's not going to work here. The kind of shit who'd threaten a couple of kids is unlikely to play by the rules. Either they're totally psychotic, or disastrously misinformed – but whatever the reason, they think that Elaine's investigation, or your involvement, is a personal threat to them. They're not playing games. Why else would they respond that way? The stakes aren't limited to just the crazy consultancy fee CapG are paying you anymore. There's an icy nugget of indigestible anxiety in your stomach, and it's telling you that you need to find Mr. Wu Chen and his stolen stash of vorpal blades and djinn lamps before he disposes of them and fades into the background, leaving you to blunder about in the darkness until someone tries to chain you to another lamppost or frame you for child abduction: or something almost unimaginably worse.

You're panting as you take the escalator steps two at a time, racing up them and along the corridor against the flow of bodies coming out of the conference room. It's bang on the hour, and the program items are all changing in lockstep, creating swirling vortices of bodies to drown in. Room 112 is round a corner, and as you get to it, you see that the door's wedged open and it's almost empty. There are tables up and down each wall, with laptops open on them in neat rows linked together with security cables: they've been running some kind of demo. A dozen or so people are milling around, some of them poking at keyboards and some of them just chatting. You look at them with Zone-enabled eyes and see blank-faced noobs and a solitary, glum-looking Orc pounding a keyboard. An azure gemstone revolves above his head, his guilt engraved upon it.

You twitch all your personae except Theodore G. Bear into invisibility as you walk up to him. 'I'm here about the auction,' you say to his hunched shoulder.

The Orc yelps and spins round, catching the edge of the laptop screen with one sleeve and nearly sending it flying. 'I don't know what you're talking about!'

'Get real,' you say. Then you remember to be polite: *You might have to hand this over to the cops, right?* 'You're auctioning a bunch of Kensu content, prestige items. You didn't get them the usual way. Did you expect nobody would notice?'

The Orc cowers. His Zonespace muscles may be green and rippling, but in meatspace he's just a scrawny little guy, possibly not even out of his teens. You're no muscle-bound hulk, but you don't look as if a strong breeze could blow you away: and besides, you've got the advantage of surprise on your side. 'What do you want?' he quavers.

'Information.' You fabricate an unfriendly smile. 'How you got the items, for starters. Who from, and when, and where. Right now, this is still an internal investigation, but Kensu are looking to set their lawyers on whoever carried out the heist. You can reduce your exposure by co-operating fully.'

Chen glances from side to side, hunting a way out. 'I don't know anything!' he protests. 'I got this loot from the club-house basement! Someone else put it there—'

'Tell me where the clubhouse is. Tell me when you got it.'

'You think I'm stupid?'

He's selling loot behind their backs; that's a weak spot. You tweak your smile slightly. 'No, I think you're trying to make some extra money. Which is why I'm here. We can do this off-line, if you want – nobody needs to know.'

His sidelong glances slow down. 'You're crazy, man,' he hisses. 'I don't know anything.'

'You know about the clubhouse.' He tenses: *Oops, back off.* 'Look, I'm not after you. I'm trying to get my teeth into *them*. Ten thousand euros in blind DigiCash for what you know, starting with the clubhouse's Zone co-ordinates.'

Ten K is a respectable sum – it's more than you used to earn in a month – but you're pretty sure that Elaine will sign off on it without blinking if it gets you hard information. Chen looks like he's considering it. Then he shakes his head rapidly. 'Not enough. You think I'm crazy? Guoanbu will have my kidneys if I give you that!'

'Fifteen,' you say without waiting. He begins to turn his head away. 'Twenty.' He looks back at you.

'Not enough. This conversation is over.'

'I can go higher, but I need clearance,' you tell him. Which is bending the truth – you couldn't even make either of the earlier figures stick without permission – but it's a hook; question is, will he bite?

'Two million, and witness protection, and I tell you everything,' he says flatly. 'A new identity. You can arrange that, yes?'

'Huh?' You gape at the Orc like he's grown a second head. It's an *out-of-context* problem, you suddenly realize. 'You think I'm the government?'

He looks at you with an expression of equal parts contempt and desperation, then flicks down his glasses and bangs out on the wings of a teleport spell, elsewhere into Avalon. But spells have echoes, and the fleeing Orc isn't as hot as he thinks; you've got admin permissions thanks to Hayek Associates' pull, and you IM Venkmann a brisk note as you follow him. You find yourself in a cellar, dank and stone-floored: the walls are almost completely hidden by racks of weapons and closed treasure-chests. There's also a very surprised Orc. He reaches over his back and pulls a sword on you, then attacks. 'Leave me alone!' he yells.

Simultaneously, back in the real world, something punches you hard in your side, rocking you back on your feet. You stagger, and the motion sensors in your glasses cut them back to semi-transparent – an emergency measure – and you see Mr. Wu Chen run through the doorway. You feel a little dizzy and instinctively raise your hand. It's just a dagger strike – no real hit points to it – so you stagger after Chen.

The translucent Orc tries to bring his big blue-glowing cleaver of a broadsword down on your ursine head, but you're armoured up to munchkin levels and deflect it with ease. You stumble as you go through the doorway, chasing the fleeing student, and there's something odd about your jacket, a crunching, broken feeling. Something is hanging out of your left pocket. You grab hold of it and there's a sudden sharp flash of pain as you stick something sharp into your hand. 'Shit!' you swear, and turn your glasses fully transparent.

There's a short-bladed knife embedded in the remains of what used to be your pocket folding keyboard, and your hand is dripping blood where you grabbed hold of the blade. Elaine is coming through the door, looking annoyed. 'He stabbed me,' you say, and sit down hard on the nearest chair. 'He . . . stabbed . . . me . . . ?'

The keyboard caught it. No surprise there – you rarely go outdoors without a keyboard, mouse, phone, spare PDA, and selection of witty repartee – but you're at a loss for words. You flick your glasses back to the fight scene as Elaine swears and grabs your left hand. The Orc is backed into a corner, whaling away at you with a virtual pigsticker.

WHATS UP? IMs Venkmann.

'Track me in Zone,' you tell the half-empty room as Elaine presses a tissue onto your hand. 'I'm where the loot is, and the guy beating up on me knows how it got there.'

'Next time leave the fighting to me,' Elaine tells you. She sounds pissed.

'But he stabbed me—' Your hand is hurting.

'No, he stabbed a piece of junk in one of your pockets.'

'I'm going to nail him!' You twitch your right hand, unlimbering the blunderbuss of +6 dungeon clearing.

'No, you're going to come with me and file a report to Security, then we're going to sit down and have a nice cup of tea and a chat with Constable Friendly. Believe me, you don't want to be chasing after a violent assailant—'

'No, I mean, in Avalon Four.' You're seeing red now. The

blunder-buss booms, sparking and filling the cellar with smoke. There's a very badly damaged Orc in front of you, backing desperately towards a doorway, as Theodore G. Bear snarls a bass rumble and reloads. 'I said I was here for the auction, and he freaked. But I found the loot.'

'You.' She crowds you back against the table and abruptly reaches forward and pulls your gaming glasses right off your face.

'Hey!' you protest, nose to nose with her, so uncomfortably close that you can smell her breath, a mixture of stale coffee and a faint fragrance you can't quite identify, eyeball to eyeball with her worried expression. 'I was getting somewhere—'

'Russell can track him through Zone. You've got a confirmed ID, but more importantly, you got yourself assaulted. *This isn't a game*, Jack. You don't want to find him! You want the police to deal with it. Don't worry about evidence, there are two security cams in every room and hallway.'

You feel embarrassed: she's absolutely right. You're also feeling a little shaky. You don't know quite how you expected Wu Chen to react, but trying to stab you and making a run for it – if he'd had a real sharpie instead of a penknife, or if he'd missed the keyboard, which you're going to have to replace, dammit – it's outside the playbook and there's no GM to appeal to. 'Crap,' you mumble.

'You can say that again.' Elaine pauses. For a moment you made naked eye contact with her, unscreened by enhanced reality: it's acutely embarrassing, the kind of out-of-context behaviour that business etiquette is intended to avoid. She looks shaken, too, but she's keeping a good lid on it. 'Come on, let's get you patched up,' she says, taking a step backwards, and breaking whatever information transfer it was that was going on between you via some kind of sub-verbal mammalian protocol layer.

Then she takes you by the undamaged hand and leads you back into the real world.

SUE: PIGS IN A CHINA SHOP

By the time you reach your destination in Leith, there's a full-dress panic in progress. Liz has IM'd Detective Superintendent Verity direct – with Kemal from Europol's encouragement – and Verity has hit the panic button and sent every warm body south of Pilton on a wild goose chase to cordon off the block around the warehouse on Lindsay Road. Which is more than slightly inconvenient, because it's about a hundred metres up the road from the National Executive complex on Victoria Quay, which is home to about five thousand civil service PowerPoint pushers and the population of designer furniture stores, ethnic restaurants, exclusive health clubs, real ale pubs, and cheap hookers who serve them. If Verity – or his boss, because this kind of shit tends to rise to the top – has to evacuate Victoria Quay, Questions Will be Asked in Parliament, not to mention generating many megabytes of editorial wittering in the virtual birdcage liners, and possibly some discreet resignations if the shit overflows and ends up in the air-conditioning. In fact, you wouldn't be surprised if Verity is crapping his britches by now: this has the potential to turn into an Ian Blair moment, the kind of policing SNAFU that remains the stuff of legend decades later. Kemal and his crack squad of dark-suited mirrorshade-wearing super-cops may be used to this sort of shit, but Edinburgh's a wee little regional boutique capital of some half million souls, about as far off the terrorism map as Oklahoma City. Which probably explains why events unfold like the Keystone Kops on crack, only with better special effects.

The remote control BMWs slow down as they hit Starbank Road and rumble alongside the docks, then pull in just past the old Newhaven fish market. 'Everybody out,' says the man in black. 'We walk from here.' There's a vanload of uniforms parked up ahead: they're setting up a barricade and preparing to divert the flow of traffic into town. It's going to cause a real clusterfuck in short order, because half the delivery trucks for the Ocean Terminal Shopping Centre, and all the consumers, go this way – not to mention the buses and the Line Two supertrams. In fact, it's going to be nearly as bad as that time some prize tit invited Tony Blair to come out of retirement and give the graduation speech up at Heriot-Watt. 'Liz, are you sure you need me for this? Because Mac's going to be needing every warm body he can get—'

'Stick around,' Liz hisses, trying to keep it down so the MIBs don't notice. 'You're right, but I want to keep a second pair of eye-balls on these clowns. *With* your phone's life-recorder running, if you please.' She's wound up as tense as a spring surprise.

'Thinking of the enquiry?'

She gives a surprised little laugh. 'Of course I am, Sergeant.' She looks over to the fence around the Western Harbour complex. 'We're too low on the totem pole to catch the flak for this one, but if the chief super himself isn't out here in the next hour, I'd be very much surprised, and he's going to want to know *exactly* what's been going on.'

'Ah. Okay.' You discreetly switch all your cameras to continuous evidence logging and tap your ear with one finger.

'I'm on it.' Then you fiddle with the menus in the MilSpec glasses Kemal gave you until you dredge up a local CopSpace overlay so you can see what the hell's going on. Your earlier diagnosis of a traffic clusterfuck is confirmed: flashing red diversion routes are springing up all over the north side of the city like chicken-pox. Overhead, a vast swirly cylinder delineates a no-fly zone – they're diverting flights in and out of Turnhouse, airliners that would normally be on final approach over the Firth of Forth. You wince, involuntarily. *What do they think –*

Whoops. You're halfway along the block, behind Liz, and now you notice a bunch of support vehicles parked just round the corner: fire engines, a fire brigade support truck, a couple of ambulances, and the big mobile HQ from Fettes Row. There are even a couple of olive drab landies . . . 'Skipper, they brought the *army*?'

Up ahead, Kemal's control is slipping: 'What's this? I didn't call for backup! You were to divert the traffic and keep a low profile, not throw a party!' He gestures at the self-kicking ant-hill ahead, his expression disgusted.

'What did you expect?' Liz sounds resigned. 'If you didn't want to make a fuss, you shouldn't have told anyone you were coming. Everyone's scared that if there's a blow-up on their turf, they'll catch it in the neck, so they're all dancing the major incident whisky tango foxtrot. At a guess, I'd say the first national-level news cameras will be along in another minute.'

'*Merde.*' He touches his earpiece. 'We're going to have to go in immediately.'

The target is just round the corner: it's a big eighteenth-century stone pile, probably a bonded warehouse back in the day, now fallen upon less industrious times. The news just keeps on getting better: CopSpace shows you that the warehouses either side of it have been converted into yuppie dormitories full of lawyers and civil servants and the like. A sign over the front door proclaims it to be a branch of a well-known outdoors and extreme sports retail chain, which might be plausible if it wasn't so clearly shuttered and padlocked. The Euro-cops have staked it out – video cameras up and down the street have been logging a metric shitload of data for weeks, capturing the faces of everyone going in and out and feeding them into some arcane international anti-terrorism database, and your glasses are just brimming with playback options – but they don't seem to have noticed that it's slap bang in the middle of a high-density residential area. 'Aren't you going to evacuate the neighbours first?' asks Liz. 'Because if not, someone needs to tell the brass.'

Kemal swears quietly. 'Go tell your commissioner,' he says tersely. 'We're starting in sixty seconds.'

The men (and women) in black are spreading around the building, not bothering to conceal themselves. Kemal's brought nearly a dozen bodies along, and they're getting set up: so far, it looks like a normal forced entry, except they're all dressed like accountants and carrying paintball guns and briefcases. They seem to be listening for something, waiting on the word of a distant control centre to which you have no access. Liz taps you on the shoulder. 'Stick with me,' she warns. 'I don't want you catching any of their shit.' Then she heads for the mobile HQ at the double. A couple of dibbles are waiting outside, looking pissed – probably missing their mid-shift break thanks to the entirely unplanned crisis. 'I need to see the chief,' she announces, holding her warrant card where they can see it. They look relieved to see the two of you: *At last, someone who looks as if they know what's going on.* If only they knew . . .

The control room in the HQ truck smells of stale coffee and sweat from all the bodies crowded inside it. One wall is a gigantic screen, presumably for those brass who could never get the hang of gestural inputs and eyeball tracking: it puts you in mind of the old joke about the mouse shaped like a pepper spray. Half a dozen dispatchers are hunched over battered HQ laptops, directing the traffic teams outside and fighting a losing battle with the inevitable tailbacks. Verity is leaning over a desk in front of it, yakking on one phone while another one trills for attention at his left elbow. He rolls his eyes as soon as he sees Liz. 'I'll be sure to do that, sir,' he says, 'but the inspector's just arrived and I need to find out what's going on from her before I can tell you anything more. If you'll excuse me . . . ' He hangs up. 'Save me from micromanaging' – he spots your cammy lights in time – 'gentlemen. Right. What's going on, Kavanaugh?' Verity using surnames is a *very* bad sign. 'The deputy minister wants to know.'

Aw, shite. Liz makes the best of it. 'They're not telling me sir, but it's some kind of national-security flap. The good news is, it's not your usual bampot bomb-throwers this time. The bad news is, they're about to shut down every communications link in—'

There's a faint popping noise, and the entire wall of the incident room shifts to the colour of the night sky above a Japanese city. The words NO SIGNAL blink for a moment above Verity's livid face. 'Get after them!' he snaps. 'I need eyeballs on the ground!'

Behind him the dispatchers are swearing and scribbling Post-it notes: their sergeant's telling them off to bring up the fall-back paper system, but it's not going to do any good – they're already deep into SFPD territory. System Fails, People Die. From the doorway you can hear an eerie chorus of burglar alarms and car-location sensors: they're all panicking at the lonely air-waves. There are more traffic lights in Leith than individual officers to replace them, and right now they're all going out of sequence. You follow Liz down the steps into the cold midmorning light, just as there's a bang from the front door of the warehouse. 'Come on,' she says urgently, and heads across the road at a trot.

You rush after her, through the blizzard of milspace warning messages about fields of fire from overlooking windows and roof-tops – the MIBs have broken the door open and are into the warehouse. Seagulls squawk and wheel in the empty blue sky overhead as you take the front step, the worn sandstone gritty beneath your boots. One of the MIBs holds up a hand, standing in the twilight vestibule – there's a rapid sequence of banging noises, then a solid *thump*. 'Not clear yet,' she says, in a thick German accent. Looking at the walls, you see translucent shadows through them – there's some kind of cute mapping system built into the MIB glasses, so that as the spooks move through the building, they feed a map of it into a shared overlay. It's a bit like having X-ray vision. Then you begin to get a headache: the rooms are ghosting, not matching up. *'Scheisse,'* says your MIB, raising her paintball gun.

Red ideograms drip down the walls, bloody trails of information bleeding into the edges of your visual field. There's a harsh squawking noise as the MIB spins round and unloads two rounds into the wall, half-deafening you. She shouts something in German and dashes towards an inner door, beyond which the ghostly outline of a lift shaft is superimposed over a spiral staircase and a small office, alternate realities competing for your attention. There's another bang from inside the building, and the lights flicker. Liz looks round at you, her face white, and begins to say something, but a noise like grinding metal drowns her out, and pale tentacles vomit from her mouth. You can't see the door you came in at anymore – the ideograms are everywhere, mocking you, and none of the walls match up. You take the nearest entrance, which is roughly where you remember the front desk as being. The room is slowly spinning around you, and there are bugs crawling on the walls. Your stomach twists, bile rising at the back of your throat: then someone touches you. You jump a mile before your realize it's Liz, tugging at your glasses. With them off, the room turns out to be insect- and rotation-free, but the grinding noise continues, mingling with shouts and the occasional banging of paint guns. 'Get out!' she shouts, close enough to your ear that you can actually hear her. 'Tell Verity!'

You nod, and she shoves you towards the doorway – visible now you've gotten out of the treacherous glasses. You pause in the entrance and fumble your official specs onto your face, but they've crashed completely; a rolling curtain of many-coloured hash blocks out your visual field. You pull them off hastily. Better to face the world barefaced than risk whatever chaos is fucking up your CopSpace.

You stumble out into the daylight, blink like a startled hedgehog while you get your bearings back, then home in on the chief, who is standing beside the HQ truck. 'It's a right mess in there,' you begin.

He cuts you off immediately: 'Do they need backup?'

'I'm not rightly sure, CopSpace is fucked. The inspector told me to tell you, they've hit resistance. They're flailing about in the toy box, you know?'

'Right.' He takes a deep breath. 'Go back in and find Liz. Keep us in the loop. You, over here!' He gestures at the heavies from S Division, who're waiting about near their response cars. 'Get your goggles off, follow the sergeant here, and get ready to find out what the feds have got themselves hung up on.'

'But I—' It's no use complaining: the chief has got it into his head that this is some kind of ned-in-a-china-shop problem, and unless you can get Kemal to stop laying about and get the hell out, Verity'll send in the armed response boys after him. And won't *that* be a fine mess? 'On my way, sir.'

You rush back over to the warehouse and dive in the door, staying low. 'Inspector,' you yell, over the noise – it's like someone's running a sawmill in there – 'where are you?'

'Through here!' You just about hear her voice and home in on it. There's a doorway behind the counter and an office. Chairs have been knocked over, and there's a huge smear of purple paint on one wall. More to the point, it's *dark*. Hitting the light switch doesn't achieve much – someone's cut the power. You draw your torch and flick it to wide-angle, lighting up the ceiling with it at arm's length, then duck-walk towards the second, inner door.

The room looks to have been halfway converted into open-plan offices, once upon a time. Cast-iron pillars spaced every four metres or so support a high ceiling of wooden timbers – but the floor has been raised and covered in those beige tiles they use to cover cable ducts, and the arched, shuttered window casements all have air-conditioning units bolted to the wall below them. The lights are out, and the room is not only dark, but sweltering hot and spectacularly noisy. Between each pair of pillars a glass-fronted box like an old-style telephone booth rises most of the way to the ceiling, and these are the source of the racket: there must be at least twenty of them. You glance through one smoked-glass front, somewhat spooked, and see rows of green-and-violet LEDs blinking from a sea of aluminium fascias. They're routers or telephone switch gear or something. Each pillar emits a blast of hot air and a variety of hissing, crackling, and whining noises, but the real source of the noise is somewhere deeper inside the building.

You find Liz near the centre of the room, kneeling over a Eurocop who is retching himself dry over a waste-paper basket. She's got his glasses off, and when she glances at you, she looks haggard. 'Don't go anywhere near the stairwell,' she warns you. 'Maurice and Jacques are still making sure the site's clear before they scram the backup generator.'

Backup generator? 'The chief's about sixty seconds away from sending in S Division,' you tell her. 'He told me to be your runner.'

'I see.' The Man in Black stops puking long enough to groan and sit back, leaning against a pillar. Liz thinks for a moment: 'Tell the chief it's all under control, but we hit electronic countermeasures. So far all we've got is lights on and nobody home, but if S Div come in shooting, it's going to go blue on blue.'

'Electronic countermeasures.' You look around in disbelief. 'Is that all this is?'

'No,' she says tightly, 'but we'll have it off-line in a couple of minutes. Go!'

You'll say this for Verity, the old fart doesn't believe in stomping on his subordinates' chilblains. 'Tell Kavanaugh she's got fifteen minutes, or until she calls for backup.' You high-tail it back to the room of servers and pass the word on.

'Good. Mario, are you feeling better yet?' Mario, now sitting with his back to the pillar and the bin within arm's reach, nods wearily. His glasses lie on the floor nearby, lighting the carpet up with a jagged lightning show.

'I will be alright.' He doesn't sound it. 'The others will . . .' He stops talking and takes a couple of deep breaths. 'They're upstairs now, except Hilda and Franz. They are looking for the generator.'

It's almost as if someone is listening to him: there's a tremendous double bang that shakes the floor, followed by the moan of a thousand fans whirring down into silence.

You can't stop yourself. 'It sounds like they found it,' you say, and – despite yourself – giggle. After a moment, you realize Mario and Liz are both staring at you as if you've grown a second head. So you stop.

'Let's go and find Kemal,' says Liz. 'What *are* these things, anyway?'

'Multi-core blade servers,' Mario pushes himself laboriously to his feet. 'Each rack houses two hundred and fifty-six blades, each blade has that many processor cores – and each core is a thousand times as powerful as your phone. We are standing inside a million euros' worth of mainframe.' He shuffles towards the interior of the data centre, back bowed like an old man. 'This is an odd place to put a data centre, yes?'

You look at Liz: Liz looks back at you and shrugs. You mouth 'ICE' at her, and she just twitches. 'Who owns them? Where are they from?' she asks.

'That is an interesting question.' And one that Mario, who is rapidly recovering his composure, does not appear to want to answer. You peer at one of the glass doors, shining your torch through: the panel inside is labelled LENOVO.

He heads towards the other end of the server room, and Liz follows him closely. You stick behind her, logging everything (you hope). At the other end of the room there's a set of fire doors and a stairwell leading up – as well as another pair of fire doors with some kind of blinking fire-alarm and gas sensor mounted next to them, and Kemal himself clattering down the stairs towards you. 'Not in there!' he calls.

'Why not?' asks Liz, peering at the blinkenlights by the door.

'It might not be safe.' Kemal's eyes look hollow without the goggles. You shine your torch on the panel; it *seems* to be saying there's no problem.

'Right,' she says with heavy irony. 'I see.' She pushes the door open before Kemal or Mario can stop her. 'What *is* this?'

It's another server room, but a lot smaller than the last one, and there's a Frankenstein machine squatting in the middle of it all, like a cheap horror prop. There are cylinders of compressed gas and lots of narrow pipes and valves, all converging on something that looks like the stainless steel thermos flask from hell, sitting under an industrial-grade cooker hood with a gigantic duct vanishing into the ceiling. There's another rack of boxes with blinkenlights sitting next to it, flashing and winking – evidently they're on a separate power supply. And it's *steaming*, a trickle of chilly smoky vapour wreathing its neck. 'Hey, is this dangerous?' you ask.

'Stay away from it, Sergeant!' Kemal insists sharply. 'It might be explosive.'

That's a thought, but you've heard enough bullshit already that you're not about to take his word for it. What kind of bampot builds a bomb with dry ice special effects and blinking LEDs, anyway? You unhook your cams and walk around it slowly, panning up and down to capture the lot.

'Wait!' Kemal hisses. 'Don't get too close.' He steps towards you. At the same moment, you feel an odd tugging. It's almost as if your cam has acquired a life of its own. Startled, you pull back, then glance at the thermos flask. You're two metres away from it. You can feel the chilly vapour on your skin: you try not to inhale as you sweep the camera across the scene, then take a step back.

'Is it *dangerous?*' Liz demands, 'Because if so, we've got to evacuate—'

'It's another server,' Kemal says carefully, 'but not a kind you can buy in a shop. In fact, what it's doing here . . . ' He trails off. 'The power's down,' he remarks quietly. 'The refrigerator fans are quiet.'

'How long until it reaches its critical temperature?' asks Mario, right behind him.

Kemal nearly jumps. 'We can't risk that! We need it intact.'

'Tell me what's going on,' Liz insists.

Kemal grunts, a sound like an irritated pig. 'This whole installation shouldn't exist. You don't just drop data centres in the middle of suburbs; you'd need to get the power company to run extra cables in from the substation. There are enough processor blades in the next room to listen in on every Internet packet and voice call in Scotland; we think' – he points at the steaming Frankenstein machine – 'this is probably the refrigeration vessel for a quantum processor—'

A door slams in the next room. You hear raised voices. *Angry* voices, and footsteps coming closer. Liz gestures you to one side of the door, and you quietly pull your can of whoop-ass. She nods minutely and takes a step back.

'—don't care! You shouldn't be here!'

'—idiots had checked with eurocontrol first—'

The doors bang open. Liz is already standing to one side, and she's drawn her warrant card.

Standing in the doorway is one of Kemal's henchmen, caught in vituperative argumentation with a familiar figure – Barry Michaels, CTO of Hayek Associates – and someone else behind him, middle-aged and red-faced. Barry's hair is even more fly-away than it was when you turned up in his boardroom last Thursday, and he's the one who's doing most of the shouting. Henchman Number One, for his part, has lost his Man in Black poise. Possibly this is something to do with the way Barry – who, you notice, not only looks like an old public-school boy but is built like an old public-school rugby squad front row forward – has got him by the scruff of his immaculate suit jacket and is almost frog-marching him –

'Stop right there,' Liz says firmly. 'You're under arrest.'

You step sideways, keeping them both covered with your pepper spray.

Barry snorts, disgustedly. 'No I'm not. Chief Constable?'

You look past him, at the man in the hounds-tooth check trousers and scary canary-yellow cardigan, with the golfing shoes and the somehow familiar face. So does Liz.

'Oh shit,' she says faintly.

'You can say that again. If you like,' says Deputy Chief Constable McMullen, who right this moment is looking distinctly peevish about been pulled away from the golf course on his day off. 'Inspector, I'm here to tell you to do whatever this man tells you to do. Do you understand?'

Liz's face is a picture. 'Sir?'

Barry clears his throat. 'Inspector, please turn around and face the wall. Try and forget everything you've seen in this building.' After a moment, he glances your way. 'That goes for you, too, Sergeant.'

'But—'

'Do as he says,' McMullen says firmly. He sounds more resigned than anything else. 'He's in charge here.'

You lower your pepper spray reluctantly. 'What's going on?' you ask, inexplicably pleased with yourself for stifling your initial instinct to yell *whae the fuck?* instead.

'It's a mix-up,' says Michaels. 'Not your fault – not your

force's fault, Mr. McMullen, nobody local is blameworthy –
but Kemal here forgot to notify eurocontrol about what he was
doing. They'd have told him to leave well alone, but he had to
go for gold, didn't you? Now we're just going to have to sit
tight until the clean-up crew arrive to sweep the mess under
the rug and put everything back where it belongs.
Otherwise . . . ' He sniffs. 'I was serious about facing the wall,
Sergeant.'

You glance at Liz. She nods. You turn around.

'I'm going to have to confiscate your evidence footage,' he
adds, apologetically.

'What?' You can't stop yourself. 'That's illegal!'

'I think you'll find my department has a specific exemp-
tion.' He speaks with the Olympian certainty of a man who
can use a deputy chief constable as his personal warrant card.
He clearly outranks Kemal and his merry Men in Black. Hell,
he probably outranks the minister. What does *that* mean?
'We'll just have to wait here for the cleaners. Shouldn't be too
long.'

Kemal clears his throat. 'The power's off. Is your quantum
gadget stable? If it warms up?'

'Not my field, old boy, I'm a peopleware person. I suppose
the cleaner chappies will sort it out once we get the power
back up – we'll be invoicing you for the downtime—'

At which moment, the big electromagnet quenches.

ELAINE: System Fails,
People Die

It's your fault Jack nearly got arrested. But what did you expect?

Luckily there's camera footage of the incident, and he's the one with a hole in his jacket and a broken chunk of electronics, not to mention the fact that the nearest thing to a knife on his person is a multitool with a one-inch blade. But afterwards, you're so angry you could kick yourself – or preferably the jobsworth in the security guard's uniform who called the police over and told the constable that *Jack* had assaulted *someone else* – a someone else who by that time had probably legged it all the way over the great firewall of China and was, to put it in copspeak, Unable to Testify.

Equally luckily, the constable was willing to listen to your eye-witness account before doing anything hasty. So instead of filling out an arrest form, a disclosure notice for the CCTV footage was served, and sometime in the next couple of weeks Strathclyde's finest will review the take and see if a crime was, in fact, committed.

Of course, you'd been labouring under the misapprehension that the men and women in uniforms wearing SECURITY badges were actually there to provide *security*, as opposed to preventing attendees from chugging the free plastic cups of sherry provided by some of the more optimistic exhibitors: but that's par for the course in Glasgow, it seems; the commission of an actual crime fills their dour Presbyterian hearts with joy (*look, a member of the criminal classes is actually* working!) while a complaint from the victim is an occasion for much swithering about clean-up rates and blackening the name of our good town and so on and so forth.

Which is why you find yourself, about two hours later, standing on a street outside the conference centre, miles from anything (except for a couple of high-rise hotels, a preserved dockyard crane the size of the Eiffel Tower, and a Foster Associates' mothership that looks to have suffered a wee navigation mishap on final approach into London's docklands), trying to cajole a shocky and stressed-out Jack in the direction of shelter. Because it's Glasgow, where the weather offers you a creative combination of hypothermia and sunburn simultaneously: and right now it's playing a DJ mix with six El Nino events, a monsoon, and a drought on the turntables.

Anyway. Blood sugar is the most important thing to get under control after a stressful confrontation, so that's what you decide to tackle first. 'C'mon, Jack, let's get back to the city centre and try to find some lunch.'

Jack groans and mutters something inaudible. He's been withdrawn, like a snail pulling itself tightly back into its shell, ever since the security goons ejected you both from the giant wood-louse; and it's not just his lack of an umbrella. ''M an idiot.'

You know better than to agree with that self-summary, and you also know better than to disagree with it. 'No, that idiot with the badge was the idiot. You aren't an idiot yet – but you will be if you don't get something to eat and a chance to chill out. You're taking the rest of the day off. Understand?'

That raises the ghost of a smile. 'The train journey's not billable time, anyway.' But he unhunches slightly and begins to walk, face screwed up in distaste. 'Who are Guoanbu?' he asks, pronouncing the word carefully. 'Some kind of Chinese farming clan?'

You shake your head. 'Never heard of them. Try Googling?'

'Okay.' He twitches. 'Mind if I call a taxi?'

'I'll do it.' You phone the first cab company that comes up in your glasses and they promise that a car will be with you inside of two minutes. 'Getting anywhere?'

You notice his face. Jack's gaping stupidly again, the way he does when he's been surprised by something and hasn't remembered he's in public: he was probably wearing an embryonic version of that expression when the midwife spanked him on the bum. 'Oh fuck,' he says, then his facial muscles twitch and come back under control. 'Oh dear baby fucking Jesus Christ on a roller-skate.'

'What?' It's raining, you're irritated with yourself, now you're annoyed at Jack: fists on hips, you feel a strong urge to bite somebody's head off. (It's just a shame you'd regret the consequences.) 'Would you care to *explain* yourself? Or are we just swearing in the rain because it's wet, or something?'

He swallows. 'I found out who Guoanbu are,' he says. 'Here.' And he flicks a tag at your glasses. It takes you a moment to open it. And then you see: **GUOJIA ANQUAN BU. MINISTRY OF STATE SECURITY**. Guoanbu is an abbreviation or acronym or whatever the Mandarin equivalent is for KGB, CIA, MI5, Mossad. **EXTRAORDINARY RENDITION ON THE NIGHT FLIGHT TO GUANZHOU**. 'Chen was scared that they'd, they'd "have my kidneys" if he squealed. Said he wanted two million, plus witness protection. That's when he ran.' Jack's face is pale in the chilly drizzle. 'What have we gotten ourselves into?'

A driverless black minivan wearing a TAXI sign on its bonnet glides up to the kerb beside you and unlocks its doors. 'Sounds like a game of **SPOOKS** to me,' you say lightly, and get in. 'Come on, the rain's getting heavier.'

Your map tells you there's a cluster of interesting-sounding restaurants in the West End, so you tell the call-centre driver to take you there. He has a bit of trouble making out your accent at first, but you convey your desires successfully at the third attempt and settle back to watch the steering wheel twitch in the grip of a poltergeist, beneath the rain-streaked windscreen. There are probably webcams in the headlight and brake light assemblies; you certainly hope your driver can see better than you can. 'Do you know where we're going?' Jack asks anxiously. 'I'm lost in Glasgow.'

He's speaking metaphorically: of course nobody is ever really lost, not anymore. 'Never been here in my life,' you say cheerfully enough, 'but I've found a couple of restaurant review forums and a mashup overlay. What do you think of this – contemporary Russian/Eastern European fusion cuisine, German beers, vodka bar next door, and old Soviet décor? It's called Stavka.'

'Stavka? There's one of those up in Dundee,' he says dismissively. 'It's okay, but a bit heavy on the cabbage and mutton.'

'Well then' – the taxi circles a roundabout closely then accelerates hard, forcing you to grab one of the handles – 'we can see what's next door.'

'Next door, that'd be on Sauchiehall Street, right? Hey, why are we going this way?'

Something in Jack's tone of voice makes you sit up sharply: your seat belt brings you up short. 'What do you mean?'

'Sauchiehall Street is *that* way,' he says.

'It could be a one-way—' You stop trying. Obviously he's been over here often enough that he knows some of the street names. A moped whizzes past on the other side of the road as the taxi accelerates. Then your phone rings. 'What's going on?'

'Your phone,' Jack suggests. 'I'll sort this out. Hey, driver—' He's talking to the mike under the red LED behind the empty driver's seat as you see the phone call is from an unlisted number.

'Who is this?' You run the volume up so you can hear over the traffic noises.

There's a familiar three-bar jingle, then: 'Agent Barnaby, this is Spooks Control.' You muffle a groan; this is almost exactly the worst possible time for **SPOOKS**' GMs to assign you another task. On the other hand, you can record it and deal with it later. 'Your authenticator is: Mapplethorpe Paints Roses.'

'Talk to my voicemail please, I'm busy right now.' You try to keep your tone brisk but professional.

'You are in a taxi in Glasgow,' the **SPOOKS** call-centre droid continues, an edge of urgency creeping into his voice. 'Unfortunately, its remote driver service has been penetrated by a Guoanbu black operations team. *This is not a game.*'

'What. The. Hell?' You stare at the wiperless windscreen, where Jack is now speaking very loudly and urgently into the microphone, and you realize the taxi's accelerated to match the speed limit, and the central locking is engaged, and there's a perspex screen between the two of you and the controls.

'Guoanbu assassins have used this technique in the past: they hijack a taxi or car, drive it to a sufficiently isolated location, and crash it. Your investigation of the leak at Hayek Associates has made you a target. We can't give you a police intercept without exposing our knowledge of their penetration of our infrastructure, which might provoke a major incident. You must break out of the taxi while it is stationary at traffic lights, or break into the driver's compartment and disable it.' Jack is shouting and thumping the electric window control. 'Call in when you have time,' says the spook. Then your phone goes dead.

'Shit.' Swearing doesn't achieve anything, but under the circumstances . . . You look left, right, left again: traffic, rain, a blurring wall of four-story tenements stacked out of red sandstone blocks rushing by. 'We've got to get out of here, Jack!'

Jack turns. There's panic in his eyes. 'I heard!' He thumps the latch on the polycarbonate screen with the flat of his hand, then swears. The taxi's doing about sixty kilometres per hour, bearing right onto a two-lane-wide stretch of concrete underpass – they're big on brutalist road-building on this side of the country, it seems – and he's unfastened his seat belt so he can get at the screen. If the carjacker just decides to aim for the nearest bridge abutment, it'll be curtains for Jack – but no, the webcam in the passenger compartment is dangling from its socket like a popped eyeball. Your mind flashes through scenarios. *Bridge*: no, too much chance of an ambulance rescuing someone. They'll wait until you're out of town, then drive over the edge of a quarry, or into a river, or the sea. Webcams popped to prevent blackboxing, doubtless a necessary safety precaution for the careful automotive assassin.

The unruly passengers broke into the driver's compartment, nobody to blame but themselves: that's what this is all about, it's an SFPD assassination, after all. Oddly, you can feel an icy sheen of sweat in the small of your back, but you're not frightened or panicking: you've played this game a hundred times before, planted plastic boxes on the walls of consulates, tailed another spook through a busy city's streets, made the dead-letter drop . . .

Oh.

'Jack. We've got to get into the cab. I know what to do.' The buttons on the steering column are mocking you: so easy to press, but impossibly inaccessible. Your hands unfasten your seat belt on autopilot. 'Give me your multitool.'

He reaches into his pocket and pulls it out, passing it to you handle first: 'Why?'

You turn it over in your hands – a lump of machined titanium with weirdly recessed slots and bumps in it, frustratingly opaque when you're in a hurry. 'I want to unscrew that latch.'

'Oh.' He hunches round on the jump-seat. 'But—'

'We've got time,' you reassure him, even though you're not entirely sure of it yourself. The cold sweat is spreading.

'Give me that.' He takes the multitool: his hands are large and warm, his nails evenly clipped, but there's an odd twist to his index fingers, almost as if their tips are curved. You notice this as you place the tool in his palm. It's funny what you notice when you're skating on the thin ice above a chilly pool of panic.

Jack crouches, flips the jump-seat out of the way, and kneels on the floor so he can peer at the catch on the sliding panel. Things flip out and latch into place as he twists the tool, then begins swearing continuously in a conversational tone of voice. 'Got it.' A black screw pops out and disappears onto the similarly black carpet. Then another. The buildings are thinning out on either side as the taxi sways and bounces, slowing as it merges with a stream of out-bound traffic, always sticking to the overtaking lanes, keeping close to the speed limit. You twitch in the grip of second thoughts – *shouldn't we have tried to get a door or window open?* – but then you have visions of falling out of a fast-moving taxi in traffic. A third screw comes loose. 'Shit. This one's stripped.'

'What—'

'Lend me a shoe.'

He's wearing trainers, you realize. You quickly unlace one of your shoes, thanking providence that round toes and plat-form heels are in again. Yours are only a couple of centimetres high, but it's enough for Jack to use it as a hammer, whacking the flat rasp-blade of his tool between the catch and the panel, levering away, until – 'Gotcha!' He looks over his shoulder at you, sheepishly. 'What do I do now?'

'Reach over and engage the autopilot,' you explain. 'Once it goes into automatic drive, it'll lock on to the roadside beacons and cut the remote driver out of the loop.' You hope. 'Then you can take back manual control if nothing goes wrong.'

He looks befuddled. 'But I can't drive!'

'Then strap yourself in and stay out of my way.' You're not sure you can do this – you're a Londoner, you don't own a car, your driving license is just another form of ID – but the taxi's speeding up, and the traffic is thinning out, and there are only occasional buildings now. 'Okay. Brace yourself.'

You slide the panel sideways and grab the steering wheel. There isn't room to fit your body through the window, just your left arm, reaching around to the driver's seat on the right, and the alarm that starts screaming in your ears as soon as you get the panel open is deafening: the taxi lurches horribly towards the near side, and you stab at the buttons, bending a fingernail back and painfully clouting your knuckles as the steering wheel begins to spin –

And straightens out as the autopilot locks on to the mark-ings on the open road –

Too hard.

There are limits to what idiot servos are capable of. You hear the blare of horns from outside, then a horrible crunching thump from behind that whacks you back into the passenger compartment, as the taxi spins across the central reservation and slides towards the on-coming lights.

Then everything stops making sense.

JACK: THE ANTI-NUTCASE EULA

When you were young, you had a recurring dream about being in a car crash. You'd be behind the wheel, peering over the dash – you were too short to reach the pedals, too young to know how to drive – and the car would be careening along the road, weaving from side to side, engine roaring and moaning in mounting chaos, and you'd see on-coming lights rushing towards you in a symphony of bent metal and pain – then you'd startle awake, shivering with fright between the sweat-slick sheets.

This is nothing like that dream. For one thing, the dream didn't smell of burning plastic and gunpowder, or explode out of the floor and punch you in the face like a demented yellow mushroom while turgid blinds snap down across the windows with a sound like gun-fire. For another thing, you were always on your own, not shit-scared about being trapped inside a crumple zone with a friend being thrown around like a rag doll.

The taxi isn't entirely stupid. Freed from the homicidal wishes of the hijacker, it sensibly determined that its new controller was intoxicated or otherwise incapacitated. Even as it crossed the central reservation it was braking hard enough to leave a thick black slug-trail of rubber on the tarmac, triggering air-bags – inside and out – and yammering a warning at the on-coming autodrive convoy. By the time the first collision hammered home, it was already down to twenty kilometres per hour, and the unfortunate impactor was in the middle of an emergency stop from sixty. The sound of tearing, crumpling metal seems to go on forever, a background string symphony almost drowned out by the percussive rattle of the air-bags and the screaming in your head. In reality, it's all over in a couple of seconds.

The stench of nitrate explosives is overpowering, and the air is full of dust. The air-bags, their job now done, begin to detumesce. You fumble with your seat belt, hunting around for the release button, then try to reach around the bulging central pillar of yellow plastic. 'Elaine?' You can barely hear the sound of your own voice. 'Are you okay—'

You edge the pillar out of the way and see Elaine's legs and torso embedded in a mass of plastic bubbles. (The driver's cab is a solid wall of yellow balloons). You stare in horror at the end of your world, half-certain that she's been chopped in half. But there's no blood, and her legs are twitching. 'Help me, can't breathe—' You almost faint with relief as the yellow walls part, and Elaine falls into your arms. 'Ow, *shit*!' She takes a deep breath and tenses. 'Fuck, ow, shit, I think I bruised my ribs.' You gape with slack-jawed relief as the yammering lizard in your hindbrain slowly realizes that the nightmare is over.

Her voice sounds wrong. The multiple air-bags in the passenger compartment are slowly going down, and there's a smear of blood on the side of one of them. Smart bags; or maybe she was just caught between them and immobilized like a fly in amber – once upon a time she'd be dead, through the windscreen and torn apart on the unforgiving road, or neck broken by a dumb stupid boxing-glove full of hot gases erupting in her face, but these bags know where you are and fire in synchrony to bounce the airborne passenger into a safe space and immobilize them.

You feel weak, your guts mushy and your head spinning. The mummy lobe is yelling about Consequences, not to mention dangerous driving and calling the emergency services, but for once it's outvoted: you're just glad she's alive and unmutilated and you're here to catch her.

'Let's get out of here,' you hear a different you say firmly: the risk of someone else driving into the wreck isn't that great, but you're not in a fate-tempting mode just now. 'You really worried me . . . '

'Me, too. Let's move.' She takes a deep breath. 'My phone—'

'Allow me.' You fumble with the multitool – somehow you kept track of it – and puncture some of the air-bags, and she twists round and grubs around on the floor for a moment while you fight your way to the near-side door. The door is jammed solid and crumpled inwards, the window a spider-web of cracks: but there's an emergency handle, and when you pull it there's a rattling bump from the door, and it falls away from your hand, hinges severed. *You broke it!* yammers the mummy lobe. *Now you'll pay!*

'Got it,' she says, and a moment later you're both standing in a cold grey shower. 'Hey, the other cars—'

Your stomach knots up, and you swallow back acid, holding your breath, and look past the taxi. There's a shiny new Range Rover with its bonnet pushed up: the driver's door is open, but the air-bags are still in place. The traffic has slowed. For a moment you're back in the nightmare again. 'Call your friends,' you tell her, a betraying wobble in your voice, 'then call the police.' Your feet feel like lead weights while your head is too light, and they're held together by knees made of jelly, but you find yourself walking towards the SUV, terrified of what you'll find.

The backdoor of the Range Rover opens and a pair of feet appear. *They're too small,* you tell yourself. They fumble around for the running-board then step down onto the road, and you suddenly realize they belong to a kid – *a girl?* In school uniform. Blonde, about ten years old, very serious-looking. She looks around, puzzled, and you wave. 'Over here! On the pavement.'

Behind you, Elaine is on the phone, shoulders hunched. The girl walks towards you slowly, head swivelling between the Range Rover and the wreck of the taxi. 'Mummy's going to be very unhappy,' she says, her voice dripping with innocent menace. Speculatively: 'Is the driver in there? Did you make it crash? Is he dead?'

'No!' You glance at Elaine. 'We were passengers, it's on remote drive. Something went wrong, my friend's calling the police now. Are you alright? Is there anyone else in your car?'

'Just me. Mummy sent the car because I had to come home early.' You realize your heart is hammering and you feel faint. 'Your hand is bleeding. Did you cut it?'

'I must have.' You sit down hard. The world is spinning. A van moves slowly past the taxi, pulls in just down the road. You hear yourself laughing, distantly: it takes you a few seconds to realize it's your phone ringing.

What happens next is this:

The first responder to arrive is a police officer. He parks up the road with his lights flickering red highlights across the broken glass and water, gets out, and immediately calls dispatch for an ambulance crew. 'Dinna move,' he advises you gingerly, then Elaine is talking to him animatedly, saying something. A few minutes later the ambulance arrives, and two nice people in green with name tags reading SUSAN and ANDRE ask you some pointed questions.

'I'm Jack,' you say, tiredly. 'I know who I am, and I know what year it is. I'm just a bit dizzy.' *And cold, and shivery.* At which point they quite unnecessarily strap a board to your back and shoulders and bring out the stretcher and lift you into a big white box full of inscrutable medical gadgets. During this process your phone rings again, so you switch it to silent.

An indeterminate time later SUSAN comes and sits on the jump-seat beside you while the ambulance starts to go places. 'Where are we going?' you ask.

'We're just taking you to the local A&E,' SUSAN explains pleasantly, 'just so they can look you over. Don't worry about your friend, she's sitting up front.'

There follows an uncomfortable interlude with wah-wah noises and many jaw-cracking jolts across homicidally inclined speed bumps: then a brisk insertion into a bay at the Accident and Emergency unit, where a nurse efficiently plugs you into a multifunction monitor and a couple of triage people conclude that you're just suffering from mild shock rather than, say, a broken neck. Whereupon they leave you alone.

An indeterminate time later — just long enough for you to begin getting grumpy and thinking *but what if I really* was *ill?* — the curtain twitches. You try to sit up, just as Elaine sneaks inside. 'How are you feeling?' she asks.

'Not wonderful, but better than I was. Bored.' You try to shrug, but it's difficult when you're lying down. You don't want her to notice how happy you are to see her, so you try to keep her talking. 'Did the police make any trouble?'

She pulls a face. 'No. Turns out the taxi was breaking the

speed limit: when I said we thought it was out of control, they were all tea and sympathy. Turns out it's the third one this week.'

'The third—'

'Yeah.' She looks at you thoughtfully. 'Stinks, doesn't it? I think we ought to head back to Hayek, find Sergeant Smith, and sing like a Welsh mining choir.'

Stinks, doesn't it? That's one way of putting it: a thousand an hour is good money, but it's not good enough to cover being stabbed, crushed, drowned, or otherwise bent, spindled, and mutilated in the line of duty. *Especially* not in a goddamn live-action role-playing game. You find yourself nodding. 'Yeah. And the call from **SPOOKS**. In the taxi. I didn't know you played **SPOOKS**.'

'Any particular reason?' She narrows her eyes, searching for contempt.

'I think it's an interesting coincidence.' You pause. 'I used to play **SPOOKS** quite a lot. But it never told me I was being kidnapped before.' There, it's out in the open.

'Yes. By the Guoanbu.'

There it is again: you try to pull your scattered thoughts together. 'When he tried to stab me. No, I mean before then. He wanted asylum, Elaine. What kind of game did he think we're playing?'

'**SPOOKS**.' She's watching you, as if she expects you to laugh at her.

'Well, that figures.' A thought strikes you. 'Maybe he was just nuts. You get that sometimes, a schizophrenic who mistakes their LARP controller for God or "M" or something. One of the things we were working on for **STEAMING** was a sign-up wizard that does some personality profiling to weed them out.'

'But' – she bites her lip – 'I don't think you're nuts. Do you think *I'm* nuts?' She asks.

No. 'How long have you been playing it?' you ask.

''Bout three years. Why?'

'Just thinking.' You've been into the game for even longer, LupuSoft *expected* you to play it back when they were in the conceptual development stage for **STEAMING** . . . 'My account lapsed about a year ago, I was too busy working on a, a competitor. Only – hey, you're not supposed to use your phone in here.'

'Bullshit, they just say that to force you to pay through the nose for the PatientLine services.' She dials a number. 'Come on . . . hello? Yes?'

It's really weird watching her face as she slips into the player's headspace. The skin around her eyes goes slightly slack, her posture changes: like a cat that's spotted a bird, she's all focus. It's even weirder when you stop to think about it: because you know all the statistics, nearly 45 per cent of gamers are women, even though if you look at the biz from outside it seems to be focussed on an attention-deficient twelve-year-old male with a breast fixation and a sugar high. Something you read about **SPOOKS** comes back to you, that it was deliberately designed to punch female escapist buttons. Back in prehistory, when there were two Germanys, the East German spies used to recruit lonely female secretarial and administrative staff on the other side, using sex . . . but also sometimes just the promise of a life less ordinary. People will pay through the nose for excitement: is it any surprise that they'll take it if you're giving it away for free?

'Yes, here he is.' She holds her phone out towards you. 'It's Spooks Control.'

'Yeah?' You take the phone. 'Who is—'

'Hello, Jack. Your authenticator is Gold Koala Dictionary.' Which is flaky because even after a year you remember the three random words: they should have dumped you off their player database months ago. The voice is faintly familiar.

'I don't play **SPOOKS** anymore,' you say automatically.

'**SPOOKS** hasn't finished playing *you*, Agent Reed,' Control replies snippily. 'Constable Patel will be along to see you in a minute or two. He'll give you each a form to sign, then you'll discharge yourself from hospital and he will give you both a ride back to Edinburgh. You have a meeting at four o'clock sharp.'

'What if I don't want to go to any meeting?' You know it's futile as the words leave your mouth, but that's not the point. 'I'm not in your bloody LARP anymore! I unsubscribed!'

'Agent Reed, this is no longer a game. If you don't play along, we'll have to have you taken into custody for your own protection. The recent attempt to abduct you was not an isolated incident: we've been informed that your niece Elsie went missing two hours ago. The local police assigned a Family Liaison Officer to the case after your reported threats and were preparing to move them to a safe house but—'

The voice continues to make buzzing noises, but you're not paying attention: you're staring at the back of your own head, wondering when you stepped through the looking-glass. Nothing makes sense, but looming at the edge of your universe is a thing of horror. The games have imploded into reality. You suppose you ought to be relieved that *they* told you about it, so that it's not a figment of your imagination . . . but it feels like your world is ending. As indeed it should have, all those years ago.

'Jack?' It's Elaine. She looks like she's seen a ghost. 'Jack? Talk to me!'

You hold the phone out. She takes it. 'Yes?' she asks. Then she listens for a minute, nodding, occasionally saying 'yes' quietly. 'He looks shocked,' she says. 'Put yourself in his shoes, for a — yes, I will. Yes.'

Eventually she hangs up. 'Jack?'

'What?'

'Get up.' She looks like her dog's just been put down. 'We've got to go.'

You bundle up the thin hospital sheet and swing your legs over the side of the bed. 'Why?'

'They told me about your niece. That's awful . . .'

'Yes,' you say, unsure what else is expected of you. 'But there's nothing I can do about that right now.'

'They told me we've been drafted,' she adds, stiffly, looking at you with an air of uncertainty, as if she's half-expecting your head to start spinning round, or something. Maybe you ought to be getting emotional, but it's just one weird blow on top of another today. People are trying to *kill* you, repeatedly: all you really feel is a numb sense of dread.

'I figured that much. As well?'

'It's in the end-user license agreement to **SPOOKS**. The usual, we let them do background checks to determine credit worthiness and "eligibility to participate", it says. The anti-nutcase clause. And we signed to let them vary the T's and C's.'

'So?'

'The anti-nutcase clause is effectively a privacy waiver for positive vetting. And the T's and C's—'

'Official Secrets Act, as a click-through?'

'Something like that.' She shifts from one foot to the other restlessly, as if thinking about running away. 'About your niece, Elsie is it? Are you close to her? Spooks Control says it was the other side.'

The other side. A nice turn of phrase, but who exactly *are* the other side? And what does it *mean*? 'They would say that, wouldn't they.' You suppose you ought to feel angry, but you're actually just filled with a monstrous sense of surprise. 'I'm . . . not that close, really.' *It's just my niece.* If it wasn't *you* at the centre of it all, if it was some other poor bastard on the receiving end of this sinister postmodern joke, you'd be laughing hysterically. As it is, maybe crying *is* an appropriate response. 'Let's—'

The curtain jerks open, admitting a police officer, goggle-eyed and cammed up like a paratrooper wearing a spider-eyed mask. 'Mr. Reed and Ms. Barnaby? I'm to take you across to Edinburgh. If you'd like to put your chop here . . . '

He hands you a clipboard and a pen, old-fashioned ink and a sticky panel for you to thumbprint at the bottom of the page of small print with the Saltire and red lion rampant, and as you sign your name to the revised EULA, you can feel the waters closing in over your head.

SUE: Cover-up

When the big electromagnet quenches, your first panicky thought is that it fucking *is* a bomb, and that slimy shite Michaels is lying through his pants. Then you realize that you're still alive and, in fact, nobody is hurt – but it's no thanks to *les Hommes de l'ONCLE*.

(Later you find an article in Wikipedia that explains it. Apparently when you warm up a superconductor to its critical temperature, and it stops superconducting, any electrons circulating in it suddenly stop circulating freely, and the energy all comes out as heat instantly. Which heats up the liquid nitrogen refrigerant the magnet is sitting in from about minus two hundred degrees to minus fifty degrees in a fraction of a second, vapourizing it – and the vapour occupies a whole lot more space than the liquid. So it's not *far* off being a bomb.)

But when it happened, you weren't expecting it. So one moment you were sitting there, listening to Barry Michaels out himself as some kind of spook, and the next thing you heard was a faint popping sound – more like a bump than anything, or maybe it's a figment of your imagination – and then God's own steam-whistle went off about two metres away from the back of your heid.

(In hospitals with body scanners, they put the magnets under a metal duct, venting through the ceiling and walls to

the outside air, and they make sure the windows are all tough-
ened glass and all the window units and doors are designed to
blow open but not to pop out of their frames. And indeed,
there's a thing like a giant extractor hood hunching over the
smoking thermos from hell in the warehouse from which
Michaels has so signally failed to dismisseth the Leith police.
And that's probably what saves your life.)

For a few seconds the roaring whistling sound fills the
room, bashing on your ear-drums and battering at your guts
like the afterburning exhaust of a fighter at an air show, more
like a jackhammer than an actual noise. Then it begins to die
down. You take a deep breath, feeling light-headed, and the
room begins to spin. It keeps spinning, and it's really funny,
you've got to laugh – it's the aftermath of the explosion. Has
somebody slipped you a popper? Because that's what it feels
like, it's like you've gone from sober to six pints drunk in five
seconds flat. And then your head begins to clear, and you feel
sick with fright. 'What's happening? Liz! Tell me!'

Liz is gasping for breath, too, and there's a rattling thunder
of fans, a tangible blast sucking a draft of air in through the
suddenly flapping doorway. 'Be. Okay. In a minute.'

The door slams open again as the S Division boyos race in,
guns drawn and twitchy. 'On the ground! On the ground!'
One of them shouts at Kemal, obviously getting completely
the wrong end of the stick. 'On the ground, motherfucker!'

'He's ours,' calls out McMullen. 'Call an ambulance crew,
we, we need oxygen in here.' *No shit,* you think: Kemal is on
the floor, gasping and twitching and generally not looking terribly healthy. 'Evac, evacuate the building.'

Three minutes later you're arguing with a paramedic who
wants you to lie down on his wee stretcher so he can play doctors and constables. 'I'm fine, dinna worry about me,' you

reassure him. Which isn't entirely true – you've got a splitting headache left over from when the gadget blew out its load – but the only person who's really in need of help seems to be Kemal, and he's on his way to the Western General in the back of an ambulance with a mask strapped to his face. 'I gotta fill in the chief.'

You manage to make your way over to the mobile incident headquarters, where the uniform on duty nods you through to the back office. Liz is already there, with McMullen and Michaels, and Detective Superintendent Verity, and Kemal's deputy Mario, none of them looking terribly happy. 'Shut the door, Smith,' snaps Verity. McMullen, looking very out of place in his golfing duds, points a finger at Michaels. 'You have some explaining to do.'

Michaels glances at his watch. 'Not as much as you will if you don't come up with a good cover story,' he mutters. He sounds genuinely rattled. *So it's pass the exploding surprise whoopee cushion public enquiry parcel, is it?* you wonder. 'If it wasn't for the damned meddling flying squad, or that prize twat Wayne . . .'

McMullen takes a deep breath. Judging by the expression on his face, you figure he's keeping a tight lid on. Poor bastard – this isn't the kind of hole in one he'd been expecting to handle on his day off. 'Would one or the other of you please explain the situation in words of one syllable?' he finally manages.

'I suppose so.' Michaels pats back a fly-away wisp of blond hair. 'Hayek Associates are what used to be called a front company. On the one hand, they do what it says on the tin – stabilize in-game economies, maximize stakeholder fun, that kind of thing. On the other hand, they give us a good opportunity to keep an eye on certain disorderly elements who like to meet up in one game space or another to swap dragon-slaying hints, as it were.'

'Who is "us"?' Liz asks.

Michaels frowns. 'You don't need to know that, but Mr. McMullen' – the deputy chief nods, lugubriously – 'can vouch for us. In any case, you need to understand that most of Hayek Associates' employees are just what they appear to be. When the robbery took place, Wayne panicked – I can confirm that he's a civilian – and called you. Which caused us to acquire an audit trail in CopSpace, which is monitored by—'

'They have no need to know,' interrupts Mario. He looks at Michaels, pleadingly. 'Can this wait for Kemal?'

'Other agencies, as I was saying,' Michaels continues, as if the interruption hadn't taken place. 'An elite pan-European counter-espionage police task force. Who promptly put two and two together and got five, hence this morning's little excursion.'

'The warehouse.' McMullen gives Michaels a hard stare. 'It's yours?'

There's a brief pause, then Michaels inclines his head. 'Yes. Nothing to do with that blacknet you're looking for in Leith. All those machines are just there to feed data in and out of the 5-million-pound quantum processor that your *idiot friend*' – he almost snarls at Mario – 'has comprehensively broken.'

You try to catch Liz's eye, but she's doing the Botox thing, cheek muscles virtually paralysed. *Pounds not euros* – so it's an English thing. Under the articles of independence MI5 and MI6 and GCHQ and SOCA and the rest of the southern intelligence apparat have got the free run of Scotland; meanwhile, the Republic's own intel capabilities are strictly local, mainly focussed on keeping an eye on the local Muj bampots down the pub and suchlike. It's on a level with the rest of Scotland's military and diplomatic clout — strictly toytown. (After all, who on earth would want to invade Scotland?) But more importantly, you can hear the well-nigh-deafening silence of Michaels lying by omission. If this was Saturday night down the shop, he'd be clamming up and calling for his solicitor rather than answering the next question, which is, *Why is MI6 (or whoever) running a multi-million-pound operation to bug gamers down in Leith?*

'You could tell them the truth,' Liz volunteers slowly.

'Yes?' McMullen looks thoughtful.

'Faulty intelligence led to a major counter-terrorism raid in Leith. Which turned over a sporting goods warehouse instead of an Al Qaida cell.' She shrugs. 'It's bad PR, but we explain we were overruled by the suits from Brussels who organized it without consulting us. Blame Kemal' — she nods at Mario, who looks outraged — 'and we're off the hook, and more importantly, the spotlight is off Mr. Michaels as well.'

'Suits me,' Michaels says dismissively.

'I'll have to run that one by the chief, but it ought to fly.' McMullen nods thoughtfully. 'You' — he points at Mario — 'you can keep your mouth shut. With your boss in the hospital, you're off the hook, and with your boss in the hospital and not answering any damn fool questions, there's nobody who can tell the press otherwise.'

'It is an outrage!' Mario vents. 'We are not responsible!'

'So?' Liz glares at him, then turns to look at Michaels. 'Next you're going to tell us you want this burying so deep it's in danger of coming up in China. Am I right?'

Michaels splutters. 'Absolutely! Of course — what do you think we are?'

She regards him coolly. 'I think you've got a leak.'

He stares right back. 'That's none of your business, and I'd appreciate it if you would desist from further speculation along those lines.'

'That's enough.' McMullen rounds on Michaels. 'You've done enough damage already, or have you not noticed we've had to shut down traffic to half the north side of the city? So I'd appreciate it if you'd cease with your high-minded requests and leave us to sort things out.' He's building up a head of steam, is the deputy chief constable, and you're torn between fascination at this fly-on-the-wall opportunity to see the boss in action, and the fear that he's going to take it out on someone under his authority. 'And then you and me and the super and Kavanaugh here are going to sit down, and you're going to tell us what you can about what's going on so we can stop blundering around in the dark and stamping on your corns.'

'What about us?' Mario demands plaintively.

McMullen finally blows his top. 'Fuck off back tae Brussels, and I won't have to prosecute you for wasting police time!'

Three hours later you're back at the station. It's been a busy morning, mopping up after the horrendous mess Kemal's flying circus left behind, but eventually you get a chance to catch a late lunch. Unfortunately, before you can cut and run, Liz Kavanaugh catches your eye. 'Sergeant, let's do lunch together.'

Ah, fuck it. You know an order when you hear one. You were planning on catching up on your paperwork – there's that wee ned to keep track of, and the incontinent dog owner the council keeps yammering on about, not to mention last week's B&E cases – but Liz obviously has something else in mind. So you nod dutifully and play along. 'Where'd ye have in mind, skipper?'

'There's a nice little Turkish bistro on the Shore, they do excellent meze.' She holds up a car keyfob. 'I'm buying.'

Well, that's no' so bad. You follow Liz out of the station, and she lets you into her car – a compact Volvo, very nice – then drives down into Leith and parks next to the Shore. 'What do you want to talk about?' you ask her receding back, as she heads up the pavement.

'Patience, Sergeant.'

Okay, so it's *serious*. (If it wasn't, she wouldn't mind nattering about it.) You trot along after her as she ducks round a corner and leads you to a couple of pavement tables outside a small diner, opposite a aquatic appendix pinched off from the harbour by a low bridge that appears to have been built on.

'Have a seat, Sergeant – Sue. We've got plenty of time for lunch: I've booked this as a meeting.' She smiles, but there's something uneasy about the expression. It doesn't reach her eyes. She's got her back to the glass front window of the bistro and keeps scanning the road as if she's expecting someone. 'I think you should go off-line.'

'You sure, skipper?' You raise one eyebrow at that, and when you blink, the speech-stress plug-in is showing red spikes all over Liz.

'Yes.'

You slip your glasses off and physically unplug them, slipping their battery out. Then you reach into your left upper-front torso pocket, pull the PDA, and pop the fuel cell. 'Satisfied?'

A bendy-bus slinks by and blasts you with a haze of biodiesel, power pack roaring. Liz nods wordlessly, then pulls her own PDA out and gives it the miser's standby. 'Position your chair so you're talking away from the window,' she says. 'I don't want anyone bouncing a laser off it.'

'Whae the fuck?' But you do as she says, more surprised than anything else.

A thin smile. 'You can buy laser-acoustic mikes for thirty euros in Maplins online these days, Sue. And the people I'm worried about won't think twice about breaking the law by using them.'

'You think Michaels sold us a line of bullshit?' you burst out, finally unable to contain yourself.

'I don't think so, I *know* so.' She rubs the side of her cheek, where the headset normally rides. 'Problem is, I don't know whether he did it to keep us distracted or to make us do some dirty work for him, or what.'

'But if he's lyin', he's a—'

She waves a hand, cutting you off. 'One thing you can be sure of is, he *is* what he said he is. It checks out. There's a . . . a restricted access file. Hard copy only, the best kind of security: they keep it in a locked room at Fettes Road. I had a look at it while you were in de-brief. Michaels is on the list. We can't touch him.'

A waitress wanders outside, sees you both, and smiles: a moment later you're puzzling over a menu as Liz continues to lay the situation out.

'Hayek Associates are a front for some sort of intelligence-gathering operation. Something went wrong, and the non-spook employees hit the panic button before anyone could stop them. They've got a quantum processor down in Leith. Those things don't grow on trees, Sue, I've been doing some reading about them and it scares me. Kemal saying TETRA is compromised scares me even more. And so does that flaky set-up in Nigel MacDonald's flat, because it's a dead ringer for a blacknet node we took down last year.'

'What's a quantum processor for?' That one's been puzzling

you all morning. It looked more like Dr. Frankenstein's work-bench than any other machine you've ever seen.

'Not my field, I don't know much more about IT than you do.' She frowns. 'But I know what they *do* – they're used for special types of calculation. Not doing your word processing or playing games, but things like calculating how proteins fold, or breaking codes. And you know what? This whole thing with Hayek Associates and the robbery in Avalon Four is about codes, isn't it? The codes your programmers were going on about, that pin down where a magic sword or whatever *is*.'

'But they wouldna buy a quantum processor just so's they could rip off their customers, is that what you're sayin'?'

'Yup.' Her cheek twitches. Liz is clearly not a happy camper today. 'Who's to say precisely *what* bunch of codes they've been cracking with it? Say what you will, mobile gaming takes bandwidth, so Hayek have a great excuse for running lots of fat pipes in and out of the exchanges. And I don't think they're going to tell us what they're doing with it, do you? So if we want to crack this case, we've got to go after it from other angles. Did you get anywhere looking for the mysterious Mr. MacDonald?'

'Not a whisper.' You shrug. Just then, the waitress reappears with your latte and something black and villainous-looking in a small glass for Liz. 'It's as if he just vanished right off the face of the earth.'

'Maybe he did.' You look at her sharply, but she's just staring at her coffee as if she's afraid it'll bite her. 'I am having second thoughts about our mysterious Mr. MacDonald. I think he's a snipe – in the American sense.'

You can find snipe all over Fife, they're not endangered or anything, but you take her point. 'Then why did that wee fool Wayne send me off after him? Wayne's a civilian.'

'Yes? I wouldn't be so sure of that.' She's visibly falling into a dreicht, dour mood. 'They've all got their little angles to play, and I wouldn't be surprised if some of them aren't playing against each other. And anyway, there's that body in Pilton. Very convenient that would be, don't you think?'

You have the uncomfortable feeling that the inspector is trying to tell you exactly the opposite of the words she's using. 'Aye, *too* convenient.'

'My thoughts exactly. I don't buy that line about this being unconnected. And I'm really worried about that blacknet setup in MacDonald's house. It doesn't *fit*.' She takes a sip of her Turkish coffee, and it's at that exact point that you realize what's going on.

Liz is scared shitless. She thinks she's got a sleeping dragon by the tail, and she's not sure it isn't about to wake up. So she's decided to designate you as her insurance policy.

'Jesus, skipper.'

'He's not answering his IMs this century.'

'If we can't get ahold of MacDonald, who're we going to go after?'

'Haven't you heard from your two new contacts today? The nerd and the librarian?'

'No, I—' You pause. 'They were dead keen to be helpful yesterday,' you say doubtfully.

The waitress is back with a platter of meze for Liz and a traditional Scottish fry-up breakfast for you.

'After lunch I want you to plug yourself back in and see what's keeping them from you,' says the inspector. 'Then I'd like you to go and talk to them, *off* the record. They're not suspects, but if what I think is happening is actually happening, they might be in danger if too much information about them shows up in CopSpace.'

'In CopSpace? But—'

'Sergeant, this is way out of my league, but I'm not convinced that idiot Kemal from Brussels was wrong. I think there's some kind of shitty infowar nonsense going on, some kind of nasty little intra-European diplomatic espionage spat. I've got a nasty feeling that someone's already been murdered because of it, and if we don't call time, there may be a bunch more bodies showing up. And worst of all – I think whoever's behind it has got their claws into CopSpace, maybe a blacknet, too. And you know something? I don't intend to do their dirty work for them . . .'

ELAINE: SHANGHAIED

Sitting in the back of the police car as it careens along the M8 with its lights flashing, you suddenly realize you feel deathly tired – and sick. Not nauseous, not period pain, just the kind of gut-deep malaise that comes from being stressed to the breaking point. Everything's happened too fast for you to get a handle on it: from Jack stumbling on a Chinese student who thought you were working for the security services, to Jack being stabbed, then the insane call from Spooks Control and the taxi trying to kill you both, then the word that one of Jack's nieces had been kidnapped, and now this . . . it's *too fucking much*. You want to hit pause, make yourself a nice mug of Horlicks, put your feet up, and watch a fluffy romantic comedy before curling up in bed. Or maybe get your shiny new claymore, find a gymnasium, and spend half an hour walloping the living shit out of a dummy. Your mental overload light is flashing red. It's too fucking much: and you're not getting any time off to assimilate it.

Sucks to be you.

Constable Patel isn't being a whole bag of laughs – he's so keyed up and focussed on the head-up display and the steering wheel that you're terrified he'll explode if you ask him anything (like, oh, 'are we nearly there?' for values of *there* that map onto *wherever you're taking us*), and in any case the speed with which he's zipping past the cars and trucks in the slow lane clues you in that maybe he's exceeding the speed limit just a little – and Jack's not much use right now, either. Come to think of it, if you're feeling like a pile of crap, what's he going through right now? You glance sideways, just enough to see that he's slumped against the opposite door, cheek leaning against the window, looking half-asleep. *Just mild shock,* the paramedics said, but that's not the half of it. You know what it's like to get home after a burglary, or to hear that a friend's died suddenly – more's the pity, from personal experience – and right now Jack shouldn't be here: he should be at home and in bed. A million spy thrillers and hard-boiled detective capers insist that the hero bounces back right after being slugged upside the head, but real life's not like that. Sucks to be *him,* too. You're torn between sympathy and a despicable little sense of warmth that comes from knowing that he's got it even worse than you have. That's not nice, and it's making you feel guilty, so you shove it to the back of your head. Sympathy is respectable; that'll do for now.

Your left spectacle frame vibrates, signalling that your phone wants to talk to you about something. Annoyed, you hit the display sync button. It's an instant message from –

JACK: dont look at me dont act suspicious

You nearly bite your tongue, so hard is the urge to look round or speak aloud. Instead, you start finger-typing. And what you type is –

ELAINE: WTF?

JACK: our driver is listening

ELAINE: so?

JACK: need 2 talk l8r not near phones

ELAINE: LOL, afraid of bugs???

JACK: yes

ELAINE: got crypto on fone lines

JACK: HA keys compromised. who else?

ELAINE: U R paranoid

JACK: ORLY?

A cold shiver runs up your spine as Officer Friendly slows, then accelerates up a slip road towards the gyratory that connects the motorway to the city bypass.

ELAINE: l8r

JACK: OK

You clear the chat log from your phone, then switch it to standby again. What Jack's saying is clear enough, and for all that you think he's being a bit paranoid, he's got a point. *You're sitting in the back of a fucking police car, for crying out loud!*

Of course, if Jack's afraid they're monitoring your phone and using it as an omnidirectional bug, why the hell did he have to IM you? He's not stupid enough to think that they won't be snooping on his texts as well, is he? Or maybe he *wants* them to think he's paranoid and needs to talk to you in private? But if that's the case, surely they're going to realize he's trying to make them think he's paranoid and – that way madness lies, the infinite receding mirror-walled tunnel of spy-versus-spy. Which, let's be honest, is what you both signed up for in a fit of boredom or a burst of manic competitive analysis, never suspecting that **SPOOKS** wasn't simply a game but is some kind of Machiavellian ploy to get thousands of willing agents' boots on the ground. *Useful idiots*, the real spymasters used to call them, the cannon-fodder of human intelligence gathering.

You're hitting traffic now, surging along one of the main arteries into the western suburbs. Your driver's still going fast, but he's not using his siren or overtaking: he's just relying on folks to get out of his way. Evidently you don't rate stunt-driving. A few moments later you recognize where you're going. The police car is taking you back to Hayek Associates' offices: you recognize the wide, straight main road with trees to one side and a hill on the other. But before you can figure out a way to warn Jack, the car is turning right, up the hill, and into the car-park outside the bunker.

The slippery public-schoolboy type, Barry Michaels, is bouncing up and down on his toes in the entrance like the floor's red-hot. Which is a definite *oh shit* moment, because it crystallizes an uneasy nagging suspicion you couldn't quite bring yourself to articulate earlier: if **SPOOKS** is for real, then why can't there be more to Hayek Associates than meets the eye?

'Come with me, please, Mr. Reed, Ms. Barnaby.' Barry manages to sound completely in control of the situation, and judging by the presence of the police, he's not wrong. You manage to nod, and follow him into the lift.

'Marcus is out of the office on business, and I sent Wayne on a wild goose chase,' Michaels confides, as the lift drops down towards the underworld. 'So you don't have to worry about the civilians getting underfoot.' As the lift stops, he jams his thumb on the close button and simultaneously pokes the call button. The lift jerks into motion again, descending. 'This is the sub-basement. I'll have to ask you to leave all your personal electronics in the basket, I'm afraid.'

The sub-basement is walled in concrete and smells of mould and neglect. What light there is comes from a caged incandescent bulb that dates to the Cold War, or maybe the Battle of Britain.

'What *is* this place?' asks Jack, sounding more than slightly dazed.

'I told you, it's the sub-basement.' Michaels points to a

wire supermarket shopping basket. 'Your gadgets, please. *Now.*' At first you think he's taking the piss, but then he shoves his left shirt cuff up and unfastens a very expensive Breitling chronometer. 'You can collect them again on the way out.' You obediently place your handbag on the counter, then put your glasses in the basket. Jack, meanwhile, is building a small pyramid: keyboard (very much the worse for wear), phone, specs, something that looks like a multifunction power pack, other less identifiable stuff . . . It's a wonder he doesn't clank when he moves. Michaels nods approvingly, then opens the single door. It's thin plywood, but the frame looks more like an airport metal detector. 'Go on. Third door on the right.'

There's a short corridor. Michaels carefully shuts the door behind himself. For a moment you think about opening one of the wrong doors – but it's very Bluebeard's castle down here, and you know what happens to girls who open the wrong doors in *that* story, don't you? The lights are all naked bulbs behind wire shields, hard-wired to switches that look like something out of the Stone Age. *No electronics.* Go figure.

Finally, the three of you are alone in a whitewashed room with half a dozen battered office chairs, a wooden table, and a sideboard with a kettle sitting on it. 'Sorry about the lack of amenities,' Michaels says brusquely. 'Help yourself to tea or coffee, I'll be back in a minute.' He ducks out the door before you can say anything.

Jack looks at you. You look at Jack. He raises an eyebrow. 'So what do *you* think?' he asks suddenly.

'Don't ask me, I'm in over my head.' You look around curiously. There's no network cabling, no phone sockets, no nothing except for an old tin kettle on a camping gas-ring and a light bulb out of the last century. You've got a creepy feeling that if they could, they'd have rigged this bunker up for gas-light. 'I think we're under a shielded nuclear bunker, and there are no cables.' You walk round the table and light the burner. The kettle's already full of water. 'Judging from what Michaels said, we're going to be here a while. How do you take your coffee?'

The kettle is just about coming up to the boil when Michaels returns. He's carrying a fat cardboard folder full of paper. 'Ah, good.' He plants the folder on the desk, then he sits down limply, as if he's been on his feet for hours. 'You're both probably looking for an explanation for what's going on here. Unfortunately, I can't give you one.' He glances from you to Jack and back again, and there's very little of the bumptious ex-public-school boy left in his expression. 'Not because I don't want to, or I'm not allowed to, but because we don't have much more than pieces of a puzzle right now.'

Jack, who has been slumped in a chair for the past minute or so, suddenly stiffens. 'What's this shit about Elsie being kidnapped?'

'I'm very sorry to say, we don't have any news of her yet.' Michaels opens the folder and pulls out a stapled memo – you try to read it, but you can't make out much more than a certain familiar coat of arms at the top of the page. 'If it's any consolation, it's quite likely that nothing's happened to her yet, and probably nothing will.'

'Nothing . . . ' Jack's at a loss for words, grasping at straws: and that makes you quietly angry at Michaels, who should know better than to string Jack along like this. The kettle's bumping, so you stand up and walk round the table to fill the mugs you set out earlier. Moving is easier than sitting still.

'Are you looking for Elsie?' you ask Michaels. 'Because it

seems to me that this wouldn't have happened if not for your games . . . '

'We traced Jack's calls and the photographs,' says Michaels. 'There's an ARG called **SPYTRAP** – you've heard of it? The photographs were pulled off a roadside traffic camera, the printing and envelope delivery were care of an unwitting **SPY-TRAP** player, and the phone call . . . ' He shrugs. 'Best guess right now is that the whole thing was automatic – one of the other side's data-mining bots determined that you were in a position to threaten their scheme and began yanking strings, starting with getting you arrested in Amsterdam.'

'Huh?' Jack somehow manages to look endearingly stupid when he gapes like an idiot, more like a large but thick sheep-dog than a village idiot. 'But it's not—'

'You're flagged as a **SPOOKS** player.' Michaels taps the folio, then glances straight at you. 'And you live within ten kilo-metres of a subject of interest, and have near enough *exactly* the same skill set. Locking you down for a couple of days while they make their move would be prudent, don't you think?'

Well. 'Who's the subject of interest?' you ask. It's not as if you haven't guessed already, but some confirmation would be nice.

'Nigel MacDonald. Who doesn't actually exist – *Yesterday upon the stair, I met a man who wasn't there: He wasn't there again today, I wish that man would go away* – he's a figment of our real-ity-fabrication department's imagination.'

'Which organization's division?' asks Jack: 'Hayek Associates, or **SPOOKS**, or whoever you are?'

Michaels nods. 'Jolly good question. As you've probably surmised, Hayek Associates are a front. It's a real enough com-pany and Wayne and Marcus are real enough businessmen, and it's even profitable – but that's not what it's here for. It – I should say "we" – are a listening post on the virtual frontier. It's our job to keep an eye open for certain activities that . . . well, for a last-decade example, do you remember the flap some years ago over terrorists holding training camps in Second Life? Not that that's quite what was going on – they weren't training camps, it was just a convenient place to go and swap intelligence or give orders, once the web and email and telephone networks were all being tapped – but, the thing is, for the past twenty years we've been trying to nail down every communications channel that the bad guys might use, and the trouble is, *it doesn't work*.' He shoves his hair back with one hand, and for a moment the boyish good looks collapse in haggard disarray. 'Because bandwidth expands faster than storage, and every time we think we've got one type of channel locked down, a new one comes along, and we can't back-track to hunt traffic in a medium we didn't know existed. And then some disruptive new technology comes down the pipeline and makes everything we're doing obsolete in a couple of months . . .'

Jack glances at you sidelong while the middle-aged spook-master is fumbling to articulate whatever it is he's got stuck in his mind. His expression is so dry you have to bite your lip. Dry as in tinder-dry. Jack's finally getting angry, and you've got a feeling that you don't want to be inside the blast radius when he goes off. 'Jack's niece,' you prompt Michaels. 'What makes you think she's safe?'

'Well, for starters there's the fact that she's been abducted by the procedural content engine from a role-playing game, rather than a slavering paedophile. In fact, if this is the usual way these things play out, she probably doesn't even know she's been kidnapped as such, any more than you realized you were being taken out of circulation by a rival intelligence agency in Amsterdam. It's all just a game to her. Look, I can promise you that we're working on it, and I won't be lying. But, in all honesty – we can't just call the local police and tell them to go in with tasers drawn. Firstly, we're not sure where she is, yet, and secondly, if the police find her too fast, it'll tip the opposition off that we're onto their game. That would be disastrous – it would invite escalation—'

And then Jack blows his top.

'What the fuck is *that* supposed to mean? It seems to me that we've already been pretty fucking escalated, all the way into a gravel quarry if we hadn't broken out! Chen was scared shitless – he thought someone was going to try to kill him – and I'll bet you that if he shows up again, it'll be in an organ bank. These fuckers aren't playing games, Mister Spook, sir, in case you've forgotten there are several million euros missing—'

You've got a very peculiar feeling that Jack is playing some kind of game with Michaels, but you haven't got a clue what the rules are. And then Michaels shakes his head. 'That's irrelevant.'

You can't keep your mouth shut at that. 'What do you mean, it's irrelevant? What are we here for, then?'

'That's what I'm trying to tell you.' Michaels breathes heavily. 'Are you going to listen?'

'*Fuck* no, I'm trying to tell you you've been—' But that's just the tail-end of Jack's venting, and he manages to shut himself up before he really puts his foot in his mouth. He's not stupid, is Jack; unlike some of the geeks you've known in your time, he can get a message if you hit him over the head with it hard enough. (He seems to be house-trained, he's not pushy, and he doesn't smell bad: if it wasn't for the tee-shirts and furtive programming runs, he'd have trouble hanging on to his geek licence.) 'Go on, please,' he says, with a very odd look on his face.

'Thank you. Let me lay out a few things first, by way of establishing a context. This is about national security, and, if you're anything like the civilians I've dealt with in the past, you're about to ask what it's got to do with you. So I'd like to nail that down first so we can skip the stupid questions later. Clear?'

You nod, warily. *National security* is a weasel term that covers a multitude of sins, but you'll let it pass for now. *Whose national security?* is the next question you've got in mind . . .

'This is the twenty-first century, and we're in the developed world. You're probably thinking wars are something that happens in third-world shit-holes a long way away. And to a degree, you'd be right. Modern warfare is capital-intensive, and it hasn't really been profitable for decades; it was already a marginal proposition back in 1939 when Hitler embarked on his pan-European asset-stripping spree – his government would have been bankrupt by March 1940 if he hadn't invaded Poland and France – and it's even worse today. When the Americans tried it in Iraq, they spent nine times the value of the country's entire oil reserves conquering a patch of desert full of – sorry, I'm rambling. Pet hobby-horse. But anyway: back in the eighteenth century, von Clauswitz was right about war being the continuation of diplomacy by other means. But today, in the twenty-first, the picture's changed. It's all about enforcing economic hegemony, which is maintained by broadcasting your vision of how the global trade system should be structured. And what we're facing is a real headache – a three-way struggle to be the next economic hegemon.'

Who is we? That's the question you're asking yourself . . .

'"We", for these purposes, is the intellectual property regime we live in – call it the European System. The other hegemonic candidates are the People's Republic of China, and India. America isn't in play – they've only got about three hundred and fifty million people, and once we finish setting up the convergence criteria for Russian accession to the Group of Thirty, the EU will be over seven hundred. China and India are even bigger. More to the point, the USA went post-industrial first. Their infrastructure is out-of-date and replacing it, now oil is no longer cheap, is costing them tens of trillions of euros to modernize. Plus, they've got all those rusty aircraft carriers to keep afloat. It's exactly the same problem Britain faced in the 1930s, the one that ultimately bankrupted the empire. But today, our infrastructure – Europe's – is in better shape, and the eastern states are even newer. They went post-industrial relatively recently, so their network infrastructure is almost as new as the shiny new stuff in Shanghai and New Delhi. So there's this constant jockeying for position between three hyperpowers while the USA takes time out, and you live in one of those powers, in case you hadn't noticed.'

'I live in Scotland,' Jack points out.

'But Scotland is part of the British Isles Derogation Zone, which in turn is part of the European Union, yes? What I'm trying to make clear here is that what's good for the EU is good for Scotland, and England. And what's playing out here is potentially *very bad indeed*, both for the country you live in, and eventually, for you.'

If you let them badger each other indefinitely, you could be stuck in this bunker until Christmas. And that would never do: the instant coffee is bogging, and you can't check your email. 'Okay, so just what *is* going on?' you ask Michaels, smiling as sweetly as possible to conceal your irritation.

'Quantum key exchange!' Michaels snaps. As far as you're

concerned, he might as well have said 'abracadabra,' but the effect on Jack is electrifying.

Michaels smiles. 'Now that I've got your attention . . . '

Jack nods like a puppet on a string.

'Until about five years ago, progress in electronics was governed by something called Moore's Law — are you familiar with it? Make a circuit smaller, it dissipates less heat, so it can run faster, and you can cram more components onto a chip of a given size. It began to bottom out in the oughties, when we began hitting the quantum-scale limits to conventional electronics. But at about the same time, scientists began trying to develop so-called quantum processors, and don't tell me how they work — it's all gibberish to me. But the long and the short of it is, a quantum processor can do certain types of calculation not simply very fast, but to all intents and purposes *instantaneously*. And among the classes of operations they're good for, the foremost is code-breaking.'

'But if you use quantum key distribution,' Jack says slowly, 'that resets the balance point in the arms race. Doesn't it?'

This is already about two steps beyond you, but you focus on it intently: there'll be time to do the homework once you get your mobile back.

'Yes and no. Quantum key distribution' — Michaels looks at you — 'lets you secure your regular encryption keys so that there's no risk of anyone else getting their hands on them, which is what makes them vulnerable to quantum code-breaking. But it's something you do strictly over secure fibre-optic cable. Our entire mobile communications infrastructure, from 3G on up through 4G and NG and 802.20, is impossible to upgrade to QKD. The next generation system *will* be secure — but right now, we're wide-open to anyone with a couple of million euros and a bunch of carrier-grade fibre — and a copy of the one-time pad used to secure supervisor access to our core backbone routers. Which, incidentally, is why we're sitting in a shielded bunker equipped with no communications technology invented after 1940. About the only consolation is that the opposition is *also* wide-open, right now, and that's why we're going through the biggest renaissance in HUMINT – HUMan INTelligence – since the Cold War. It's all mediated through artificial reality and live-action role-playing games like **SPOOKS**, in case you hadn't guessed: adding the power of electronic information gathering to human espionage. Would you believe it used to cost us ten thousand euros a day to put a full surveillance team on a suspect? Now we've got volunteers who'll pay us to let them do our legwork!'

You shake your head. Michaels is dropping a bunch of random jigsaw pieces on the table in front of you, all shaken up, and expecting you to put them together, and you're not sure you've got the big photograph to work from yet. 'What are you getting at?' you ask. 'Because I don't see what this has got to do with us.'

'It's a lot to take in all at once.' Michaels shrugs self-deprecatingly. *Aw, shucks.* 'Let's just say . . . I'd like you to imagine that somewhere in the bowels of a shopping mall in Beijing, some game-obsessed otaku types are really getting into a multiplayer game called, oh, something like whatever's the mandarin for "Global Conquest". There's a whole bunch of them, in two gaming clans: call them Team Red and Team Blue. And somewhere in an office block, some differently game-obsessed intelligence officers working for the Guoanbu have decided that maybe, just maybe, these gaming clans are what the Soviet KGB used to call *useful idiots*, back in the day, and give them their head. The Chinese have a short way with hackers. Time was, they'd end up in pieces in an organ bank: these days it's cheaper to grow organs, so they're more likely to get twenty years' hard labour, but it's still not exactly something they encourage. But it's a different matter if the hacking is directed at an enemy of the state. And so these gaming clans, these useful idiots, they're playing out their game of "Global Conquest", and, rather than shitting on them from a great height, someone high up in the Guoanbu has given them limited access to one of the quantum processors in the basement of the State Academy of Sciences.'

'And what's the objective of their game?' you ask.

'As far as we can tell, it's capture the flag – the first team to take control of the backbone routers of a medium-sized EU member state wins. And guess what? They were all set to succeed, because some bastard – no, I have no idea who it is – leaked them a copy of the back-bone authentication pad. They've still got it, and they're running all over our telecoms infrastructure in hobnailed boots, because we don't dare shut down and reboot everything until we know where they got the keys. And you know what? We wouldn't have had any idea at all, if one of their low-level grunts hadn't hatched a plan to make some money on the side. Which is where you come in . . .'

JACK: SEX OFFENDER

Two hours after Michaels drops his cluster bomb of revelations, you stumble out of the rabbit-hole under Hayek Associates, exhausted, hungry, and not sure whether to be angry or scared.

At least Elaine looks as coolly imperturbable and spotless as ever: maybe her suit's made of Teflon. She glances up at the grey overcast, already spitting fat, isolated rain-drops in preparation for the main program. 'Let's get you home,' she says, and taps her ear-piece with a knowing expression. 'We need to talk.'

'You don't need to,' you say, because it's the right thing to do, according to the manners gland (which normally reports directly to the mummy lobe, except the mummy lobe is off-line right now, gibbering and sucking its thumb). 'We could head back to your hotel.'

'Rubbish.' She looks at you oddly. 'You're at the end of your tether. Which way is the bus-stop?'

'It's just uphill from the end of the drive . . .'

Another five minutes, and you're ensconced in adjacent seats on a two-thirds-empty LRT special, slowly climbing Drum Brae with a whining from its rapeseed-fuelled power pack that bodes ill for the future. It's electric blue inside, with orange grab rails, and the sky outside the advertisement-obscured windows is a louring slate-grey promise of things to come. Your mind's spinning like a Scottish Hydro turbine, chasing your own tail from pillar to post. Tracking down the Orcish thieves and their stolen stash of vorpal blades is neither here nor there anymore – what's important is keeping your head, while all around you other folks are losing theirs to the *snicker-snack* of the twenty-first-century yellow peril.

'Did you buy that line of bullshit?' you ask her.

'You're tired,' she repeats. She rolls her eyes sideways, and you follow the direction of her gaze, coming up hard against the little black eyeball of a camera. *Oops.* No wonder they call these fuckers Optares – there're at least eight of them visible, and no telling if they're broken *or*— 'Let's get home. No chit-chat.'

Paranoid thoughts begin spooling through your mind, following a multiplicity of threads. You've just come out of Hayek Associates, with a whole bunch of random fragments and the blinding revelation that Michaels's operation has been penetrated, and he either doesn't know, or isn't going to tell you. Now, let's suppose that Michaels was right, that one or other of the Beijing clans have their hooks into, well, *everything*. Can you get home safely? They've got the buses' cams – no more fallible video recorders behind the driver's seat, not after 7/7 – and the traffic cams and . . . but no, HA pointedly *don't* have any cameras overlooking their car-park, do they? And face recognition off a camera is notoriously CPU-intensive and not the kind of thing a quantum shoe-box under the server rack will help with, not with the current state of the art. *Good.* If you'd called a taxi, you might be up shit creek again, but buses still have drivers to extract the pocket change from tourists and ne'er-do-wells who don't have a RiderPass. It's not anonymous transport – that probably doesn't exist anymore, unless you go on horseback or ride a bicycle – but it's the next best thing: transport with no real-time ID tracking. The bad guys might well know where you live and where HA's offices are, and make the logical public transport connection . . . or would they? Who knows? Put yourself in the head of a puppet master in an office in downtown Guanzhou, pulling the strings for an ARG played by foreign devils. *This is not a game.* Which means –

The bus lurches away from the kerb and trundles towards your stop. You reach up and push the button, then stand: catching Elaine's eye, you nod at the exit. 'Next stop.'

Pervasive game-play. They've got reality by the short-and-curlies, thanks to the cryptography gap Michaels kindly pointed out to you. 'It's not as if this stuff is new,' he explained. 'The NSA were doing it years before anyone else, before their recent unfortunate circumstances.' They got Elsie, Michaels tells you – and there's a big black belly-laugh hanging over a yawning pit of terror you don't have the guts to think about yet. Michaels hung your virtual alter ego out as bait, and now you and Elaine are *it*, the plot coupon at the heart of the next level of the game that *he* is spinning for the unseen masters of reality in Beijing. If Chen – Team Red's non-virtual eyes and ears on the ground, a foreign student at large in Scotland – hadn't fucked up by getting greedy and trying to abuse his access to their key cracker to line his own pocket, you'd all still be flailing around in the dark as opposed to this turbid twilight.

How do you roll up a foreign spy network when the spies don't even know what they're doing? Not to mention your own counter-espionage fools . . .

You're on the pavement now, and the rain is splattering around you. You glance, longingly, in the direction of Burt's Bar, just over the road – good beer and excellent pies – but there'll be too many people about, too many pairs of flapping ears and unblinking video eyes and mobile phones that double as bugging devices. And you're feeling bruised and paranoid enough that you need some privacy. 'This way,' you tell Elaine, still not quite sure why she insisted on coming home with you rather than having a natter in some coffee shop.

You shamble across the cobbled road at a near trot, turn towards Glenogle and your wee Colonies house, and the heavens open all at once. Suddenly you're dashing for cover beneath an artillery barrage of water-bombs, Elaine stamping along behind you – and it's a couple of hundred metres to go. While you're both paused at a kerbside to check for traffic, an SUV aquaplanes past, malevolently hugging the gutter and spraying a mucky sheet of water across your legs. Elaine swears quietly behind your back as you cross the road, but then you're at the right side street, and heading for the cast-iron gate.

She grabs your arm. 'Stop,' she hisses.

'But it's pouring—' You stop. 'Yes?'

'This the door?' *You nod.* 'Give me your keys, okay? And hang back.'

Oh, for fuck's sake. 'I'm not stupid,' you grunt. And you drop into **SPOOKS** mode and scan the hedges and parked cars to either side for signs, eyeballs wide open for watchers and lurking booby-traps. Sidling up your own garden path like you expect to find a ninja hiding in the recycling bin would make you feel like an idiot even without the cold rain dripping down the back of your neck, but you've done this often enough in role-play that the tradecraft is almost automatic: and then you're at your own keyhole, glancing round the door-frame for signs and portents like anonymous black boxes that weren't there the day before.

Nothing. And it's your house. As you stick the key in the lock, you say, over your shoulder, 'Is your phone switched off?'

'Whoops.' She's fumbling in the darkness and the rain as you step inside and turn the hall light on.

'Come on in and close the door, then.'

There's no rain inside the house except for that which drips off your sodden jacket and trousers and trickles down your hair and into your eyes. You stumble into the hall wearily and shrug out of your soaking jacket. Reaching into the pockets, you pull out your phone – off – and your keyboard (also off, probably terminally so) and glasses. The sound of the cloudburst fades as Elaine locks the front door and stomps her feet dry on the mat. 'I'm soaked. That fucking Chelsea tractor really got me.'

'Me, too. I think they do it deliberately.' Drive with their near-side wheels in the overflowing gutter, just to inundate the automotively challenged who can't afford the ruinous road tax. You kick your trainers off, stumble up to the bedroom door, and grab the dressing-gown off the back of the door. 'Here, make yourself at home. Is your suit machine-washable?'

'Of course.' She looks at you warily, then takes the dressing-gown. 'Hey, you don't need to—'

'It's no trouble. Look, let me stick some real coffee in the pot, then we can talk.'

'Talk is good.' She looks around the living room, at the tangles of wires plugged into the overloaded ten-way gang in the corner and the bookcase with its middle shelves bowed beneath a stack of old d20 game supplements and graphic novels; then she plants herself in the far corner of the newer of the two IKEA futons that constitute 90 per cent of the soft furnishings and bends down to remove her shoes. You shake your head and duck into the kitchen to grapple with your feelings. It's smaller than the galley of an Airbus, but you can get the coffee started while giving her a modicum of privacy. And it gives you a chance to gibber quietly for a couple of minutes and try to calm yourself down.

When you emerge again, calm and collected and bearing two reasonably clean mugs full of organic fairtrade espresso, it's to find a twilight surprise. Elaine is bending over the power hub, systematically following cables from wall wart to blinkenlight. She seems to be trying to turn everything off. She's wearing your dressing-gown: her trousers and jacket are an untidy puddle in the middle of the rug. You clear your throat. 'Oh, hi,' she says. 'Any idea how many gadgets you've got plugged in here?'

'Um. Too many?' She's got you bang to rights. 'What are you doing?'

She pushes the off button on the video receiver. 'If we're going to talk, we might as well do it in private. Besides, the lights were bugging me. I counted sixteen before I lost track.'

A moment's stock-taking tells you that she's not about to do any damage – everything here's an embedded appliance except for the household disk farm next to the fireplace. 'One moment.' You bend down and rummage for the wall plug, then flick the switch. Everything on the power hub flickers and dies simultaneously. 'That do you?'

'Let's see.' She picks up her phone from the precarious pile of coffee-ringed magazines on the side-table and frowns at it. 'Yeah. The snitch is muzzled.'

'Snitch?'

'Spooks Control sent me a bug detector. Something about it reprogramming my phone's processor to sniff for different emission sources? Does that sound right?'

It sounds like a high-end cognitive radio application, and

probably illegal as hell – one that can override the built-in standards firmware and turn a handset into a scanner that can monitor any radio-based protocol its antenna can pull in. (Radio interference, after all, is purely an artefact of buggy receiver design.) Back when you thought **SPOOKS** was a game, it would just have been a prop, but now . . . 'It's plausible. What does it say?'

'It *said* something in here was transmitting, but it stopped when you pulled the plug.' She closes her phone. 'Sound like a bug to you?'

You glance at the streaming media hub, LEDs dark and lifeless. *That's your musical life, buddy, right there in the corner.* 'Might be.'

If someone was going to plant a bug on you, where better to put it than in the firmware of a gizmo that's transmitting all the time? 'Coffee?'

'Thanks.' She accepts the mug gratefully. 'About your washing-machine—'

'It'll take about three hours, if you still want to use it. But I can lend you a spare pair of jeans and a jacket if you don't.'

'You don't need to, but thanks.' A certain tension goes out of her. 'Show me where you keep the machine?' The washer/dryer is under the kitchen work-top. It's fully automatic, setting its cycle from the RFIDs in her jacket and trousers. Thirty seconds later she curls up on the futon opposite you with her coffee mug, eyes dark and serious in the gloom. (You hadn't realized just quite how much illumination the various gizmos contributed to your den.) 'Okay. What do *you* think is going on?'

'Well—' You stop, half-tongue-tied by the sight of her sitting opposite you, large as life, wearing your dressing-gown. There's a subtext here that you'd barely allowed yourself to

notice, consciously: *Do you suppose she's here because she likes you?*
The mummy lobe wants to kick up a censorious fuss, but it's
at a loss for words: you're not terribly good at dealing with the
rules of the game Elaine seems to be playing, or even recog-
nizing when a game's in progress, so you retreat hastily in the
direction of something you understand.

'I think we can trust Barry about as far as we can throw
him. He's definitely part of **SPOOKS**, and **SPOOKS** ties into the
police or intelligence services at some level – otherwise, we
wouldn't have gotten the taxi ride. And he's fed us a great
story-line. Beyond that . . . '

She stares at you from the darkness. 'Your niece, Elsie.
You're . . . you don't seem to be worrying about her. Is *that* just
a story? Jack?'

The roaring in your ears is like the engine of an on-coming
juggernaut on the wrong side of the road, headlights blazing
and horn blaring. 'I can't' – *don't want to* – 'face . . . '

'Jack?' She leans forward, visibly concerned. 'What is it?'

You force yourself to take a breath and try to nail down the
mess of emotions she's stirred up. 'I can't . . . look, trust me on
this?'

'Trust you?' She's still tense.

Another deeper breath. 'It's complicated. I'll try to explain
later. For now, let's just say there's stuff Michaels knows about
if he's plugged into the police. And there's nothing – from
here – *I* can do for her.'

'But I'd have thought—' She stops, with a visible effort.
'You're sure?'

You nod, not trusting yourself to say any more. You feel
shaky. It's all true – Elsie is beyond your ability to help – but
you don't like to think about it. It's just too painful.

Elaine sits back, looking thoughtful. After a moment, she

glances away. 'You trust Barry to look after Elsie, but you don't trust his operation as far as you can throw him. Is that right?'

That's an easy one to catch. 'They've been penetrated by the other side. And what about the rest of it? That piece of paper? How do we know it's genuine?'

She shakes her head. You trace the outline of her face against the dim light from the street filtering through the net curtains. 'The paperwork's the real thing. Either that, or the cop who handed it to us wasn't. And with the lights and the way he bent the speed limit on the way over . . . no.'

'Bugger.' You take an experimental sip of coffee. 'Okay. So **SPOOKS** is basically a tool that permits an electronic intelligence agency to run a metric shitload of unwitting human intelligence agents, weekend spies. They trained us, and now we've been activated to deal with a threat. The alleged threat, the one they *say* they *want* us to look at, is a different kind of gaming gambit: a botnet attack on a small European state, where the zombies are obedient human gamers who think they're just having fun and the director is a procedural content generator—'

'Huh.' The tip of her nose crinkles slightly when she frowns. 'I'm not a gamer, you'll have to define your terms.'

'Terms?' You back-track, trying to work out what confused her. 'Procedural content?' She nods. 'Content is, well, the map of the dungeon, location of treasure, where the monsters live, what the wallpaper looks like. Any game is full of the stuff, and it's expensive to do by hand – you need tile illustrators, narrators, musicians, programmers, a whole bunch of skills. So over the past couple of decades the industry's put a lot of effort into procedural game design – AI tools that can design a virtual-reality environment on the fly for players to explore. It's not just multiplayer games like Avalon Four; there's been work on ARG – artificial reality games – that can take a set of starting hints and design a conspiracy to drop on top of the players. You know, generate scripts for phone calls, order up custom gadgets to be planted at certain locations, hire actors . . . ?'

She looks blank, the same way she did right before you hit on your spreadsheet-as-programming metaphor, but this time you can't quite see a way around it. 'Artificial reality?'

'Yeah! **SPOOKS** is a variant on it, heavily mediated via the net, but you get ones in which there are actors and sets – you sign up to be inside the story. Like **I LOVE BEES** – that was the first one to go large – or **DARK DESIGNS**.'

'Pay to be inside the story.' She looks distant. 'So, uh. Suppose someone's set up a content generator to try and hijack a country. Bribe police constable A to ignore game-player B – who thinks it's a game – to carry bomb C (which is a firework, modified by a pyrotechnics geek who thinks they're building it for a special effects outfit) into a parliament building where useful idiot D will install the detonator. That sort of thing. Right?'

'Something like that.' You take another sip of coffee. 'They're exploiting our shitty wide-open crypto infrastructure, of course. Everything, phones, Internet, the lot, runs over TCP/IP these days – blame some really stupid decisions back in the oughties. They should have known better; it's hackable as hell, so, in an attempt to lock things down, the government decreed that access to the national-level routers, the boxes that manage all the traffic, would be secured using a code called a one-time pad. OTP codes are great – they're totally unbreakable if you don't have a copy of the key – but they've got a big draw-back: you need a copy of the key, a long sequence of random numbers, at each end-point. And if some-one who's not supposed to have a copy of the key gets hold of it, the whole thing is blown wide open. Anyway, what Michaels was telling us was, someone leaked those keys to Team Red. As the actual connections between routers are secured using symmetric cyphers that are easy to crack if you've got a quantum processor, it means they can snoop on *anything*. The National ID Register – never mind that it's poisoned, full of bogus records – the ID cards themselves use last-generation public-key encryption that a quantum processor can break almost instantly. And if Team Red have got a copy of the backbone keys, they can impersonate anyone they want to be, up to a point. The content engine can fake the ID of the first minister, but it still takes a voice actor to impersonate the first minister on the phone, right? So they've got this amazing backdoor, but wherever possible, they're doing stuff via the net. And as the net is so heavily surveilled, they're focussing on the bits that are hardest to monitor – stuff that goes on inside the big distributed games in Zonespace, where the rules change from minute to minute, and the players can implement their own in-game game engines.'

'Right. Right.' She nods, her expression intent. 'So we've got these two, uh, clans. Teams? Red versus Blue, playing for Scotland or Poland. And it's all happening quietly when Chen and his accomplice . . . ?'

'Chen's over here, being a pair of hands for Team Red. And he's got access to their key cracker back home, and he thinks, why shouldn't I make some money on the side? It's typical, really: great plan, but the operational security is blown wide open because a team member got greedy and ran a bank robbery in Avalon Four. Which must have netted him, oh, all of about ten thousand euros' worth of loot, and maybe a death sentence from the Guoanbu when they find out. Which is why he was so desperate to spill his guts when we showed up.' Unconsciously, you find yourself rubbing your ribs. Right where the pocket with your keyboard was. 'Jesus. He probably thought we were zombies closing on him, and we were going to put him in a taxi.'

'The taxi was already waiting.' Elaine shudders delicately. 'We weren't its real target, we were just the useful idiots who were going to shanghai Chen. Only we screwed up.' She's staring at you, you realize.

Timing is everything. (But at least the mummy lobe has shut its trap, leaving you to coldly consider the picture with your Spy Sensibility, or maybe your Gamer's Gonads.) 'I was arrested in Amsterdam.'

'I know.' She sits up straighter.

'On Friday night, last week. The bank robbery on the Island of Valiant Dreams happened on Thursday morning, didn't it? Triggering Michaels's man-trap.'

'The man who never was, Nigel MacDonald – the fake identity built around your résumé.' She's still staring at you. It's as if you've fallen into the centre of her world. 'How long have you been playing **SPOOKS**?'

'Huh? Like I said, I did it years ago – on-the-job research, actually.'

'Okay.' She makes deliberate eye contact. 'So you expect me to believe that Hayek Associates had a Jack-shaped hole in its corporate structure *just waiting* for Mr. Chen to try a penetration attack on them?'

'No, I—' You look away, embarrassed. Then an idea surfaces in your imagination like an iceberg. It's too preposterous for words, but it fits the observable facts – 'whoops.'

'Yes?' She leans forward.

'What if the whole reason **STEAMING** was shitcanned last week was because Michaels was planning to hire me anyway? Or rather . . . they've got a hole in their org chart with my name on it – or rather, "Nigel MacDonald", but I'm there if they need to activate me – and it's not the only hole, they've probably got a bunch of other ones. Hell, there's probably an agency somewhere with an Elaine-Barnaby–shaped hole in it by any other name, just waiting. Let's suppose Michaels already had the wind up that something shitty was stinking up the Beijing gutters, and was getting ready to activate a counter-espionage unit to go looking for it. He was planning on running most of the team via **SPOOKS**, but he'd need some clueful people on the inside – I suspect he tapped me for the job of GM. But then the robbery pointed to the bad guys having penetrated a lot further than anyone realized, and the idiot marketing manager called in the cops. So he ensured that when you asked for a native guide, I was hired' – you flash back to that weird interview, with Mr. Pin-Stripe and Mr. Grey and the not-quite-right uncanny valley graphical overlay – 'and he probably leaned on your boss to make sure you were left up here because, after all, you're one of his pawns.'

'Sounds plausible. I think you're right about him tapping you for a job – but it's not just the matter of your old employment being terminated. I think he had you arrested in Amsterdam just to drive you home with your tail between your legs.' She puts her coffee mug down.

'Agh!' The mummy lobe manages to blurt out an indignant denial of your innocence, then shuts down in complete catatonic withdrawal.

She grins at you impishly. 'That's how I'd have done it, anyway.'

'You have an evil mind!'

'And this is a bad thing how, exactly?'

You find yourself returning her grin. 'We're going to need it if we're going to figure out what Barry isn't telling us. As long as you can remember only to use your powers for good.'

'I'll do my best. But anyway, Team Red are dug in, they can listen in on any communications in Scotland, and they can crack any of the common encryption systems in use.' She looks dubious. 'Are we safe?'

'I don't know. Certainly Barry's man-behind-the-curtain operation has got stuff that Team Red don't know about or can't break. And' – another iceberg heaves into view – 'I think I just got it.'

'Got what?' She looks anxious. 'Is it catching?'

'Skill set: Nigel MacDonald. Let's suppose . . . yeah. Let's say Barry got wind of Team Red's existence and also got wind of Chen's little bank robbery before it happened. Yes? Or even just the capability Chen had tucked up his post-graduate-student sleeve. "Nigel MacDonald" shows up, encourages Chen to do the deed, then vanishes after the robbery. Team Red are trying to figure out what the ingenious Mr. Chen was up to, and they realize MacDonald has done a runner, so they focus on him as the accomplice. Then I turn up in their trawl, and—'

Her eyes go wide. 'Carry on, Nigel.'

Nigel? It's not a name you'd have picked for yourself, but *if the hat fits* . . .

'Whoops. They set me up – and you – to go and poke Team Red with a pointy stick, and Team Red are primed to think that I'm their rogue member's partner, right? They don't know what Nigel MacDonald looks like, other than through his NIR entry. Shit, I bet you he's my spitting image!'

'What's the opposite of identity theft? Identity donation?'

She shakes her head. 'Okay, so they've set you up as bait for Team Red. So that makes me . . . the sniper. Right?' She stands up. 'Where's the bathroom?'

You point wordlessly and track her as she heads upstairs. The street light filtering through the hall window outlines the calves of her legs beneath the robe, drawing your eyes after her. It's as if your mind is split three ways. Part of you is still trying to assimilate the fact that the other side play for keeps, and you are *it*. Not the People's Republic of Scotland, but *you*, personally, are facing the sharp end of the best and the brightest of the Chinese Ministry of State Affairs, and you are not qualified to dabble in their games. Another part of you is now almost certain that Elaine is considering inviting you to play a different game, the oldest game there is – and the mummy lobe is tongue-tied and stricken with horror, realizing that, if you take up her invitation, you'll have to explain *both* your little problems . . . And, finally, there's the little fact that you're playing a game you don't understand the rules of against an artificial reality engine that Barry Michaels says has taken Elsie hostage, and that he thought it'd be a good idea to cross-link your National Identity Register files with those of an imaginary double agent. Slick public-school dog-fucker.

With a creak of floor-boards, Elaine sits down beside you on the futon, graceful and elegant as only a gawky collection of librarian-shaped elbows and knees can be. 'I'm trying to figure out what they expect me to do,' she says, arranging the dressing-gown so that it covers her bare toes. 'And you,' she adds. 'I know what role you're meant to play, but who am I?'

She's eerily focussed, and you're not entirely sure which game she's talking about at this point. 'What do you want to be?' you ask, not quite looking at her directly.

'I think' – she licks her upper lip nervously – 'I want to be a spook.' Her pupils are wide and black in the twilight. 'I know what I *don't* want to be.'

'Well, then. I think you're already halfway there. You're a forensic analyst with a security clearance, and you're positioned so uncomfortably close to, uh, "Nigel MacDonald" that if Team Red are tracking our meatspace location, they'll figure MacDonald is under extreme close-up examination.'

'But that's not what you should have asked,' she says, nodding at the stack of dead home-entertainment gear.

'Oh?'

'You should have said, *who* do you want' – she looks you in the eye, and you realize it's *game on*, and you freeze in her path like a pheasant in front of a highland Land Rover; because there's one special unfair rule to this game that applies to you but not to anybody else: and now it's time to tell her, you find you're terrified, but you can't *not* tell her, either, and retain a shred of self-respect – 'to be?'

Which is how Elaine ends up staying the night at your flat.

Face it, it was probably inevitable from the moment you offered to lend her the use of the washing-machine *and* a spare pair of jeans. If you'd realized she was halfway to fancying you, you'd have panicked and stuck your foot so far down your throat you could have kicked yourself in the ass: but by being considerate and friendly, you accidentally convinced her that you're not a desperate loser. So she sat on your futon in the twilight, and you both chewed the paranoid cud and realized how isolated you were. And the next thing you noticed it was dark outside and the washing-machine was still running. 'How do I get back to the hotel from here?' she asked. 'Without using a taxi,' she added with the ghost of a smile.

'There's a bus that'll take you most of the way – or I could walk you' – and then you stood up and looked out the window and saw the rain: not the roaring waterfall that had ambushed you on the way home, but a normal Edinburgh evening's worth of rain, a sporadic tinkling of liquid shrapnel – 'or you can use the futon if you like: there's plenty of spare bedding.'

'Thanks,' she said, a genuine smile now, and patted the futon beside her. 'How about we order in a pizza? You've still got a land-line, right?'

A pizza in the darkness demanded accompaniment – the neglected litre-bottle of Belgian beer in the fridge – and you rummaged around with the cables and plugged your pod straight into the speakers, and then she started rummaging through your music collection until she found a bunch of tracks by Miranda Sex Garden that you'd completely forgotten about to *ooh* and *ah* over, and made small-talk about gigs she'd been to (with a friend, you inferred, conveniently airbrushed out of the frame), and her gaming/re-enactment habit. There'd been an odd moment when she found a project you'd forgotten about sitting under the stack of magazines in the bathroom, but then you'd explained it was your knitting, not an ex's, and she'd taken it in her stride; and that got you both onto talking about how your respective jobs had got in the way of you having a life, and opened the second (unchilled) bottle of Belgian beer. She'd asked how you were feeling after the crash, and confessed her neck was stiff, and you'd gingerly, inexpertly, rubbed it by way of confirmation. Until you'd tipsily noticed how late it was getting and had suggested maybe it was time to go to bed, and fetch the spare bedding – and she'd somehow managed to imply that this was unnecessary. She kissed you like a small, cold creature seeking warmth, and you'd tried desperately to remember how to kiss someone back passionately, half-paralysed with fear that the moment wasn't going to last.

And then you had to say it.

'There's something I've got to tell you,' you said, through a throat that felt like bricks lined with cobwebs.

'Mm?' She tensed slightly and pulled back.

'When I was fourteen, at school' – she stopped moving in your arms, going limp, listening – 'I got caught on camera.'

It was the old shame and embarrassment tap-dance. It took you a moment to gather your wits: during which she tensed. 'What were you doing?'

'I was' – you took a deep breath – 'she was fifteen. We were doing this, more or less. Kissing.'

You felt the tension go out of her. 'That's all?'

'The head teacher was having a, a demonstration. Showing his new camera system to the community relations constable. Who noticed it officially. They called me up.'

'What?' The tension in her arms is systolic, squeezing you like an ocean.

'Under the Sexual Offences Act, the new one they'd just passed, *any* sexual contact with an under-sixteen was – well, we didn't know any better, and it was before they passed the amendment a couple of years later. I accepted a caution. And so did Claire.'

'*What?*' Her arms tightened around you.

'I'm just trying to say.' You took a deep breath: 'You may not want to go any further. With someone who's listed on the sex offender's register as a paedophile.'

She shuddered slightly. 'A *what?*' She sounded incredulous.

'Sexual contact with a minor. It covers kissing or copping a feel, you know? She was nearly a year older than I was; another twelve months and we'd have been legal, anyway, but the trouble is, neither of us knew better than to accept a caution. It means they won't prosecute; but it's an admission of guilt, it gets you a criminal record, and unlike a conviction in court which carries a sentence with an expiry date, a caution is never spent. If I'd kicked up a fuss and demanded a trial, the children's panel would have told the police to piss off and stop wasting their time, but as it is . . . it follows me around.' Your breath was coming too fast. 'I'm *scared*.'

You realized after a moment that she was still holding on to you tightly. Almost like she was drowning. 'Jack.' She spoke into the base of your throat. 'I have to ask you this. Are you a nonce?'

'No, but I have to tell—' No, *you* don't have to tell, but the mummy lobe, the five-year-old who believed what the grown-ups said about always telling the truth, had to confess to *everything*, just like that horrible morning in the head's office –

'Honestly, Jack, you *don't*.' Her nose was at the side of your neck.

You could feel her tongue, exploring your clavicle. 'It's just a bug in the legal code. You don't need to punish yourself any more.'

'What they'll do – Michaels says Elsie is missing—'

'Shut up!' She was fierce, angrier than Lucy was when she found out and dumped you, hotter than the coldly venomous whispering behind your back during that last, miserable (not to mention celibate) year at university. But the strength of her hug told you it wasn't you she was angry at. 'Idiot. How old do you think I was the first time I kissed a boy?'

'I'm afraid—'

She kissed you again. 'They didn't catch me on camera. That's the only difference between us.'

And now she's breathing evenly and slowly, a faint draught

of cool, slightly beery breath riffling through the fine hairs on your arm: and you're studying her closed eyelids and relaxed face, her dark eyebrows relaxed in sleep, by the faint glow of the red LED street-lamp outside the bedroom window, and you're feeling a tenderness almost as vast as the sea of surprise that's crashed through your front door and made itself at home under the duvet, warm and naked and sleeping next to you as if it's the most natural thing in the world.

And you think, *This probably changes everything.* But whether it changes it for better or worse, only time will tell.

SUE: Missing in Action

You know what Liz wants you to do, don't you? She wants you to go and find the nerd and the librarian, Jack Reed and Elaine Barnaby, and put it to them that they can be of help in your investigation. (That, and she wants you to switch all your network services off and wear a tinfoil hat under your four-leafed clover.) Which would be easy enough, if you could only bloody locate the terrible twosome. As it is, when you get back to the station and go live again, you bounce in quick succession off their voice mailboxes, IM receptionists, and social websites. Which tells you a lot about them (Jack's into extreme knitting, Elaine likes dressing up as Maid Marian and hitting people with a sword) but nothing particularly useful like where they're hiding. After half an hour of persistently not finding them – you know they headed over to Glasgow in the morning, but, by the time you get to the point of escalating your search, both their mobies are off-line – you're out of ideas. So it's time to get all twentieth-century and hit the pavement.

Except these two aren't your usual neds. They've got no pavement to hang out on, just a hotel room and a recycled nuclear bunker. By the time you've confirmed they're not filling up a conference room at the hotel, you've narrowed it down a wee bit: but then you hit a blank wall down at the bunker.

'They're not here.' It's Beccy Webster, the Market Stabilization Executive, coming on all Lady Macbeth at you. 'I haven't seen them, they haven't been signed in, and you're wasting your time.' She sniffs and stares down her nose, like you're from the cleaning agency, and you've just smeared printer toner all over her nice clean walls.

'Oh really?' You raise an eyebrow at her, but your authority field is down below half strength. She just looks at you icily and nods.

'Yes. We've tightened up security a lot since last week.'

Fuck. 'Is Mr. Richardson in his office, then?'

'Of course. But he won't tell you any different.' One more sniff, and she signs you in, then stalks off in a huff. *Bitch.* But you've been here before, and you know the way. So you go and knock on Wayne's door, and when it opens, you give him your best shit-eating grin.

'Mr. Richardson. I was hoping to find you here!'

Wayne gives you a rabbit-in-the-headlights look and backs into his room. 'Really?' he asks cautiously.

You follow him in. It's a dingy little hole, lit by a strip of blue-white daylight LEDs strung around the upper edges of the walls. He's got a bunch of tattooed sheepskins with his name on them up on the wall behind his desk, framed so you can't really miss them (ALL-ANGLESEY MIDDLE MANAGEMENT SHEEP SHAGGING CHAMPION, 2014) and a suspiciously large monitor parked on the blotter. 'Have you by any chance seen Jack Reed or Elaine Barnaby today?' you ask him. And this time you've got the speech-stress monitor on real time, just out of curiosity.

'I'm sorry, I haven't,' he says, and he's telling the truth, dammit.

'Do you know where they've gone?' you ask.

'I'm sorry, but no. They haven't been in all day.' He frowns pensively. 'That's odd, now you mention it.' He's green-lit within the error bars, all the way: telling the truth again. *How inconvenient.* 'They were running some sort of database trawl overnight, I think. They demanded access to a lot of rather sensitive data yesterday evening and left a big batch job running.'

'What kind of data were they after?' you ask, just cross-referencing in case it spooks Wayne into putting a foot wrong.

'A bunch of stolen magic plot coupons, described in Structured Treasure Language. I gave him read-only access to our code repository, so he could compile in some modules, and hooks into a bunch of the online auction-houses who buy and trade prestige goodies. I think that's all, but I may be wrong – they were haggling with Sam.'

'Sam . . . ?'

'Sam Couper.'

You twitch up a mug shot you captured earlier, back when you first parachuted into their full-metal panic. 'Is he in today?'

'Sure!' Wayne looks surprised. 'Third door down the hall on your left, you can't miss it: it's the one with the sign saying "Real programmers do it with a float".'

He's right, you can't really miss it. So you walk right up to the door and, hearing voices, open it.

You are in a windowless room, with a huge, curved desk extending around three walls. The desk is covered in flat-panel displays, electronic gadgets, wires, books, print-outs, and half-eaten pizza crusts. The walls are covered with many-coloured maps gridded out with hexagonal overlays: what bare space there is is taken up by an Ansari Space Camp calendar. Three adult males sit bolt-upright in expensive wheelie chairs, facing the centre of the room, whistling a vaguely familiar melody while one of them — balding, thirtyish, red-faced — frowns furiously, concentrating as he juggles four or five small plush Cthulhu dolls. (After a moment you realize they're all trying to whistle the *Twilight Zone* theme, slightly out of key.)

It takes a moment for them to notice you: then the whistling falters to a diminuendo, followed by a splattering of bat-winged beanie-monsters crashing to the institutional blue-green carpet. For a moment there is a guilt-stricken silence so thick you could hear a snowflake fall, then one of them finds his voice. 'What do *you* want?' he demands. It's Sam 'tracer-oute is my bitch' Couper, and his associates Darren and Mike. (Darren is the juggler of eldritch horrors.)

You smile evilly. 'I want to pick your brains.'

Darren shudders, but Sam is made of tougher stuff. 'I already told you everything I know.'

You can't help it. Something about this room seems to exclude you. It must be all the frustrated testosterone sweated into the concrete walls over the years: but whatever it is, it gets right up your nose. 'You told me everything you knew as of three days ago, Mr. Couper. I'd like to know what transpired between yourself and Jack Reed and Elaine Barnaby yesterday afternoon or evening.'

'Huh?' Sam looks surprised. 'It was Wayne. He brought them in and told me, give them what they want. They wanted a list of what we could drag out of the journal logs from the bank, right before the robbery. And the source code to some of our in-house tools so that Reed could hack on them to go search for the missing loot. That's all, I didn't have anything to do with them afterwards.'

'I see.' *Dammit, he's telling the truth, too! How unhelpful.* 'Do you know when they left?'

'When they . . . ? No, I don't. Reed was still here when I went home, around 7:00 p.m. I think he was pulling an all-nighter.'

'Uh-huh.' Whatever else you can say about him, he sounds like a hard worker. You glance at Darren and Mike. 'Do either of you know anything else? Your help would be very much appreciated.'

'Know—' Mike stops. 'Yesterday Jack saved my ass.'

'What do you mean, he saved your ass?' you ask.

'We were – I was being Venkmann, one of the house avatars. Your two pet auditors were messing around in Avalon, and they called me in because they'd tracked down the entry point for the Orcs. Turns out it was a hacked Iron Maiden and someone had converted it into a shredder and added a bunch of traps. We were jumped by slaadi while I was immobilized, but they got me out of it. The other end of the shredder turns out to be in Zhongguo, where we don't have any administrative access.'

It's so much gibberish to you, but you pull one piece out of it as sounding like it needs further clarification. 'Zhongguo?' You mangle his pronunciation. 'Where's that?'

'It's another Zonespace game, run by Hentai Animatics. I captured the fight, if you want I can send you an AVI of it?'

He's trying to be helpful, you realize with a sinking heart. That's just what you don't need – what you're looking for is pushback, not volunteers. 'Aye, if you could forward it to me that would maybe help,' you tell him to shut him up. 'Well, I'll be going.' You hesitate for a moment, looking at the plushies sleeping on the ocean-blue carpet. 'Would you mind telling me what was that all about?' You manage to maintain an even tone of voice that would probably make Liz proud.

'Focus break,' says Russell. 'We work till it gets too much, and then . . . juggling elder gods just seems to help with the stress, you know?'

'I see.' You beat a hasty retreat and manage to hold a lid on it until the door behind you is shut tight on the juggling rocket scientists and their mad ritual.

Hentai Animatics. At least you can see if that tentacle leads somewhere interesting . . .

When you step out of the lift back up to the car-park you discover that a cold drizzle is falling – and you've got even more voice mail to put a damper on the occasion. 'Elaine from Dietrich-Brunner here – can you call me when you get this? I believe we've got a lead for you on the items that were stolen from Hayek Associates.' This does not improve your mood, especially when you check the time-stamp and realize it's at least four hours old.

You call her back, but get put straight through to *her* voice mail. 'Ms. Barnaby? This is Sergeant Smith, returning your call. Could you, or Mr. Reed if you are with him, call me back as soon as possible, please? Thanks.'

You're getting a bad feeling about this. You're supposed to be on top of things, but getting traction on this case is proving remarkably difficult – and that was before your voice mail started keeping its own counsel. Liz's words float back to you: *Whoever's behind it has got their claws into CopSpace.* Normally you wouldn't credit such hallucinations, but Inspector Kavanaugh with her sharp suits and her degrees in criminology and social science isn't so much climbing the greasy pole as riding up it on a personal jet pack; not so much a straight arrow as a guided missile aimed at making chief constable. If she's going all swivel-eyed on you and muttering about spies and cloak-and-dagger stuff, but hasn't gone completely off the deep end (and the arrival of Kemal's bumbling gang of Keystone Kops this morning suggests that if she *is* nuts, the funny farm should be expecting a bumper crop), then you bloody ought to keep your eyes peeled for secret agents doing the funny handshake two-step down by the water of Leith.

So. What else can you do, besides waiting for the nerd and the librarian to surface? You consult your conscience and realize that: (a) you still haven't recorded your evidence in the Hastie breaking-and-entering case, (b) you've been shamelessly neglecting Bob (who, despite your recent abduction to Liz's firm, is still your responsibility), and (c) you've deadended, unless you want to put the Hentai Animatics lead into CopSpace and see where it goes. Which, now you think about it, isn't a bad idea at all. So you wheech out your personal mobie – the one you usually use to keep tabs on Davey – and phone Bob on his, just on the off chance: and he picks up on the second ring. 'Yes?'

'Bob? Sergeant Smith here. You busy?'

'Bus— uh, no, Sergeant! What can I do for you?' He's like an over-eager puppy: you can see him drooling and wagging his tail while clenching a pair of size ten DMs in his mouth.

'I've got a little project, Bob. When you get a chance, I want you to hop along to the nearest library and borrow one of their public terminals. Dig up everything you can find on a company called Hentai Animatics – they run games' – you take time to spell it out to him— 'then text it to me. Don't bother going through CopSpace yet. If you can get it to me by end of shift, I'll be happy.'

'I'll do what I can, Sergeant.' You don't need telepathy to sense the doubt in his voice.

'If you think it sounds flaky, Constable, take it to Inspector Kavanaugh. She's who I'm working for right now.'

'Oh. Well, if you say so, ma'am! I'll get onto it right away. Or as soon as Constable Wilson goes on his next coffee break.'

You end the call, shaking your head slightly at the thought of Paul 'two lumps' Wilson running Bob ragged: stranger things have happened, but not recently. On the other hand, that's your lead taken care of. Now you can piss off back to the station to *finally* record your statement, catch up with big Mac in case he's forgotten you used to work for him, and sort out the paperwork that's been building up since last Thursday. Tomorrow is another day.

ELAINE: MORNING AFTER

There's a subterranean snuffling sound from somewhere under the duvet, then a sense of warmth. You freeze for a moment while the recoil-reflex dies away, then relax into it. An arm slowly reaches across you, an animal comfort — or maybe *he* can't quite believe he isn't alone (and is having second thoughts).

This is not the first time you've woken up with the dawn to find yourself in a strange man's bed. (Well, not a complete stranger — but you've known him for less than a week, and what's that in real terms?) Mind you, on second thoughts, if you're mutually attracted to someone, a week in close proximity is enough time to figure out what you've both got in mind: and no number of extra months will make one whit of difference if one or the other of you isn't interested. And yesterday was more than a little crazy, which always tends to speed things up. But if you lie awake for much longer staring at the floral Rorschach patterns on the inside of the curtains — *where did he get them?* or, more realistically, *who inflicted them on him and why did they hate him so much?* — you're going to start worrying morbidly about whether it was really a good idea, about whether it was *sensible*, rather than being what you both needed at the time. And if you start tugging at the loose ends of your self-doubt like that, not only will you bury the memory of comfort under a cairn of *buts*, you'll stifle any prospect of continuing to explore this thorny maze of insecurity and need that hems you in . . . just like you did last time. Trust you to get involved with a man who's even more insecure than you are.

'Jack?'

He shuffles closer, spooning up to your back. 'Mm?'

'Been awake long?'

He pauses for a long time. 'Had difficulty sleeping.'

'Well.' You press your back against him. 'We're going to have to face the music later.'

'If there *is* a later.'

You bite the inside of your cheek. *Ah well.* 'Isn't there going to be one?' *Please don't tell me he's bailing out already . . .*

'I've been working through what Michaels said—'

You unromantic sod! you think, somewhat relieved.

'—about the implications of a core-router exploit on a national level.'

Oh for fuck's sake. You resist the urge to elbow him in the ribs. 'Yes? Is it bad?'

'Very . . . especially the worst case. Imagine you can't get any money out of a cashpoint, even though there's money in your bank account. That's annoying, right? Now imagine the entire APACS network goes down. And, oh, the contents of your bank account are randomized, along with everyone else's. And all the supermarket stock-control databases go down, so they don't know what's moving and what's on the shelves. And all their suppliers' networks go down, so nobody knows what stock they've got, and where it is. And finally, all the Internet service providers and telcos and cellcos go down hard, and stay down—'

You're fully awake now. 'Stop. You're saying, no communications? No money? No food? What are you saying?'

'That's the start of it.' His tone of voice is maddeningly reasonable. 'No transport, because you can't trust the remote driver services or the online navigation systems and the road-pricing and speed-control systems are down. Medical services are knocked back to emergency-only because NHSNet is down. The police are forced back to relying on runners and whistles, and as for the fire service . . . better hope there aren't any. When people start dying, you can't even identify them, because the identity register's been scrambled, too, so the biometrics point to the wrong personal files.'

'That sounds more like an act of war than a hack.' You roll away from him.

'That's what it would be.' He sounds almost pleased with himself. You don't see why: it's not as if Michaels is paying him to do this kind of freelance analysis while he's in bed, is it? 'And that's the *twentieth-century* model, what they used to call an electronic Pearl Harbour. Things have moved on since then. More likely, it would be a lot more subtle. Footnotes inserted in government reports feeding into World Trade Organization negotiating positions. Nothing we'd notice at first, nothing that would be obvious for a couple of years. You don't want to halt the state in its tracks, you simply want to divert it into a siding of your choice. And if a couple of auditors die in a taxi crash, who cares?'

'What—' You stop, feeling cold. Despite your carefully cultivated habit of keeping work and private life separate, he's got you to put your thinking cap on. Any vague thoughts about a pre-prandial cuddle go out the window. 'You're messing with my head! I need coffee first.'

'You want coffee at a time like this?' You can feel him shaking his head through the mattress.

Fuck him, you think, heavy with regret. *Or not, as the case may be.* You lift the duvet back and sit up, shivering in the cool air. 'Coffee, slave.'

'It doesn't have to happen,' he says hopefully. 'Nobody in their right mind would *do* such a thing, not short of actual pre-existing hostilities. The Guoanbu for sure doesn't want to destroy Scotland's infrastructure – we're part of the EU, their biggest trading partner. On the other hand, by demonstrating that they've got such a capability, they force us to pay attention to it . . . we're into diplomacy here, aren't we?'

There's doubt in his voice, and suddenly you can see what's going through his mind: lying awake at night, next to your sleeping form, thinking morbid thoughts about the future, self-doubt gnawing at him – it's the mirror image of your own uncertainty, only he's externalizing it, projecting it on the big picture rather than worrying about his own prospects. So you swallow your cutting response and instead nod at him, encouraging. Maybe you can salvage something more than memories if you help him get this out of his system first.

'A "capture the flag" exercise by a bunch of deniable hackers – well, either it works, or it doesn't. If it works, they've got the kind of espionage edge that the old-time CIA or KGB would have creamed themselves over, and if it fails, they've learned something.' He pulls on a tee-shirt by the light of the bedside lamp and pads around to your side of the room. 'Want to stay here? Or come downstairs and talk?'

You slide out of bed and pick up his dressing-gown, from where you dropped it last night. 'I'm listening.'

'Michaels wants to use us to flush out Team Red's resident agent so he can then back-track through their audit trail and roll up the hole Team Red came in through. Assuming we trust him when he says **SPOOKS** isn't compromised, all we have to do is set up a situation where they come for Nigel

MacDonald, then wrap them up . . . And there's always the chance that my filter tool has caught some more stolen prestige items overnight.'

His happy babble is slowing down, his uncertainty finally rising to the level of consciousness. 'Jack. Listen.' You're standing behind him. It'd be really easy to reach out and put your arms around his waist, if you could just break through his preoccupation. 'You're talking about people who have, at best, been involved in a criminal conspiracy to commit robbery, and at worst, have been involved in preparing the groundwork for a major act of terrorism. Who come from a country where people who do that sort of thing usually end up dead, and who know they're expendable, and we're sniffing around after them.' He tenses. 'Remember last time? Remember your niece is still missing? And you think getting in deeper is a good idea?'

You can see it all laid out before you. All you have to do is draft a whitewash report, *nothing found*, and scurry back to London with your tail between your legs before the shit hits the fan. Maggie and Chris will pat you on the head, and you can get back onto the Dietrich-Brunner promotion treadmill (even without the funny handshake, nod, and wink from Barry Michaels that says *she's one of us, look after her*). And you can put Jack on a flight to Amsterdam to continue installing the hangover he was working on when this whole mad whirlwind blew out of nowhere to engulf you both. You don't have to see each other ever again, and nobody needs to get hurt. Jack can go back to biting his belly raw over an unjust wound, and you can go back to keeping the world at bay. Chalk it up to experience and leave Michaels to swear over the wreckage of his intricately planned human-engineering hack. Jump back into your emotional coffin and slam the lid; nobody needs to get hurt.

And if this wasn't the morning after, that's exactly what you'd do.

He shudders and begins to turn round. 'Elaine, I don't think they'll just let me leave. There's stuff I used to do in my last job, I can see why they'd want me—'

You can feel his breath on your cheek, shallow and anxious. You lean towards him. 'If you get yourself stabbed again, I will be *very angry* with you.'

'I' – he reaches out to you hesitantly – 'know.'

And then the doorbell rings.

JACK: BODY OF EVIDENCE

The moment is as fragile as a painted eggshell. The doorbell rings just as Elaine's early-morning chill seems to be thawing: just as you pick up her first indication that she isn't, actually, embarrassed or mad at you or wishing she'd chewed her arm off at the shoulder and slipped out the window rather than waiting for dawn. It is an instant laden with profundity – and the bell shatters it.

'You'd better answer that,' she says, looking at you as calmly as a robot, the urgency of the moment suddenly masked.

'Okay.' You grab your underpants and hop towards the staircase, pausing to get one foot in at a time.

The doorbell chimes again just as you get to it. You pause for a moment, then stick your face up to the security lens. The fish-eye view is hard to interpret, but it looks like a police uniform. Your stomach does a double back-flip of Olympic-qualifying proportions as you twist the Yale lock and pull. 'Hello?'

'Mr . . . Reed? Jack Reed?' There's something odd about the constable, and then it clicks: he's reading from a hand-written piece of paper. (That, and he looks very young and inexperienced.) 'Inspector Kavanaugh sent me. Would you be aware of the location of a Ms. Barnaby?'

'I'm Jack. She's here, too.' The handwritten note gives you a sudden flicker of optimism. 'What can we do for you?'

'If I can come inside, sir?' You take a step back, involuntarily. The constable looks a little unhappy about something, as if he's steeling himself to deliver some bad news. 'I'm told that yesterday you were in Glasgow. Is that correct?'

An icy moment of clarity: *Should I call my solicitor now?* you wonder.

'Yes,' calls Elaine, and you look round automatically. She's standing at the top of the staircase, huddled inside your dressing-gown.

'I see, ma'am.' The cop nods, and you notice something else that's odd – he's not wearing heavy-framed glasses, and there's no webcam Velcro'd to the front of his anti-stabby vest. You peer at the name tag on his chest: LOCKHART. 'Well, in that case, the inspector said to pass on her apologies, and would you mind coming down to the city mortuary to attempt to' – he swallows – 'identify a deceased person for us?'

'Oh *fuck*,' you say, just as Elaine expresses a similar sentiment. You glance at her and see your own shock, mirrored and multiplied.

'I'm sorry, sir.' PC Lockhart sounds mortified.

It's got to be Mr. Wu Chen, prize bastard and the only person you know who was angling to get himself killed. One James Bond movie too many tries to bubble past your tongue, but the mummy lobe clamps down before you can say something you might regret later, like *he knew the shortest way to my heart* or *the bastard owes me a new keyboard*. Because that would be Inappropriate, and saying Inappropriate things at the Wrong Time in front of a Police Officer is bound to get you into Hot Water, and despite the fact that the past week has somewhat taken the shine off your virginal relationship with the forces of law'n'order, and despite the fact that Elaine (astonishingly) doesn't think you're some kind of pervert and (even more astonishingly) seems to want to install herself in your life, you have no desire to become any more intimate with their ways than you already are.

'We'll come along,' you hear yourself say. 'We're just . . . up. Do you mind if we get dressed first?'

Lockhart looks mortified, as if he's dreaming and has just realized he's wearing a pink tutu under his tunic. 'No! No! I'll just be waiting . . . '

'Down here, yes.' You retreat upstairs towards Elaine, who is mouthing something at you furiously but completely inaudibly. She waits until you're in the bedroom, then shuts the door. 'What about my suit?'

'Oh.' You stop to think, one leg in your jeans and the other out. 'I'll go get it out of the machine.' Too late you realize that what she was *really* asking was, *Do you have an ironing board?* The miracles of modern fabric technology only stretch so far.

'Never mind.' She rummages through the closet and pulls out a pair of your combat pants that have seen better days, and a SIMS 4: NOW IT'S REAL tee-shirt. 'Have you got a belt? I'll drop in at the hotel afterwards . . . '

A couple of minutes later you're both downstairs and pulling your boots on. PC Lockhart is hovering and havering as if he's not quite sure what to do with himself. You duck into the kitchen and scoop Elaine's business weeds into a spare carrier bag while she pointedly makes small-talk in the living room, grab your own jacket, wallet, and phone – and then it's time to go. 'If you'll follow me, please?' asks Lockhart.

Unlike the Glaswegian cop, Lockhart doesn't rate a souped-up Volvo with a stack of electronic countermeasures and a boot full of hazard warning signs. You end up knee-cap to knee-cap with Elaine in the back of a wee white Toyota hybrid that looks like something a real car would carry as a life-boat. Lockhart drives like a myopic granny, slowing for every speed pillow and chicane as he potters along the road to Canonmills, then uphill towards the city centre with the power pack whining like an overloaded dentist's drill (from back in your childhood, before dentists got their hands on the orbital death-rays they use nowadays for hunting down unfortunate plaques of bacteria and nuking them back into the pre-Cambrian).

Edinburgh's city mortuary is a flat-roofed brutalist brick-and-concrete bunker occupying a hole between two of the tall stone buildings of the Cowgate, in the heart of the old town. Time runs differently in Edinburgh: the old town is old because it dates to the middle ages. (There are rumours of entire lost streets down here within the mediaeval city walls, barricaded, buried, and built-over after the plague carried away their denizens.) Lockhart approaches the mortuary directly, driving up the Mound and over and down through the Grassmarket, where they used to hang witches and heretics. Picturesque and gingerbread it might be, but this ain city has a dark history, and no mistake. You travel in silence, shoulder to shoulder, and when Elaine takes hold of your hand, her fingers are cold and tense.

Finally, Lockhart turns sharply uphill and then slides into the carpark. There's a loading bay at the gloomy back for the ambulances and hearses, but the ordinary traffic gets the view of the pub opposite. Lockhart gets out and holds the door for you while you clamber into the daylight and blink as Elaine unpacks herself. 'Where's the inspector?' she asks, looking round.

'She said she'd be here.' Lockhart fumbles with his handset, which takes a moment to boot. 'Go on inside.'

He's still fumbling with the handset as you go through the mirrored doors and find yourself facing a woman who could pass for Elaine's elder sister – the tougher, short-haired one carved from cold, grey northern marble. 'Mr. Reed, Ms. Barnaby? I'm Inspector Kavanaugh. Sue Smith – Sergeant Smith – has been telling me about you.' She doesn't look like a happy camper, and for an instant the mummy lobe starts yammering about guilt, urging you to confess to something, anything, *everything* – the eighth of slate in the stash tin that PC Lockhart failed to spot under the sofa cushions, or the time you swiped Paul Doulton's Mars Bar in Secondary Two. You keep a lid on it: you seem to be getting better about not incriminating yourself the moment an officer of the law blinks at you. 'I was hoping to make your acquaintance yesterday.'

'Really?' asks Elaine, with every appearance of being intensely interested. 'We were in Glasgow in the morning, then in a meeting.'

'A *meeting*.' The way Kavanaugh pronounces the word makes it sound like a criminal conspiracy to conduct business in accordance with the rules of procedure: or maybe it's just her mouth wash disagreeing with her. (A quick tongue around your teeth convinces you that perhaps taking the time for a brush and shave wouldn't have been a bad idea.) 'Well, that's as may be. Barry Michaels called me – at home, on a voice line, I might add – to tell me you were working for him. And he suggested you might be able to help me clear up a little problem.'

'A problem——' you begin to echo, as Elaine elbows you in the ribs.

'Of course we'd be happy to help,' she butts in smoothly: 'Insofar as it's compatible with our duties.' *Ouch,* you think. 'What can we do for you?'

You've got a sinking feeling about this. 'I'd like to ask you if you can formally identify a deceased gentleman.'

Elaine grabs your hand. You tense as she draws close. 'What happened?'

'I can tell you more afterwards,' says Kavanaugh. She glances at the inner doorway. 'Jimmy? I've got your witnesses.' The speakerphone crackles, and then there's a buzz as the door unlatches.

You've seen mortuaries a hundred times on television, but that doesn't do the place justice. For one thing they smell a bit like a hospital . . . only, not. And the quiet. It's like the offices at the funeral home after Mum died. Sure, there are people going in and out of small rooms with tablets and bundles of paperwork, but there's a marked shortage of levity in this place. If you could bottle whatever it is and sell it to schools, they'd give you a gong: it's the concentrated essence of sobriety. And you've just been dragged into it without even a shave and a hang-over.

Elaine trots along after the long-legged inspector, dragging you along in her wake. Her lips are a thin blue slash beneath the old-fashioned fluorescents. 'In here,' says the inspector, holding an office door open. For a moment you worry — but it's just an office, with a desk and a half-bald man in a white coat but no stethoscope. 'Dr. Hughes? These are my witnesses. You might want to go easy, they haven't had much warning.'

Hughes raises an eyebrow. 'That makes three of us,' he comments. A deep breath: 'Well, I assume you know where you are?' You force yourself to nod. 'Good. Well, I'm the duty pathologist today, and I gather the inspector here would like you to confirm a positive identification. Have either of you ever done this before?' You shake your head. Elaine's grip on your hand tightens as Hughes gives the inspector a sharp look. 'They're not next of kin, are they?'

Your heart flops around madly, missing a beat. *Who can it be?* Your hands are sweating. You've been here before, hungover in the presence of the law to witness something you don't want to admit –

'Adult male.' Kavanaugh shakes her head, then glances at you. 'Is something the matter, Mr. Reed?'

'No – I mean, not this: I don't think so.' You take a deep breath. The mummy lobe kicks up a cacophonous din, demanding that you unload everything you know on the inspector *right now*, but you manage to beat it into submission: 'I have a weak stomach.' Which is an exaggeration, but not by much.

'Alright.' That's Dr. Hughes. He glances at Inspector Kavanaugh. 'In that case I'll take Ms . . .'

'Ms. Barnaby and Mr. Reed.'

'Yes. Ms. Barnaby? If you're comfortable with this, in a moment I shall show you into the, ah, viewing room. Mr. Reed, if you'd like to wait here. After you've had enough time, I'll bring you back here and take Mr. Reed in while the inspector records your statement.'

'Is it' – Elaine's voice is uncharacteristically weak – 'I mean, is this necessary?'

Dr. Hughes glances at the inspector. Kavanaugh clears her throat. 'I'm afraid it is, under the circumstances.' She gives you a significant look. 'I believe you know enough about image filtering to explain why to me.'

The bottom drops out of your stomach again, just after you thought you'd gotten a grip on yourself. Elaine's hand slips away, lubricated by the sweat of your palm. 'I'm ready,' she says.

They disappear through a disappointingly ordinary-looking

inner-office door, and Kavanaugh focusses on you. 'Yes?' she asks.

'Did Michaels . . .' You swallow. 'Did he tell you about my niece?'

'About who?' In the bright office light you can see her pupils dilate.

'He says his people are looking for her,' the mummy lobe pushes out. Then you add, consciously: 'And I don't trust him.'

'Christ, I don't blame you for *that*.' She looks concerned. 'What's the story?'

You explain the background, weird calls, and the photographs, and the police reports – and that last call. It's not true that the inspector has a Botox-frozen face: it goes through quite a few expressions in just thirty seconds, running through a spectrum of surprise and outrage. But then she cuts you off with a brief gesture. 'Later.' She glances at the door. 'If you can identify the person in there, I'd be very grateful. But I—' The door opens and she swallows whatever she was about to come out with. Framed in the opening is a whey-faced Elaine, looking between you and the inspector as if she's certain one of you killed Colonel Mustard in the Drawing Room with the Candlestick.

It's your turn. Dr. Hughes beckons. 'Just follow me,' he says, not unkindly. There's a short corridor, then another door, and – *a window running along one wall?* 'Take your time,' he says. 'When you've seen enough, or if you feel at all unwell, we'll go outside.' Which is all very easy to say, but you *do* feel unwell: it's giving you a horrible sense of déjà vu, and not in a good way.

A light comes on in the room on the other side of the window. It's small and bare, with tiled walls, and a trolley with a draped form.

You blink, trying to bring it into focus. He looks like he's deeply asleep, what you can see of him: head and shoulders only. And something is *very* wrong indeed, you realize immediately. Your mouth is dry. You work your jaw, trying to get your salivary glands to lubricate your tongue. 'I saw him yesterday,' you say, and you're pretty sure you're telling the truth. 'That's enough.'

'Thank you.' This time you see Hughes flip the switch. 'Are you feeling alright?' he asks, solicitously. 'The toilets are just round here—'

'No.' You take a deep breath and try to pull yourself together. 'I'm okay.'

Hughes leads you back out through the short corridor and into his office, where Inspector Kavanaugh is waiting, with Elaine, whose expression of numb surprise you can feel mirrored on your own face.

'Well?' Asks Kavanaugh. She glances at Elaine warningly. 'Would you please state for the record the name of the person in the observation room as it is known to you?'

'Certainly.' You lick your lips. And now for the surprise package. 'He's called Wayne, uh, Richmond? No, Richardson. And he was the Marketing Director at Hayek Associates.'

SUE: CIVIL CONTINGENCIES

Morning. It's Mary's day off work, and you've just about got the wild wee one into his school uniform and fed, and you are about to strap your kit on and hie thee to the cop shop when Davey's phone rings. It's a kiddie-phone, bright orange-and-black plastic bristling with gadgets, and he listens for a moment before handing it to you: 'It's for yiz, maw.'

'Who is it?' you ask, as you try to find a clear spot to dump your kit.

'It's some wummun,' he says. *Very helpful.*

'Aw, fer crying out—' You dump your overladen webbing belt on the floor and make a grab for the phone. It's probably some telesales bot – they've been pesting him lately – 'Yes?'

'Sergeant?' Your back stiffens instinctively: you know that voice.

'Skipper?' You glance round, warily. Davey's looking at you, round-eyed and mischievous like some kind of self-propelled phone tap. 'Go comb your hair, Davey.'

Davey legs it. 'What's up, boss?'

Liz Kavanaugh is matter-of-fact. 'We've got a big problem, Sue. First, I want you to switch your kit off and pull the batteries. You're not wired yet, are you?'

'Jesus, skipper, that's against—'

'Don't I fucking know it!' she snarls, and your hair stands

on end. 'Sorry, Sergeant, I don't want anyone else to get . . . Quick. Are you wired?'

'Not yet, I was just sorting out the wee one first. I'm not on shift for another forty minutes.'

'You'll be putting in for overtime and expenses before today's over, I'm afraid. Okay, here's what I want you to do; you may want to make notes on paper, but do not, *under any circumstances*, put them into any kind of machine. First, I want you to get over to the nearest Tesco's and buy six prepaid mobies, using your own credit card. We'll put them through expenses later, so keep the paper receipt. Second, I want you to get over to Fettes Row. Get one of the phones registered and charged up, then find Detective Inspector Long, give him the phone, and tell him to phone me. The number I'm carrying today is – you've got a pen?'

She goes on like this for a couple of minutes as you frantically scribble on the guts of an organic Weetabix box. Finally: 'Are there any questions, Sergeant?'

You don't know where to begin. *Are you off your meds, skipper?* Would be a good starting place, if a wee bit tactless: *Have you cleared this with the military?* Might be another. Liz isn't simply not going by the book, she's just about throwing it in the shredder. Finally, you clear your throat. 'Aye, skipper. Isn't this a bit, kind of, irregular?'

The giggle that blasts out of Davey's phone nearly makes you drop it in the cereal bowl. 'You just noticed? How perceptive of you!' She takes a moment to collect herself. 'Sorry, Sue, we're a bit stressed around here right now. The situation is, ah, at least as serious as the possibilities I outlined to you yesterday. I have in my hand a written letter from the chief constable – typed on a manual typewriter – citing his orders from the minister of justice – which were *handwritten* – invoking the Civil

Contingencies Act. It's fall-out from yesterday. Have you got that? This time the shit's *really* going to hit the fan . . .'

At the local Tesco you find yourself in the automatic checkout aisle behind two other officers who you know by sight. Your hand-baskets are full of mobies. You all carefully avoid making eye contact with one another, but you can't help noticing that one of them is also stocking up on water bottles.

You're not that slow on the uptake; before you left home you washed out your backpack hydration system, the one you use for football matches, and filled it with freshly filtered water: and you made sure to give Davey an extra-large packed lunch, and five times as much bus fare as he's likely to need to get home. He's wearing his good shoes and has a spare pair of socks and a dog-eared old A-Z in his pack with gran's address and a couple of other safe houses marked in red crayon – just in case. Liz Kavanaugh seems to think it's going to be manageable, but paper doesn't fail when the critical infrastructure goes down. About the only reason you don't crack and put the bairn on a train to see his uncle in Liverpool is the worry that it might break down or get lost in the middle of nowhere. Which might be worse. Wouldn't it?

After you drop five of the six cheap mobies off with Inspector Long, he gives you two more anonymous cereal-packet phones to carry, along with a long handwritten list of phone numbers and names. You don't have to be a rocket scientist to figure out it's a skeletal org chart, division heads and support units etched in hard black pencil. So you go downstairs and draw out a car – unsurprisingly, almost everything with wheels that turn is already on the road, somewhere – then head over to Meadowplace Road to find the inspector.

What you find at the station is something like an ants' nest that's been doused in paraffin but not yet set alight. There's a frazzled constable on the front desk, and he's splitting his time between turning MOPs away – 'come back tomorrow, we're too busy to take complaints right now' (which is just *not* how it's done) – and grilling every uniform who comes in late. He sees you immediately. 'Sergeant Smith? You got any numbers for me, miss?'

You plonk your ad hoc phone book on the blotter in front of him. 'Is this what you're after? I cannae let you keep it – it's for Inspector Kavanaugh.'

'Just give me a minute . . . ' He goes over it with a pen, copying lines into the gaps on his own list. 'We're not to use the photocopiers, the chief said. Not till they've been vetted by ICE.'

You take a deep breath. *Well, if that's how it is . . .* 'There's a team meeting on the Hayek Associates job. You know where it is? I'm due there.'

'Room 204.' He glances up. 'I havenae seen the inspector yet, miss. You go up there, and I'll send someone up with yer list when I'm through with it.'

You thank him and head for the staircase. On your way through the office you notice that the monitors are all turned to face the walls and there's an unusual clattering, thudding noise – someone's wheeched out a metal box with a keyboard on the front of it and they're banging the keys like they're wee trip-hammers. There's a sheet of paper sticking out the top, and it vibrates whenever they hit it: a *typewriter?* Phones are ringing everywhere, the bleeping of cheap no-name mobies, and there's a big red plastic thing with a rotary dial on the front on the duty sergeant's desk, like something out of an Agatha Christie video. *Jesus,* you think, *if we're knocked back into the twentieth century, how're we going to know what to charge the customers with?* It's a scary thought: the succession of criminal justice acts that the old British government passed, and then the revised justice acts since independence, replaced the old catch-all offences like 'breach of the peace' with a huge array of very specific charges ('being aggressive in charge of a Segway or similar scooter after midnight in a residential area'), such that you really need the expert system on your phone to figure out precisely how to throw the charge book at them. Never mind the fact that the station doesn't have a bloody paper ledger anymore and you can't actually book a customer into the cells without a worki . . .

You slip in the back of room 204 and find it's already crowded. You've seen the faces before, at last week's video conference – this time they're all present and correct and not wearing their goggles. Verity looks royally fucked-off about something or other, and the detective suits aren't looking too happy either. And there are others present – what looks like the whole of the murder team from St. Leonard's, who were working on the Pilton case, chasing Liz's chimerical blacknet. *Full house.* Verity glares directly at you. 'I believe you've got a phone for me, Sergeant?'

'Certainly, sir.' You walk right on up to the front and hand it to him, along with its box. 'The front desk is copying the phone book for you. By hand.'

His cheek twitches as he turns the gadget over in his hands. 'I see a camera.' He mimes snapping a shot as he turns to Bill the Suit. 'Tell 'em to photograph the pages and text me the picture. That'll do for now. Get the list typed up and reshoot it, then send it to one of those online OCR services.' Bill looks shocked. 'Go on! If they're Googling all the civilian traffic in Scotland, it's too late, already.' Behind you, the door opens again; you glance round and recognize Liz Kavanaugh. 'Ah, good,' rasps Verity, as Bill heads for the door to engage in his amateur photography. 'I was wondering when you'd get here!'

'Yes, well, I was regrettably delayed.' Liz looks at you pointedly.

'You've got a phone for me?' You hand the mobie over. She takes it and goes over to the vacant chair next to Verity. 'I had to stop to get eyeball confirmation of a murder victim's ID.'

'*Another* . . . ?' Verity's eyebrows go up. 'Is it connected?'

'Definitely.' Liz grins like a skull.

'Well, shite. If you'll pardon my French.' Verity doesn't hold with bad language, which makes him something of an anomaly north of the border. 'Who is it this time?'

'Wayne Richardson, a Hayek Associates' employee who has been helping with our investigations this past week.' She nods at you, and you tense. 'He was the source of the original crime report and the first indication that, uh, Nigel MacDonald was *missing*. I caught up with our two external investigators, Mr. Reed and Ms. Barnaby, and they confirmed his identity.'

'That makes it, what? Four this week?'

'Three, sir,' Liz says firmly. 'Because Nigel MacDonald doesn't exist.'

Verity rolls his eyes. 'Explain.'

'Sir.' Liz faces the roomful of faces. 'There's a body in Pilton. Last night, there was another body in Strathclyde – looked like a foreign-exchange student who'd gone for a midnight walk on the Clockwork Orange tracks, except his blood alcohol was zero, serum cortisol was sky-high, and there were other phys-ical signs of stress – and, earlier in the day, he'd tried to stab a person of interest in my other case. This morning Wayne Richardson of Hayek Associates shows up dead: hit and run, apparently on his way to work, except that the hit and run in question was a taxi under remote drive authority by persons unknown.' There's an audible wave of angry muttering from around the room. 'These events are connected to an *alleged* kidnapping down south the day before yesterday, to yesterday's fun and games involving Europol, a warehouse in Leith, and a bunch of very expensive servers' – you can see Verity wincing at the memory – 'and this morning's major incident alert and to the flat on the meadows with a satellite uplink on the roof we did over earlier in the week, so if anyone hasn't got the message already, if you've got a PDA, or an official phone, or a personal phone you owned more than twenty-four hours ago, switch the bloody thing off *right now*.'

Verity glares at the assembled roomful of dibbles. '*Do* it!' There's another wave of fidgeting and you get the feeling that most of it is make-show to clue the boss in that various folks aren't totally fucked in the heid – Liz said *Civil Contingencies Act* earlier, and that's enough to put the wind right up you because that bland-sounding piece of legislation lays out the rules for declaring a State of Emergency, and you'd bet good money that every other one of the lads and lasses here got tipped off about it before they started their shift, just like you. 'Continue, Inspector.'

'I don't know who our Pilton body is, and I doubt we're going to find out via the normal channels, because he wasn't listed in the National Identity Register.' Which is a pish-poor excuse for a mess of an identity system, has been ever since the idiots who brought it in got the wind up them over the civil disobedience campaign and turned it into a dumping ground for every buggy civil service client tracking database the pre-defederalization UK owned – but still, *not listed* is a headache: it's a synonym for *up to no good* in copspeak. 'I *do* know that Nigel MacDonald, who we've pegged as missing in suspicious circumstances in the Hayek Associates investigation, is in the register but doesn't actually exist, but I've been ordered not to investigate him further because it's a matter of national security. His flat was rented by parties unknown and seems to have been used as a remixer by the blacknet we've been looking for, and I suspect the late Mr. Richardson could have told us some more about that if he wasn't currently occupying a drawer in the mortuary.'

At that point, the muttering gets loud enough that Kavanaugh stops talking and waits for it to die down. 'If you'll permit me to continue? Yes? The third one, the exchange student, was implicated in the same business, and so are Hayek Associates, who employed the fourth, although I am *assured'* — at this point she stares, unreassuringly, at Verity — 'that they're on our side. This is a national-security clusterfuck rather than a police investigation, and we would be shutting it down forthwith, as soon as we've dotted the i's and crossed the t's, except for the small problem that we've been told by the intel community that whoever we're up against has penetrated not only the national switched telecommunications backbone but CopSpace from top to bottom *and* we're to go on standby for a major terrorist incident within the next twenty-four hours.' Liz pauses to take a deep breath, but nobody interrupts: 'I don't know where they got hold of all this, but they're taking it seriously enough that the minister of justice has just issued an Emergency Regulations order as set out under Part 2 of the Civil Contingencies Act, while they redistribute fresh authentication keys to every telco and ISP in the country. And I believe that's what the chief inspector is just about to tell us all about . . .'

ELAINE: Gentleman and Players

It is a hell of a shock, being expected to identify a dead body before breakfast, and you do not appreciate it – especially when you're also trying to digest the significance of whatever happened between you and Jack last night (and won't *that* suck, if Margaret or Chris or one of the other friendly piranhas at the office find out that you've been shagging the gamekeeper?) and you're spending your sanity points worrying about what the hell the two of you have got yourselves into at a practical, spy-versus-spy, level. Not to mention Jack's criminal-record equivalent of a lousy credit history with fries on top. Which is why you're really quite relieved when the inspector has to rush off somewhere, pausing only to extract from you a promise that you'll keep your phone switched on in case she wants to talk to you later. She witnesses for Dr. Hughes while the two of you sign a great big ledger – on real bleached wood-pulp – to agree that on this day you have confirmed the identity of Richardson, Wayne, lately employed by Hayek Associates. And you're hanging around in the lobby (waiting while Jack uses the toilet) when the doors open again and none other than Barry Michaels of Hayek Associates walks in.

'Ah, Miss Barnaby.' He smiles, affably. 'And Mr. Reed is about, I take it?' He holds up a keyfob. 'Come drive with me.'

You know an order when you hear one, but you still bridle at it: 'You'll have to do better than that!'

'Yes.' He puts his smile back in its box. 'It's time to do breakfast. Today's going to be a busy day.'

'The hell it is.' Seeing Wayne laid out on the slab turned your stomach. 'I didn't sign on for this, Barry, I signed on for an artificial reality game, not Raw-head and Bloody-bones. We – I – quit.'

He shakes his head. 'I wish you could, believe me, I wish you could.'

'Could what?' Jack chooses just this exact moment to pop out of the lavatory, shaking his head in ground-hog confusion. 'What's up?'

'We're doing breakfast. I was just explaining to Miss Barnaby that it's too late to opt out.'

'The hell it is—'

You turn away, but he's too fast: '*They have your number,* Elaine. *I'd* let you go – but Team Red won't.'

Whoops. You stop, and take a deep, angry breath. 'I think you owe us an explanation.'

'Over breakfast? I'm buying.'

'Mm, *breakfast,*' says Jack, doing a convincing imitation of a dumb-ass cartoon character.

'Fuck off . . .' But it's too late, you're outvoted, and besides, you're wearing his trousers. What else is there to do but listen to Michaels's pitch?

Michaels leads you down an alleyway, across a main road, and into a gloomy-looking pub built into what looks to have been a mediaeval dungeon – all vaulted stone archways a metre and a half high, complete with blackened oak barrels wearing restaurant-drag table-tops. There are TV screens everywhere, as if trying to deny the essentially antediluvian origins of the place, but they can't cover up the pervasive smell of rising damp. 'The cooked breakfast here is really quite good,' Michaels asserts, 'very twentieth-century Scottish.'

You let yourself be steered into ordering the cooked breakfast. You're a good girl and you take your prophylactic statins every evening religiously: saturated fats can hold no fear for you, at least in moderation and followed by a penance of tossed green salad.

'We should be secure in here,' Michaels explains over the top of the menu: 'The walls are three feet thick and made of solid stone. People used to avoid the place – they couldn't get a phone signal inside, and installing wifi was pointless – until a particularly bright landlord figured out she could make money by pitching it as a stuckist hang-out.' And indeed when you look at your phone you see you've got zero bars of signal, even though you're within sight of a window looking out onto the canyonlike depths of the Cowgate.

'So you wanted to tenderize us before breakfast.' Jack leans back against the bare stone wall. 'Was that what that little piece of Grand Guignol back at the mortuary was all about, then?'

Michaels has the decency to look abashed. 'That's a bit unfair.'

'Really?' You glare at him. 'The police roust us out of bed to come and view a body, and you *just happen* to be passing? Pull the other one!'

Michaels picks up a fork and stabs it in your direction: 'Next you'll be accusing me of murdering poor Wayne. Can you get it through your thick head that *it's not about you?*'

'If it's not about us, then who killed Wayne?' asks Jack.

Michaels frowns. 'I wish I knew,' he mutters, shoving his unruly forelock back into place. 'Oh, I mean it was clearly Team Red who did it – but the *why* of it is another matter.'

Jack tenses. 'I heard something,' he says, reluctantly.

'Yes?' Michaels raises an eyebrow.

'When I was working late. Day before yesterday.'

You feel like shaking him. 'What did you—' Michaels holds up a hand.

'I was on my way out, about elevenish. Most of the lights were out. I heard a couple of voices arguing in one of the meeting rooms. One of them was – I'm pretty sure of this – Wayne Richardson.' He winces. 'I don't know who the other was. Male, that's all. I thought you might know.'

Michaels is looking at Jack incredulously. 'You don't know who it was?'

'No.' Jack looks frustrated. 'It's rude to listen at doors, did you know that . . . ?'

You bite your lower lip. It would not do to giggle at this point, they'd both get entirely the wrong idea about you, and that would be a mistake. *Poor Jack: too honest for his own good.* But you knew that already, didn't you?

'Oh Jesus fucking Christ,' Michaels says disgustedly. 'You thought it was *me*?'

Jack just sits there, looking defensive.

'Well, why didn't you say so before?' Michaels demands.

This has gone far enough. 'Stop that!' you tell him. 'Jack had no good reason to trust you, yesterday.' You're not sure he has any reason to do so today, either. You take a stab in the dark. 'Why should we trust you?'

Michaels is about to say something, but Jack beats him to it. 'Someone's penetrated your operation,' he says, remarkably calmly. 'And you don't know who. They were working with Wayne, weren't they?'

'Go on.' Michaels rolls with the punch.

Jack swallows. 'Let's start with, who is Nigel MacDonald a

cover for?' When Michaels doesn't respond, he raises an eyebrow. 'Well?'

Michaels shakes his head pensively. 'There used to be an old joke in role-playing circles – it isn't funny, these days – that there were only a thousand real people in the UK – everybody else was a non-player character. Now it's pretty much the reverse.'

That's worth blinking at. You can't quite picture the urbane establishment-issue Barry Michaels as a spotty teenage D&Der, but it would explain his current position, wouldn't it? **SPOOKS** has got to have taken years to develop – it's clearly a long-term project – which implies funding and pilot projects and all sorts of R&D behind it.

'Nigel MacDonald was a useful sock-puppet for the **SPOOKS** development group at CESG,' he says slowly. 'He was there so they could interact with the staff quants without tipping them off that they were actually talking to various people inside the Doughnut.'

'The Doughnut?'

'Cheltenham.' He frowns. 'So we had this telecommuter on the payroll. Wayne tapped me on the shoulder about him a year ago when he realized Nigel didn't actually live anywhere – he figured there was a payroll scam going on. So I rolled out the cover story and told Wayne to play along.'

Jack nods thoughtfully. 'What's the cover?' He sounds resigned, almost as if he can guess what's coming.

'Hayek Associates play by the rules – officially.' Michaels bares his teeth, briefly. 'We don't have a dirty-tricks department, *officially*.'

'Ah.' Jack looks satisfied, but you're anything but. 'What kind of dirty tricks?' you demand.

'The industry – the games biz – has a habit of playing

dirty. Keeping players happy is all about fun, isn't it?' says Michaels. 'So by extension, a tool that can tweak how much *fun* you're having in a given game can also . . . '

'He's talking about sabotage tools,' Jack cuts in. He gives Michaels a hard look. 'That was your story for Wayne?'

Michaels nods. 'Yes, basically. If we ever had to do anything deniable, we wanted a scapegoat to pin it on.'

'What did Wayne do after you told him that?' Jacks asks.

'He played along.' Michaels looks thoughtful. 'He suggested we flesh out the role, actually. Rent a flat, pay the bills, work up a credit history, so we'd have something to look shocked about if anyone ever started digging.' He looks straight at you: 'When the police broke down the MacDonald residence door and found a blacknet node, *that* was a shock. But by that point the cover story was out, so it could have been anyone at Hayek Associates, really. But that' – he nods at Jack, with an expression something like respect – 'is when we realized we had a real problem. Now we know that part of the problem was Wayne. The question is, who else is involved?'

You swallow. It's time to lay some cards of your own on the table. 'I don't like this game, Barry. I came up here to audit a bank, not identify murder victims.' (Or be abducted by kamikaze taxis, or conscripted by the secret service.) 'I'm not cut out for this, and neither is Jack.'

'Really? I'd never have guessed,' he snarks at you. 'Before you get on your high horse, I'd like to say that you're absolutely wrong about that last bit. You're here because you're both graduates of an extensive training course. Only you didn't see it as training, you paid to subscribe to it; it's the difference between work and play, nothing more. You're complaining *now* because something you used to do for fun turns out to be a paying career—'

'Paying?' Jack asks sharply.

'Who the hell do you think is footing the bill for the contract you gouged out of CapG?' Michaels raises an eyebrow. 'It wasn't just the stuff you listed on your CV, Jack. We know about the other. The tools. You've got *exactly* what we need for this job.' Then he turns to you: 'You also, even though three-quarters of what we're paying for your services is going into Dietrich-Brunner's coffers – you'd do better to go freelance.' While you're gasping indignantly, he adds, 'I'm not going to make the mistake of appealing to your patriotism: it's a deflating currency these days, and an ambiguous one. But I *would* like to put a word in for ethics, fair play, and enlightened self-interest. It's not good for any of us to let Team Red run around hijacking certain, ah, critical systems – and killing people.' (He's clearly got something in mind other than Avalon Four or the Zonespace game platform, and you find his fastidious reluctance to name things extremely disturbing.) 'This isn't the Great Game as it was played in the 1870s, in the high plateaus of central Asia; it's the extension of diplomacy by other means into the medium of virtual worlds. It wouldn't be necessary if those virtual worlds didn't have entry points back into the net at large, or if we used virtual realms only for gaming – but you get the picture.'

And indeed you do. It's a heady mixture of blackmail, flattery, appeals to your idealism, and a play for your self-interest, all rolled into one. You'd resent it even more if you weren't compelled to sit back and admire the sheer brass-necked cheek of his approach. 'You forgot to mention the kitten,' you say.

'The kitten?' Michaels looks nonplussed.

'If we don't help you, you'll have to drown the cute widdle kitten, and it'll all be *our* fault.' You glare at him, but it just glances off the glacis of his self-confidence. Michaels's confidence is disturbing, almost religious in its unshakable faith. *Never trust a man who thinks his religion gives him all the answers.* 'Never mind. What are you trying so hard to get us to do?'

'What you've already been doing. You've already spooked one of our security problems into running and given us a handle on another.' He contrives to look innocent as one of the bar staff slopes by and deposits a bowl stuffed with small condiment sachets on your barrel top.

'But you've been penetrated—'

'Not just us, the entire country. Which is why there's a very quiet panic going on today as the police go onto a civil contingencies footing and couriers distribute new one-time pads to all the telcos. Once *that's* done, we can re-authenticate the entire backbone, and at that point we'll have locked out Team Red. The trouble is, someone on the inside – and I doubt it was Wayne, he wasn't clueful enough to pull a stunt like that – sold them a copy of the old pad via the blacknet, and I want to know who. If we don't identify them, the whole operation's a waste of time. But I think there's a very good chance that if you just keep doing what you've been doing, you'll make them break cover.'

The waiter is back, with two portions of coronary artery disease and a heart attack on the side. Michaels waits while he slides the traditional Scottish cuisine under your respective noses, then clears his throat. 'Someone inside Hayek Associates used the Nigel MacDonald sock-puppet as a safe house for a criminal blacknet, then sold the crown jewels.' He bares his teeth as he hacks away at something that looks like a square of deep-fried sausage meat with his steak knife. 'None of us is safe until they're out of the way.'

Jack glances at you and silently shakes his head. There's

something speared on his fork, waiting in front of his open mouth – the naked cooked Scottish breakfast. You don't want to look at it.

'Why?' you persist.

'Because . . .' Michaels looks confused.

'Why *us*? As opposed to any other specialists you might have on tap, already working in your department?'

'Oh.' His face clears. 'Because you're not part of the core intelligence group – sorry, but that's the fact of it. You don't know enough about us to give anything significant away: you're outsiders. Skilled, highly trained outsiders. Just like Team Red, actually. Nobody sends real spies these days; everything's very hands-off. Anyway, once the mole is out of the way and the backbone is secure, their controls will realize that Team Red are blown, and they'll withdraw. We want to send them a message – don't mess around on our patch.'

It sounds superficially plausible, but you've got a feeling that things are never simple where Michaels is concerned. The strange cross-linkage between Jack's ID and the non-existent Nigel MacDonald tells you there's more to this than meets the eye, as does the business in the taxi, and Chen's terror. Not to mention Jack's Elsie. 'You expect me to swallow that whole?' you ask, holding up a forkful of slowly congealing baked beans.

'Of course I don't!' Michaels carves away at an egg that appears to have been fried in sump oil and lard. 'But I can't tell you everything. It'd be a hideous security breach for starters, despite the variable EULA you signed . . . What I *can* assure you is that your role is significant, your co-operation is highly desirable, and if you do what we want, you will be rewarded, both financially and with the knowledge that you've helped secure your country's borders against a probe by an unfriendly foreign agency.'

'Which country?' Jack asks helpfully: 'Scotland, England, the British Isles Derogation Zone, or the EU?'

'All of the above.' Barry taps his fork on the side of his plate, as if it's a gavel. 'Do you want fries with that?'

You put your knife down carefully. 'What if I just say "no"?'

Michaels looks at you with jailhouse eyes. 'You can't. So I'll pretend I didn't hear that.'

You're getting really fucking sick of slick public-school boys telling you what you do or do not want to do, and saluting the flag and *being constructive* is nearing the point of diminishing returns; but you get the message. Chris and Maggie and Brendan and the gang can just fire your ass and make sure you never work in the forensic accounting field again, but Michaels can really screw you if he puts his mind to it: he can screw you as thoroughly as only a vindictive civil servant can. *On the other hand* . . . 'On the other hand, you can't get my willing co-operation if you twist my arm. If you want *that*, you're going to have to pay.' You pick up the coffee cup that came with your breakfast. 'Like this: I quit Dietrich-Brunner Associates. Retroactively, with effect from yesterday morning at 9:00 A.M. And you hire me on a freelance basis and pay me the same rate you're giving Jack. Also retroactive, with effect from yesterday morning at 9:00 A.M.'

Michaels picks up his coffee cup. 'You enjoy living dangerously, do you?'

'You need her, don't you? You need her as much as you need me.' Jack flashes a worried look at you from behind Michaels's shoulder.

Your mouth is dry. You take a sip of coffee to moisten it, as you realize what you're gambling for. 'Do you want me *motivated*, Mr. Michaels?' (You've just demanded two months' pay,

minimum. Your instincts are yelling *don't give up the day job!* –
but logic tells you that if he agrees to pay you this once, he'll
pay and pay again for what you can do for him. You and Jack,
if you're sensible about it. Because the agency behind Hayek
Associates clearly need you far more badly than Dietrich-
Brunner ever did. If only you knew *why*!) 'You know what I
can do for you, that's why I'm here.'

Michaels grunts as if someone kicked his ankle, then looks
away. 'That falls within my discretionary allowance.' He puts
his empty coffee cup down and winces. 'But don't push your
luck.'

'And I want you to do something about Elsie,' says Jack.
His guarded expression promises many more words for you,
when Michaels isn't around to hear them.

'Right,' you agree. 'Or we go to the police.'

'Really?' Michaels gives you a very odd look. Jack is frantically trying to tell you something without moving his face or
his lips, but it'll just have to wait. 'I said we were making
enquiries, yesterday. I can ask our SOCA liaison how things are
going, but they don't appreciate having their elbows jogged.'

He might as well be wearing an LED signboard flashing
phony, but there's nothing more you can demand right now –
and Jack looks as if he's about to explode, which would be bad,
so you nod and finish your coffee, then smile. 'So that's everything settled,' you say. 'So how about we go someplace where
there's some signal and place some calls?'

JACK: SCHRÖDINGER'S GIRL

You emerge from the depths of Bannerman's blinking like a hung-over bat, and glance up and down the canyonlike length of the Cowgate. *Someplace where there's some signal* indeed: the stone tenements to either side are nine stories high, and they predate lifts and indoor plumbing. Michaels spots an oncoming taxi (subtype: one with a human driver) and flags it down without waiting for you, so you glance over your shoulder at Elaine, who is glaring at her mobile and fuming. 'Come on, let's take a walk,' you propose.

'We've got work to be doing,' she points out.

'Well, the hotel is about a mile and a half that way' – you point along the canyon towards the Grassmarket and beyond, in the direction of Tollcross or maybe the West End – 'and we need to talk. Might be a good idea to take the battery out of your phone first.'

'Right, right.' She fiddles intently with the plastic case of the gizmo, then shoves it in a back pocket. 'What now?'

You begin walking towards the looming arch where North Bridge vaults across the Cowgate, perpetually confusing tourists who think that if two roads intersect on their moving map it should be possible to cross between them without abseiling. 'What did you pick up there?'

'He's scared, very scared. And he knows more about your Elsie than he's letting on.'

You keep going, legs pumping, arms swinging, even though you want to stop and have a good scream at the underside of the stone bridge. That's what you'd concluded, too – but grabbing Michaels and trying to throttle the truth out of him seemed inadvisable. And besides, you have three different hypotheses – and only the sheer terror of finding out that they're *all* wrong keeps you from making the final phone call. That, and the little problem that you're in too deep and you'd have to tell Elaine about – no, let's not go there now. There'll be plenty of time later.

You fumble around for a conversational token. 'Were you serious about quitting your job?'

'Are you kidding?' She catches up beside you as you sidle past the puddles under the bridge, the loading bay for the nightclub ahead on the left. 'Look, Barry's desperate. And . . . long-term, his operation needs us. What does that suggest to you?'

'I really don't know where you're going there.' You shake your head.

Small fingers force their way into your hand. After a moment you relax your fist and try to slow down to her pace. 'There's the cover story, and there's the truth. Everybody here's playing games, Jack, everyone but you – the game developer.'

'Huh? How do you figure that?' She's wrong, as it happens, but it's an interesting mistake. The buildings are opening out ahead, towards the homeless shelter and the weird little shops that cluster on the edge of the Grassmarket.

'Michaels – I'm pretty sure he's responsible – made damn sure I stayed up here after Maggie and Chris and the rest of the home team scuttled back to London with their tails between their legs. He wanted an auditor present, someone to act as a disruptive influence – but not to keep the place crawling with strangers. I was containable. So I have to ask, *why me?*'

You can play this game straight, and that seems to be what she wants, so: 'Why you?'

'Nobody else at Dietrich-Brunner plays games. No RPGs, no LARPs, no re-enactment, no ARGs. Doesn't that strike you as slightly strange, in this day and age?'

'Strange?' It's downright freakish, but you decide to play it straight. 'Wow. What were you doing there?'

'I'm not sure. But now I think about it, I wonder if the real reason I was there wasn't the reason I *thought* I was there at all.'

'Try me. Why did you think you were there?'

'Why the hell do you work *anywhere*? I was sending out job applications, and they offered me a job, straight out of university with a golden handshake to cover my tuition fees and professional registration. The only question is whether that's all there ever was to it. I don't know . . . I've got a feeling I was set up. Maybe it was a long-term thing: if **SPOOKS** is a pilot project, maybe they figured that if they went into widespread deployment, they'd eventually need a way of guaranteeing their own transactional integrity? Wanted: one forensic accountant, trained in HUMINT fieldwork, with gaming experience and security clearance, for counter-penetration duties. They don't exactly grow on trees, do they?'

'So what am *I* doing here?' You look around, then cross the road quickly. There's a shop selling beautifully unearthed fossils opposite the site of the old gallows, then a straight uphill march past the most dangerous run of second-hand bookshops in town.

'That's obvious: you were being groomed to join the **SPOOKS** dev team. Or **SPOOKS 2.0**. Then the shit hit the fan, and Michaels decided to use you as bait in his little trap instead.'

How reassuring, you tell yourself. 'So we're lost in a maze of shiny little mirrors, all alike, spies to the left of us, spooks to the right. And you quit your day job?'

'Tripling my pay, and . . . Michaels is scared, Jack. So am I, to be perfectly truthful – what happened to Wayne is no joke. The sooner we call time on the bastards, the safer I'll feel.'

'Oh yes?' You slow down to a dawdle and look sidelong at her focussed expression. When you first met her, you thought: *librarian on crystal meth.* Now you think: *ferret.* Then she breaks the effect by smiling hesitantly at you, and it messes with your head because there's no way a mustelid could make you feel warm and fuzzily protective like that.

'There's what Barry wants us to know, and there's what the situation really is as Barry and his core intelligence group understand it, and there's the *truth.* I'd draw you a Venn diagram, but it's more like peeling a hyperdimensional onion – not all the layers that look like they're concentric spheres actually enclose one another. We can peel it ourselves and risk uncovering something that'll make us cry . . . or we can play by his rules. And he's rigged the game to keep us in it – you with Elsie, and by the way, have you called your sister to check that it's not just a crock of lies he's feeding you? – and me with—' She stops. 'You haven't called your sister. Why not? Is it just your . . . record?'

You really don't want to have to explain the truth about Elsie, and your sister, and the rest of your non-standard family arrangements, so you endeavour to tiptoe around the elephant in the living room without actually making eye contact with the pachyderm. 'You know about Schrödinger's cat? The superposition of quantum states? Michaels has put my niece in a box, and I'd rather not know for the time being who's more ruthless — the other side, or the bastards we're working for.' Because Team Red *might* have done something, like Barry says, *or* Barry's cell might be running a really nasty Augmented Reality game against you to secure your co-operation. And *neither* possibility is pleasant to contemplate. 'I pointed Inspector Kavanaugh at it. Hopefully, she'll tell me to stop wasting police time.' Or maybe she'll find out who's pushing your buttons — whether it's Team Red or Michaels.

Elaine lets go of your hand. A moment later you feel her hand on your shoulder, pulling you close. 'That wasn't a bad choice.'

'Believe me, I know all about bad choices.' You're conflicted. You crave her touch, but feeling her hand on your shoulder, in front of all the cameras . . . in the end, you don't shake it off. 'Real life isn't a game, there's no undo, no reload. I've played too many games: real life scares me.'

'Is it much farther?'

'We're nearly halfway.' Which is a little white lie, but with her phone turned off, she's capable of being deceived — she'd actually be lost, without your local knowledge. And hopefully so will be anyone who's tracking her location, or your location. You can discount face recognition, despite all those cameras surreptitiously filing away your misdemeanours for later (like back when you were fifteen and stupid) because it's CPU-intensive as hell, but your mobie is a tracking device par excellence, and you've got to assume that Team Red know who you both are, by now. 'Let's stay off-line until we get to the hotel.' By which point, Team Red won't have a fucking clue where you are, which is exactly how you want things to be.

'I hate being lost,' she mutters.

'Really?' You're taken aback. 'It used to be normal.'

'Lots of things used to be normal. No indoor plumbing and dying in childbirth used to be normal. Where *are* we?'

'We're on, um, the road that leads from the Grassmarket to Lothian Road, dammit. I can't remember.' It's an itch you can't scratch, like not being able to check a watch or pull up the news headlines. 'Just think, it used to be like this for everybody, just twenty years ago!'

'I suppose.'

'Imagine you were a time-traveller from the 1980s, say 1984, and you stepped out of your TARDIS right here, outside, uh, West Port Books.' (Which tells you where you are.) 'Looking around, what would you see that tells you you're not in Thatcherland anymore?'

'You're playing a game, right?'

'If you want it to be a game, it's a game.' Actually it's not a game, it's a stratagem, but let's hope she doesn't spot it.

'Okay.' She points at the office building opposite. 'But that . . . okay, the lights are modern, and there are the flat screens inside the window. Does that help?'

'A little.' Traffic lights change: cars drive past. 'Look at the cars. They're a little bit different, more melted-looking, and some of them don't have drivers. But most of the buildings – they're the same as they've ever been. The people, they're the same. Okay, so fashions change a little. But how'd you tell you weren't in 1988? As opposed to '98? Or '08? Or today?'

'I don't—' She blinks rapidly, then something clicks: 'The mobile phones! Everyone's got them, and they're a lot smaller, right?'

'I picked 1984 for a reason. They didn't *have* mobies then – they were just coming in. No Internet, except a few university research departments. No cable TV, no laptops, no websites, no games—'

'Didn't they have Space Invaders?'

You feel like kicking yourself. 'I guess. But apart from that . . . everything out here on the street *looks* the same, near enough, but it doesn't *work* the same. They had pocket calculators back then, and I remember my dad showing me what they used before that – books of tables, and a thing like a ruler with a log scale on it, a slide-rule. Do *you* have a pocket calculator? Do you use one to do your job, your old job?'

'No, of course I—' She waves at the bookshop opposite. 'I'm a forensic accountant! What use is a pocket calculator?'

'Well, that's my point in a nutshell. We used to have slide-rules and log tables, then calculators made them obsolete. Even though old folks can still do division and multiplication in their heads, we don't *use* that. We *used* to have maps, on paper. But these are all small things.' The traffic lights sense your presence and trigger the pedestrian crossing: you pause while she catches up with you. 'The city looks the same, but underneath its stony hide, nothing is quite the way it used to be. Somewhere along the line we ripped its nervous systems and muscles out and replaced them with a different architecture. In a few years it'll all run on quantum key-exchange magic, and everything will have changed again. But our time-traveller – they won't know that. It *looks* like the twentieth century.' (Bits of it look like the eighteenth century, for that matter: this is Edinburgh, and you're deep in the World Heritage Conservation Zone.) 'Nothing works the way it used to, exactly. And knowing how it works now is the edge we've got over Michaels.'

You lead her up through the pubic triangle (which is not a patch on Amsterdam's famous red light district, but sleazy enough for a cheap shiver if you're so inclined) and onto Lothian Road (tame by daylight, wild West End by night). 'We can catch a bus from here,' you suggest, and she looks slightly pained, but nods. And so you do, taking the hit for paying cash: and ten minutes later you step off the bus nearly opposite the West End Malmaison hotel. 'Do you know where you are now?' you ask her, trying not to pay too much attention to the police vans parked outside.

'How the hell should I—' She catches your expression. 'Oh. Right.'

'*They* don't know either, because we've been off-line for over an hour,' you point out. 'So let's grab the laptops and go to work where they won't be expecting us!'

'Do you have somewhere in mind?' She raises an eyebrow.

And now you feel yourself smiling. 'Right here. Why do you think we've been off-line for an hour?'

The hotel is surrounded by cops. It's not an obvious cordon, there are no crowds of uniforms with riot shields drawn up – but as you cross the road you notice a couple of police motorbikes drawn up outside the power tool emporium opposite the hotel car-park. And there's a van parked up a side street. A couple of officers are standing at the corner by the hotel entrance, looking around, their eyes invisible behind heavy goggles and their jaws working as they subvocalize. If you weren't actively looking, you might not notice more than a couple at any one time, but when you add it all up, there's a heavy presence on the street. You squirm as you open the heavy glass door for Elaine: it's the same reflex you get when walking past guard dogs – they're unpredictable, capable of attacking. You can cope with them in ones or twos – a homeo-pathic dose of policing, so to speak – but this heavy cordon sanitaire is awakening the old phobia, even before you take into account your current state of unease.

'Come on!' Elaine nudges you impatiently. 'What are you waiting for?' She heads towards the lifts.

'A pony.' You follow her – this is her territory, you don't generally do plush hotels – up to the second floor, then into a conference room that opens to her thumbprint. 'Laptops?' You raise an eyebrow.

'Go on.' At least they're still here, and so are the cheap back-packs you stuck on top of the purchase nearly three infinite days ago. 'Where are we going to go?'

'Nowhere, yet.' You sit down at the desk and unfold your machine's display. It's chunky and old-fashioned but vastly faster than your phone and glasses: you log on to the hotel's network, bounce into Zonespace using the passwords Russell gave you, and proceed to take your bear for a romp around the tourist sites. 'I suggest . . . go get your stuff from your room, anything you may want later, as if you're checking out: I'm going to make damn sure Team Red know where I am. Alright?'

'Got it.' She studies your screen, which is repeating the display on your glasses. 'That's not Avalon Four. Where are you?'

'On the high plateau of Leng. That's where the Pabodie expedition came adrift: there should be some Old Ones hereabouts if the rampaging hordes of Antarctic explorers haven't been through since they last reset the shard. They're guarding some loot I need to get my hands on.' About a quarter of a million lines of source code, squirreled away among the skeletons and treasures guarded by a fearsomely large shoggoth; if you want to keep some data secure, there's nothing quite like sticking it in a record in a holographic distributed database that's guarded by Lovecraftian horrors. And it's not as if you took the intellectual property with you when you left LupuSoft, is it? This is just a backup copy, buried in one of their own databases. One that it's just possible for a random stranger to get his hands on if he knows *exactly* where the body's buried and the correct ritual for digging it up.

'Riiiight.' She sounds sceptical. 'So, let's see. You're deliberately drawing attention to yourself, and getting your hands on something you stashed earlier. And you want me to grab my bags. What exactly are you planning on doing?'

You stretch your arms above your head, lace your fingers together, and yawn widely. 'I want to look like I'm the bait in Barry's trap that he asked for. Do you trust the police?'

'I trust Inspector Kavanaugh to find your niece, that's about it.' You give her a long look. *Should have expected her to say something like that*. Lowering your arms: 'Why?'

'Just asking. Barry wants us to flush someone out of the woodwork. A distraction, probably – some nuisance to attract the cops' attention, something they can't ignore. When that happens, we can expect things to get hot. Question is, do we duck and run when that happens? Or do we stay here?'

'It depends. What do you mean by hot?' The ferret is back: she's not taken in by the line you fed Michaels. Well, you figure she's in this with you, and she deserves to know.

'Barry's wrong.'

'Wrong about . . . ?'

'He thinks this is a game of spooks, that he's up against the Guoanbu, who are professionals. He figures that when he rolls up their network and serves the ASBO, they'll just pack up their kit and go home.' (The hoard is just around the corner of this icicle-lined tunnel into hell, once you sweet-talk its guardian into going to sleep and letting you through. So you hit the PAUSE key.) 'He's as wrong as a very wrong noob can be. We're not playing against the Guoanbu, we're playing against *Team Red*. They're a gaming clan, and by all the evidence a fucking hot one, and they've got the technical backup from hell. The Chinese gamers, they're vicious. I've gone up against those fluffy bunnies before, and they play for keeps and they co-ordinate really well. And they, they don't really *believe* we *exist*. We're pale ghosts, trapped on the other side of a screen for their amusement. They're going to grief us hard, and if they've got access to the sort of kit Barry's talking about, they could have done all sorts of . . . stuff.'

It's more than a decade since a bunch of crackers – who nobody ever identified – managed to sneak password and credit card sniffers onto the core Cisco routers at MAE-East; things have gotten far worse since then, in the covert war of sysadmin on hacker that the public don't get to hear about. Entire telco companies have been compromised with no one the wiser until months afterwards. The public, with their wee fingerprint-authorized smart cards to supply them with the response to their e-commerce challenges, don't really have a clue what's going on. And there are much worse things a black hat troupe on a capture-the-flag rampage can do these days than just grabbing passwords and borking hospital networks. Lots of critical engineering systems rely on encrypted tunnels running over the Internet, lots of SCADA systems and worse – remote medical telemetry ('but you said you wanted your blood test results analysing as fast as possible!'), stock-market transactions, civil airliner flight plans, and exercise program updates to coffin dodgers' programmable pace-makers. The spooks in Guoanbu probably *are* professional, they wouldn't mess with the European SCADA infrastructure short of an outright shooting war . . . but are they likely to realize that they've almost certainly been pwn3d by their own pet griefer clan, and all their electronic armoured divisions are in the hands of a dozen Asperger's cases with attention-deficit disorder and a quantum magic wand?

It's not a risk you can take. And it's not a risk you can explain to Barry Michaels, because you know his type, and after seventy years of data processing, they *still* think that coders can be hired and fired; that the engineers who ripped out the muscles and nerves of the modern world and replaced it with something entirely alien under the skin are still little artisans who will put their tools down and go home if you tell them to leave the job half-done.

You're half-worried that Elaine will make a big deal of it, but instead she nods quickly, walks up behind your chair, and pecks you on top of the head. 'Don't go 'way,' she says, then backs out of the room in a hurry. You find yourself staring after her with a warm interior glow of confusion to keep you company: the idea that you might *go away* while she's counting on you being here is just plain bizarre.

You dive back into the tunnel into the mountains of madness. It's icy cold and very dark except where your head-mounted lamp is pointing, and the walls are covered with intricate hieroglyphs beneath their thin layer of rime. The floor is uneven and worn, and you shuffle forward slowly, sniffing suspiciously. The Guardian of the Depths lives hereabouts, but frequently sorties from its chamber of horrors to patrol the upper levels. You can't hear the faint leathery susurration of its progress as it worms its way around the Antarctic catacombs like a vast, malignant slug, but that doesn't mean you're safe: it's smart enough to lurk in ambush if it hears an unwary human or ursinoid.

In this Zone shard, you've tooled up to the tech limit – the blunderbuss has given way to a monstrous Steyr IWS-2000, and you've got an RPG-30 slung over your shoulder in case the Anti-Materiel Rifle fails to dent the Guardian's hide – but you're unlikely to triumph by force of arms in Lovecraftland. In fact, just tiptoeing around here on your own would be suicidally foolhardy if you didn't have a couple of very unfair safewords up your sleeve.

You shuffle along the passageway. A T-junction looms out of the gloom in front of you, empty twin dark tunnels mocking you like vacant eye-sockets. You grunt and shine your torch down the left-hand branch, consulting the map you summoned from the vasty deeps of your phone's memory earlier (carefully misspelled and misfiled to throw the inevitable googlebots off, lest some gameco crawler stumble across it in the public search indices and flag this complex as spoilered). There should be a landmark around here –

Aha! *Landmark 192* humps up out of the frosty trail on the floor. The unfortunate explorer is curled foetally in his sealskin parka, facing the wall as if in his last moments he imagined that hiding his face from the crawling horror might save him. Which means you're about ten metres away from the oubliette. You rise to your knees and lope forward until the darkness gives back a greater shadow, the round mouth of the Guardian's cavern.

Summoning your words of power – and shouldering the IWS-2000 – you step in front of the black pit of despair. The Guardian, as your torch beam rapidly informs you, is out: therefore you get to play another day. (There are two ways around the Guardian: admin mode, or a ten-kiloton tacnuke. And unfortunately Lovecraftland is owned by your former employers and they didn't give you either of the magic keys when they showed you the door.) So you step down the weirdly reticulated snail's-tongue slope that leads into the conical pit, paying no attention to the eldritch bioluminescent glow from the ceiling or the piles of bones and other debris that line the floor of the huge space, and lope across to the irregular, pentagonal altar at the far side of the dungeon. Ten more seconds, and you'll have your buried loot –

Bamf.

Oh bugger, you think, as no less than four glowing indigo holes appear in the air, occupying an arc between you and the altar. *Someone got creative . . .*

You flick the safety off and shoulder the AMR, aiming at the first eerie shape as it begins to take on humanoid form. In the real world, only a complete lunatic would fire the IWS-2000 from the shoulder or in a confined space – it's a crew-served weapon – but when you're a quarter-ton bull ursus, reality gets to take a back seat; besides, you've got the musculature and bone structure to take the recoil at least once.

Darkness grins at you and takes a step forward as you squeeze the trigger.

Things get a little confusing at this point, because you've run up against one of the limits of Zonespace: the lack of haptic feedback. But when the view stops jittering and clipping, you realize that the recoil has flung you all the way back to the altar, and the thing you shot at isn't there anymore – spooks and shades may be nasty enough for normal adventurers, but they're not up to stopping twenty grams of armour-piercing fin-stabilized discarding sabot love missile when it comes knocking at fifteen hundred metres per second. You track on the second shade as it raises its arms and does the zombie-lurch towards you, and pull the trigger again. This time you see what happens as the hypersonic shock wave turns the bogeyman into a humanoid smoke-ring, but your vision flickers red, and you notice that you're down 30 per cent on your stamina. Which is not good at all as bogey three looms closer, baring teeth that stretch and waver like a mirage –

Another round, and another palpable hit. But your vision's reddening now and you see you're down to 50 per cent: *What the fuck?* You think, then blink up the medical chart and realize to your horror that it's the AMR: you're turning your own shoulder into ground hamburger with the recoil. Which is pants – in the real world the AMR just has a kick like a mule, that's what the shock absorbers and the muzzle brake are for – but the Zone weapons committee clearly got it wrong, and you're stuck taking damage from your own gun like you're a seventy-kilo noob or something.

There's no time to switch to a different weapon – bogey four is crouching in readiness for a cavern-crossing leap, its claws and fangs lengthening – so you grit your teeth and aim, squeezing off another shot. The magazine's down to one round, but bogey four disintegrates in mid-air. There's a crash and a cloud of dust and icy gravel showers down from the roof, almost blocking the doorway, and your stamina read-out begins to flash: at 20 per cent you're in big trouble, medevac territory in a guild scenario, but there are no healers around right now. *Never mind . . .*

You put the anti-tank rifle down and turn around. The ghastly altar is still there. It's made of pale granite, and it seems to throb slightly as you look at it, as if it's on the verge of turning inside out like a Necker cube: the hieroglyphs are as alien and incomprehensible as ever, but somehow horrible, bringing to mind echoes of alien anatomy, organs ripped from the abdominal cavities of human sacrifices, and other, hidden things. 'Great,' you mutter. 'Attention, object able charlie sixteen. This is your creator speaking. Give me a cookie and initiate debug mode.'

The altar flashes emerald and turns inside out, injecting the stolen hoard straight into your character's inventory. And you're tooled up! Now let the games begin.

SUE: MAKING PLANS FOR NIGEL

After the briefing, Liz held you back for a couple of extra minutes. 'I met your nerd and librarian this morning,' she says. 'You didn't tell me they were a couple.'

'You—' You blink. 'What makes you think that?'

'Well, Sergeant, only the fact that she's wearing his spare trousers. And Bob Lockhart picked them both up at Mr. Reed's address. It does tend to complicate things, doesn't it?'

You blink again. 'Christ, skipper, that's news to me.' You try to square the memory with how they'd acted earlier: not a sniff of any office hanky-panky, that was for sure, not that it's any of your business what they get up to in their spare time. 'I didnae get any sign of it earlier.'

'Well, they're working for Michaels now, I am informed. That's where this shitstorm is blowing in from.' She gives you an odd look. 'When CopSpace comes back up, call me before you look up Mr. Reed's previous, Sue. It's misleading.'

Huh? 'Okay.' You look around. Everyone else has already left the briefing room, off to their various tasks. 'What do you want me to do now?'

'I want you to get yourself over to the West End Malmaison hotel and find them as soon as they show up. Then stick to them like glue. That clown Michaels is up to something, and while everyone else is running around looking for terrorists under the bed, I want someone competent – you – on the spot.'

'You think Jack and Elaine are going to piss on our patch, skipper?' You don't bother to hide your scepticism.

'No, Sue, I think they're very likely the target!' And she doesn't bother to hide her urgency either.

'But I haven't done the course—'

'You think I don't already *know* that? Jesus, Sue, we're at full stretch here; do you think I'd put you on protection duty if I had someone qualified? If you need advice, call me. Now get moving.'

You've never seen Liz that close to losing her rag, and it's not a pretty sight – especially when you're on the receiving end of it. She must be close to doing her nut. 'Reet! Right! I get the picture! I'm off.'

'Take Bob with you, he needs the education!' she calls as she strides off towards the incident control room.

That's you telled off. You're about to IM Bob when you remember: TETRA's been pwn3d. So you ask yourself, *If I were Bob, where would I be right now? Ah,* that's *where.* And you head down to the back yard.

Mary badgered you unconscionably until you gave up the habit a year or two ago, but Bob's still young and unencumbered by health insurance worries. And he is indeed having a furtive fag out round the bike rack. 'Bob. Got yourself a cheap mobie? Then send me your number.'

'My number—' He twitches nervously. 'Really? You want my number?'

'Bob. Bob.' You lean closer. Technically, smoking isn't allowed anywhere on the station, even outdoors in the car-park, but nobody in their right mind's going to push the button that suspends half the force and leaves the other half pulling double shifts, as long as the tobacco junkies are prudent enough to keep their filthy habit out of the public gaze. 'I'm your sergeant, Bob. Which means I need to be able to contact you at all times. Are you with me?'

Bob nods reluctantly.

'And you got the message to buy yourself a prepay mobie this morning, like everyone else. And now I want your number. Yes? So show me.'

He glances around anxiously. 'Promise you won't tell anyone?' He stubs the fag out on the underside of his size twelve and pulls the phone out. It's pink and has frilly unicorns frolicking on it.

You take a moment to get your coughing fit under control. 'Whae did ye get *that*?' you splutter.

'It was all they had left, Sarge, honest – it was in Toys "R" Us, see? Because all the big phone shops had already sold out.' You roll your eyes: he's right, now you think about it – it's not going to be just the Polis who're tooling up with prepays for today's big switch-over. He looks mortified as he punches up his pin number and shows it to you. (The display has little explodey pink love-hearts, twinkling and falling to either side of the multi-coloured numbers.)

'Aw, Jesus.' You haul your own playground special out – it's a big boy's model, black and chunky with yellow chevrons – and pair it with his. 'You poor bastard.'

'It was down to either My Little Unicorn or the Hello Kitty Ballerina Special when I got there,' he confesses.

'Just put the bloody thing away, before anyone sees it!' He obeys with alacrity. Look on the bright side, if you get called to deal with any hypo diabetics, he's got *just* the right thing.

'Has Inspector Mac given you anything to be doing today? Or just the general . . . ?'

'Me? Nothing, Sarge. Why?'

'Just checking. Alright, you're assigned to me today – by Inspector Kavanaugh. Yeah, I know she's not in your line, but you've met Mr. Reed and Ms. Barnaby this morning, I gather? Our job's to stick to them like glue today. They haven't done anything, but the skipper figures they're trouble magnets, and with the upcoming disruption, she wants humans in contact all the way.'

'Wow.' His eyes go wide. 'I haven't done the protection duty course, Sarge.'

'Between you and me, neither have I,' you confide. 'But we know the targets, and we've got our orders, so we're going to have to wing it.' So much for ISO9000-certified policing. You head for the door to see where your driver's gotten to. 'Come on, I'll tell you what we're supposed to be doing on the way.'

Traffic is heavy out on Corstorphine Road, and the van's full of irritated constables fiddling clumsily with their unfamiliar mobies, swapping numbers and muttering voice dialling tags. Even though CopSpace is going down in a couple of hours, and they've been ordered in the most fearsome terms to keep their fingers out of the files, most of them are still wearing their goggles: an old protective reflex, tinted windows to keep the compromised world at bay. You're an old enough sweat to remember a time before policing was something you did through augmented reality – a time when it wasnae just stumbling-down drunks who were dumb enough to swear at cops – and you're not looking forward to today's fun and games. It'll be okay if they get CopSpace rebooted before chucking-out time, but the Council's going through one of its usual barkingly stupid attempts to get all the pubs to close simultaneously on the stroke of half past midnight, and you're not looking forward to Friday night once the local pissheads realize that the cops' liferecorders aren't running, and the cameras overhead are unmanned. It'll be extra pepper spray and tasers all round, with double paperwork on the morrow when you go to explain the festivities to the hard-faced sheriff sitting in court: like a throwback to the nineties.

The van pulls in opposite the hotel, and you hop out. Bob bumbles along after you like an obedient puppy. You head for the front desk, where the polished-looking receptionists are handling the morning's fall-out of crumblies – the problem cases who're too old to cope with the automated checkout, or whose requirements don't fall in one of the neat boxes in the business work flow. You slide deftly round the shambling sequential headache and slot yourself in at the end of the desk. Finally, one of the receptionists finishes processing a coffin dodger and comes over to get you off her plate before you lower the tone of her lobby. 'Can I help?'

'Yes.' You smile politely. 'I'm looking for one of your residents, a Ms. Barnaby. I believe she's leasing an office suite from you? Dietrich-Brunner Associates?'

She looks at you as if you're something that's died under her nose. 'Is there a problem?'

It's time to tighten the smile and go a little glassy-eyed. 'No problem. But I need to see Ms. Barnaby immediately. Police business.'

The two magic words finally sink in: you can almost hear the gears and cam-shafts engage in her head. 'Oh, in that case . . . ' She bends over her terminal. 'Room 402, second floor, the lifts are over to your left. She was in there a minute ago.' Then she turns to the next tourist. 'Can I help you?'

You can tell when you're not wanted. 'C'mon,' you mutter to Bob. 'Let's go upstairs.'

It's a plush wee hotel, to be sure; the lifts have indirect lighting and subtle forest scents, and when you go out onto the landing, you see a strip of glass running floor to ceiling embedded in one wall, overlooking the high street. Room 402 isn't far off the landing, and you approach it cautiously. The door's not locked, so you open it and barge on in, regardless.

Here's Jack! Sitting at a table, playing some kind of game. You glance over his shoulder at the big, unfolded screens of his laptop: some kind of cavern, luminous green text marching across the left-hand screen. 'Mr. Reed,' you say, quite loudly, and he jumps and spins round, wincing as he nearly pulls his headphones out of their wired socket.

'You!' he says, for all the world like one of the villains in those cheesy Saturday-morning cartoons Davey keeps downloading. For a moment you think he's about to freak on you, but he's looking past your shoulder, with his face slowly crinkling with worry. 'What's up?'

'Nothing's up—' you begin, but someone behind you is speaking: the librarian, Barnaby.

'Someone's been in my room,' she says, angrily. 'And it wasn't room service. They don't make up the rooms until after check-out.'

You turn round. She's wearing jeans and a leather jacket and that's an expensive kit-bag she's got there. Something long is poking out of it, a black bin-liner wrapped around one end – a hockey stick, maybe? 'Ah, Ms. Barnaby. I was looking for you both. Inspector Kavanaugh says—'

She raises a hand. 'Don't tell me, she wants you to stick to us like glue. Right?'

'Reet.' You stare at her hard. 'You planning to be a nuisance? Or know somebody else who is?'

She meets your eyes. 'I'm planning on doing what I've been told to do, Sergeant.' She puts the bag down. 'I haven't been told to expect you.' She stonewalls like a defence solicitor: you snort and turn aside.

Behind you, Bob clears his throat. 'Sergeant?'

Jack is hammering away at the keyboard, typing like a mad thing in a pop-up window while the game he's in unrolls in real time behind it. 'What is it, Bob?'

Barnaby's phone trills for attention: she turns away. Bob shuffles uneasily. 'I think you'd better come and see for yourself, boss.'

You follow him out onto the landing outside the room. Bob points out the strip of floor-to-ceiling window. 'Look.'

You stare out onto the high street. It's the usual congested mess of buses and taxis queuing for Haymarket Interchange, with a couple of supertrams parked nose-to-tail and gumming everything up. Things have never been right there since they installed the light rail system, but nobody on the Council's about to admit that they should have knocked down about a billion euros' worth of historic listed buildings before they built the bloody tracks. It looks like pedestrian hell down there, even without the shambling crowd of people getting off the trams, moving oddly.

'What am I meant to be looking for, Bob?' you ask, forcing yourself to be patient.

'Zombies, skipper. What do they look like to you?'

You stare, wishing you could use your goggles – the digital zoom would be right handy at this point. It looks like any other crowd to you, at first, so you squint and look at the edges. They're walking funny, lurching from side to side. And why has that guy got his arms outstretched? He blunders about, colliding with a woman in a business suit that's ripped from shoulder to sleeve, and her face –

'Jesus, Bob.' You blink, then swallow. 'There's no such thing as zombies.' A little niggling doubt worries away at you. 'But get yerself down to reception and tell them to shut the doors, just in case. I'm going to make some calls.'

You pull your phone out and speed-dial Liz. There's no wait, just an immediate canned message. 'Hello, you are through to Detective Inspector Kavanaugh's voice mail. Please leave a message.'

Shit. Why's her phone switched off? You glance out of the window again, just to confirm what you can see. 'Skipper, Sue here. Ye dinna have tae take ma wuird fer it, I'll text you a photie' – you pause, trying to get a grip on your accent, which is making a bid for freedom (as it often does in moments of stress) – 'but we're holed up in the Malmaison and there's a bunch of zombies on the pavement outside.' You swallow. 'Whit should I do?' You end the call, then take a couple of snaps of the shambling horde and send them to Liz's mailbox. It's probably one of those old-time flash mobs, but why here, why now, and why zombies?

You go back into the conference room just as Elaine, nodding furiously at no one in particular, ends *her* call and glances at you. 'Sorry I was rude earlier, Sergeant. Nobody told me to expect you.'

'Reet.' You shake your head. 'What're you doing?'

'Being bait.' She swings an office chair round and sits down on it, facing you. 'Actually, Jack's the bait, I'm supposed to co-ordinate the response.'

Bait? Response? 'Bait for who?' you ask cautiously.

'A bunch of gamers in China.' She sniffs. 'They're all over

our critical infrastructure, but they made a few mistakes, and now Jack's wearing a false identity – Nigel MacDonald, the guy you've been looking for – and *we*' – her emphasis on the last word is extremely odd – 'expect the bad guys to expose themselves, trying to locate him so they can shut him up. They don't know MacDonald is a sock-puppet, you see.'

'And you are . . . ?' *Scrabbling for traction*, springs to mind.

'I'm secret agent X, it seems.' She grimaces. 'Thing is, we don't know how they're going to try to get at Jack, but he's raising a fuss to make them pay attention—'

'Got it,' says the man himself, still hunched over his gaming box. There's a pause in his incessant typing.

'Got what?' you and Elaine ask, almost simultaneously.

'What they're fucking doing,' says Jack, triumphantly. 'At least, I *think* I know what they're doing.'

'What are they doing, Jack?' asks Elaine. She's flexing her hands unconsciously, so that for a moment you think she's fantasizing about strangling him.

'They've set up a botnet, and now they're controlling it through Zonespace. Zonespace runs distributed across most mobile phones – just about any multi-user game you play relies on one or another version of Zone/DB to handle transactions. They're sending control packets disguised as flocks of birds or patterns of trees in the forests, or something, you know? Updating the database, and relying on the zombies in the botnet to pick up the changes. It's their backdoor into the public network, by the way – they feed instructions to the zombies, and the zombies with the stolen authentication pad update the routing tables. The traffic looks like game-play to GCHQ or CESG or NSA or whoever's sniffing packets; looking in-game for characters run by Abdullah and Salim holding private chat about blowing up the White House garden gnomes won't get you a handle on what's going on because they're not using the game as a ludic universe to chat in, they're using it as a transport layer! They're tunnelling TCP/IP over AD&D!'

You look at Elaine. 'Is he usually like this?'

She sniffs. 'I'm beginning to wonder.' Looking at Jack: 'What can we expect?'

'Besides the big-time griefing? Michaels figures the Guoanbu will pull Team Red off us as soon as he hands them a list of names and faces. Nigel MacDonald is there to distract their attention – they're meant to think his oppo are just a branch of the existing security services with a super-programmer on board, sort of a Ken Thompson figure – rather than understanding what Hayek Associates and **SPOOKS** are really about. But I reckon Team Red are going to be reluctant to go back in their box. They'll take advantage of whatever chaos they can create to go after MacDonald, which means *me*.'

Griefing is what Davey got suspended from school for last year, not something you associate with spies and terrorists: but on the other hand . . . they seem to know what they're doing, and you've been told to look after them, right? So you open your mouth: 'I'm told there's a blacknet operating in Edinburgh, and the inspector figures it's possible it organized what happened to Wayne Richardson. Would this be something your bad guys might use?'

'Fuck!' Jack jerks in his chair like you've brought out a car battery and clamped the shockers to his wedding tackle. 'Of course it would be!' (*Make it a truck battery.*) 'That would explain—' He turns back to his laptop and starts typing again. 'Fuck, fuck . . .' It seems that under pressure Jack comes down with a wee dose of the Tourette's: a good thing you aren't logging evidence right now, isn't it?

'Is a blacknet what I think it is?' asks Elaine. There's some kind of racket from outside the window: you're thinking you ought to go and keep an eye on it.

'Probably.' *Where's Bob?* You can understand the skipper taking her time phoning you back, but Bob's running late. 'At the protocol level, it's an anonymous peer-to-peer currency system. It asks you to do favours, it does you favours. Like, be in front of a building with a running motor at such a time with the backdoors open, and drive to an address where some-one'll be waiting for you with a wallet full of cash and another stolen car.' At least, that's the innocent-sounding version, because, let's face it, burglary and criminal damage go together like love and marriage, or robbery and a get-away carriage – and most of the stuff blacknets get used for starts there and gets worse *real* fast. None of the perps know each other, because it's all done with zero-knowledge proofs and anony-mous remixers running out of zombie servers on some poor victim's home-entertainment system that's downloaded one piece of X-rated malware too many. 'That's why I'm here, to make sure nobody tries to kill Nigel MacDonald.'

There's a roar from outside, the sound of a crowd yelling a single word over and over again.

'What's that?' asks Elaine.

'Sounds like' – *shit, where's Bob?* – 'brains,' you say faintly.

Outside the window, the zombies are holding a pavement sit-in. 'What do we want? *Brains!* When do we want them? *Nowwwww . . .*'

'I'd better go sort this out, before they try to storm the hotel.'

ELAINE: ZOMBIE MUSH

'What am I looking at?' you ask.

'A map of Zonespace, with shard frontiers and zombies.'

'What kind of zombies?'

'In this context, gamers who've been subverted. See them over there? The blue dots are your tribe, **SPOOKS** players who're also Zone gamers.' There are surprisingly few of them on the map. 'The distortion – that's latency time. Things are really fucked up, I can't see any websites outside . . . shit. I think the bad guys must have decided to make happy with all the backbone bandwidth in Scotland. They've gotten the authentication keys, so they can mess with the routers in SCOLocate, and the main telcos – there are only a couple of dozen who own their own fibre.'

You grapple with the magnitude of the problem. 'I don't understand why I'm looking at this, Jack.'

'The question isn't where Team Red got the keys to the realm from: Hayek Associates have a copy of the one-time pad, because they're sniffing on *everything*. The question is, *Who inside Hayek Associates leaked the pad, via the blacknet?* Barry's gotten through to the disaster planning people. They've generated fresh master pads, and they're pushing copies out to the main switches by courier – they're implementing the national zero-day exploit plan. The goal is to throw the switch at noon, at which point all Team Red's careful work goes down the toilet. Then they'll reboot CopSpace completely *and* load freshly signed certificates for the dot-sco domain by hand on the root servers, and a bunch more fiddly stuff. But the main thing is, once they change the one-time pads for admin access to the national backbone routers, Team Red will be unable to tap traffic at will. Zonespace will go down at noon, too, and *that* won't be coming back up for a wee while: when it does, they'll be frozen out. Our problem is to locate Team Red's avatars and kill them repeatedly until they stay dead – that should tie them up in PvP until it's too late, and sends them the message: we know who they are, and if they fuck with us, we'll take them down. And whoever their inside man or woman at Hayek Associates is, will probably bolt . . . So get co-ordinating, okay?'

'Right.' You shuftie over to your own laptop and blink at the screens until you stop feeling cross-eyed. 'Don't you have macros for this?'

Jack gives you a toothy grin. 'Macros for combat would be a breach of the T&Cs, wouldn't they?'

'I knew you were going to say something about that.' *Grind, grind, grind your foes* . . . Something about this whole set-up doesn't add up, but you can't quite put your finger on what feels wrong.

'That's what I was digging out of Lovecraftland.' He pulls his phone out and sets it on the desk next to his laptop. 'It's a stress-testing framework I wrote, ages back. Give it a bunch of Zone character accounts, and it'll run them as a swarm, targeting whatever you put in their path.' He rolls his eyes.

'That doesn't sound right.' You stare at him.

'Dead right it's not.' He stares right back. 'That's why I buried a backup copy out in the boonies: insurance.'

'Insurance—'

'It's the flip side of a coyote tunnel they wanted installing. You find a bunch of gamers who're not having any fun, and you lure them to your new setting, see? Come play with us, we're more fun. Give us your account, and we'll migrate your players into our new game and give you three months extra time, free. Which is where the stress tester comes in. Because if you give it a bunch of moribund characters in the old game, you can, uh, *stress-test* it. Just to make it even *less* fun for the stay-behinds.'

'*You* wrote that?' The more you think about it, the less you like the sound of it.

'Yup. On instructions from management at LupuSoft.' He grins humourlessly. 'For stress-testing our own products, *honest*. This sort of thing happens all the time in a mature market – it's all about ensuring your customers have fun, and the other side don't. It's all okay, as long as you don't actually use it for immoral, illegal, or fattening purposes: it has entirely legitimate applications. And it's not the sort of thing you can easily explain *not* wanting to write in front of an employment tribunal. So there I was, thinking there was *some mistake* about Dietrich-Brunner Associates needing my particular skill set after all.' He clicks on a button, and another window opens, more text scrolling. 'Look in your controls, under DM, options, stress.'

You bring up the pie menu and see it at once. 'Now, let me just load the bunch of accounts that Barry beamed at my phone this morning . . . '

His phone is blinking its wee sapphire light for attention. *Transfer in progress.* A whole bunch of blue dots are showing up on the map of Zonespace, like a toxic rash infecting it from Jack's mobie. You move your cursor towards them – it's got a funny lasso icon now – and herd them all together. This is a god mode – you can drop in behind their eyes and drive them, one-on-one, or you can string a whole bundle of them together in a mob and tell them to follow the leader. Who can be another zombie, with an assigned target, or you can run them yourself. It's a deeply ugly trick, a custom-built griefing tool, but it's just what you need right now and you have to ask yourself, *How much of this did Barry Michaels expect?*

You drop into Stheno's eyes. It comes easily. You're standing in the middle of a dirt track, woods to one side and a mountain range just visible in the distance across a field of maize to the other. You look round and see the most bizarre assortment of thuggish allies you can imagine. Orcs, humans, dwarfs, ice elves, a couple of giants, and a solitary dalek: they're milling around like a flock of sheep. 'Listen up!' you yell, trusting the rudimentary speech-to-text capabilities of the mobies they're running on. 'Follow me! Kill anything that's wearing this!' You hold up the scroll Jack hands you and show them the design inscribed on it in blood, an ideogram of chaos. 'Get moving!' And then you hit the GM menu and drop god-level privileges on every last one of Jack's zombie horde.

It's Zonespace, and there's a city here, a city built on the glacier-rasped basalt plug of an extinct volcano. Huge lumps of steep granite rear from the pine-forested flanks of a huge loch, and the swampy slopes down to a rough timber-crafted coastal harbour in which galleons and triremes swing at anchor. Someone's obviously been having fun with a bunch of historical maps, because you recognize bits of it from context – a huge castle looming from the top of a basalt spine, a proud royal palace sprawling at the opposite end of the Royal Mile – but you're pretty certain the real Dunedin never had a mangrove swamp where now the railway station sits, nor was there a rainforest in Leith or an Aztec step-pyramid out by the Gyle.

But that's all by the by. You've got an army of hundreds and a sword in your hand (not to mention snakes in your hair) and a job to do of killing every Orc you can see, repeatedly, until they stop coming back from the dead. *Maybe it's going to work out,* you think. *Now all I need to do is figure out how to run god mode in* **SPOOKS** *and establish a perimeter.* And so you flip back to the desktop and log in to the call-centre application Michaels gave *you,* just as the office door opens.

JACK: IN THE BOX

You're watching over Elaine's shoulder to see if she's got the hang of riding the horde of zombie griefers you've just unleashed, which is why you're puzzled in the extreme when she zips out of the game interface and flips over to the laptop's other screen to start messing with some other application. 'What are you—' *doing?* you begin to say, as the door opens and you look round expecting to see Sergeant Smith or her big goon of a trainee, and instead find yourself looking at Marcus Hackman, who is staring at you with an expression of concentrated loathing that is rendered even more frightening by what he's pointing at you: an extremely illegal black-market automatic pistol.

'Don't move,' he says. 'Keep your hands where I can see them. *Both* of you,' he adds, as Elaine begins to turn round to see what's going on – her back is to the door. He steps sideways, out of the doorway, and kicks it shut, keeping his back to the wall.

What the fuck? you think, a sick, sinking sensation loosening your guts. A lot of things come into abrupt focus. Hackman is wearing his usual expensive suit, but he hasn't shaved recently, and his normally lacquered hairstyle is giving way to minor chaos, strands and tufts out of place. His left shoe, highly polished, has a scuff mark on its toe. And the gun, a Yarygin PYa if you're any judge of such things (and you swallowed the Zone Weapons Bible whole during your probationary period, lo those many years ago, as young men are wont to do) has seen better days since it fell off the back of a Russian army lorry and into the hands of some blacknet-connected *mafiya* scumbag.

'Mr. Reed. If you don't do exactly as I say, I shall shoot Ms. Barnaby. Ms. Barnaby, if you disobey an instruction, I shall shoot Mr. Reed. If you understand what I'm saying, you may nod.'

You swallow and make like a parcel-shelf ornament. After a momentary hesitation, Elaine does likewise. The small of your back is chilly with perspiration.

'Very good,' says Hackman, as if he's speaking to a small child. 'Where's your phone, Ms. Barnaby? Quickly.'

'In my hip pocket,' she says, again hesitating slightly.

'Good. Ms. Barnaby, when I finish talking, I want you to take Mr. Reed's phone – there on the desk – and *without standing up* I want you to drop it in the trash can.' The bin is under the desk, between your right leg and her left. 'Do it.'

Shit. You watch as she reaches across you with her left arm and takes your mobie from where it's sitting next to the laptop and slowly moves it over the bin. *Double shit.* Of course it can't recognize her, so she can't speed-dial the distress number even if CopSpace was working –

Clonk.

'Good. Now, Mr. Reed, when I finish talking, you will reach over and take Ms. Barnaby's phone from her pocket and put it in the bin. Without standing up.'

'But it's—'

'*Shut up,*' he snarls, and you put a sock in it fast. 'Ms. Barnaby may rise slightly to give you access. She will keep both hands on the table as she does so. If she takes either hand off the table or moves either foot while she is standing, I will shoot you. If you understand, nod.'

You feel yourself nodding. *This can't be happening, can it?* He's about three metres away, too damn far to try and get to him – he'd shoot one of you first. If it was just you, you might try something (*poor impulse control* said Miss Fuller in elementary fourth, a damning diagnosis of potential heroism), but he's aiming at Elaine, and just the thought of him putting a bullet in her makes your heart hammer and turns your vision grey at the edges.

'Do it,' he says. 'Ms. Barnaby first.'

Elaine puts her hands on the table and tenses, rising out of her chair slowly. She's got her head cranked round, looking over her shoulder with an expression of profound apprehension (*or is it calculation?*) on her face. You reach out and slowly slide your fingers into her pocket, finger the warm soap-bar shape of her mobile, and retract. 'In the bin, Mr. Reed. *Now*.'

Clonk. And a faint sigh as the gas strut under the chair takes Elaine's weight again.

'Take your glasses off and put them in the bin. Then put your hands behind your neck. Stay away from the keyboards.' Hackman is stripping you naked – not of clothing, but in a more significant way: stripping you of the right to volitional speech, stripping you of the ability to communicate, stripping you of identity. But he hasn't reached your skin yet – *if Sergeant Smith comes back . . .* 'Now turn round to face the door. *Slowly*.'

'What do you want?' Elaine asks, getting the words out in a hurry.

Hackman twitches. 'Shut up.' He glances at you. 'If I don't call a certain number in sixteen minutes, your niece dies. Do you understand?'

You nod, your heart in your mouth. You understand all too well: Hackman's got hold of Barry's crock of shit about Elsie, and now you *know* he's lying. But *he* probably doesn't know he's lying, not if he's going through Team Red – there's no reason for any of them to know the truth about your family. Or for Elaine to know, for that matter. Which puts an uncomfortable complexion on things. Because if Sue Smith *isn't* coming back, if Hackman's used Team Red's favours to lure her away, thinking Elsie is at risk from his friends could stop Elaine getting away. *Inconvenient*, and then some. You're going to have to bite a bullet, if not take one for a team you never asked to join.

'Why?' you croak.

'Shut up. I've got a car downstairs, round the back. Auto-drive. We're going for a little ride into the borders, then you're going to spend an uncomfortable twenty-eight . . . no, twenty-seven . . . hours locked in a cellar. Then I'll be in the clear, and you'll be free. Do you understand?'

Elaine is shaking her head. 'Why?'

'Follow the money, stupid.' He looks angry, and a bit bewildered now. 'It was working fine until you showed up.' *If it wasn't for you pesky interfering kids, I'd have gotten away with it . . .*

'How much money?' Maybe, you think, you can convince him that you're venal enough to switch sides to an obvious liar.

'Twenty million in put options hedged against Hayek going down the tubes within two months of IPO, bought through a blind trust.' His cheek twitches. 'I'm into covering my bets. Barry and Wayne were just way too confident. The writing's been on the walls for months.'

You realize your jaw's gaping wide open. 'You've been betting on your own company *failing*?'

'You youngsters.' His expression is coolly cynical: 'You were still in short trousers during the first dot-com bubble, weren't you? Fucking amateur get-rich-quick schemes. I made my first fortune and lost it before you were even out of school. I know the signs.' He twitches the gun barrel towards you, then back to Elaine. 'Seen it before, twice over. But this time I was ready. All it takes is a couple of million and the right suit, and you can buy in, and be out before the starry-eyed optimists notice what's going on.'

'But you can't . . . be . . . ' Elaine is almost stuttering with surprise. And you can tell what's going through her head. *You were onto a winner! Chief executive of a Potemkin corporation, backed by the security services! Just lie back and let the money roll in!* 'I don't believe it.'

'Is that your bag?' Hackman asks, deceptively casual, with a nod towards the duffel bag and its cylindrical protuberance, where it sits beside the window.

'Yes.' Elaine nods.

'Stand up, slowly. *Slowly* now, go and stand beside it. You'll notice I'm pointing my gun at Ms. Barnaby, Mr. Reed, so don't do anything silly, or I shall have to shoot her.'

Realizations crystallize in parallel as you see Elaine slide sideways towards the bag. Like: *Hackman is a fruitcake.* And: *He doesn't know you know about Wayne.* And: *Wayne's dead, and who the hell do you think killed him?* 'Are you working for Team Red?' you ask.

'Shut up. I'm working for myself.' So he's been going through the blacknet, not knowing who's on the other side of it, also tapping it for what it can give them. And he's still pointing the gun at Elaine. *Oh shit.* Elaine is tense: she glances at you wide-eyed, like a woman about to stick her head in a hangman's noose. You can read her expression, clear as day –

I'm doing this for Elsie. And that's what triggers the honesty attack as the mummy lobe, hitherto catatonic with fright, finally takes over your tongue:

'Elsie died six years ago, Hackman. Your blacknet friends are lying to you.'

And it's true, and the confession rips you back to that horrible morning in the mortuary down south where they showed you the photographs, then waited while you got a grip on yourself and blew your nose and wiped your eyes — you didn't throw up until later, after the sixth pint of the evening — and were *very sorry, sir, to put you through this, but we need to know,* we need to know *who was in the car* because after it came out from underneath the articulated lorry you had no family *at all*, you had *no life*, and that was when you began paying the Absent Friends subscription, because even the simulacrum of your sister and nieces gives you something to talk about, it's better than nothing at all. People instinctively know when a member of the herd is the last of their kind, and you can't live with the sympathetic glances, and you can't live with the isolation, either, and how were you to know? It's just your reality, these days, an embarrassing ghost you've dragged around with you ever since the accident. A bodyguard of ghosts.

The ghosts surround you as you stand up and take a step away from Elaine, away from the desk where the zombie-haunted laptop is co-ordinating the automatic mop-up operation to a war Hackman doesn't even know is happening, a second step to widen the gap and close with Marcus as the gun barrel turns to track you and shoots.

BANG.

You didn't know it could be that loud: it's not just a noise, like in the games, it's a solid force hammering on your eardrums and punching at you. But you take another step and reach for the gun.

BANG.

This time you feel something like a punch in the ribs. But you're close enough to grab at Hackman's arm, now, even though your legs don't seem to want to work properly. It's very odd: you've almost got your hand on the gun-barrel, but it's getting farther away, and what's the ceiling doing? Something hits you appallingly hard in the back, and then your head's in agony as you whack it on the floor, and the gun is still pointing at you, with Hackman's face behind it, snarling like a shark that's scented blood on the boardroom carpet and is about to bite your throat out –

Then Elaine takes a brisk step forward, straightening up from where she's grabbed something from her bag with both hands, pivots smartly on her left ankle, and swings a huge sword over him in a motion like the windscreen wiper from hell. Through your ringing ears you hear a crunch of bone. And the last thing you see is Hackman, a surprised expression on his face, toppling towards you, as Elaine staggers with the effort of halting the instinctive backstroke that would take his face off.

Restart:

A white plastic ceiling above you, lights, and a green shape hunched over your face. Some kind of mask. Whatever you're lying on jars painfully as the wheels ride over speed pillows. And you wish they'd turn off the siren.

Been here before. Didn't like it any better the first time. 'Looks like he's coming round.'

Nope, sorry.

Restart:

You've been shot in the chest, in case you hadn't guessed. Twice – once wasn't enough for you? So you had to go and be a hero, because you knew what Hackman didn't know you knew, which is that his friends on the other end of the anonymously remixed blacknet link, Team Red, had already tried to kill you a couple of times over: and to make things better, Hackman had already iced his partner in insider trading, Wayne Richardson, and it therefore followed that he wasn't about to leave you or Elaine behind to point the finger at him. Because that's what blacknets are good for: buying illegal handguns, arranging executions, raising dirty money at insane short-term interest rates to invest in a gamble that your own corporation is going to tank within weeks.

And you'd been meaning to tell Elaine about your lack of a real life sometime, anyway.

But getting yourself shot wasn't clever, was it? It hurts. It's down to a dull ache now – either you're dying, or they whacked you full of morphine – and you can breathe, but there's something annoying in your nose. Maybe opening your eyes would be a good idea, although they're hot and gummy, and you feel almost as fuzzy as that time in Amsterdam, sitting in a burning chair by a canal and a broken shop window.

(*Burning?* Why did you think the chair was on fire?)

You manage to crowbar your eyelids apart. It's a huge effort, but it's rewarded by a worried face, blurred but recognizable, a ferret sniffing over its prey as if unable to decide whether to bite or groom it. 'Jack?' She squeezes your hand. 'Jack?'

'Grrrrumph.' That's a highly compressed shorthand version of *are you alright? Did Hackman get away? Where are the police? And what's happening?* Unfortunately, your throat didn't work too well, so you cough and try again: ' 'Laine?'

She squeezes your hand so hard you're afraid she's going to crush it. 'Don't you *ever* do that to me again!' Then she lets go abruptly, as if she's suddenly realized what she's doing and got self-conscious. 'For fuck's sake,' she bursts out suddenly. 'You really scared me!'

I *scared you*? you think, but it's too much of an effort to say that. 'Hackman?'

She sniffs, misunderstanding. 'Untrained handgun versus trained sword at that range? I was just waiting for a chance to draw on him.' She's still holding your hand. There's steel in those fingers, you realize. 'Good thing for his sake it was blunt when I went into *krumphau* on him, or he'd be missing both hands.'

Well, duh. You blink, feeling stupid. She *told* you she was into mediaeval sword-fighting, didn't she? What did you expect?

'Sorry. You scared the crap out of me, Jack.' Pause. 'How do you feel?'

Your throat feels like it's on fire, and there's definitely something wrong with your chest: it makes odd crackling noises when you breathe, and you can't quite get enough air. 'Water,' you say hopefully. You're too tired to worry about anything else. Besides, she's here, and she's in the chair by your – *hospital bed?* – so she must be okay. 'Phone?'

'I phoned Sophie,' she says. 'After they rebooted the phone system.' She looks apprehensive: that same facing-the-noose expression you saw earlier, back when . . .

'You know, then.'

She nods. 'They told me everything.'

The mummy lobe – what's left of it – closes your eyes, out of embarrassment, or respect for the dead, or something. 'I couldn't handle it back then. Not six months after Mum died.

I just couldn't handle being on my own.' The mummy lobe is tired, too: tired of holding you together through lonely years of death-march work and playing at real life, tired of emulating the society you've been so cut off from for so long.

'But to try blackmailing you—' She breaks off.

'How were *they* to know that Sophie wasn't real? They were sub-contracting hands-on stuff to a local blacknet. Probably gave it to some local muscle down south who's laughing his rocks off. Like the story about the police who send this guy a photograph of his car, speeding, and a fine: so he sends them a photograph of a cheque. And they send him back a photograph of a pair of handcuffs . . .'

Cold little fingers insert themselves into your hand, kneading. 'But you don't need to be alone, if you don't want to,' she says hesitantly. 'You do know that, don't you?'

'I do *now*.' You squeeze her fingers, as hard as you can, which is about drowned-rat strength right now. 'Game over.'

SUE: PLEA BARGAIN

'. . . So I was nattering wi' the heid zombie in the hotel lobby when I heard the shots. The front-desk video take will show me lookin' scunnered. It was two stories up, but I knew what they was immediately – that's when I called, as I ran upstairs. It was all history by the time I got there, she had him on the floor with that sword of hers, and it was all over bar the bleedin'. But I feel like a right wally, skipper.'

'You and me both, Sergeant, and you know who the enquiry's going to blame for assigning an uncertified officer to personal protection duty.'

That's scant comfort, and ye ken the inspector knows it, but it's a worse mess for her, you've got to admit – you're not climbing the greasy pole after all. On the other hand – 'We wuz in a collective tizzy, Liz, thanks to those bloody spooks and their full-dress crapfest. If they hadna sprung the terrorism alert at the same time we had to shut down CopSpace, we'd maybe hae stood a chance, and if we'd had CopSpace, again, we'd hae known what was happening. I blame myself – I should have told Bob to get his boots back upstairs the instant he'd spoken to the front desk.'

'You're trying to second-guess an IPCC enquiry, Sue. My advice? Drop it, it's over.' Liz looks irritated. 'Besides, we shouldn't talk about it outside of school. It looks like collusion in the wrong light, and that would never do.'

'Oh, okay.' *Collusion* is a political word, and you'll take Liz's word for it looking bad. You tighten your grip on your hat, realize what you're doing, twitch it round in your lap, then let go again. It's too much like sitting in a dentist's waiting room for comfort. All it would need is a NO PHONES sign and a ticking clock on the mantelpiece above a dysfunctional gas fire to drive the message home. But this particular waiting room's in better shape than your tooth doctor's front room, right down to the extra-uncomfortable chairs and the civilian receptionist outside.

Kavanaugh looks at her watch. 'Not long now,' she remarks, and you realize she's bloody nervous, too. And then the inner-office door opens.

'Inspector Kavanaugh, Sergeant Smith, please take a seat.'

There are two chairs waiting for you, opposite a desk the size of a wee conference-table. And on the other side of it is the top brass – Deputy Chief Constable McMullen, who is definitely *not* dressed for the golf course this morning, sitting with a face like a hanging judge beneath a photie of *his* boss, Andrew Sampson, chief constable of South East Scotland force, shaking hands with the last-but-one justice minister on the back steps outside Holyrood, just to rub it in. But you have to work hard not to raise an eyebrow, because sitting next to him is that fly-case, Michaels – and another character in a grey suit with a face like a horse and a look that says *high-altitude civil service*, so high you need an oxygen mask just to breathe up there.

'At ease, sit down.' That's McMullen. He glances to either side. 'I want to make it clear right now that this is not a disciplinary hearing. Nothing is being recorded, and nothing you say here will go on any record. Is that understood?'

You don't dare look round, but you can just about hear the

sonic boom from Liz's eyebrows as they head for the strato-sphere. *It's policing, but not as we know it – everything* is on the record, these days, lest the clients start throwing themselves down the stairs and suing the force for compensation. 'Isnae that a bit . . . *radical?*' you hear yourself asking, somewhat to your own disbelief.

'It's necessary.' McMullen doesn't look terribly happy. 'As Mr. Jones from the Joint Defense Ministry will explain . . . ?'

Jones – the high-flyer – has been looking at something in a leather folio. Now he closes it, puts in on the desk, and clears his throat. 'I'm here to inform you that the events that took place at the West End Malmaison the Thursday before last are the subject of a classification order issued by the Ministry of Justice, at our request. The Home Office down south is also playing along. You may not discuss those events with anyone outside this room, other than the direct partici-pants, without breach of the Official Secrets Act. You will need to sign these forms before you leave' – he taps the folder – 'to confirm that you have been so informed. That's the bad news.' He pauses for a moment. 'On the other hand, you won't be facing a board of enquiry.'

Really? But they didn't need to call you here to tell you that in person, did they? So what's going on?

McMullen clears his throat. 'This leaves us with a little problem.' He pointedly doesn't glance at Michaels, who's got his arms crossed and is looking smugly dishevelled, or at Jones, who appears to have turned back into a cardboard statue of a civil servant. 'The disposal of one Marcus Hackman. Who I believe you arrested and charged with attempted murder, possessing an unlicensed firearm, and, Inspector . . . ?'

Liz clears her throat. 'Also, two counts of murder – Wayne Richardson and Wu Chen – and that's before we get into the

esoteric stuff – solicitation of murder, conspiracy, membership of an organized criminal enterprise, whatever we can pin
on him for the blacknet node he was running out of the
MacDonald safe house, the various securities violations, insider
trading, fraud, and you could probably nail him for spying if
you were willing to drag everything up in court.' *Now* you
spare her a glance: she rolls her eyes. 'Of course, that's all just
fall-out from trying to cover up his first mistake, which was to
have so little confidence in his own business venture that he
expected it to fail and configured it as a honey trap for
investors.'

Across the desk, Michaels is finally looking a bit less smug.
'Hayek Associates wouldn't be able to do their job if they
didn't look and function like a real company, Inspector. And
this may come as a surprise to you, but we in the intelligence
community aren't *actually* experts in running dot-com start-
ups. We went and took on board some people with good
experience and a solid background that checked out, relying
on them to make most of the running, and one of them turned
out to be a particularly bad egg, and another of them was a
slightly less bad egg. The problem was figuring out who was
who without trucking everyone who worked at Hayek
Associates into a secret bunker and interrogating them, which
would have risked blowing the cover operation sky-high. All
it takes is one contrarian who doesn't approve of being used as
a stalking-horse by the government and leaks it via a backnet
or a blog or a newspaper, and . . . ' He shrugs.

Oh, so that's *the way the wind is blowing!* You smile politely
and try to look like a dumb cop. Let Michaels incriminate
himself if he wants to.

'What about **SPOOKS**?' asks Liz, and you blink. 'And where
did the zombies come from?'

'The zombies were from just about every AR and LARP in town,' says Michaels. 'When Hackman realized his blacknet friends – Team Red in fact, but he probably thought he was dealing with the Russian *mafiya* – fucked up on killing Mr. Reed and Ms. Barnaby, he got them to organize a flash mob for him – an organized zombie fest outside the hotel, promise of prizes for the best-dressed undead, word out that it had been cleared with yourselves and there'd be a couple of TV crews in attendance. You've got to admire it as a piece of improvisation – it got your attention, didn't it? It also distracted everyone while Hackman was trying to work out his own solution to the problem.'

'Wayne Richardson?' prompts Liz.

'Wayne, Wayne.' Michaels looks pained. 'Wayne was just the weakest link. Hackman was the bad one. When he found out about the MacDonald identity, he suggested setting up a better back story. I should have realized earlier, but he really wanted the flat so he could loan it out to some shady characters he owed a favour or two. Local gangsters. They installed the blacknet node to replace the one you shut down last year; where better to put it than in the apartment of someone who doesn't exist? Then Hackman realized it had other uses. *Wayne* he got to via the usual mixture of fear, uncertainty, and doubt. Thick as thieves – but there's always a leader, and when Wayne panicked and tried to cut a deal, Hackman got rid of him.'

At which point things fall into place in your head. Except for one thing. 'Why did you get Jack fired from his job?' you ask.

'Because we wanted to recruit him,' Michaels explains. 'ARGs like **SPOOKS** don't grow on trees, they take years to develop. **SPOOKS** was our first toe in the water. It taught us a lot about what we need to do to run a virtual HUMINT operation, and it fed into the design process for **SPOOKS 2.0**, which will roll out next year. Most of the developers don't need to know what they're doing – we pointed them at a similar development project, used it to break the back of the coding, then cancelled it and disbanded the team once it was nearly done. But we need some of them – the smart ones, who can take the ninety-five per cent complete code for **STEAMING** and turn it into **SPOOKS 2.0** then keep it running. And we needed Elaine for two reasons – to flush Hackman from cover, and because we wanted to recruit her, too.'

And things *are* falling into place. Because it all comes back to Hackman, and the inadequate job Michaels did of positively vetting his tame sociopathic CEO and the chancer of a marketing manager. All CEOs are a bit sociopathic – it takes a really obsessive personality type to take a business public, especially in the fevered climate of a bubble, not just any bubble but the third one in a row – and Michaels had no way of getting into Hackman's skull and realize that underneath the confident reptilian exterior there lurked a huge ball of neuroses and a psychotic rage at the world for having taken his toys away from him twice already. Hackman wanted to have his cake and eat it, and didn't think Michaels and his old-school buddies (who kept dropping in for no obvious reason that Hackman could see) were capable of holding up their end. And Wayne Richardson was Hackman's cat's-paw. They hedged their bets, taking out derivatives geared against the company's success. Get in, get the VC set-up, float on the market, get out as much of your own shares as you can, *then* clean up when the bottom falls out, even though you're holding most of your visible assets in options that haven't vested yet. Only it didn't work, because Hayek Associates were doomed to succeed: Michaels's friends in the shadowy machinery of state simply kept pouring liquidity into their Potemkin dot-com. The bottom persistently refused to fall out — and Hackman was getting desperate.

But Hackman had an ace up his sleeve: he was already hooked into the local blacknet. Probably it started with his cocaine habit, or something like that; but he ended up scratching backs and hosting a node, and before long he found a way in and a seat at the table: and he found people there who wanted to pay him for information about a company he knew an awful lot about. Which is how blacknets work — people put stuff up for sale, or issue tenders, and other folks see the goods and buy them. It's a market, just like any other, except the things that are bought and sold are illegal — drugs, confidential information, murderous favours. It was the obvious way for those spooks Liz was so uptight about to get into Hayek Associates, and they used it. Hackman sold them the company's copy of the authentication pad for the backbone routers and the private authentication keys to Zonespace, told them how everything worked, played the part of a disgruntled employee — all to raise money to bet against his company's inevitable success. He even solicited a final raid on their most public asset in an attempt to blow the foundations out from under them.

Only he miscalculated.

Reputations were at stake. Phone calls were made: investigators were sent in — auditors, not spooks for the most part. Michaels wasn't going to let his surveillance operation go down the toilet. He needed to know who was leaking secrets, and why. But as he rolled back the carpet, what he found underneath was much worse than he'd anticipated. The leaker hadn't simply sold the family silver to a gang of thieves, they'd managed to attract the attention of the opposition. Events began to snowball – you can't really guess just how far it went, but the arrival of Kemal's Keystone Kops is suggestive – until it all ended up in the kind of counter-intelligence clusterfuck that is the stuff of legend thirty years later when it is declassified.

'So Hackman and Richardson were just in it for the money?' you ask. 'You expect us to believe that he'd kill three folks – trying for five – just to cover it up?'

Michaels slumps very slightly: for a moment he looks his age. 'Twenty-six million euros, Sergeant. That's what Hackman was in it for, after all. The two things that motivate CEOs: money and winning.'

And you get the message. Because in the final analysis, that's a load of dosh, dosh beyond the wildest imagining of the wee neds you get to deal with – like Jimmy Hastie – and you know damn well what they'd get up to for a tinny of Carlsberg, never mind a tax-free twenty-six million. 'Are we looking to recover it?' you ask.

'That's for the proceeds of crime unit.' McMullen sniffs dismissively. 'I'm sure they'll find wherever he put it sooner or later. But first, there's the small matter of the prosecution. Everything happened while CopSpace was compromised, so there's a slight lack of visuals – and the lifelog transcripts for yourself and the inspector are going to be misplaced. On the other hand, we've got the hotel camera footage from the business in the Malmaison, so we're going to have to run with that. If we can't nail him for attempted murder and firearms possession in front of a jury on the basis of video evidence and witnesses, one of whom has holes, we're idiots. The heavy stuff – Chen and Richardson and the blacknet and the penetration at Hayek Associates – we don't need to bring it up to put him away, and if we keep it out of the picture, there's no reason why anyone would start digging. So.' He glances at Jones: 'I'm told the Procurator Fiscal will be laying charges against Mr. Hackman, and he's going to be offered a discreet plea bargain.'

Which is very much *not* how things are done in Scotland, where plea-bargaining is seen as some kind of perverted transatlantic phenomenon, but ye ken why the security services might not want to advertise that their pilot project in the virtual world was penetrated by a bunch of Chinese script kiddies because the guy running the cover operation didn't believe his own story.

'Well, if that's the course of action you've decided on, I'll co-operate,' says Liz. 'Although' – she glances between Jones and Michaels – 'I'd be happier hanging the bastard out to dry.'

Jones just sits there with a pained look on his face, but Michaels nods. 'So would I, Inspector. And maybe we'll be able to let you re-open the case in a couple of years, when our critical infrastructure is nailed down tight. But I hope you understand the need for discretion here?' He looks at you suddenly, and there's nowt of the public-school boy in his eyes. 'We're not playing games anymore.'

EPILOGUE:
BANKER MARTIN MASE

Mail-Allegedly-From: Martin.Mase@NNPB.co.ng
Subject: URGENT FINANCIAL INFORMATION SOLICITED REGARD-
ING OVERDUE SUSPENSE ACCOUNT
Auto-Summary: Typical 419 scam.
Spam-Weighting: 95% probable, don't waste your time.

Dear Mr. Hackman,

I fervently pray that this letter soliciting for your kind assistance will not cause any embarrassment to you. I am aware that we have never seen each other before, neither have we exchanged any form of formal contact or correspondence before. I am also aware that this world is full of dishonest people, but I sincerely hope that my humble letter will touch your kind heart to assist us in establishing mutual identity authentication and a profitable and happy future business relationship.

I, on behalf of my other colleague in the office (NNPB) have decided to solicit your assistance as regards to the disposition of the sum of €26,023,691.47 deposited into your bank account two months ago. This fund arose from the liquidation of certain security assets deposited on your behalf by our colleagues in the Pyongyang subdivision of my parastatal over the preceding accounting period.

We understand that the amount will be transferred into a bank account provided by yourself, but this must be supplied by you, as the code of conduct of the federal civil service does not allow us to operate with foreign accounts. We are therefore seeking for your assistance based on the agreement been made within our selves the documents of this fund will be speedily processed for immediate remittance of the fund into your bank account.

We will avail you with our identities as regards our respective offices when relationship is fully established and smooth operation commences. We are at your disposition to entertain any question from you in respect of this transaction, so, contact me immediately through my email or the above telephone numbers for further information on the requirements and procedure. We are in particular eager to receive your suspense account details and required biometrics (e.g. left fingertip, letter signed in blood) for completion of this transaction.

Please, note that this Deal needs utmost confidentiality and observe suitable secrecy.

Yours faithfully,

DR. MARTIN MASE

Nigerian National Petroleum Bank

Lagos

Nigeria

extras

www.orbitbooks.net

about the author

Charles Stross is a full-time writer who was born in Leeds, England in 1964. He studied in London and Bradford, gaining degrees in pharmacy and computer science, and has worked in a variety of jobs, including pharmacist, technical author, software engineer and freelance journalist.

Find out more about Charles Stross at www.antipope.org/charlie/index.html or you can read more about Charles and other Orbit authors by visiting www.orbitbooks.net

interview

What's the story behind the title *Halting State*? I looked it up on Wikipedia, but a simpler explanation would be much appreciated!

The title is a pun. In computer science, all computational processes (programs) proceed through a series of state changes governed by rules, until they reach what is termed a halting state – a state in which no further state transitions may occur. (It may, however, take an infinitely long time for them to get there.) And one of the major plot elements of the book hinges on a conspiracy to grab control over a nation-state by means of networked computers, with the implicit ability to bring the state to a standstill. (I have a bad pun habit . . .)

And can you tell us a little bit about the background to *Halting State*, the book?

Halting State is an attempt to explore the very real virtual realities that are now coming into existence. VR was meat and drink for SF from 1984 – with William Gibson's

Neuromancer — until some time after Neal Stephenson published *Snow Crash*, but it hasn't had a lot of love since then. Which is odd, because we finally have broadband internet and massively multiplayer online role-playing games which actually fit the model for large VR communities! So I decided to revisit the whole VR in SF thing, but on the basis of existing technologies, and see where it was set to take us in the near future.

Halting State is an exploration of some of the cultural changes we're likely to see when certain trends we're seeing today (pervasive wireless broadband communications, ubiquitous location services, and massively multiplayer online role-playing games) are likely to go in another decade. Obviously, some of the forerunners of those changes are visible today, if you know where to look — but there's a big difference between being able to look at, say, amazon.com in 1996, and see the potential there, and grasping the full implications of e-commerce in 2007.

One of the things that watching the birth of the world wide web and the initial dot-com rush taught me — I had a ringside seat, as the first programmer hired into the software development team of a successful dot-com — is that the attitude of the bleeding edge early adopters to a new tech field is rather different from the mass culture that will subsequently emerge. There's a qualitative difference between what geeks do with a new toy, and what happens when you hit the mass adoption stage and the whole world and their dog get their hands on it. It was pretty obvious that while the trappings of *Halting State* are already out there (there's only one technology in the book that isn't actually commercially available right now), the impact they'd have on society at large would be radically different in ten years' time. And so, while I could have written a novel about MMORPGs and computer crime set in 2007, I figured 2016-2018 was a much more interesting period to aim for — when there's a generation of young professionals who don't remember a time before YouTube, MySpace and transparency, and a cohort of teenagers behind them who don't even understand the concept of being lost in a strange city because they *always* know where they are.

Did the idea for the book come to you fully realised or did you have one particular starting point from which it grew?

Oh, it went through a lot of revisions along the way! First there was the embryonic form — the non-fiction birth-of-a-dot-com book I was pitching in 1998, and which went nowhere (luckily). Then the bubble burst and I had other, pressing priorities, like earning a living as a freelance journalist and writer, and selling novels. Around 2003 I began thinking about a novel set in a dot-com, but who wants to read a historical cyberpunk novel? (Apart from William Gibson . . .)

So I realised I needed a science fictional angle to stick on the semi-autobiographical dot-com novel. For a while I toyed with the idea of a hard-SF vampire theme, although I abandoned that idea around 2004. (For what it's worth, the ideas I was working with are not dissimilar to those Scott Westerfeld used in *Parasite Positive* and Peter Watts used in *Blindsight*. We're not talking paranormal romance here, we're talking infectious diseases with side-effects as charming as leprosy.)

And then, I began noticing stuff about the culture of computer games.

Now, I try to avoid gaming like the plague. I can easily lose days (or weeks!) at a time if I start on one, so for the most part I don't do that. But I've had intermittent bouts with gaming, and with multiplayer games at that; I remember one morning in 1986 when I watched the sun rise over the back of a university computer terminal, after spending the entire night online via JANET (the pre-TCP/IP Joint Academic Network that linked the UK's universities), exploring one of the original MUDs, or multi-user dungeon, running on a mainframe at Essex University. And I couldn't help noticing stuff happening in the gaming world. A couple in South Korea, who'd met via an MMO, were getting divorced – and wanted the judge to divide up their in-game property. A man in South London walked into a police station to report a crime – he'd been sold an enchanted sword, and it turned out not to be magic after all. (An in-game item, sold via eBay or an online auction house – when the police finally got their head around the crime they filed it under 'fraud'.) And so on.

The games were generating social fallout in the real world. Which in turn implied that they were, in some sense, very real to the people who played them. And so I began reading and researching, and rapidly realized that something big was going on: the first wave of real, commercially viable, multi-user virtual reality had finally reached the shore of public consciousness. And if that's not meat and drink for an SF writer, what is?

Halting State is set in a similar world to our own, but the technology available to the police, for example, exceeds our own. When do you think we might catch up? And would this be a good idea?

I think most of the tech in *Halting State* is pretty much here today, or on the drawing boards. There are only two hardware items that aren't on sale right now, at least in embryonic form; the quantum computer that plays a role in the book (and they're clearly a field undergoing a ferment of commercial R&D right now, with several companies claiming to have plans to bring them to market in the next few years), and the glasses that the protagonists use. We're used to the idea of clunky goggles with tiny LCD screens built into them for watching movies on our iPods; you can buy them right now. And we're used to the idea of having camera chips in our mobile phones. What struck me is that there's no reason not to combine the two – to have glasses with a screen in front of each eye, and a camera chip on the outside. You can then 'blend' the view through the camera with whatever graphics the screen is being fed by its computer (or cellphone, or iPod) to either merge real world and computer-generated imagery, or to provide an enhanced view of your surroundings.

Think, for example, of how the police would use such goggles: with decent cameras they'd have infra-red night vision, or zoom capability, along with the ability to call up crime reports or local information. Or think again about how live-action gamers might use such goggles: to see Orcs and Dwarves in place of commuters, and dank dungeon walls in place of hotel wallpaper. Or students: to watch a movie while the professor lectures, leaving the goggles to record their notes for later. This is a technology that *could* exist today, and which I suspect will show up suddenly and in large numbers in the next few years.

Of course, the effects of these technologies on society are part of what I was trying to explore in *Halting State* . . .

The interaction between the virtual and the real feels very natural in *Halting State*. Would you enjoy living in such a world?

I think, on balance, it'd be a better world to live in than many of the alternatives on offer. All too often, SF focuses on futures wracked by strife and pain – distinctly unpleasant places to live. In contrast, the future of *Halting State* is grounded in today; many trends already visible in our current civilization are present and amplified, and some of them aren't good, but it's still a future with room for ordinary people to live. They've got expensive oil and annoying traffic jams and they're worried about global climate change and international relations – but that's a far cry from living in a bombed-out radioactive wilderness while being hunted by killer robots! And they've got computer games to die for.

Your writing has been called 'information dense' and *Halting State* does contain a fair amount of technological content and industry-specific jargon. Do you self-edit to make sure your material is as accessible as possible, or do you think that this is what your fan-base wants and expects from you? Or is there a middle ground?

I'm trying to write a specific kind of fiction here, for an audience that is being ill-served by traditional science fiction.

Back in the golden age of SF, it was fairly clear that the bright shining future lay in speed and transport technologies. Everything was getting faster; I think it was the late Jack Williamson whose career as an SF writer began not long after his family migrated across the prairies in a covered wagon, and lived through the Apollo program to see the current international space station being assembled in orbit above him. SF reflects the spirit of the age it's written in; and so the nuts and bolts engineering-oriented SF of the 1930s to the 1960s reflected a confident belief that as things were getting faster, the moon and the planets and then the stars would come within our grasp. And as readers we learned to deal with concepts like nuclear rockets, and anti-gravity, and faster-than-light travel, and a whole slew of other specialized jargon and technological content that we tend to take for granted as the stage sets and furniture of SF.

But something went wrong. In the mid-1960s the curve of increasing transportation speed – which had been getting faster since about 1800 – reached a plateau and stagnated. Today's fastest spacecraft travel at barely twice the velocity of the Apollo missions. We don't use nuclear motive technologies (unless you count the French railway network), and as Newton first noticed, it turns out that to go twice as fast, you need to square the energy input to your propulsion system. Today's fastest airliners are actually *slower* than those of 1988! (Although they carry far more travellers and cost comparatively less.)

Just as the curve of increasing speed flattened out, a new slew of technologies for processing information were coming along. And the explosion in computing, networking, and IT sucked up the energies of the next two generations of bright, engineering-obsessed geeks. But for some reason, we SF writers seem to have missed the bus. We're still largely writing stories about thrilling space adventures, even though this is talking *past* the experience and internal dialog of the geek community from whom our audience is drawn. Meanwhile, as we learn more about the solar system and our niche in it, those space adventures are becoming increasingly hard to distinguish from fantasy.

There are exceptions, of course. Neal Stephenson's phenomenal popularity among IT workers and geeks should be no surprise, because he's writing for them, not for nostalgic fantasists and dreamers of a final frontier. And I'm trying to do likewise, to speak to a different audience from the traditional SF readership – or rather, to speak to a broader audience. The existing SF readers are already with us; I want to recapture the interest of the people who gave up reading SF in their teens because it seemed to be shallow escapism that had nothing to say to them. And that's why I'm using industry-specific jargon – but stuff these readers understand – to deal with different concepts in place of the rocketry and ray-guns jargon of traditional SF.

Do you think that it is possible for the speed of communications and quantity of information we are expected to absorb to continue to increase exponentially?

No. There are actually quite tight limits on human cognitive bandwidth and multi-tasking; we can multi-task up to a point, but our effectiveness falls off dramatically if we try to juggle just three or four tasks. (While I'm writing this interview I'm not checking my email, surfing the web, or working on a novel, for example – I *could* but it'd be stupid to try; everything would take twice as long.)

So if anything, the real challenge in software today is to pre-filter the information out there before it reaches us, so that the relevant stuff comes up first and the irrelevant is discarded. One reason Google is so popular is because of their use of the PageRank algorithm, to present search results to users in a cunningly-sorted order that prioritises web pages that other human readers found useful; it harnesses human attention spans to determine what is of interest to human beings. A flipside of this coin: I always browse the web with a formidable array of image and pop-up blockers switched on, tools to actually damp down and discard irritants and distractions like animated advertisements.

These are two aspects of the internet that would have boggled its early users twenty years ago, and they're aspects of the cognitive arms race we're fighting in order to maintain open access to information.

Surely there will come a point where the human brain can't cope with all this data? Or will that have to change too?!

The human brain is remarkably adaptable, and there's some research that indicates we're better at processing this sort of information than our ancestors – but then, we've grown up doing it; spending eighty hours a week watching the southbound end of a north-bound plough horse doesn't train you to rapidly correlate large volumes of data. But yes, there are probably hard limits beyond which we can't push ourselves without having to take drastic steps that may redefine what it means to be human – electronic neural prosthesis, genetic engineering, you name it.

The pace of change is also accelerating all the time. Do you think it is becoming harder for science fiction writers to stay ahead of the game, channelling the future for the rest of us?

It's very hard indeed to write near-future SF these days; you can open the newspapers any day of the week and read a lot of news reports about technology and medical innovations that would have been seen as science-fictional just decades ago. By the same token, to design realistic-looking near-future worlds (in which to set convincing near-future SF) you need to maintain a death-grip on the state of progress in a variety of loosely-interlocking fields. Some of the broad trends are fairly obvious (energy is getting more expensive, climate change is increasingly hard to ignore, electronics is getting smaller, faster, and cheaper) but others seem to come out of nowhere. GPS navigation started out as a tool for keeping US Navy warships off reefs, but suddenly it's in your car telling you which road to drive down; next it'll be in commercial goods (along with tiny, data-only cell-phone modems), phoning home to tell head office where they've gotten to, or in convicts' electronic tags, telling the parole officer which pub they've sneaked off to. And then, bang! You've got a generation who grew up not knowing what it's like to be lost. And what does *that* mean, really?

You've gained degrees in pharmacy and computer science and worked as a pharmacist, software engineer and freelance journalist (to quote your biography!). Has the hunt for the right day job been hard, or has your career been an organic and enjoyable journey up to this point?

I figured out I wasn't well suited to being a pharmacist pretty early on – I have too much imagination. (The ideal pharmacist is meticulous, learned, has infinite attention to detail, and doesn't lie awake at night worrying about how many people they may have poisoned by accident the day before.) Programming was fascinating and enjoyable, and also obsessive, but the half-life of a programmer is about a decade: most people who're good at it find they burn out sooner or later. Freelance computer journalism was a side-effect of the computing background and the writing; it was a useful and interesting area to be in (and it saved my bacon when I cleverly accepted a very nice job offer with a different dot-com – in March 2000, just as the bottom dropped out of the bubble economy – only to finish my notice period and discover that the job I was going to, and indeed the company, no longer existed).

This varied work history must be useful when writing your technologically sophisticated novels. Do you find you draw on this much when writing, or have you moved beyond that?

I've worked in a variety of organizations, ranging from a three-man start-up through to a large NHS teaching hospital and a multinational software corporation. The patterns of social and managerial politics start to look familiar after a while, and you begin to see similarities between the way different organisations work. (And between people in what appear at first to be very different roles in different organisations.)

It gets increasingly hard to project myself back into some of those niches now – I've been self-employed full time for going on eight years, which is a lifestyle that, for a writer, is disturbingly like being on the dole (only with more money, you hope); personal experience recedes into the distance and you have to rely more on what other people bring to you.

Most genre authors find a niche and write consistently within it. However, you've written far-future space opera, near future crime, science fiction spy thrillers (with lashings of Lovecraft) and alternative history/fantasy.

As for the range I write, there are some common underpinnings. Mostly I write about people working within a larger organization. There are exceptions, but I find the idea of a lone hero somewhat anaemic; what do they do when they're not off in the wilderness, hero-ing? (And what do they put in their tax forms?) We're a social species, and most of us don't thrive in the absence of structure and companionship. So there's a common theme (in fact, there are several common themes) running through my writing – and the struggle for organisational change seems to be a big element of it.

So do you have a set writing routine and if so, what is it?

I have no set writing routine (and this is a problem). This year, I started out with a new year's resolution, to write a thousand words a day; it worked fine until the second overseas trip of the year. It turns out that I don't work well when I'm not in comfortable or familiar surroundings – typically at home, because if I'm away from home and paying for a hotel room I have a neurotic twitch about getting my money's worth by exploring whatever town or city the hotel is located in.

On a similar theme, how extensively do you plot your novels before you start writing them? Or do you prefer to let the story roam where it will?

It depends. No two novels work the same way, and no two writers; anyone who tells you they've got the one true method for writing the perfect novel is misguided at best or a charlatan at worst. When working on a novel in a series, a detailed outline usually helps – if I drive off the road, at least I've got a map to consult as I bump through the long grass alongside it. But sometimes I start with a situation, a character, a lot of background notes on the world the story is happening in, and some waypoints to navigate by – but getting from one pivotal scene to the next is an exercise for me to engage in while I'm writing. At least it means the job is full of surprises!

When reading your books, I am always impressed by their inventiveness, and your enthusiasm and wealth of ideas has been consistently praised in the genre press. Do the ideas just keep on coming?

Yes. And here's the weird thing; ideas *breed*. They multiply in dark corners when I'm not looking. I learn something new and trivial and the next thing I know, it's jumped a hoary old cliché and they're enthusiastically breeding a new master-race of cockroach-like plot tropes that scurry off and hide behind the wainscoting of a novel!

(I am very grateful for this, incidentally.)

And do you ever feel the need to rest? Or isn't rest restful for you?!

I'm getting older, like the rest of us, at one year per 365.25 days. And I can't keep the rate of output up the way I used to. For the past several years I've been scrabbling to establish a career; I've had about two vacations that *didn't* involve a work-related meeting or convention in the past four years, and meanwhile have been averaging two novels a year.

After ten books or so it begins to grind you down. Hopefully over the next year or two I can reduce my working commitments enough that I can catch some down-time; I'll be able to polish my work more, make sure it's fully developed before I send it out the door to fend for itself, and also find it less draining.

On the other hand, I enjoy this stuff, really. If I didn't, I could always go back to a day job.

So, what's next for you?

I'm currently working on an original novella (as yet untitled) that's going to go into my next SF book after *Saturn's Children* — a short story collection.

Looking further ahead, I'm working on notes towards a sequel to *Halting State*, tentatively titled *419* — it's about the future of distraction in a networked world (and the largest advance-fee fraud in history). And I'm planning the third Laundry novel, a sequel to *The Atrocity Archives* and *The Jennifer Morgue*, currently titled *The Fuller Memorandum*. Like the others, it's a Cold War spy thriller homage — in this case paying tribute to Anthony Price — in which Bob gets to meet the Laundry's Russian counterparts.

Beyond that, who knows? That's enough to keep me busy until 2010!

if you enjoyed
HALTING STATE

look out for

THE NIGHT SESSIONS

by

Ken MacLeod

'Science fiction,' said the robot, 'has *become science fact*!'

John Richard Campbell groaned, as much at the cliché as at having been wakened from his uncomfortable doze. He shifted in his seat, pushed the blanket away from his face, resettled his phone clip and sat up. As he adjusted the back-rest to vertical he noticed only a score or so of other passengers stirring. The great majority were sleeping on, and even most of those awake were staring blankly at what-ever was playing in their eyewear. Business flyers, he guessed, who'd already seen the sight often enough. Campbell had opted to be wakened at the approach to the equator, for the same reason as he'd chosen a window seat. He didn't want to miss seeing the Pacific Space Elevator. With its Atlantic counterpart – or rival – it was possibly the most impressive, and certainly the most massive, work of man. A new Tower of Babel, he'd called it once, but he had to see it.

'The elevator is now visible to passengers on the right-hand side of the plane,' the robot's voice murmured in the phone clip. 'Passengers on the left will be able to see it in a few minutes, after we turn slightly to avoid the exclusion zone.'

Campbell pressed his cheek against the window and his chin against his shoulder, cupped his left hand to his temple to cut out the reflections from the dim cabin lighting, and peered ahead and to starboard. In the dark below he saw a spire of pinprick lights. From its summit a bright line extended straight up, for what seemed a short distance. Carefully angling his gaze upward along the line, Campbell spotted a tiny clump of bright lights directly above the spire, about level with the aircraft along the line of sight. He had time to see its almost imperceptible upward motion before the nose of the plane slowly swung starboard and cut it from view. Campbell felt the window press harder against his cheekbone as the aircraft banked.

'You can no longer see the crawler,' said the robot voice, 'but if you look farther up, to the sky, you may just be able to see the elevator in space. From this angle it appears as a shorter line than you may expect, but as bright as a star.'

And so it was. Campbell stared at the hairline crack in the night sky until it passed from view. Near its far end, he fancied, he could see a small brightening of the line, like a lone bead about to drop off the string, but he couldn't be sure: at 35,786 kilometres (less twelve, for the height the aircraft was flying at) the Geostation was tiny, and even the more massive counterweight beyond it, at the very end of the cable, was hardly more visible.

Campbell settled back. The sight had been worth seeing, but he could understand why the frequent fliers hadn't stirred for it. At the cockpit end of the aisle the cabin-crew robot had turned its fixed gaze towards the left-hand window seats and was no doubt murmuring in the phone clips of those passengers now craning their necks and peering out. Campbell guessed that they had a better view. He decided to book a window seat on the other side on the way back; the return-flight corridor passed on the western side of the elevator.

He turned to the window and let his eyes adjust again to the dark. The viewing conditions weren't perfect by any means, but he could make out the brighter stars. After a few minutes' watching he saw a meteor, burning bright orange; then, shortly afterward, another. Each time it was his own intake of breath that he heard, but the fiery meteors seemed so close he imagined he could hear the whoosh.

After a while the position became uncomfortable. He switched off the robot commentary channel, tilted the backrest as far as it would go, pulled the blanket over his head and tried to sleep. He was sure he wouldn't, but the next thing he noticed was that the blanket was on his knees and light from the window was in his eyes. The dawn sky glowed innumerable shades of green, from lemon to duck-egg to almost blue, like the background colour in a Hindu painting, and turned slowly to a pure deep blue over ten minutes or more as he watched. He dozed again.

The cabin bell chimed. The robot channel clicked itself back on. The drop-down screen above the seat in front showed the aircraft approaching the US West Coast, the local time as two p.m. Up front, and far behind, cabin-crew robots had begun shoving trolleys and handing out coffees. Campbell looked out, seeing white wakes like comets on the blue sea; wavy cliffs like the edge of a corrugated roof. Campbell's legs ached. He stood, apologised his way past the two other passengers beside him, and made for the midship toilet. By the time he got back the trolley and its dollies were two rows away. He settled again.

The trolley locked, the trolley-dolly halted. It had an oval head with two lenticular eyes and a smile-shaped speaker grille, and a torso of more or less feminine proportions, joined at a black flexible concertina waist to an inverted cone resembling a long skirt.

'Black, no sugar, please,' Campbell said.

The machine's arm extended, without its body having to lean, and handed him a small tray with coffee to spec, kiwi-fruit juice and a cereal bar.

'Thank you,' he said.

'You're welcome,' said the robot.

The passenger next to him, a middle-aged woman, accepted her breakfast without saying anything but: 'White, two sugars.'

'No need for the please and thank you,' she said, as the dolly glided on. 'They're no smarter than ATMs.'

Campbell tore open the wrapper of his cereal bar and smiled at the woman.

'I thank ATMs,' he said.

Campbell turned the robot commentary back on as the aircraft flew over LA. He couldn't take his gaze from the ground: the black plain, the grey ribbons of freeways, the grid of faint lines that marked where streets had been.

'. . . At this point the Christian forces struck back with a ten-kiloton nuclear warhead . . .'

Irritated, Campbell cut the commentary and sat back in his seat. The woman beside him, leaning a little in front of him to look out herself, noticed his annoyance.

'What's the matter?' she asked.

Campbell grimaced. 'Calling the rebels "the Christian forces". There were just as many Christians on the government side.' He shook his head, smiling apologetically. 'It's just a bug of mine.'

'Yeah, well, it isn't the government side that has plagued us in NZ ever since,' the woman said. She folded a scrap of her breakfast wrapper and worried at a seed stuck between two of her broad white teeth. 'It's the fucking Christians.'

'I'm a fu— a fundamentalist Christian myself,' said Campbell, stung into remonstrance.

'The more fool you, young man,' the woman said. She probed with her tongue behind her upper lip, made a sucking sound and then swallowed. 'I used to go to church too, you know, when I was your age. Nice little church we had, all wooden, lovely carvings. Kind of like a marae, you know? Then these American Christians came along and started yelling at us that we were heathen for having a church that looked Maori. Well, the hell with them, I thought. Walked out through their picket line, went to the nearest kaori tree to talk to my ancestors, and never looked back.'

'I'm very sorry to hear that,' Campbell said. 'A lot of these American exiles aren't true Christians, and even those that are are sometimes high-handed. So I don't approve of what happened to you. Not at all.'

'Well, thanks for that!' She didn't sound grateful. 'And what would "true" Christians have done, huh?'

'Oh,' said Campbell, 'they'd have first of all proclaimed the gospel to you, and only after they'd established that you or some of you were seriously and genuinely trying to follow Christ – and the apostolic form of church government – would they have raised the secondary matter of church decoration.'

'Jesus!' the woman said, blasphemously but aptly. 'You mean you think just the same as they did, you'd just be more tactful about it.'

Campbell smiled, trying to defuse the situation.

'Not many people call me tactful.'

'Yeah, I can see that. OK, let's leave it. What do you do?'

'I'm a robotics engineer,' Campbell said.

'My son's studying that,' the woman said, sounding more friendly. 'Where do you work?'

'Waimangu Science Park,' Campbell said.

'That place!' The woman shook her head, back to hostility again. 'You know, that's one of the things I resent the most about these goddamn Yank exiles. Cluttering one of our NZ natural wonders with their creationist rubbish!' She gave him a sharp look. 'Robotics engineer, huh? I suppose that means you maintain the animatronic Adam and Eve and the dinosaurs and all the rest of that crap.'

She crushed her empty coffee cup and threw it on the floor, apparently by reflex, as she spoke. Her anger took Campbell aback.

'The displays aren't as intrusive as you might think,' he

said. 'There's only a handful of animatronics, and a few robots. Most of the displays are virtual, a package that visitors can download to their frames.'

The woman compressed her lips, shook her head, turned away and put her frames on. Campbell shrugged and looked out of the window. The afternoon sun picked out the tablelands and mesas and escarpments, and after a while the landscape below opened up into a single enormous feature. Campbell became aware of the woman leaning sideways again. He leaned back, to give her a better view. She looked down, her eyewear pushed up on her forehead, until the Grand Canyon was out of sight.

'Doesn't look much like Waimangu,' she said.

Campbell found himself giving her a complicit grin.

'You're right about that,' he said. 'I don't believe in flood geology.'

'What *do* you believe in, then?'

'I believe the Bible,' said Campbell. 'Which means I believe it about the Creation and the Flood, and the dates when these happened. I just think it's presumptuous to look for *evidence*. We should take God's word for it.'

'So you don't think the fossils were left by the Flood?'

'No.'

'So how do you explain them?'

'I don't *have* to explain them,' said Campbell. 'But I can point out that it's a *presumption* that they're the remains of animals. What we *find* in the rocks are bone-shaped stones.'

The woman gave him a look of amused disbelief. 'And feather-shaped stones, skin-shaped stones, footprint-shaped stones . . . ?'

'As you say, stones.'

'So God planted them to test our faith?'

'No, no! We can't say that. Before people started *believing* that these stones were remains, they believed they were natural created forms of rock. It didn't trouble their faith at all.'

She bumped her forehead with the heel of a hand. 'And how do you explain the stars, millions of light years away?'

'How do we know they're millions of light years away?'

'By measuring their parallax,' the woman said.

'Good,' said Campbell. 'Most people don't even know that, they just believe it because they were told. But what the astronomers actually measure, when they work out a stellar parallax, is the angles between beams of light. They then *assume* that these beams come from bodies like the Sun, for which they have no independent evidence at all.'

'Oh yes, they do! They have spectrograms that show the composition of the stars.'

'Spectrograms of beams of light, yes.'

'And now we have the space telescopes, we can see the actual planets – heck, we can even see the clouds and continents on Earth-sized planets, with that probes-flying-in-formation set-up, what's it called?'

'The Hoyle Telescope. Which gathers together beams of light.'

'Which just *happen* to form images of stars and planets!'

'It doesn't just happen. God designed them that way. Not to fool us, of course not, but to show us His power, His infinite creativity. He *told* us He had made lights in the sky. It's *we* who are responsible if we make the unwarranted assumption that these lights come from other suns and other worlds that God told us nothing about.'

'So the entire universe, outside the solar system, is just some kind of light show?'

'That's as far as the evidence goes at the moment,' said Campbell. 'And speaking of evidence, I'll remind you that if these supposed galaxies were real physical bodies billions of years old, then they wouldn't hold together gravitationally. They'd long since have spun apart. The only explanation the astronomers have for *that* is dark matter, matter they can't see and have never found or identified, but which they postulate because it's necessary to explain away the evidence of a young universe on the basis of their assumptions.'

The woman screwed up her eyes for a moment.

'This is like a nightmare,' she said. 'Don't tell me any more of what you believe in. I just don't want to know.'

Campbell had several replies primed for that, but he just nodded.

'Fair enough,' he said.

He turned back to the window.